LIEUTENANT ABLS

To Michael,

Hope you enjoy it. As a retired law officer, your comments would be welcome

Matt [signature]

12/13/08

Lieutenant ABLS

MATTHEW J DUFFIN

YELLOWBACK MYSTERIES
JAMES A. ROCK & COMPANY, PUBLISHERS
ROCKVILLE • MARYLAND

Lieutenant ABLS by Matthew J Duffin

is an imprint of JAMES A. ROCK & CO., PUBLISHERS

Address comments and inquiries to:

YELLOWBACK MYSTERIES
James A. Rock & Company, Publishers
9710 Traville Gateway Drive, #305
Rockville, MD 20850

E-mail:

jrock@rockpublishing.com lrock@rockpublishing.com
Internet URL: www.rockpublishing.com

Paperback ISBN-13/EAN: 978-1-59663-647-7

Library of Congress Control Number: 2008920590

Printed in the United States of America

First Edition: 2008

This book is dedicated to my father, who in later years became something even more important.

He became my friend.

PROLOGUE

Philadelphia, May 19th, 1993, 10:10 P.M.

The drunk staggered up Tasker Street toward the Broad Street Subway Line. As he crossed Clarion Street, four sets of teenaged eyes locked onto him as tenaciously as any radar. "He's headed for the subway, sure as shit," the leader said to the youngest. "Go!"

The little point man jogged up Tasker, swung left on Juniper, right on Morris, and quickly arrived at Broad Street. He hurried to the Tasker-Morris Station, scanning the area quickly. Cops were about, but uninterested in him or the immediate area. He disappeared down the steps.

SEPTA Police Officer Theresa Altez came up the steps on the other side of the street several moments later. Done for the night, she crossed the street and started to head down Tasker Street toward Kirkbride Elementary, near where she lived. Coming toward her, almost in a straight line, was a fairly well dressed man with a briefcase and a load-on. *Jeez, another stupid white man walking drunk in this neighborhood. Unbelievable!*

She stopped him about a hundred feet from the corner. "Sir, are you lost?"

"Nooow, not now ofishur," he replied. "I think I found the subtway. Jest tryin' to get home." A boozy cloud escaped his mouth with his words.

"O.K. then," she said. "You just keep going straight up there and try not to fall down the steps, O.K.?"

"Yesh ma'am, ofishur sir. Off I go."

She watched him move off for a moment and then turned and continued on home. "Fucking drunks," she muttered. *Oh well,* she thought. *Not my problem.* Home to the kids and her mama's nagging. And that *was* her problem. She did not see the three young men glide north up Broad Street, and walk silently down the steps to the Tasker Street Station.

The leader, who missed nothing, had observed the meeting of the drunk and the SEPTA cop. *Good break*, he thought. It had given them an extra minute or two for recon. He too had noticed the cops in their cars sitting up the street, but everything was calm.

The three youths slid their tokens in the slots, and walked onto the northbound platform. Rowdy and rambunctious as any young black kids, they were muted tonight. They were on a mission. The leader's two companions carried backpack school bags actually filled with books and class notes from the evening remedial classes for high school students given at Temple University. The classes were given in a small off-campus building at Carlisle Street and Cecil B. Moore Avenue. Special curfew passes were given to these students. All three boys, and their point man, had them.

So far, so good, the leader thought. The point man was gone. The boys did carry on a bit, mugging and messing with each other, but their young eyes watched everything as they jostled. Cold, hard young eyes.

Here came the drunk. He lurched left, then right, but eventually hit the token gate. Literally. He slammed into the post, fumbled his token into the slot, and fell into the turnstile. Only its slow, revolving give prevented him from falling. He regained his balance, and emerged onto the platform. The boys studiously ignored him, and moved further up the platform so they could catch the forward car of the next train.

Now, as they turned about and looked down the tracks for the approaching subway, they all watched the drunk without staring. Medium height, well-dressed but casual, with beard, mustache, and glasses. Tan Jeff and matching sports coat over a pair of Levis and decent kicks. *Looks like those new Jordans*, the leader thought. It was just an observation; they weren't after the shoes. They *were* after the briefcase and the wallet, of course.

The leader was proud of his men and himself. They had been in operation for almost a year. He had prepared for months before they started, and had carefully picked his team. They were all street smart, but they were all very intelligent also. It took a while, but he had finally convinced them his way would work. Two years, he had told them, maybe three, and then they would be set. They laughed at first at his frequent use of big words and military terms, but they understood everything he said.

Then one day in January of 1992 he put it all on the table, and he finally had them. "Look at all the kids we know in jail. And if they ain't in jail, they're fucked up or dead. The ones who play it Whitey's way go to school in shitty threads, and come home to empty fridges. They do their homework every night because it keeps their mind off their empty stomachs and empty lives."

They were all staring at him very intently.

"Every night, all over this town, rich drunks walk the streets. We go after the loners, the real alkies. Most of 'em won't remember nothin' about us, except that we're young and black. Let the PO-LICE try to deal with that. There'll only be about a hundred-thousand suspects."

They had sniggered at this, but he had them and they all knew it.

They had planned and rehearsed. This had taken some extra convincing on his part, because they were eager to get started. But he reined them in. He never threatened or yelled. He used calm, quiet logic, and it worked. Before their first mission they knew SEPTA, the public transportation system, forward and backward. One of the backpackers once asked him about boosting a car, and then dumping it afterwards.

"Listen, cars mean prints, chases, the whole bad deal. We be quick, we be silent, and we be rich. We use The System."

"The System" was SEPTA's nickname.

The other boy laughed. "Yeah, you can't beat The System," he said, referring to the little ad jingo of SEPTA's that everybody knew.

"That's right," the leader replied. "It'll get us anywhere and everywhere, and no traces."

And so it went. They were very disciplined. They even aborted missions if the point man waved them off. There were other nights, and many drunks. Everything was split evenly and they all had some money stashed away. They did not flash their cash, and they all dressed modestly. "In a couple years, when we're done, and we have real jobs, then we spend. We go our separate ways, and we'll all have a big leg up on all the good niggers. Don't worry about the bad niggers. By the time we're twenty-five, most of them will be dead or doin' time."

At their last meeting before their first mission, he insisted on his military terminology, he talked about the absolute necessity of secrecy.

"Don't ever tell nobody nothin'. On mission nights we'll always be back early enough. Just tell whoever needs to know that you were just hangin' out. Keep up your schoolwork, do your homework, and let them think you're good little Uncle Tommys. Never, ever talk, and we'll all be sitting pretty on the kitty. Always go home with a soda or candy bar, and be good little boys. Remember, never talk!"

* * *

They heard the far away rumble and saw the distant headlight. Soon the train roared into the station. The noise of a subway screaming into a platform is loud and unique. It cannot be described, only experienced.

As they jumped into the first car, they saw the target get in the next-to-last one. As the train moved out, the butterflies started. But after they passed the Lombard Street Stop, calm settled over all of them, and preparation took over. At City Hall, they got off and headed slowly thru the free interchange for the Market-Frankford EL Line. The target had gotten off too, like he always did, and staggered their way.

The leader looked to the end of the passage. There was the point man. He signaled all clear. A Go! One of the boys "accidentally" dropped his backpack, and stopped to gather the books that had fallen out.

The drunk walked past the boys, seemingly oblivious. Here we go! Here we go! The rear was clear. The leader slammed the drunk against the wall, and took the briefcase. The second backpacker quickly found and took his wallet. The first backpacker rushed up, sealed the drunk's mouth with plumbers tape, and after the leader had spun him around, he quickly taped his wrists together, just enough to confuse him and slow him down. The leader slammed the target to the ground, and they all moved out. Up through the concourse they went, moving fast, but not running. They hit the westbound EL platform, and waited patiently for a train. One came quickly. They got off at 34th and Market, climbed the stairs, walked over to 33rd Street, and caught a Subway Surface Car east. They got off at 17th Street, walked up to Cherry Street, made a right, and made their way to North Broad Street. Here they waited for a southbound C Bus to take them home.

* * *

The drunk sat up and leaned forward. He pressed hard on his inner forearms, and the rigged switchblade shot open. The double-edged, razor sharp knife caught a small portion of the tape, and cut a small tear. Once a cut is started, plumbers tape rips easily. He freed his wrists quickly, stood up, and ripped the tape off his mouth. The mustache came with it. As he was smoothing his beard, a man from the southbound platform yelled at him.

"Hey mister, what happened—you O.K.?"

The drunk quickly walked off, rolling the mustache-laden tape into a ball. He pulled the rest of the tape off his wrists, and put the whole wad in his jacket pocket. He headed for an eastbound EL. The other man was still yelling, and now he was walking quickly to the interchange.

The target moved to a large, wooden revolving door for access to the EL. As he went through it, he quickly removed his coat, and ripped off the beard. The glasses, Jeff, and beard went into a coat pocket, which he quickly reversed and slung over his arm. It all took about three seconds. And eastbound train was approaching.

The Good Samaritan emerged into the broad concourse. He had lost sight of the man. The place was practically empty; he should be easy to spot. He was nowhere to be seen. There was a man on the eastbound EL platform, but there was no resemblance. He spotted a cop.

"Officer, Officer, I think somebody was just robbed!"

* * *

The boys hopped on the C Bus. The first backpacker gave his pack to the point man, and took the briefcase from the leader. The second backpacker gave the leader the wallet. They remained quiet. He had conditioned them to this. If they started jabbering now, none of them would be able to shut up.

The bus rolled around City Hall, and continued down South Broad Street. The point man got off at Christian Street, and headed home. The two original backpackers got off at Wharton Street, and walked to the playground at Passyunk Avenue. The leader continued on.

The two boys cut through the playground. They passed behind a rundown, graffiti-scarred building, and scrambled down a dirt slope filled with weeds, small trees, and lots of trash. They had their knives out now, for their own protection. They crawled into a little opening through some tall, dense weeds, and entered a tiny clearing.

They sat down with the briefcase; it was scuffed, beat up, and locked. Pulling out their penlights, they centered it in front of them, and each pried at a clasp. First one, then the other popped up. They looked at each other and grinned. This was always the best part.

They flipped open the lid of the briefcase, and two 40mm CS grenade rounds exploded in their faces.

* * *

The leader got off at Dickerson Street, and headed west. After several blocks he turned left onto Woodstock. He ducked down a small alley, and squeezed between two little outbuildings. He jumped over a small fence, and was in his backyard, next to his grandfather's old tool shed. His Rotweiller charged without barking. He had trained it to sniff first and bark later. The dog settled down and whined happily.

"Shhh! Good boy," he whispered.

He unlocked the shed, and quickly moved in and shut the door, leaving the dog outside. He went to the bench, and brought out the wallet. He set his penlight and the wallet on the bench. He would bury any good stuff under the floorboard, and lose the wallet later. He flicked the penlight on, and flipped the wallet open. The large bill slot had two twenties in it. Oh, well. Some of the drunks didn't carry large amounts of cash. It was the credit cards he was most interested in.

Funny. Most credit cards in their slots showed at least some of their logo. All he could see was colored plastic. He pulled one out. There was a sizzle, a bright flash, and a loud bang.

It was hard to tell what was louder, his screaming or the dog's howling.

* * *

The target got off the EL at Allegheny Avenue and caught the 60 Bus down to Richmond Terminal. He got off and walked toward Westmoreland Street, and faded quietly into his Port Richmond neighborhood.

Lunacy is in the eyes
of the reflection.

—Matthew J Duffin

What the hell's that
supposed to mean?

—Richard D Head

CHAPTER ONE

May 20th, 1993

Detective Lieutenant Matt Gallagher strode into the office at 7:55 A.M. He was never first in. He gave that shit up years ago. Many nights he was last out; but the hell with that dawn at your desk nonsense.

As Head of Detectives for the 3rd and 4th combined Police Districts, he didn't delegate, per se. He let his gold shields do their duties as they saw fit. He was aware peripherally of all their cases. For any specifics, he had daily reports and updates from all his people.

And all his people were watching him now. Winston Smythe, a Special Task Unit detective, stealthily slid back the typewriter support from his desk. Mounted on it was a plain calendar with each month for 1993 boxed off, and each individual day squared off also. All the days except yesterday, Wednesday, May 19th, were X'ed off in black magic marker. He waited.

Sergeant Vargas looked at Sergeant Patrillo, who shook her head no. He looked at Sergeant Godwin. Ditto. He made it unanimous. Without even looking at Smythe, he gave a field goal no good wave, barely moving his hands. That was enough. Smythe crossed off May 19th. Other than the months and days, there was only one label on the calendar. In large red block letters at the top was just this: "ABLS." Smythe slid the support back into the slot in the desk. He had this duty because they figured if he got caught, Gallagher wouldn't come down too hard on him. The Loo liked Smythe. Everybody did.

"Mornin', Loo," called Vargas. Several other detectives chimed in with greetings. "Hey everybody," replied Gallagher.

"Good morning, Lieutenant," smiled Sergeant Emma Godwin as she brought him a cup of tea. She was an absolutely gorgeous black woman, tough as nails, and the best shot in the office.

"Emma, how many times have I asked you not bring me my tea?" Gallagher asked.

"Just about every time I do it," she replied laughingly.

She was a happily married mother of three, and at age thirty-five, could have posed for the cover of any magazine in the world. She was one of Gallagher's two unofficial deputies, and besides helping him run the office, she went well out of her way to be nice to him, and make his days easier. She didn't mother him, but she did watch over him. Fiercely.

Gallagher was enamored of her, but he never let it go beyond that in his own mind. She was a policewoman, and a damn good one. To him, that was what really counted. That she was a great human being was a big plus. Her doings concerning Gallagher didn't bother anybody in this office. She was going places with or without him. She was taking the Lieutenant exam in September. When asked why she was waiting so long, she would say, "I'm still studying. I'm not going to just pass it, I'm going to max it." The way she prepared, no one doubted it. She was no brown nose. She just liked Gallagher, and was genuinely concerned for him

Julio Vargas, Gallagher's other "deputy," came up to the boss's desk. Gallagher ostensibly had a little office in the back of the squad room, but that wasn't his style. He was "born on this floor" and would stay on this floor. They used his office for files and other storage. Gallagher's presence wasn't overbearing, and it didn't inhibit his troops. If they needed to talk out of his presence, they waited until they were on the streets, which was often. There were few whisperings in this squad, and no major discord. There were far worse places to work in The Philadelphia Police Department.

"I better clue you in before you go to your morning meeting," Vargas said. "You're not gonna believe this shit. It's gonna hit the fan from here to the Schuylkill."

"All right," Matt said. "Sit down and let me have it." Matt sat in his chair, and Vargas sat down next to the desk and started in.

"It was about ten forty-five last night. They could hear the screams in here."

* * *

Vargas related as how the dicks on the night shift had run to the front door to see a couple of Uniforms, guns drawn, running down Wharton Street towards the playground. Two detectives took off after them, while another got on the horn and sent a patrol car down Federal Street.

The two Uniforms had arrived at the trash-strewn slope inside the playground and hesitated. The ungodly screams were coming from right below. Detective Sergeant Grady ran up and whipped out his hand-held. He could see the unit on Federal as it slammed to a stop.

"Watch for anything coming out of those weeds," he shouted into his radio.

"Roger," came the reply.

"O.K.," he pointed to one of the Uniforms, "me and you. You watch our six," he yelled to the other.

"Right, Sarge," she said.

"Stay with her, Bill," he shouted to the other detective as he ran up.

"Here we go," said Grady. "Watch your front, Officer."

They plunged down the slope, and moved quickly to the almost inhuman sounds.

"Oh, God, my eyes! My fuckin' eyes!" they heard.

They burst thru the weeds into the small clearing, and now the gas was all over them.

"What the fuck?" Officer Radell yelled.

"It's teargas, don't touch your eyes," Grady shouted.

He then saw the two youngsters writhing on the ground. They all had to get out of there.

"Come on, grab one and drag him back to the hill."

It wasn't easy. Both kids were in agony, and the cops were succumbing now, too.

When they got to the hill, Grady, coughing and retching, called up, "Bill, get Company Ten and an ambulance here ASAP."

"Right," he heard back.

He heard Radell coughing over the noise of the kids, and he was about to tell him to help get these kids up the hill and away from the gas, but he stopped. Something was goofy here. He was still suffering and coughing, but he was halfway up the little hill where he had moved to get Bill's attention. If somebody had fired or thrown tear gas (he knew now it was CS, a super-potent tear gas named after two early 20th Century chemists: B.B. Corson and R.W. Stoughton) into those weeds, there would be a large cloud there, billowing up into the air. But there was just a small plume, sitting low in the weeds. And coming out of the weeds were two trails of it where they had dragged the kids out. He looked down.

Holy shit! The gas was coming from them. Radell had just noticed it too, and had backed away.

"Sarge!" he coughed. "It's all over them!"

Grady jumped down the slope. He put his handkerchief over his mouth, bent down, and furiously waved his hand in front of one kid's face to get a clear look. He saw raw hamburger embedded with diced onions. The eyes were bubbling, hissing green orbs.

He jumped back. "Oh my God!"

That face finished the job the gas had started. He fell back on his ass, and threw up all over himself.

* * *

"They got the kids over at Sinai," said Vargas.

The reports, already on the Captain's desk, were not good.

"They're not dead," Vargas said. "But from what I hear, they're gonna wish they were."

"How're Radell and Grady?" asked Gallagher.

"Well, both got pretty sick from the CS, but they'll be O.K."

* * *

The firemen had declared an immediate Hazmat, and sealed off the area. The two Hazmat guys suited up and went in. They were back out in two minutes. This was no accident, they told their boss. "We found a briefcase with two CS rounds mounted in the bottom," one of them said. "Looks like a booby trap to me." His partner nodded in agreement.

"Captain, I recommend we let it blow off and dissipate, and designate this area a Hazmat crime scene."

The Fire Captain quickly assented. This was more than a little bizarre.

"Captain, you know once we do that, the crap's really gonna start flying."

"You boys are just doing your job, John," the Captain replied. "The shit'll all hit me. That's what I'm here for. Get to it."

"Yessir."

* * *

"The boss has been on the phone for about a half-hour now," Emma said. "He hasn't asked for you yet."

"O.K.," Matt said. "Can everything else wait?"

"Yeah," Vargas said. "Everything else on our plate is just veggies compared to this shit."

"You got that right," Matt replied. "Are Halston and Johnson in?"

"Yep, they're hanging around Cap's office."

"All right," said Matt. "I'll be back."

Gallagher went through a connecting door and through the Desk Sergeant's lobby (and you had better believe it was *his* lobby), waving as he went. He might have received a grunt in reply. It didn't matter. He always waved or said hi. He went past the double doors leading into the patrol area, down a hall, and walked into an open area of desks and partitions. Near the last desk were Johnson and Halston.

Lieutenant Ralph Halston was in charge of all daytime patrol units, mobile. Short and lean, he was a nervous bundle of energy. *A good cop*, Gallagher thought. He was almost always out on the streets with his men.

Lieutenant Larry Johnson was an absolute Sherman Tank of a man, and if there was any fat on him, only his wife knew about it. He was in charge of beat cops, and he *was* always on the streets with his men. After the morning meeting with the Captain, he wouldn't be seen again until six or seven in the evening. He was big, black, and bad. His men adored him.

"Gentlemen," Gallagher greeted them. "How they hangin'?"

"High," said Ralph.

"Low," said Larry.

They laughed. It was an old joke and it matched the two of them perfectly.

"Tsk, tsk," came from the desk's occupant. Jane Wilson was Captain Parmalee's secretary. She was middle-aged, competent, and this was not well-known, very street smart. "That joke's older than me," she said. "You boys have got to get new material."

"Aw shucks, Miss Jane," said Johnson. "You ain't old. You jest a spry young thang."

Larry Johnson was about as much an "Aw, shucks" guy as The Incredible Hulk, but he was putty in Jane's hands. *It was pretty hilarious*, Gallagher thought. She made all of them feel like they were standing in front of their grade school principal, but she never had a mean look or a bad word for anybody. She just had that effect.

"Go on with you, Lawrence," she said, as a blue button lit on her phone. "He's ready for you boys."

Captain Richard Parmalee was ready for them, indeed. As the three Lieutenants entered his office, he gestured to the folding chairs against the wall. They each took one and sat down.

"Ralph, Larry, I'll be brief," Parmalee said. "Somebody on the street has to know about these kids getting gassed. Naturally, the dicks will handle the investigation, but anything you get, let 'em know. Don't worry about paper; call it in right away. If you have to, call Vargas' squad or Matt direct on your radio. O.K.?"

"Right, Cap," Ralph replied.

Larry nodded and asked, "How bad are them kids, Captain?"

"Real bad. They're heavily sedated—induced comas. They may not make it. Now, I need some time with Matt."

"Yessir," Larry and Ralph chorused in reply, and left the office.

Gallagher shifted in his seat. He knew what was coming. He also knew Parmalee didn't like it. But Parmalee was "management," and he had to play it this way, or leave the field. Matt didn't hold it against him.

"Right in your lap, Matt. I wasn't calling your shots about Vargas earlier. It has to go to him, and it has to go to him yesterday."

"I understand Cap. Your finger hurtin' yet?"

"Not too bad. But if I pull it out to suck on it, the dike won't just leak; it'll collapse on both of us. Look at this." He handed the report across the desk, and picked up his phone.

Matt started reading. Unbelievable! Somehow these kids had gotten hold of a briefcase booby-trapped with CS gas, which was like tear gas on steroids. When it blew, hundreds of crystals were forcibly imbedded into the upper half of their bodies. Their faces took the brunt of it, and the eyes were the worst. The chemical basically boiled their eyeballs right out of their sockets. Gallagher stopped reading.

The Captain said into the phone, "Right, Chief. Yeah, I got him right here. No, you don't have to remind me Chief; or him, either ... I know my place, Chief. I wanna make sure you know it. I'm not gonna let anybody ruin my best Loo because some sick fuck booby-trapped a couple of kids ... you do that, Chief. Goodbye."

"That was Deputy Chief Barnes," the Captain said. "Know him?"

"I know him a little. Some kind of liaison to City Hall, right?"

"His official title is 'Department Liaison to the Mayor's Office'. Unfortunately, the biggest prick in uniform. He'd bust his mother for jaywalking if he thought it would make the Mayor happy. Funny thing is, the Mayor's not that kind of guy. He hates ass kissers. Barnes is an asshole, but he's very dangerous. He has many friends among the desk riders, and they all watch each other's backs. I'll watch your six, but if you don't get this asshole, they'll fuck me and fry you. You have to know that going in."

"Anything else?" Matt asked.

"Yeah. Press wise, we couldn't have been luckier. They had those kids out of there less then ten minutes after Grady showed up. Even that asshole from *The Daily News* ain't that quick. KYW and *The Inquirer* only know we had an incident with tear gas." *The Daily News* and *The Inquirer* were also known as *The DN* and *The Inky*, respectively.

"What did *The Inky* have to say?"

"Only a small item in the local section about the Hazmat situation with The Fire Department. Jeez, Matt, if you're gonna take The System to work, at least you oughta read *The Inquirer* on the way in."

"It screws up my thought processes. I read *The Daily News* on the way home. Then when I read about how fucked up we are, it doesn't mess up my work day."

Gallagher was getting a little pissed. He avoided driving in the city between 7:00 A.M. and 7:00 P.M. as much as possible. When he had to, he took one of the unmarked cars; but he rarely took one home, although he had an open offer to officially do so.

Captain Parmalee looked at him for a long minute. "Well, we don't want to screw up those thought processes. I've always said they were the best in The Department. O.K., I won't micromanage this; you know that. But keep me posted. A lot of people are gonna wanna know how two kids got hold of a briefcase booby-trapped with CS."

"O.K., Cap. Can I take this?" he asked, indicating the report.

"Yeah. Nail this down, Matt."

"Later, Cap."

"Bye Jane," he said as he walked out of the Captain's office.

"Goodbye, Lieutenant ABLS," she replied quietly.

He had to laugh. Even Jane was human.

* * *

"O.K., gather round," he called, after he got back to the squad room. The detectives all moved to his desk.

"Here it is," Matt said. "You all know by now of the little episode down the street. Besides Special Tasks, does anyone need my immediate help with anything?"

Shrugs, headshakes, and murmured "no's" were the responses he got.

"Good, everybody else drive on. Julio, let's you and your folks go to the conference room." Julio's "folks" were the members of the Special Tasks Unit. They were: Sergeant Vargas himself; his partner, Detective Nguyen (pronounced Win) Trung; Sergeant Pablo Gonzales; and his partner, Detective Winston Smythe.

The "conference" room was the interrogation room. The gunmetal gray tables were in the corner of the room, side by side. There were also half a dozen metal folding chairs scattered about. The room was clean; surprisingly so, a visitor might think. But their entire working area was like that. Gallagher insisted on it. He had seen other squad rooms that were absolute pigsties. And the bathrooms throughout The Department were an abomination. But not here. Every other Tuesday night, Gallagher himself stayed on late, and cleaned the whole work area; he even scrubbed down the bathroom. If it set an example, fine; but he did it for himself.

He wanted a clean place to work in; and after a while, even the old warhorses watched where they threw their garbage, and stopped pissing on the bathroom floor.

They all took seats.

"It's as bad as you've heard. These boys are all fucked up." Gallagher tossed the report on the table.

"The pictures are as bad as anything you'll see at the morgue. I know the Booze Bandits were a priority with youse guys." The Booze Bandits were a group of muggers hitting drunks walking Center City and nearby environs at night. "Don't back burner that. But this is now number one. And unless the honcho himself pulls me off, I'm attaching myself to youse guys." Silence and raised eyebrows was the response.

Matt pointed. "You start, Pablo."

"You got special instructions for us, Jefe?" Pablo asked.

When he wanted to, Sergeant Gonzales could speak perfect English. He was asking this question, in this way, for a reason. And Gallagher knew the reason.

"It ain't like that Compadre, and you know it. But I'm glad you spoke up. This is Julio's squad. He's gonna run this. If Sergeant Vargas has something specific for me to do, I'll do it. Otherwise, I'll be out and about sniffin' on this thing. But Julio will always know what I'm doin' and where I'm at. I'll have one of the new hand-helds you all got. I'll speak up when I need to like I expect everybody else to. The Captain's got my back, and I got yours. But I'm also now your funny uncle, like it or not. O.K. Sarge, it's all yours." Gallagher leaned back and smiled.

For a moment, Vargas said nothing. Then he snorted a laugh. "Jeez Loo, I ain't heard you say so much at once since the 'Dude' broke his wrist on opening day last year."

They all laughed, and any tension quickly dissipated.

The "Dude" was Lenny Dykstra, the Phillies' center fielder. In front of a sold out Vet on opening day in '92, the Cubs pitcher, Gary Maddux, had broke Dykstra's wrist in his first at bat. Gallagher, a passionate Phillies fan, had ranted about it for days.

"O.K., amigos here we go," Vargas began. He pointed to Detectives Trung and Smythe. "Nguyen, you and the Limey head over to Mount Sinai and see the docs. Me and Pablo are goin' to the playground. Loo, how about you come with us and talk to the Hazmat guys?"

"Sounds good to me, Sarge," Gallagher said.

"Let's roll."

CHAPTER TWO

Trung grabbed the keys to one of the Crown Vics, and met Smythe in the parking lot. Trung drove down Wharton Street, crossed 5th, and swung in behind the hospital. Like all hospitals in Philadelphia, Sinai was always a busy place.

Even though they each usually partnered with one of their Sergeants, it was not unheard of for this odd pair to work together. On the Special Tasks Unit, the four team members did whatever it took, with whoever it took, to do a job.

Licensed to drive in the United States, Smythe, a transplanted Englishman, was still more than a little uncomfortable driving on the wrong side of the road. When they were on the job, he had no problem with anybody else at the wheel. Anybody! It was the only real beef Gallagher had with Smythe. But Gallagher had told him, "Winston, if that's the only problem I ever have with you, you'll have a long and prosperous career with The Philadelphia Police Department." And that suited Smythe just fine.

Trung parked in an official spot near the emergency room entrance, and threw the "Get Out of Jail Free" card up on the dash. It was the official police business sign. Every cop in the city knew about the new Crown Victorias, and every one of them wanted one, marked or unmarked. The sign was probably not needed, but Trung was a fanatical stickler for details.

Nguyen Trung, twenty-six, was Vietnamese, and a four-year veteran of The Department. His mother had insisted on naming him Nguyen, even though it was a last name for Vietnamese. Nguyen was pronounced "Win," and she was determined that her son be a winner in America. After graduating from The University of Pennsylvania in four years (he'd entered at age seventeen) with a major in economics, a minor in chemistry, *and* a masters in political science, Trung had thoroughly startled his family and friends by applying to The Police Department. He had never hinted to any of his friends or family about this plan. He knew that everybody he knew, from his extended family, to his extensive circle of friends would have tried to talk him out of it. Smythe (and everyone else in the detective unit) thought him to be an extraordinary human being. No one expected him to make it a career, and he wasn't yet sure himself. Both Captain Parmalee and Lieutenant Gallagher had talked to him about this. In no uncertain terms they had told him: if he wanted to, he could ride this horse all the way to the top. But both had let him know of the problems and obstacles. Captain Parmalee had had to be politically correct. Not so, Gallagher.

"Nguyen, this is a tough town," Matt had told him in private. "And an even tougher Department. The people who are right in the head will help you. But Philly is full of bigots, inside and outside the force. The real knuckleheads are the ones who'll trash you because you're better than them. They flush their paychecks down urinals all over town every week, and complain about how screwed up everybody else is."

Trung remained silent throughout this speech. Unlike Vargas, he knew Gallagher would say a lot when he had something to say. Nguyen always listened to every word. Matt was more than his boss. He was his mentor.

Matt was finishing up. "The fact that you're smart, Vietnamese, and a decent human being just means they'll fling more shit at you. Maybe in ten years that shit'll stop. Change is coming. It has to. But I don't know when. If you can survive the internal and external politics, and still be here when the changes come, you'll write your own ticket. O.K., end of lecture."

* * *

Trung and Smythe walked into the hospital and got the info on where the kids were being kept. They made their way up to the ICU, and showed their badges at the nurse's station. The nurse told them a doctor would be with them shortly.

"Have they been identified yet?" asked Trung.

"Not yet," the nurse replied. "But with some of these poor kids, that's not unusual. I know. Until my sister got help with her addiction, she didn't know or care where she was half the time, let alone her kids. If these boys have responsible adults in the house, we should know soon. If not, we'll know when mom or dad, or whoever, sobers up and reports them missing."

"I say," Smythe spoke up. "You do seem to know what you're talking about."

She nodded. "Bet your white ass, buddy," she said, not unkindly.

"I've lived and worked in this neighborhood all my life. Some—hell—half of these kids never have had any kind of decent home life. I could tell you some stories, believe me."

"I do believe you, young miss," Smythe replied. "I do indeed."

Nurse Florence Robinson blushed, unseen by Smythe because of her very dark face. *Uh-oh,* thought Florence. *All the guy did was talk to me, and already I got the hots for him. How is this possible?*

An older man in a lab coat approached the counter. He laid a clipboard down.

"I'm Doctor James, can I help you?"

Once again the detectives showed their badges.

"O.K.," the doctor said. "Come with me please."

He led them to a small break room off the hallway, stepped inside, and closed the door behind them. "Have a seat," he said.

"We're good," Trung replied.

"Well, I'll sit if you don't mind," the doctor said. "I'm on my feet most of the day. O.K., here's the deal. Short term, they'll make it. Long term, these two kids are gonna suffer for the rest of their lives. They're both horribly disfigured; and of course, they're blind. No, blind doesn't cover it. They have no eyeballs left. They boiled right out of the sockets. I'll take you down to see them in a minute."

The doctor told them the rest of it. Shortly after 11:00 P.M. the night before, the boys were brought to the emergency room. The boys, the EMTs, and the ambulance were all saturated with CS. The driver had donned a pair of goggles and a surgical mask for the short ride, or he wouldn't have been able to function. Coughing and choking, one of the EMTs had done his best to radio ahead, but he wasn't coherent to the reaction team at the emergency room, and so nobody was quite prepared for what came in. When the ambulance slammed to a halt, the doors flew open, and an EMT dove out onto the asphalt, crying and retching. The other EMT fell out onto the ground holding a cloth over his face.

"It's gas," he gasped. "CS, maybe."

The emergency room team hesitated, but the ER Resident quickly sized up the situation and began issuing orders.

Pointing to a nurse, he shouted, "I want respirators, gloves, goggles, and masks. Lots of them. Go! Everybody else, stay away until we get that stuff. We can't help anybody if we're all fuckin' puking."

The driver of the ambulance had climbed out, and he and the rest of the team helped the EMTs to their feet.

"Don't touch your eyes," the resident told them. "You'll just rub it in and make it worse. It sucks, I know, but you'll be all right. Just keep walking around the driveway and the air'll take care of it." He turned to the driver. "You O.K.?" he asked.

"Yeah," the man replied. "We had to deal with this shit once a year or so in the service for training. I'll be O.K."

"Good," the doctor told him. "Stand by. I'm gonna need you."

The respirators and other gear quickly arrived, and the reaction team immediately gloved and masked up.

"O.K., listen up people. Get 'em out of there and cut their clothes off right here. Everything. Rita, you and Jack bring out two fresh carts. Let's go!"

The boys were pulled out of the ambulance, the driver helping. Their clothes and shoes were cut off and dumped right on the ground. The team was careful around the chest and neck area. Some clothing had to be cut around and left on. The boys were lifted onto the replacement carts, and wheeled into the emergency room. Two areas had been cleared out; patients, nurses, everybody.

While the reaction team went to work, the emergency room resident stepped out of the curtained area, lifted off his respirator, and beckoned to two interns watching from down the hall. They came running.

"Pads out," he said, although they were already yanking them out of their pockets. They knew this resident's reputation well.

"First, on my say-so, call in Dr. Caponi. Then call the OR resident down here. Next, call over to Wills Eye Hospital, and tell them we need a resident if they can spare one, or somebody we can call; then make that call. Again, on my say-so, grab some nurses and send them out to help the ambulance crew. After all that, grab some respirators and gloves and come back here to help. Go!"

He stepped back into the alcove, and put his respirator back on. He should have reversed that order. He got a whiff. He choked back a retch and moved in. The patients, side by side on their carts, were aspirated and hooked up. The ventilation fans in the ceiling were not gonna be enough.

"Jack," he said to one of the nurses, "go dig up some fans, and bring 'em in here and point 'em right at the ceiling."

"Right," Jack replied, off and running.

"O.K.," the resident said. "Gimme some separation here so I can get a good look at both of 'em."

His team was good. In the two minutes he had been occupied, the boys had been aspirated, hooked up to IV's, sedated, and covered. He stepped between the two carts. What he saw looked like two copies of Freddy Kruger. No, check that. Freddy looked much better than this. He got to work.

* * *

"Well," Doctor James said. "They worked all night. Their first priority was to get the CS crystals out of their faces. All the while, the shit still in there was vaporizing. The Wills Eye guy came in, took one look, and said, 'Forget it'. He helped them scoop out the mess in their eye sockets, and left. Dr. Caponi, a burn and facial reconstruction specialist, worked with the resident surgeon in the OR, and they did the best they could for now. The ER resident, Bill Garlow, and his team did a great job. If those kids had been wheeled into the emergency room as is, they would have had to evacuate the place. It could've been total chaos. I'm gonna go change their dressings now. Come on."

They left the break room, and crossed over to the double doors at the ICU. A nurse outside the door gave them all surgical masks, and they donned them and pushed inside. The boys were in the first two spots on the left.

"We've got 'em here so we can get to 'em quick if we have to. CS is nasty enough on external skin surfaces. This stuff got underneath, and some leaked into their bloodstreams. We're flushing it out, slowly but surely; but it'll take time."

Trung and Smythe moved to the side as the doctor approached the beds. There were tubes and lines everywhere. The doctor gently removed the dressing on one boy's face. It had basically just been lying on the face, not wrapped down. The two detectives slid over to look.

"I say!" said Smythe.

"Oh boy!" said Trung.

It was as bad as they had been led to expect. The doctor worked quickly, a nurse cleaning the faces and applying a salve as he redressed them. The doctor finished and led them back to the little break room.

"They're in for all kinds of intensive care and reconstructive surgery. They'll be on, and probably hooked on, pain medication for the rest of their lives. Whoever their families are, I hope they're good people. I guess we'll find that out."

"Will they stay at Sinai?" This from Trung.

"At least until they're out of ICU," James replied. "There're all kinds of economic and legal ramifications as to their long-term care. I have no idea how that'll play out."

"Thanks, Doc," Smythe said, offering his hand. Trung also shook hands with the doctor.

As they were leaving, Dr. James said, "When you catch whoever did this, I'd like to see him get some long-term care himself."

"Bloody right, Doc," Smythe replied. "Bloody damn right."

* * *

Sergeants Vargas and Gonzales, and Lieutenant Gallagher had walked over to the Wharton playground. It was now a very active place, but not with children and their guardians. Sawhorse barricades, cones, and policemen had the grounds closed down. Inside the area was a large Fire Department van, and a smaller, yellow box truck from the United States Transportation Office, Hazmat Division.

They showed their badges to the federal guy at the access point, and after he checked with his super on his radio, he waved them through.

"Federal fuckin' puke," muttered Gonzales as they moved on. "This is our fuckin' District."

"You're right about that, Pablo," said Vargas. "But, because of the CS, this is their turf for a day or two."

"He's right, Sarge," added Gallagher. "They'll get this cleaned up, and then The Fire Department and the Feds will play phone tag for a few days as they toss this back and forth. Then they'll be a memory, and this will still be our little hot tamale.

Comprende, compadre?"

"Yeah, yeah. Comprendo. It's just that the guy looked like he was guarding the fuckin' White House."

"To him, he probably was," said Julio. "It'll give him something to talk about when he hits the singles bar tonight with his little dick."

He laughed and slapped Pablo's shoulder, and Gonzales immediately chilled out. Gallagher once again saw why he had such faith in Vargas. Besides being a great detective, he could chill anybody out, defusing tense, and potentially dangerous, situations.

They came upon the taped off area near the main building of the playground. Captain Ron Gerasimos was standing at the top of the little trash-littered hill. He was the honcho of Fire Company Ten.

"Good morning, gentlemen." he said. "You too, Matt."

Gallagher laughed. It was a stale joke, but he sometimes used it himself. A man in a blue windbreaker stood next to Captain Gerasimos. It had "U.S. TRANS DEPT" in yellow letters stenciled on the back.

"This is John Raleigh of The United States Transportation Department." They all introduced themselves and shook hands.

"I'll let him do the lowdown," Gerasimos said.

"O.K., right," Raleigh started. "Those CS canisters were old Army ordinance, forty millimeter. You might be familiar with them." Gallagher was, as were most Vietnam Vets. Fired from the M-79 grenade launcher, the canisters were used extensively in the war to flush out the enemy from tunnels and bunkers.

"As you can see," Raleigh continued, "the gas has dissipated because of the time elapsed; and because most of it was on those kids. We know this is your case Lieutenant; but the fact that it's old Army stuff means we're involved, like it or not. The way it'll go down is our Hazmat guys will turn the briefcase over to federal explosive people. I'll see that any reports I get go right to you. What any other federal departments will do I can't tell you. I'm only interested in tracing where the shit came from. O.K., lecture over." He strode off.

Gallagher and Gerasimos walked off to talk by themselves. Now Vargas looked closely down into the clearing. There was a fireman down there poking around with a photographer. He guessed he was a Hazmat guy. As he walked down the little hill, he realized he had guessed wrong. Pablo, right behind him, realized it too.

"It's fuckin' Brice," Gonzales said. "I don't believe it." Tony Brice was a police reporter for *The Daily News*, and he took all his own pictures. He said it made it easier to slip in and out of crime scenes that way.

"Hey dickhead, what the hell you doin'?" yelled Gonzales. "Who the fuck let you in here? This is our job and you ain't authorized." Vargas said nothing.

"I work for *The Daily News*, Detective. And until you start signing my paychecks, I don't answer to you," Brice calmly replied. All police beat reporters learned early to be calm around Philly cops. One loud noise too many, and it was a trip to the pokey, courtesy of "Disorderly Conduct."

Gonzales moved over to Brice. "Well, I'm in charge here, and I say you have to leave," he told him.

"And I can say he can stay, Detective. And short of giving out any compromising information, you will cooperate with the press. Is that clear?"

They all looked up. The speaker was Deputy Chief William Barnes, in full uniform. *Oh no,* thought Vargas. This was Butthole Barnes; as in, he had his nose in any higher up's butthole that could further his career.

Gonzales let out a long, audible sigh.

"What was that, Detective? I didn't get that."

"Nothing, sir. Good morning, sir. Mr. Brice and I were just discussing the First Amendment to the Constitution of the United States. Sir."

Vargas stifled a laugh. It was too late to stifle Pablo, though. *Oh, well.*

"Yeah, well hear this," Barnes said. "If my office hears of any complaints from Tony Brice or any other media people, your next civics discussion will be with me personally, and it will be very unpleasant. You get my drift, Detective?"

"Yessir. Loud and clear, sir."

"Good. Get back to work."

Gallagher was now standing near Barnes. "Good morning, Chief. Problem?" he asked.

"Not with me, Lieutenant," Barnes replied. "But your man there is borderline insubordinate. I suggest that you correct that. Promptly."

"Yessir."

"A word, Lieutenant."

"A word", from a superior, meant a talk in private. They moved away toward the playground buildings.

"Lieutenant, I know most of the force doesn't like me, and privately, I don't give a rat's ass. I'm gonna be around like white on rice until you people find out who did this. The Commissioner and the Mayor will be regularly informed; because you're gonna keep me regularly informed. Is that clear?"

"Yessir."

"And if that detective, or any of your other people fuck with me in public again, I'll take 'im down. I'll find the worst beat, in the worst District, and they'll walk it alone. Trust me on this, Lieutenant. I got friends in places the Mayor don't even know about."

"I understand, sir. Will you be wanting daily reports, sir?" Gallagher asked.

"No," Barnes replied. "I'll be calling you; often, but irregularly. I know the sugar coating that goes on reports."

"I can assure you, Chief Barnes, that there is no sugar in my bowl."

"Are you being smart with me, Lieutenant?"

"No, sir. I'm too dumb to do that."

Barnes briefly turned deep red, but it quickly passed. He looked into Matt's eyes, smiled sarcastically, and said, "Gallagher, I know you're a good cop. And we really do want this solved. But it's gonna be a political hot potato, and none of the rights groups even know yet that two poor little African-Americans have been maimed by some kind of lunatic. Do your best; because if you don't, I'll do my worst. Understood, Lieutenant?"

"Understood, sir."

"Carry on."

As Barnes moved off, Gallagher stepped to the top of the hill. The fireman was basically finishing putting away his gear, and Brice was snapping some more pictures.

"Find any good weeds today, Tony?" he asked.

"Don't bust my balls Lieutenant. O.K.? I'm just doing my job."

"Gotta have 'em to bust 'em," muttered Gonzales, as he climbed back up the short hill. Vargas was right behind him. Brice stayed at the bottom.

"Funny, Detective," he said. "Real fuckin' funny. Don't quit your day job." He turned back to Gallagher. "So, Lieutenant how goes the investigation?"

"Just started," replied Gallagher. "There'll be a press conference later, and all you hounds will get what we deem appropriate to give you."

"Can I quote you on *that*, Lieutenant?"

"Quote this!" menaced Pablo, starting back down the hill toward Brice. Vargas quickly restrained him.

"Let's go, Sergeants," said Gallagher. "Mr. Brice must stay and justify his paycheck."

As they walked back to the station, Vargas started chuckling and Gallagher soon joined him.

"What's so funny?" asked Pablo.

"You!" they chorused.

"Pablo, Pablo," sighed Julio. "You've been a Sergeant what, six months? You keep dickin' with Deputy Chiefs, let alone the press, you won't make a year."

"He's right, Sarge," Matt chimed in. "I got everybody's back on this investigation, but you gotta chill. I'd tell you to take anger management classes, but we all know that's bullshit. Ya gotta let it go some other way. Go to the gym and hit the heavy bag; or go up to the Academy and challenge one of the self-defense instructors to a workout." He laughed. "That'll work, believe me. You need some outlet, some release. Ya gettin' any lately?"

Gonzales's frown turned into a smirk. "You gotta lotta guts, Lieutenant ABLS."

They all laughed, and any tension quickly dissolved. As they crossed the street and entered the stationhouse, Vargas thought, not for the first time, that as far as he was concerned, this was Gallagher's greatest trait; it was what made him such a great leader. The guy had absolutely no ego. He never thumped his own chest, and never looked for the limelight. He backed his people one hundred percent, and truly cared about them and the environment they worked in. Shit, how many Lieutenants cleaned bathrooms? And didn't that piss off a lot of higher ups!

Yeah, Gallagher was different, real different. And Vargas would follow him into the depths of hell without a second thought.

CHAPTER THREE

Detective Sergeant Bruno Mitelli was working on his third cup of coffee while going over last night's reports for The 17th District. *The usual chaos and mayhem*, he thought, *except ... what the hell!* He read quickly, and then flipped open his Rolodex. He found the number for his counterpart on the night shift, Sergeant Barry Sykes. He dialed and let it ring. It might take a while, he knew. He almost never called Sykes at home; but this needed discussing before Captain Summers called him into his office. He was probably waking the guy up from just a few hours sleep. Tough shit!

"Yeah," a groggy voice said into his ear.

"Barry, Bruno. What's this shit about a kid blowin' himself up over on Woodstock?"

"Yeah, right. Wait a second. Lemme open my eyes." A pause. "O.K. Dispatch sent a car over Woodstock around 11:00 P.M. Time's in the report. Lots of screamin' and shoutin'." Sykes was fully awake now.

"The Uniforms found a lady in hysterics at the front of the house. They couldn't make sense outta've 'er. An older guy, her father, yelled for the cops to come through the house to the backyard. It was all real hairy I guess, because both Uniforms slapped leather. Good thing, too."

"Yeah, why's that?" Mitelli asked.

"Well," Sykes continued. "They started down the basement steps, and the old man was telling the Uniforms that his grandson was in the shed in the backyard. The grandfather thought somebody had shot him. Anyway, the Uniforms, Little Mo and Persons, got the old man away from the back door, and turned out the basement light."

"Good for them. They were thinking."

"Right, these two are pretty good. Anyways, Persons covered, and Little Mo stepped out first. The old man forgot to mention the dog. All Mo saw was a dark shape headin' right at her. She crouched, the dog jumped, and Mo put one right in his pump. The dog was dead before it crashed into her. Persons charges out and checks Little Mo. She's O.K.

She's already rolling onto her feet. She covers, and Persons heads for the shed. He finds the kid, and the rest is history, as they say. They directed the ambulance around back, and they took him over to Agnes. Somethin' blew up in his face. The explosives guys might still be over at the shed. You should be hearin' from 'em soon."

"O.K., Barry. You wanna keep this or what?"

"It's up to you, Bruno. Not to pass the buck or anything, but this one's a little strange, and daytime's always a little better for the strange ones. And actually, I think Cap'll give it to you anyway."

"Right. Alright, go back to sleep."

"Fat chance. The kids heard me talkin', and they're bangin' on the bedroom door as we speak. I'll be having dirty diapers bouncin' in my face very shortly. Later."

Mitelli laughed as he hung up. He knew that feeling. From long ago, but he knew it.

"Hey Mike," he called to a detective. "Got a minute?"

Detective Mike Robinson walked over to Mitelli's desk.

"Read this please; and then head over to the house, and check with the explosive folks. Then motor over to Agnes, and talk to the docs about the kid."

"What about the mother?" Robinson asked as he quickly scanned the report.

"I was gonna get to that. She's probably at the hospital. If she is, talk to her there. If she's at home, I'd rather you waited until you see what's up in the back of the house. If you see her first, all you're gonna hear is what a fine upstanding lad her son is, and how he would never be messin' with somethin' that might blow him out of his own shoes."

"Right, boss," Mike said. He headed back to his desk. He quickly re-read the report. Then he grabbed keys for one of the Crown Victorias and left the stationhouse.

* * *

Over on Woodstock Street, Officer Steve Archland was just finishing up. Archland was an explosives expert for The Philadelphia Police Department. He liked his job, hairy as it was; and anyway, this one had already gone off. It was the ones he had to stop from going off that gave him the sweats when he slept. But still, short of drugs, nothing gave you a rush like approaching a live boomer. It was probably a little sick. Hell, he *knew* it was a little sick. But he didn't want to do anything else. Nobody else in The Department bothered the Explosives and Demolitions Division. Even The Department psychiatrists stayed out of the picture unless you asked to see one. And if you did, they would pull you off this duty immediately. There could be no shaky fingers on these triggers.

The job was all-volunteer, and the training was long and very intense. The instructors, mostly ex-service members, never let anybody unsuited for the job get too far through the course. The Department's policy was that anybody could apply for the initial test, and take the course if they qualified. Unofficially, volunteers were highly sought and highly encouraged; because no truly sane person would want the job. Police Departments everywhere knew you had to be little nuts in the first place to want the job; but Police Departments everywhere also respected the hell out of their bomb guys. They were given lots of perks, and *lots* of space to work.

Archland and his partner, Glen Alt, had known almost immediately that it had been some kind of booby-trap. They had found a spring mechanism, and remains of a leather wallet.

The first question was whether the kid was making a bomb or had found one.

It quickly became evident that this was no factory; and the kid was no bomb maker. The kid had found it, stolen it, or something else; but that was for the detectives.

Their job was to make their report to their boss, and he would take it from there. Still, it was pretty interesting, if a little gruesome for the kid; and they were cops. They were curious.

"O.K., whadda youse guys got?" asked Sergeant Todd May, their honcho. He was standing in the door of the shed. He was also their trainer, their *constant* trainer, and he was better at this shit than they would ever be (he thought); but he let them do their work. Through the years he had only lost two fingers and part of his jaw; and in four months he was going to retire, mostly whole. He intended to keep all his remaining body parts. Especially his pendulum. It still hung, and it still swung. His wife had told him long ago that she would be a good cop's wife and stick by him through thick and thin, as long as he retired after twenty years. All she wanted him to bring away from The Department was his pension and his pendulum (with accessories). If he came out of all this with either one missing, all bets were off. He sighed inwardly. *Four fucking months*!

"O.K.," Archland started. "Definitely C-4." C-4 was a plastic explosive. "A small piece in a wallet. He had a parallel circuit, with the lower resistance going through a spring. Pull a card out of the wallet, the spring snaps open, and the battery sends the current to the detonator. Ka-boom! He used regular BB's for the shrapnel. We found colored plastic and parts of some twenty dollar bills." He showed May some bits of the dollars.

"This was a good one, Sarge," said Glen Alt, Archland's partner, and the third member of the team. "About three or four grams of C-4 spread on a piece of plastic, and layered with BB's." He also showed Sergeant May some debris. "He used a watch battery. This is what's left of it." It was a crescent shaped piece of metal with minute machine markings on. "This guy really knew what he was doing. And he was confident enough to walk around with this thing in his back pocket or whatever. He's had some training for sure." Glen pointed to a wall behind the workbench. "Bunch of BB's are still in the wall; but I understand that the victim's got most of 'em in him somewhere."

"Right," said Sergeant May. "Finish up, and let's get out of here. We'll go over to the office and get everything to the lab, and start the reports. Who're the dicks on this?"

"That would be us," said a voice outside the shed. From the shed door, May looked over his shoulder to the figure at the fence.

"Mike Robinson, Seventeenth. How ya doin? Can I come in?"

"Sure, Detective, we're just about done here," May replied. "Steve, give him a quick walk through."

"Right, Sarge. Come in, Detective. Stop just inside the door please."

May and Alt stepped outside to make room for Robinson, and Archland stood in front of the bench.

"This is what I see. The kid comes in here, and puts the wallet on the bench. He also had a flashlight. We found that on the floor." He held up a small penlight, and flicked it on. "Still works. Anyways, he opens the wallet and holds it up about here." Archland mimicked holding a small object in his left hand, about chest level. "He pulls a card out of the wallet. He probably heard a snapping noise; and then it went off. This was a really good device."

"No chance he made it?" asked Robinson.

"No chance," replied Archland. "Even with the lack of materials in here, the real clue is how sophisticated this thing was. This was a professional booby-trap. Somebody gave it to him, or he picked it up somewhere."

"O.K.," said Mike. "You'll send us the paperwork?"

"We always do, Detective," said Sergeant May from the yard.

Mike stepped outside.

"As soon as we get the prelim done," May continued, "youse guys will get that. After the lab work comes back, you'll get the final report. It won't take long. We're nowhere near as busy as you regular guys are."

"Yeah, well I don't ever want to get even a little bit busy like you guys," Robinson laughed.

"This was an easy one," said Alt. "It already talked."

"How's that?"

Archland chimed in. "The ones that haven't gone off yet are quiet. They haven't talked yet. Those are the heartbreakers and widow makers."

"Jesus!" Robinson shook his head. "You guys mind if I make a personal observation?"

All three bomb experts smiled, and shook their heads no. They knew what was coming.

"You guys don't look crazy. Must be just a myth."

"No myth," laughed Sergeant May. He pointed to his head. "We keep the craziness all in here. If we looked crazy, do you think they'd let us near one of those things?" He was pointing to the shed. They loved fucking with regular cops. It was a great tension releaser.

But Robinson was laughing now, and they all joined him. "O.K., O.K. I'm outta here. Thanks, guys. Be careful."

"We always are, Detective. We always are. See ya," Sergeant May replied. Bomb guys *always* had the last word.

Robinson walked back to this car thinking hard. As he headed down 20th Street, he realized how polite Archland had been. He had said about the wallet, "somebody gave it to him or he picked it up somewhere." Yeah, sure! He picked it up somewhere, all right. The somewhere was right out of somebody's pocket. You didn't need to be a detective to realize that *somebody* had wanted his pocket picked. A booby-trap for a potential mugger? So this goof ball carries an armed bomb around in his pocket? Everywhere he goes? Oh, brother! This was gonna get interesting. Well, he sighed. He had wanted an interesting life. That's why he had joined The Police Department. So he wouldn't be bored. *Well,* he thought, as he turned left on Tasker Street, *except for a couple of classes at the Academy, he was never bored with this job. Not yet, anyway,* he laughed to himself, as he headed toward Broad Street and Saint Agnes Hospital.

* * *

Saint Agnes Hospital, at Broad and Mifflin Streets, like Methodist Hospital a little further down the road, was huge. The grounds took up an entire square block.

The mob boys in South Philly claimed it as their own. Anytime one of their own was beat up, blown up, or shot, no matter what emergency room he wound up in, as soon as he was stabilized, arrangements were made to bring him to Agnes. This was usually done by private ambulance; but it was also not unusual for the victim himself to make a phone call and walk, assisted by friends, to a waiting car; and off to Saint Agnes they went. Doctors all over the city were used to it; and nobody raised a stink. The bills were always paid without question, and many an emergency technician, nurse, or doctor received a healthy gratuity for his or her efforts. And *nobody* ever needed to be told to keep his mouth shut. At least not more than once. This had gone on for so long that even the cops accepted it. Whenever a detective was told he had a mob shooting or beating to investigate, the first question always asked was, "They got 'im over at Agnes yet?"

But of course, Saint Agnes took in all comers in its area, and Michael Jefferson was in the Intensive Care Unit on the seventh floor. His mother sat quietly by his bed, holding a handkerchief to her face. She was in mild shock, and one of the doctors had given her a light sedative. The last normal thing she remembered was watching the news last night, and hearing a loud noise in the backyard. After that, it was total chaos. She didn't remember sleeping; but she must have; because her father had woken her this morning so she could go back to the hospital.

They had left the emergency room around 2:00 A.M. The emergency room resident had given the grandfather a sleeping pill, and told him to give it to her when they got home.

"Is Michael going to be alright, Doc?" Paul Jefferson had asked.

"He'll live," Doctor Trent had replied. "There's going to be some complications after the surgery; but they'll be able to tell you more in the morning. Get the missus home to bed; and come back tomorrow. He'll be up on the seventh floor in the ICU. Then they'll tell you everything you need to know."

"O.K., Doc. Thanks." Paul then took his daughter home, and put her to bed.

* * *

Detective Robinson stepped off the elevator on the 7th floor at Saint Agnes, and found the nurses station. He showed his badge to the nurse on duty and asked where he could find Michael Jefferson.

"The doctor's making rounds right now, Detective," she told him. "It may be a few minutes before he can talk to you. The mother is down there with Michael in the ICU. She's not in too good shape."

A man approached carrying containers of coffee and orange juice.

"Oh. Here's Mr. Jefferson, Michael's grandfather. This is a police officer, Mr. Jefferson," she said, pointing to Robinson, who again flashed his badge.

"Mr. Jefferson, I'm Detective Robinson. I need to talk to you, please."

"O.K., let me take this juice down to my daughter." He set his coffee down and walked down the corridor.

"How's the kid?" Mike asked the nurse. Nurse Hanley, he noted from her nametag.

"He's stable, that's all I can tell you," she replied. "The doctor will fill you in."

"Is there somewhere Mr. Jefferson and I can talk?"

"Sure, right there across the hall. That door with the 'Staff Only' sign. It's for breaks when we can get 'em."

Paul Jefferson came back and got his coffee, and he and Robinson went into the break room and sat at a small table. Mike got out his notebook and waited until Jefferson had flipped the top back on his coffee and taken a sip.

"Mr. Jefferson," he started "I know this is hard on you ..."

"Call me Paul," Jefferson interrupted.

"Fine. Call me Mike. Paul, tell me what you can remember about what happened before the police arrived?"

"Well, "Jefferson said, "we was watchin' TV, and we heard a bang outside. Ain't nothin' unusual for that neighborhood; but this was a little close. Then we heard screamin'; and the dog was howlin'; and I got scairt. I grabbed my baseball bat, and went out to take a look. When I found my grandson in the shed, I dammed near fainted. I ran back inside and called 911. Then I grabbed some towels and went back out. The kid was a mess. His hands and face was a mess. I wrapped his hands best I could. I left his face alone. I didn't wanna mess with that. Then the cops showed up. I went in and waved them to the backyard. I told them I thought somebody did the kid with a shotgun. Anyways, I forgot to tell them about the dog. The lady cop shot the dog."

"I know that. It was unfortunate; but any cop in that situation probably would've done the same thing."

"I know, I know. I ain't blamin' her," Jefferson said. "That dog didn't bark at strangers. The kid trained it that way."

"Say what?"

"Yeah, he always said it was because he didn't want the neighbors complainin'; and then maybe the SCPA would come take it away. It didn't bark; but one look at that bad boy chargin' the fence was enough to keep people away."

Trained not to bark? A silent guard dog? Yeah, Robinson thought. *But for who? The household or the kid?*

"O.K.," Mike said. "And then?"

"And then the cops took over. I kept Monica—that's my daughter—in the house. And that took some doin', believe me. The ambulance came, and got him to the hospital."

"What did you tell the detectives when they came?"

"I didn't see 'em 'til they came over to the hospital. They told me no shotgun. They said somethin' exploded in the shed."

"Did your grandson ever keep anything unusual in the shed, Paul?"

"He didn't keep nothin' in the shed, far's I know." Paul replied. "I didn't even know he had a key to that lock. There's one hangin' near the basement door; and I keep one on my key chain. Here's mine." He held up a small key attached to a chain. "The other one's still hangin' up in the basement. I checked when I got home last night."

Robinson caught up his notes while Jefferson sipped his coffee. He looked up and stared frankly at Jefferson. Jefferson held his gaze without flinching. *This might get a little rough,* Robinson thought.

"Mr. Jef … Paul," he said. "Please don't take offense; but I have to do my job. You seem awful calm about this. Are you telling me you didn't know Michael had been in that shed last night? Or any other night?"

Jefferson set down his cup. "I realize yir just doin' your job," he said; "but you lissun to me a minute, young buck. I done lost two grandkids already. One shot in the back, one shot in the face. Both over this fuckin' crack shit. I lost a son in Vietnam. Over the years my heart's been gettin' just a little stony, know what I mean?" He leaned forward over the table. "What heart I got left is breakin' in little pieces over this. My grandkid is maimed, and my daughter needs sedatin'. I'm stayin' calm for them. So I don't need you tellin' me I'm too calm, O.K.?"

"Yes sir, my apologies; and believe me, my condolences. But please, let's move on here." Robinson turned to a fresh page in his notebook. "We know Michael had never even been arrested, let alone had a record." This has been in the report. "Was he a problem at home?"

"No, never," Paul said immediately. "That's why this really hurts. Straight A's at school. He wanted to go to college. He always minded me and his mother, and always did his chores."

"What was in the shed?" Mike asked. He had seen a few tools and gardening implements, but he wanted to hear it from Jefferson.

"Just some tools and my gardenin' stuff," replied Paul. "I grow tamators and tators, and some greens and such in the summer. I keep it locked because them crack heads nowadays will steal anything ain't nailed down. Like I said, I didn't know the kid had his own key. I mean hell, if he wanted in there, he could've used the one hangin' in the basement anytime."

"Yeah, right," Robinson said. "Do you know if he was with anybody last night?"

"Oh sure," Jefferson said. "Same kids he was with most any night. They hang out after school and after dinner. Some nights Mike came home a little late; but like I said, he never gave us any trouble; and his homework was always done, so we cut him a little slack there."

"What are the names of these kids? We're gonna want to talk to them."

"Uh, let's see. Memory's a little slow here. There's Jamal, Jamal Woodson. Then there's Reshawn Deeds. They both live over near Jackson Elementary School. I think they both go to Roxborough High School."

Roxborough High School was in northwest Philadelphia. Philadelphia's version of bussing was to assign kids to school districts away from their neighborhoods, and let SEPTA get them there.

"And there's a Gerald Hanson," Jefferson continued, "young boy, he goes to Barratt Middle School over on Sixteenth Street. He lives over on Titan Street."

"Pretty good for a slow memory," Robinson observed.

"I seen these kids most every day. They played together, hung together. Hell, they even helped each other with their homework, even though they went to different schools. Mostly, young Gerald needed the most help. He got left back twice in grade school. He's smart, but he has trouble with readin', I think. Oh, by the way, Michael goes to Neumann."

"Thanks. That was in the report." Robinson finished writing and looked up. "You've been a big help. I gotta wait for the doctor. Here's my card. If you think of anything else, anything odd, anything strange, let us know. Somebody will always answer that number."

Jefferson got up, and opened the door to leave the room. "He's a good boy, Detective," he said. "I don't know what he was playin' with in that shed; but when you find out, please let us know."

"You'll be hearing from us, Mr. Jefferson."

The doctor came in as Jefferson left. He sat down and said, "I'm Bill Ryan. I'm the daytime doc up here."

"Mike Robinson," replied Mike, showing his badge yet again. It probably wasn't necessary; but it was so automatic that he, like most cops, wasn't even conscious of doing it.

Ryan sighed and stretched. He glanced briefly at his clipboard, and then laid it aside. "Alright, here's the deal. Last night the surgeons removed all of the plastic and leather from Michael's face. They got most of the BB's; but there's still a few lodged in his jaw and palette. He lost one eye." Ryan stopped. "Well," he continued, "it's still there; but everything that makes sight work is gone. He lost two fingers on his left hand, and parts of three others on this right. He'll recover fully as far as his overall health goes. He's gonna need rehab and therapy; but he'll make it."

"How's the mom?" Mike asked.

"Basically, in a state of shock. I'd like her to go home and rest; but she's a mother. We'll let her stay as long as she wants."

"Can I talk to the kid?'

"Not to sound like a smart ass, but you can talk to him all you want. He ain't gonna be responding for a while. His face is a mess, his hands are maimed; and we're gonna keep him on a morphine drip, and keep him sleeping as much as possible."

"O.K., Doc, don't get your dander up. I had to ask."

"You think it's related to the other kids?" Ryan asked

Robinson leaned forward intently. "What other kids?"

"Those kids over at Mount Sinai. We had a guy from Wills Eye Hospital come over to look at the kid's eye last night during the surgery. He had been over at Sinai earlier to check out two kids who had their eyes blasted out by some kind of tear gas bomb. He told our surgeons that, short of a battlefield, it was the worst thing he'd ever seen."

"Holy shit!" Robinson sat stunned; but that only lasted a few seconds. He was up and moving out the door. "Thanks, Doc. Gotta go!" And he was gone.

Oh well, Doctor Ryan thought. *Guess I'll read about it in the papers like everybody else.*

Detective Mike Robinson stepped quickly across the hall to the nurses' station. The nurse on duty looked up. "Was there something else, Detective?"

"Yes. Could I use your phone; and do you have a number over to Mount Sinai Hospital?"

The nurse picked up a phone and dialed for an outside line. "What department would you like?"

"Admissions, I would think," Mike replied.

The nurse consulted a list by the phone, dialed a number, and handed him the phone. "Here you are."

Mike took the phone. "Thank you."

"Mount Sinai. Admissions. Miss Simpson speaking."

"Miss Simpson, this is Detective Mike Robinson from The Seventeenth District. You had two young men last night admitted with wounds from a tear gas bomb of some sort, correct?"

"One moment, Detective ... yes, Detective. They were admitted after surgery."

Robinson looked at his notes. "Miss Simpson, were their names Reshawn Deeds and Jamal Woodson?" His heart was pounding.

"May I have your badge number, Detective?"

Mike had to restrain himself from shouting. "Six eight four one eight three. My supervisor is Sergeant Bruno Mitelli."

"Thank you, Detective," the woman replied, making a note. "Yes. Their names are Deeds and Woodson. We just received that information. A nurse got it from one of the boys this morning when he woke up."

"Ma'am, where were the kids brought in from?"

"The Wharton Street Playground, Detective."

"Thank you, ma'am." Mike handed back the phone, mumbled thanks to the nurse, and sprinted to the elevators.

CHAPTER FOUR

Gallagher sat at his desk re-reading the incident report on the kids. Trung and Smythe had told him and Vargas of their visit to the hospital. Then all the Special Task guys hit their desks to clear everything they could, so they could concentrate on the new case. The Vice folks were gonna be a big help; because Matt had already decided that pimps and hookers were going take a back seat until they got a handle on this lunatic. Sergeant Godwin would take everything Vargas passed on to her without a hitch or complaint. Gallagher knew this, and didn't give it a second thought. Emma, ever concerned, reassured him anyway.

"Don't worry, Matthew. We'll handle it. You guys just catch this asshole."

"Such language, Sergeant!"

"Excuse me, Lieutenant. Please catch this rectum."

"Yes, ma'am. Said rectum is definitely priority one."

Earlier Gallagher had called the Narcotics team into the interrogation room before they went out for the day. They were a scruffy lot, as all such teams are. They had to get in with the scumbags and dirtballs, make buys, and then make arrests. It was like that day in and day out, on and on and on. And it was very dangerous. Gallagher had always felt that the only way to stop the ever-escalating violence, prison overcrowding, and wrecked lives, was to legalize the shit once and for all.

"O.K.," Matt started, after they all sat down. "Youse all know about this CS booby-trap. We all know somebody out there saw something or knows something, even if they're not sure what it means. Youse guys can help us."

"Whaddya got in mind, Loo?" asked Sergeant Taggert. He knew what Gallagher wanted; but they all needed to hear it out loud. They all were loyal to Gallagher, and would do anything he asked. But he had to ask.

"Here it is, Vic. In your travels throughout the next few days, ask around. If you bag some nickel and dimer that knows somethin', and he's a two or three time loser, you can deal. On my say-so. Those kids got that briefcase from somebody. It wasn't just layin' around somewhere."

"How far can we go, Matt?" asked Sergeant Shincock. "We need to know that."

"I know, Mike," Matt replied. "No major bad guys get off for nothin'. I trust your judgment out on the street. Let us know what you get, and if we can use it, your little perp can walk."

"Still sounds kinda vague," said Detective Parmella Smith.

"It's all vague, Detective. Just do what you can."

There were only two people on the whole squad that Gallagher didn't really like. Smith was one of them, and they both knew it. Gallagher didn't analyze it. It just was. She was a good cop. As long as she did her job, he didn't care about her personality. Good thing, too. It really stunk.

Juan Pasqualez had sat silent through all this with his usual blank poker face. It was the most desired trait in undercover drug work; and Pasqualez had it in spades. A clock face showed more emotion. *Gonzales could sure take notes from this guy*, Gallagher thought.

"Talk to me, Juan," Gallagher said aloud.

"No problema aqui, Jefe," Juan responded. "We'll see what goes down."

"OK, thanks people," Matt said. "Keep in touch."

Gallagher left the room and walked over to the Robbery and Homicide desks, which were all together like a big rectangle in a corner of the room. All four detectives were busy typing, reading reports, or talking on the phone. Matt waited for the phone calls to end; and then they were all looking at him with those friendly smirks he pretended not to like. Every squad needed an oddball or two. He was lucky enough to have four of them.

"Is there something we can do for you, Lieutenant Gallagher?" Detective Costello asked, batting her eyes at him. Matt was already trying hard not to laugh.

"What's happening, Loo?" asked Detective Ladders.

"We have donuts, Matthew," Sergeant Patrillo said, as she licked jelly off her lips.

"Come on, cut it out you flakes," said Sergeant Farrel. He was trying not to laugh too. "The Lieutenant has some thing on his mind."

"Do tell," said Costello. "Is this the proper place to hear it, Matthew?"

Gallagher finally snorted laughter. Irene Costello and Imogene Patrillo teased him like this all the time. Truth to tell, Gallagher loved to be teased by beautiful women. And these two were gorgeous!

"You all know what I need," Gallagher said, still laughing. "You hear anything, let me know. But don't deviate from your caseload."

"But Matthew," Imogene cooed. "Deviation is my specialty." The whole squad room was laughing now. Matt just shook his head and walked away. It was all in fun, and Costello and Patrillo were great cops; but there was real desire in both pair of eyes as they watched Gallagher move back to his desk. Emma Godwin was well aware of this, and had warned both of them months ago.

"I'm gonna say this just once," Emma had told Irene and Imogene, when the three of them were alone. "Don't either one of you even think about jumpin' his bones just to win the pool; and if either one of you tries to lead him on emotionally, I'll have your tits in a wringer. That man's heart still ain't whole, and I'll be watchin' real close. Don't make me prove to you how much I care for that man."

And that was that. It had been a very one-sided conversation.

Before Gallagher sat back down at his desk he yelled, "How'd they do last night, Jack?"

Detective Jack Miles of Vice was in charge of this little detail, reporting on the status of the Philadelphia Phillies.

"The Marlins beat 'em five to three, boss. De Leon had 'em handcuffed, but Morandini booted one late, and Florida got three unearned runs. Inky hit one out. Still, they're looking good, boss."

"Yeah, we'll see. Same old shit. If the pitchin' holds up, we got a shot. They're home tonight against the Expos."

Miles let the discussion end. He wasn't as big a fan as Matt. Almost nobody was. But the Phillies were huge heartbreakers.

They hadn't been to the playoffs in ten years. But when they were good back in the day they didn't just break your heart, they ripped it out. They made the NLCS in 1976, 1977, and 1978, and lost all three times. They won the pennant in 1980 against Houston with a late game comeback in game five against Nolan Ryan, of all people. They then went on to win their only World Series title, beating Kansas City in six games.

Gallagher was a rabid Phillie fan, more fanatic than the Phanatic, the Phillies mascot. He had two season tickets in the 200 Level near the Phillies dugout. He went as much as his duties allowed; when he couldn't make it he gave the tickets away. But that wasn't often. Even at eight o'clock or so, he was only a ten-minute ride from the office to the Vet via the Broad Street Subway. You can't beat The System.

* * *

Meanwhile, Detective Mike Robinson had arrived back at The 17th District all fired up. He flew through the doors, and ran to Sergeant Mitelli's desk. Mitelli was on the phone, but that didn't stop Robinson.

"Sarge!" he said, breathlessly. "There was another one over at Three/Four! Another bomb!"

"I'll get back to you," Mitelli said into the phone, and hung up.

"Slow down, Mike. Take a deep breath." Mitelli waited a moment. "O.K.," he said. "Start from the top."

Robinson told him what he had learned from the bomb guys, and the doctor at the hospital. He also gave him a quick brief of his conversations with Jefferson and the woman at Sinai Admissions. "It's gotta be related, Sarge. It's two bombs."

"Maybe, maybe not," Bruno replied. "But let's go see the Captain."

The 17th wasn't as big as The 3/4 District. The Captain's office was just a few doors down. His secretary had a small alcove near the Captain's door.

"We need to see the boss, Marybeth," Bruno said. Bruno had been around long enough that he could have just knocked and walked in; but protocol was protocol. The secretary punched a button, and spoke a few words into her phone. "Go right in," she said as she hung up. Bruno tapped his knuckle on the glass, and he and Robinson walked in.

Captain Christopher Summers looked up from his desk. "You heard about the CS victims at Mount Sinai, right?"

"Yeah, Cap," Mitelli replied. "Mike heard about it over at Agnes, believe it or not."

"Have a seat." Summers pointed to two chairs. "The Roundhouse just called. My boss got it from Chief Barnes. I swear to God; Barnes has a better intelligence network than most countries. Faster, too. If we could use it, we could roll up every drug gang in The District. Anyway, tell me what you got Detective Robinson."

Looking at his notes, Mike gave them everything he had. Both Summers and Mitelli listened closely. When he finished, Captain Summers looked over at Mitelli. "You first, Bruno."

"O.K. Cap, here's what I wanna do. I'm gonna send Mike here over to pull the Hanson kid out of school, and bring 'im in for a chat. I'll use Canatta; it always works. Other than that, I'll wait on you. I know you gotta call Captain Parmalee, and work things out."

"That's right," Summers said. "If it's the same case, we'll let him have it, I think. They got more people."

"Captain," Mike said. "I'd like a piece of this."

"Detective, there's plenty of 'love' in the City of Brotherly Love to keep us all busy twenty four/seven. But if we get slow, and Sergeant Mitelli wants to send you over there, that's up to him."

"Yessir."

"O.K., guys," Summers said, standing up. As Robinson walked out the door, Summers said, "Bruno, a word." Mitelli closed the door.

"I know you're gonna use Canatta to scare the kid. But no rough stuff. Things are gonna get bad enough as it is."

"Cap, we're just gonna use Alphonse to get information from the kid. There won't be a mark on him."

"Alright. Just keep Canatta on a short leash. If I was a kid in trouble, and in a room alone with Canatta, I'd shit my pants six different ways from Sunday." Bruno was laughing as he left the room.

As it was, Detective Alphonse Canatta was just getting in because he had been up at the Academy for his annual pistol qualification.

When Bruno got back to the squad room, Canatta was at his desk.

"How'd you do, Al?" Bruno asked.

"I passed," Al replied. "But I gotta do better. I still ain't used to that Glock. I should practice more."

The Philadelphia Police Department had recently chosen the 9mm Glock as its standard handgun. With fifteen slugs in the magazine, and one in the chamber, it gave the cops the extra firepower they had been screaming about for years. Hell, they were even starting to catch up with the kids in the projects who were running around with MAC-10's with 30 round magazines.

"I got a job for ya, Al.," Mitelli said as he came over and sat next to Canatta's desk. He filled him in on the situation. "I need everything he knows. Don't hurt 'im. I mean … well, you know what to do."

"So how do I look today?" Canatta asked. Others in the squad room pretended to be doing anything but listening.

"Fine."

"Bullshit. How do I look?"

"Look Al … Gumba, whaddya want from me? I ain't countin' your zits."

"I did this morning. I estimated about what, ninety, one-ten? Just oozin' and a coozin' all down my fuckin' face."

Several people in the room were starting to look nauseous.

"Look," Bruno said. "That new Vitamin A therapy's startin' to work. You know it is. It's gonna go away eventually."

"Yeah, yeah. Alright. Let me go change."

Al left, and Bruno sighed. Everyone in the room had heard the conversation. That's the way Al had wanted it from the start. Last year, on Canatta's first day in the squad room, Bruno had introduced him to everyone; and then Canatta had surprised them all. He had walked to the center of the room and said, "Can I have everyone's attention, please?" And under the circumstances, he had immediately gotten it.

"I know what I look like. I see this face in the mirror every day. It's acne at its worst, and it's grotesque. I'll be starting a new therapy soon, and I hope it helps. If you wanna know about it, ask me. And if you're a female, please don't come up to me and say it doesn't look that bad. That's worse than anything. O.K., that's it."

Everyone had handled it well after that, at least for the first few months. But then one day last winter they found out, quite by accident, that they had a new psychological weapon in the squad room, the likes of which none of them had ever seen.

A tag team of purse-snatchers had been trolling Broad Street, near Reed. They spotted a potential victim coming down the sidewalk. One thug waited in a doorway, and the other waited just around the corner on Reed Street. As the woman passed the doorway, the kid jumped out, grabbed her purse, and started to take off with it. The victim ran right with him, holding on to the purse strap, and yelling for help. The kid started to turn the corner, and gave one final, hard yank on the purse. At the same time the woman slipped on a patch of ice, and her face slammed into a fire hydrant. The strap came free, and the snatcher threw the purse to the runner, who took off like greased lightning. But just as the snatcher himself tried to take off, a pedestrian knocked him to the ground. Several people then held him down, until a cop arrived on the scene. Seeing the woman, he called for an ambulance before he cuffed the kid.

Later, back at the Station, they had the kid in the interrogation room. Two officers were grilling the little bastard about where his friend was. Alphonse Canatta, in the squad room, had just happened to take the call from the hospital about the woman's condition. Parts of her face had been absolutely shattered, and she would need extensive reconstructive surgery. Canatta lost it, and like everyone else who got that angry that quick, blood rushed to his head, and veins in his face pulsed and throbbed. This caused some of his zits to leak, and the result was very unpleasant to look at, to say the least.

Canatta stormed into the interrogation room, and pushed right past one of the officers. He picked the kid out of his chair by his coat, brought his face right up next to his own, and yelled, "You tell me everything about you and your rat bastard friend right now, or I'm gonna beat you into a fuckin' coma!"

The kid's eyes had gotten wide, and his skin was turning gray. A low wail started in his throat, and turned into a full scream.

"Aaah, aaah, help me, help me! Please help me, Officers! I'll tell ya, I'll tell ya! Just help me, please!"

The other two cops in the room were absolutely astounded. This was a typical Philly street kid, tough as they come. They had been threatening him for twenty minutes with the worst kind of consequences if he didn't talk to them.

But they hadn't gotten a peep out of the kid, not even his name. And then in ten seconds, Canatta had the kid begging for mercy; that face had scared him to death. He had even pissed himself. Hell, it had even shaken the two cops.

Detective Alphonse Canatta became the best interrogator of juveniles The 17th District ever had.

Bruno Mitelli walked back to his desk and sat down. He had other things on his plate; but as soon as Robinson got here with the Hanson kid, he would drop what he was doing. Al walked back into the squad room wearing a clean blue sweatshirt. He also sat back at his desk.

Bruno really did feel sorry for the guy. He had once seen Al without a T-shirt on. The acne was also on his chest, shoulders, and back. And it was vicious looking stuff. You didn't have to be a detective to know Canatta didn't have a girlfriend. If Lieutenant Matt Gallagher's nickname was "*Ain't Been Laid Since*," this poor kid was "*Ain't Never Gonna Happen*."

* * *

Gallagher's intercom light blinked, and he picked up his phone. It was Captain Parmalee.

"A word, Matthew."

"On my way, Cap," Matt replied. *Geez,* he thought, *must be more trouble*. Whenever somebody in authority called him Matthew like that, it was never good news.

A minute later, with a wave at Jane Wilson, he tapped on Parmalee's door, and walked into the office and took a seat.

"Just got a call from the Seventeenth," Parmalee began. "They got a kid over at Agnes that had a booby-trapped wallet blow up in his face."

Gallagher's jaw dropped.

"Yeah, that's how I feel," Parmalee continued. "They might have a handle on the identity of our CS victims. They're gonna get back to us fairly quick. Captain Summers and I agree that if this is the same case, you keep it. But if it was a hot potato before, we got a real fire now."

"O.K., boss. How's the kid at Agnes?"

Parmalee nodded to himself approvingly. Gallagher was one of those rare people in The Department. He really, truly cared about crime victims. Most cops were so jaded by the mayhem they witnessed, that they forgot how to care. For some, it was the only way to stay sane.

"He's banged up, but he'll make it," Parmalee replied. "At least he's got one usable eye left. But both his hands are maimed."

"Captain, this is a whole new meal. I wanna go after this fuckin' nutcase with everything I got."

"You're right, Matt. This changes everything. Summers and I gotta be at the Roundhouse in twenty minutes; and we are definitely gonna hear about it. Chris and I will recommend a task force with you as boss. I'm sure Chief Loudin will go along with it." Chief Inspector Maxwell Loudin was The Philadelphia Police Department's Chief of Detectives. "Sergeant Mitelli over at the Seventeenth will be calling you as soon as he knows for sure about the ID's. I gotta go."

"Right, boss." Matt got up and left the room. *The shit was definitely gonna hit the fan now*, he thought.

* * *

Over at The 17th, Robinson brought the Hanson kid through the station doors and up to Mitelli's desk. The kid was as stone faced as any poker player.

"Take him into the question and answer room please, Detective Robinson, and give the young man a donut and a hot chocolate, please." Mitelli's exaggerated politeness was all part of the set up. When the kid came in, Canatta had had his mug buried in paperwork. And Bruno knew that Mike had been a model police officer with the little bastard on the way over from the school. Mitelli had great cop instincts, and as soon as he saw Gerald Hanson's cold, blank face, he knew the kid had what they needed. But these kids knew that all they had to do was be silent, for hours if need be, and eventually they would get a meal and a place to sleep, or be released to a parent or guardian (if one could be found). But Mitelli had his secret weapon.

After Robinson got the kid situated, Al came over to Mitelli and asked, "Whaddya wanna use this time?"

"I'll tell 'im your mother was killed by a black mugger a couple of months back. Give us about five minutes."

"O.K., Sarge. I'll be getting my game face on." Canatta laughed. "Like it ain't mostly there already."

Bruno almost gave him a friendly whack on the shoulder, but quickly pulled back. *That woulda broke about ten zits*, he thought. Mitelli called Robinson out of the interrogation room, and briefed him on the set-up. Then they both went into the room and closed the door.

The kid was sitting calmly, hands folded on the table, blank look still on his face.

"Hello, Gerald," said Mitelli. "Hot chocolate O.K.?"

"S'alright. I wanna go back to my school. We got a big math test today."

"Soon, Gerald, soon," Mitelli told him

Robinson, also sitting at the table, said, "Sergeant, his teacher told me he's a model student. Does his best, and don't cause no trouble."

"Good," said Mitelli. "Real good. Where were you last night, Gerald?"

The kid went instantly back into stone face mode. Never talk; never, ever talk.

"Gerald, your friend Michael's in Saint Agnes Hospital. He's missing an eye and some fingers; and the rest of his face is a mess. Something blew up in his hands. You know anything about that?"

Again, no response; just a slight widening of the eyes.

Robinson leaned forward. "What about Jamal and Reshawn, Gerald? Were you with them last night? It's better if you talk to us now, son, because later just might be too late. Help us, and we'll help you."

Nothing.

Outside the door, Canatta and another detective waited. "Ready?" Canatta asked. "Anytime, Al," the other cop laughed. The rest of the squad room was gathered at the one-way glass. It was always a great show.

Inside the room, Sergeant Mitelli started again. "Look Gerald, we need ..."

Bam! The door rattled. Loud voices.

"You can't go in there, man!"

"He might be the one! I want his ass!"

The door opened partway, and a blue clad arm shoved through before it was dragged back, and the door was slammed shut.

"Let go of me! Get your fuckin' hands off me!"

"Christ, help me over here! He's outta control again!"

Inside, an alarmed Bruno looked over at Robinson. "I thought he was off today."

"Me too," Mike shrugged. "Shit, ever since that black kid killed his mother, he ain't been the same."

Gerald was now paying close attention.

"Yeah," said Sergeant Mitelli. "He was a good cop until that kid killed his mom. I'll go calm him down." Bruno headed for the door.

Just as he started to pull it open, a voice yelled, "Look out Sarge!" And a man flew into the room, knocking Mitelli aside. Before Robinson could react, Canatta had the kid by the shirt, up close and personal.

"Did you kill my mother, you little bastard? Did you kill her?" Al was shouting. "Tell me, you little ratfuck!"

Gerald immediately started screaming for help. He wasn't scared of anything. Except monsters. And this thing in front of him definitely qualified.

This might be a new record, Robinson thought as he ran around the table and grabbed Canatta's arm.

"Al! Easy, man! Easy! We need this kid!"

Bruno had come up and grabbed Al's other arm.

"Let him go, Detective!"

Al still seethed and snarled in the kid's face. "Did you kill my mother, you little bastard?"

"Help me!" screamed Gerald.

"Detective Canatta!" Mitelli shouted. "I said let him go, or I'm sending you right back to the psycho ward. Drop him! Now!"

Al lowered the kid to the ground, and let go. Gerald immediately scrambled into a corner. His pants were soaked, and he was babbling.

"Keep him away from me, please! I didn't do nothin'! I'm just the lookout! The other guys did the stealin'! Please!"

Bingo!

Robinson and Mitelli turned Al around, and started to march him out of the room. Canatta half-twisted around.

"If I find out you killed my mother, I'm comin' after you, you little prick!"

Bruno and Mike shoved him out of the room, and closed the door.

"Man, that was close," Mike said.

Bruno picked it up. "Gerald, I'm sorry. We didn't know he was here today. But you gotta tell us everything you know, so we can tell him you didn't kill his mother. He's still a little nuts about it; and once he's out of this building, I can't control him."

"Alright, alright," Gerald was crying freely now. "Just keep that monster away from me." He moved back to the chair, and then looked down. "I pissed my pants," he wailed.

Back out in the squad room there were moans and cheers as money changed hands. Detective Brandon had handled all bets, as usual. The first wager was strictly for time. How long from the second Al went through the door until the little delinquent started talking. A stopwatch was used for this. The other bet was, would he wet himself or not? Some did, some didn't. Brandon kept half the money on the time bet, and whoever was closest got the other half. The piss bets were win or lose, and handled individually. It really was great fun, and the best entertainment the station ever got—at least inside the station. Mitelli looked the other way, and didn't participate in the wagering. He didn't need that aggravation.

Al Canatta had quickly retreated to the bathroom. Several zits had broken open, of course, and leaked down onto his sweatshirt. He wet a paper towel and started to clean up. The door opened, and Detective Ruth Netters, his partner, walked in and locked the door. She had a white towel in one hand, and a jar in the other.

"What do you want?' he rasped. Even though it was all an act, it still took a lot out of him. And broken zits hurt.

"I want to help you," she replied.

"No pity, Ruth."

"No pity, Al; just concern, and a little compassion. You're my partner and I happen to like you." She moved to the sink, and ran hot water onto the towel. She reached for his shoulder, and gently turned him around. She started lightly patting his face.

"What's in the jar?" he asked.

"It's a new cleansing pad and medicine. My little sister's been using it. It seems to help."

"I've tried everything, believe me."

"I know, Al; but you've got a new friend and a new partner. And we're gonna keep trying."

"Look at me closely," Al said. But she already was. "I'm grotesque."

"Oh, bullshit! Now that's pity, self-pity. The acne's grotesque, not you. You're a good man, and a good cop. Now hold still." She pulled one of the pads out of the jar.

This isn't happening, Al thought. *Not to me. Never to me.* He closed his eyes and stood still as Ruth gently patted down his face.

Ruth wondered if any or all of the other Districts were this bizarre. She could only hope.

CHAPTER FIVE

Just after 11:00 A.M. Gallagher's phone rang. "Lieutenant Gallagher, Three-Four District."

"Mornin', Matt. Bruno Mitelli here, from across the road," Sergeant Mitelli said.

"Hi, Sarge. I thought I'd be hearing from ya. What's up?"

"O.K., you know about the little wallet bomb last night, right?'

"Right."

"Well," Bruno said, "there's no doubt. The wallet and the briefcase came from the same guy."

"Oh, shit."

"Oh, shit is right," Bruno came back. "I'd like to pat myself on the back, but we just got lucky. I mean, if you can call a kid maiming himself in my District lucky."

"Alright, Bruno," Matt started to reply. "How do you want … ?"

"Wait, Matt," Mitelli interrupted. "This is the sweet part; and I will take a pat on the back for this. We caught your 'Booze Bandits'. There's four of 'em."

"GET DA FLOCK OUTTA HERE!" Gallagher shouted.

The squad room focused on Gallagher intently. This phrase, a Gallagher original, was the signal to anyone who knew him that something was seriously up. From his early teen years growing up in the Roxborough section of the city, Matt, like most kids in the city, had started using the phrase "Get da fuck outta here!" for all kinds of incredulous situations, minor and major. Trying to break the habit of using the phrase altogether had proved to be impossible. As Gallagher had moved up in The Department, he had substituted "flock" for "fuck" to make the phrase inoffensive. After Gallagher had taken over the squad room early in 1990, the phrase had morphed even further into one of the great group gags in The Philadelphia Police Department. Whenever an outsider, be it a suspect, another officer, whoever, was giving off what sounded like a lot of bullshit, one of the detectives would say, loudly and firmly, "That sounds like a bunch of sheep to me." "A bunch of sheep?" came the inevitable reply. "Yeah—GET DA FLOCK OUTTA HERE!" the whole squad room would shout at the startled questioner. The gag was famous in Districts throughout the city, and although many tried, nobody quite pulled it off like The 3/4. Gallagher still used the "f-word" occasionally, but he tried not to around Emma Godwin; and he never used it around Jane Wilson, the Captain's secretary.

"Fuckin-A right, Loo. Your boys at Sinai, the kid at Agnes, and a kid over with us. We pulled him outta Barratt Middle School this morning after the Agnes kid's grandfather talked to one of my dicks. The little bastard wouldn't tell us a fuckin' thing at first, but now he won't shut up."

"Let me guess, you used Canatta," Gallagher asked.

"Yeah, whatever works, ya know? Listen, let me fill you in real quick and then we'll bring the kid over to ya."

"O.K., shoot."

Mitelli filled Matt in on the morning's activities, and made arrangements for charges, jurisdiction, and travel for the Booze Bandits' point man, Gerald Hanson. Gallagher thanked Mitelli and hung up. He looked up at the squad room. He didn't have to ask for anyone's attention. Except for several people on the phone, everyone was looking at him.

"Well," he said loudly, standing up. "This is gonna get really interesting. We know who the kids in Mount Sinai are. They're one-half of the Booze Bandits. There's another kid at Saint Agnes who was maimed last night by a bobby-trapped wallet. The Seventeenth is bringing over the last member of our little gang; they called him 'the point man', believe it or not. Sergeant Vargas, me and your people please," Matt finished, pointing toward the interrogation room.

"Right, Matt," Julio replied.

"Emma, a word please," Matt said.

"Yes, Boss," Emma said, coming over to Matt's desk.

"A detective from the Seventeenth will be here shortly with our juvenile perp. Keep the kid handcuffed, and watch him, please. Bruno Martelli says he's really spooked."

"O.K., Matthew. What's he spooked about?"

"They used Canatta on him."

"That's terrible the way they use that man," Emma said. She had never met Canatta; but like everybody else she had heard the stories. Even if you weren't a gossip in The Philadelphia Police Department, you heard it all anyway, just by being there.

"I know, Emma," Matt said over his shoulder as he walked to the interrogation room. "But it works. And it busted this case wide open. End-a-story." This was another one of Matt's sayings. Always used politely, it always meant: conversation over.

Gallagher closed the door behind him and sat down with the Special Tasks Unit.

"Que pasa, Jefe?" Sergeant Gonzales asked.

Gallagher filled them in with as much as he knew in the short, all-business style he used in situations like this. It was one of the things that made him easy to work for. When he went into this mode, his body language, facial expressions, and voice let everybody know that this was Lieutenant Matt Gallagher, honcho, universally recognized as one of the best, if not the best, cops in The Department. Gallagher didn't use a poker face with these troops.

"Mike Robinson's bringing over the incident report about the Jefferson kid. Now before he gets here, listen up." He had their undivided attention, and he knew it was because they knew what was coming, and he knew they would take it well. Jeez, these were good cops. The whole squad was a cut above. He felt privileged to be their boss. "What I said this morning about Sergeant Vargas still being in charge, I meant that when I said it. It can't be that way anymore. I am now in charge, personally and directly, of the Special Tasks Unit. Sergeant Vargas, talk to me."

Julio looked hard at Gallagher. "You know it's cool, Matt. I like being in charge; but if not, I've had worse bosses."

"Pablo?" Matt said.

"No problema aqui, Jefe."

Matt looked down the table. "Nguyen?"

"It's good training," Trung replied.

"Please carry on, Leftenant," Smythe said before Matt could continue. "Let's Rock 'n Roll, as you Yanks are wont to say."

"Right," Matt said. Before he could continue there was a knock at the door.

"Come in," Matt said. The door opened and Mike Robinson walked in. "Hi, Mike. You know Julio and Pablo. This is Winston Smythe and Nguyen Trung. Guys, this is Mike Robinson from the Seventeenth."

They all exchanged pleasantries, and Mike sat down. He placed a folder on the table. "Here's the report on Michael Jefferson, the leader of our little military group. He's the one in Agnes. The point man's outside. Let me run it down for you before you talk to him."

"Gawhead," replied Gallagher.

"They worked as a team, like a recon team. Jefferson must have done some serious reading on tactics, somewhere." Robinson told them the story they had gotten from the sobbing little point man.

* * *

The Booze Bandits had been stalking and robbing since February of 1992, after several months of training and preparation. Operating from Cherry Street in the North to Passyunk Avenue in South Philly, the kids would recon drunks—respectable, well dressed drunks. They would watch a pub or bar, and focus on businessmen having a snort or three before heading home after a day of work downtown. They would watch for an individual who "repeated," as the leader said. They would follow their mark, and if his pattern was repeated for two or three nights, they would take him down. To qualify, a victim also had to use SEPTA, or head for a dimly lit parking lot. Then they would take him out in an alley, or quickly at one of the subway stations, or somewhere in the sprawling subterranean network under downtown Philadelphia.

* * *

"I'll let the kid give you some real details," Robinson said. "I've got to get back. Sergeant Godwin has all the processing paperwork for Hanson, and the identities and addresses for the other three kids."

"Thanks, Mike," Matt replied.

As Robinson got up to leave he said, "Lieutenant, my Captain said that if my Sergeant can spare me, and you can use me, I might be available. If you start calling in more bodies on this, I'd like in on it. It sounds like it's gonna be a real whodunit."

"I'll keep that in mind Mike. Thanks a lot," Gallagher replied, and Robinson left the room.

"O.K., here's how I see it," Matt started in. "These kids were stalking drunks like the VC used to stalk us. No offense, Nguyen."

"None taken, boss. Long before my time."

"Right. To continue then; what we somewhat affectionately called the 'Booze Bandits', were a well-organized gang. We had a dozen or so takedowns that we know of, and I think we're about to find out that there were lots more. We didn't get reports because the victims were too drunk to remember how they lost their wallets, etc., and the ones that could remember got the tape off, and for whatever reason didn't report it. Fear of wives, girlfriends, whatever." Gallagher paused. "And then the stalkers were stalked. He let himself be mugged, got out of the area, and boom! Deliberately rigged, malicious booby-traps. Not for killing, but for maiming. That's how I see it. Talk to me."

"What a mess," Pablo said. "I say let's get the kid in here right now. Two recorders. Calm him down, take off the cuffs, hear the whole story."

"Right," Matt said. "Set it up. I'm gonna get officers out to notify the families of the kids at Agnes. I might be gone more than a couple minutes. When you're ready, start without me."

Matt left the room, and walked to Sergeant Godwin's desk and picked up the file. He peripherally eyed the Hanson kid seated next to her desk. Opening the file, he took out the sheet with all the gangs' names and addresses, and walked over to the copier. As he made copies he stared hard at the little "point man," who seemed to be getting some of his composure back.

As Matt returned the originals to the file on Emma's desk, he said, almost offhandedly, "By the way Sergeant Godwin, please call over to The Seventeenth District, and make sure they have Detective Canatta under control. I don't want any incidents in my squad room."

Gerald's eyes got very big, very quickly.

"I'll take care of it, Lieutenant," Emma said. She patted Gerald's hand. "Don't worry, son. If he gets this far, we'll use our tranquilizer gun on him. It usually works."

Matt walked out of the squad room, and headed for the operations area. For the day shift, this was Corporal Raymond Bradley's territory.

After one year on the force any officer is eligible to apply for, and take, either the Detective exam or the Corporal exam. While most of those seeking promotion choose the Detective exam, or the "Dick Test" as most called it, it took a different outlook and attitude to want to be a Corporal. Corporals were assigned to "Operations" and as such, were deluged with information during the entire shift. The Operations Corporal was responsible for knowing where everybody was, and what they were doing, throughout The District. The Corporal, or "Ops" as he was called, was responsible for all equipment status, who was sick, who was on vacation, etc., etc. "Ops" did all this while monitoring Central Dispatch on one radio, and The 3/4 on another. It was hard or easy, all depending on attitude. Ex-servicemen who had served as RTO's (Radio/Telephone Operators) loved it, and stayed with it till they retired. Some could only take it for a short time, and opted out through promotion or lateral transfer.

"Ops" was fast moving and stressful, and when you stepped up to the operations area you waited to be acknowledged, regardless of rank. "Ops" wasn't ignoring you; he was clearing his plate first. Then you got his undivided attention for about fifteen seconds; and you had better be ready.

Matt stepped up and waited. Corporal Bradley was talking on a microphone and writing on a pad at the same time. He finished talking, got a 10-4, and turned to Matt.

"Whaddya got, Loo?" he asked.

Gallagher showed him the sheet. "I need officers sent to these addresses to inform next of kin for the two kids in Mount Sinai Hospital. If they got questions, they can call me or stop in first."

"Got it. Anything else?'

"That's it."

"I hear ya got the Booze Bandits." The operations people seemed to know things almost before they happened. It never ceased to amaze Gallagher.

"We didn't. The Seventeenth accidentally solved it. But yeah, we got 'em."

"Cool shit," Ops said, and turned back to his work. Matt acknowledged the cordial dismissal, and walked back to the squad room.

Matt quietly opened the door to the interrogation room, and stepped inside. There were two tape recorders on the table, and all four detectives were grouped around the table with pencils and big legal pads. They used the pads for quick notes and reminders to themselves; because once a subject started talking they rarely shut the recorders off. And Gerald was definitely talking.

Gallagher had already decided not to read the kid his rights. Nothing they got from Gerald Hanson could be used against him because of that; but Matt wanted the information on the booby-trapper, and as far as he was concerned, Hanson could walk. He was a juvenile, and he probably would've gotten off with probation or even a warning from the do-gooders at Juvenile Court. Matt didn't give a shit. He wanted the bomber. Besides, the "Booze Bandits" had definitely stalked their last victim.

"After the second or third night, we went after them. I would head for the take-down point. When the drunk showed up, the bros would be close. I always had my Walkman on. If the coast was clear, I'd be dancin' to the music. If there was somebody around or it weren't safe, I'd be lookin' at the Walkman with the batteries out, or shakin' it or somethin'. Makin' like it wasn't working. The other guys would just pass the drunk, and keep goin', or turn around and leave the way they came, and we would all go home."

"O.K., wait a minute," Pablo said. "What would make you call it off?"

"People around," Gerald replied. "Cops close by. That for sure. But Michael always told me, if it don't seem right, wave it off. He trusted me," Gerald said proudly.

He was very relaxed now because he sensed no hostility from this group of cops; and he definitely didn't want to go back to the other place, where the monster cop was. No way.

"Where did you first see the last guy you took down?" Detective Trung asked.

"That bar at Sixth and Tasker, the Red Eagle," Gerald said. "He came out of there drunk Monday, and Tuesday. We took him down on Wednesday."

"Why'd you use tape on this guy?" this from Pablo.

"Because he wasn't too blasted. He was staggerin', but he was movin'."

Matt asked, "How many guys did youse use the tape on?"

"I'm not sure," Gerald said. "Not too many of 'em. Most of 'em were so drunk that they didn't even know what was happenin'. We'd get the goods and be gone so quick they be standin' there after we left, lookin' stupid. Michael told us that people get drunk like that, they get home alright, but don't remember shit the next day. I don't understand it; but we did a lotta these drunks, and we never came close to bein' caught." Gerald stopped, and looked up at the detectives. He realized he had just been bragging. "I ain't dissin', man, but we had a lotta pickins. Ain't my fault so many honkies wander around these neighborhoods drunk."

The detectives knew the deal. They had been investigating this thing since the second drunk had been found taped up and passed out on Moravian Street, just off Samson. It was just an alley, really, and a short cut to the parking lot at 12th and Walnut.

All over downtown Philadelphia, workers streamed out of office buildings between 5:00 and 7:00 P.M. everyday. A great many—the majority—headed home by car or The System. But that left thousands who stopped somewhere for a quickie before going home. And for some, a quickie was four or five doubles of their favorite libation. They all knew people who did it, cops included. When they left the bars, they put it on automatic pilot. Most made it home. All except for the ones who crashed their cars somewhere on the way home, or who were unlucky enough to have crossed the radar of the Booze Bandits. The System got the rest of them home in one piece. Some people did this for years, Gallagher knew. What a world.

"Who picked the bars to watch?" Nguyen asked.

"Usually Michael. But it was easy. We'd hang at a corner near a bar, and just watch. The second night, we picked two or three to follow. We'd split up and follow them. The ones who headed to dark alleys, or parking lots, or the subways were picked. Michael always decided; and he was always right."

"O.K. One more time," Sergeant Vargas said. "Describe this guy and where you first spotted him."

"He was about five-eight, I think" Gerald replied. 'And he …"

"Wait a minute," Matt said. "Which build and height does he come close to with us?" All the detectives stood up.

"Him," said Gerald, pointing at Smythe.

"Good," Matt said. "Keep going." The other four detectives sat back down.

"He had beard on his chin, and a mustache. He wore glasses. All three nights he wore that same hat. Honky hat. Same color jacket and Levis. He had the new Air Jordan's on." Gerald stopped for a minute. He had only been told that Michael had blown up his hands. He didn't know much more than that. The light finally came on.

Gerald looked up at Gallagher. "You mean this guy's wallet was a bomb … oh shit!" Gerald collected himself quickly. The monster was far away. He decided to take a chance. "I want my Granmama. And I'm hungry. I wanna go home."

"Turn 'em off," Matt said, indicating the recorders. "Sergeant Vargas, a word please." Matt stepped out of the room, quickly followed by Julio.

"Here's the way I wanna go. Grab all the stuff on the Booze Bandits. Call down to Juvenile Court, and tell them you're bringing one of 'em in. They're gonna be pissed as hell that we let the kid talk without Miranda; but you tell them that was my call. Even if they don't ask you, tell them that was my call, and my call only. O.K. so far?"

"So far."

"Call the kid's folks, and have someone in the family meet you at Juvenile. If necessary, send a Uniform or one of our guys to give them a ride. O.K.?"

"O.K." Sergeant Vargas looked hard at his Lieutenant. If all that this kid said is inadmissible, and it is, the kid'll be home for supper. The DA is really gonna be pissed, Matt."

"I know, and I'll take all the heat for that. But as far as I'm concerned, case closed. Two kids are fucked up for life, and another one's gonna need a lotta therapy. Our boy Gerald's gonna get away with murder; but he'll be back. He's got a taste for it now. Maybe he'll try to start his own crew. Then he'll step on his stinger sooner or later. Take my word for it." Gallagher paused and took a deep breath. "Now this is a Direct Order. As soon as someone gets in your face down at Juvenile Court, give 'im this." Gallagher handed Vargas one of his business cards. "Got it?"

"Got it, Loo," said Julio.

"Oh, shit. Here." Gallagher handed Vargas all the cards he had on him. "It's really gonna hit the fan down there. Give one to everybody that yells at you."

Vargas laughed. Gallagher really was something else. With the possible exception of Lieutenant Larry Johnson on Beats, nobody backed their troops like this. But Johnson did it mostly on the streets, and mostly because he liked the possibility of physical action with *uncooperative citizens*, as he called them. He cared for his troops, but not like Gallagher.

"You know, you can't leave 'til I retire Matt," Vargas said. "You spoil us so much, we won't know how to act with a new boss."

Matt laughed. "Yeah, right. Listen, I'm gonna be here, there, and everywhere the rest of the day. Before I go, I'm gonna give the rest of the troops their marching orders. You sure you're O.K. with that?"

""I told you Matt, no problem. If I see something that needs to be pointed out, I'll definitely do it."

"Good," Matt said. "Let's get the kid outta here."

As Sergeant Vargas went back into the interrogation room, Matt paused, and his face went blank. Anyone from the outside who saw him like this would think he was spacing-out. Even some of his co-workers called it the "Space Cowboy Look." But Matt's wheels were spinning. "Honky Hat," the kid had said. He quickly walked to the Captain's office.

"He's still out," Jane Wilson said.

"I know. I need something out of his office. Will you come in with me?" He asked politely; but they both knew he wasn't going in there without her.

"O.K., Matthew, but you can't take any paperwork out of there."

"I know," Matt replied. "Humor me. Please."

Jane sighed, and led the way into Captain Parmalee's office. She held the door open and leaned on it, watching Gallagher with arched eyebrows. Matt walked over to Parmalee's coat rack, and plucked one of the Jeff style hats that Parmalee kept in the office—the tan one, as luck would have it.

"I'll bring it right back," Matt said.

He moved quickly back to the squad room. Since the Booze Bandits case files were all on Vargas' desk anyway, he and Detective Trung were ready to leave with the kid. They were moving to the exit when Matt opened the hall door and stood there.

"Hey kid!" Matt shouted.

The little group stopped, and Gerald looked up.

Matt placed the hat on his head. "Honky hat?" he asked

For the first time all day, Gerald Hanson smiled. "Honky Hat," he confirmed. Vargas and Trung then led the kid outside, and they were all laughing.

Detectives Gonzales and Smythe were still in the interrogation room, finishing up. Matt walked in and sat down. "O.K. I want youse guys to check out the subway area where this went down. Are you familiar with that free transfer area under City Hall?"

Before Pablo could speak, Winston said, "Intimately, Leftenant. As you know, I have your somewhat lacking Underground memorized."

"Good," Matt said. "And see if you can find out what officer or SEPTA cop was on duty. Maybe somebody saw something."

"O.K., Boss," Pablo said.

"Also, give me one tape, and keep the other one handy. If somebody screams for it let 'im have it. No need to tell 'im there's another one. Got it?"

"Got it," both detectives replied.

They were both excited, Gallagher saw. And why not? They were cops—detectives. And they had a whodunit on their hands. The fact that it was a little on the gruesome side as cases go didn't diminish the adventure. This is what they were paid to do, and they lived for it. All Gallagher's people were like this. If they weren't, they didn't stay Gallagher's people. It had taken awhile, but he had the crew he wanted. Good cops.

"O.K.," Matt said. "I'll be out and about. Use your squawkers to keep in touch."

Squawkers were the new hand-held radios the detectives carried. Uniformed officers wore versions that hooked to their equipment belts, with an attached microphone going over their shoulder and secured to an epaulet. All were tuned to Central Dispatch, and you switched to your District frequency with a flip of a switch. It made it extremely easy to keep in touch within your District, which increased safety for all concerned, especially the Uniforms. Once assigned a job by Central

Dispatch, individual officers could keep in touch with their partners and their District with no effort and no confusion. For the detectives, it allowed freedom of movement and the ability to call for help at the same time.

Gallagher went to his desk, and sat down to think. He had some unpleasant calls to make. Inspector Earl Watson, in charge of Detectives, Field Division South, was technically Matt's boss. Matt ran everything by Captain Parmalee, and took orders from him; but Watson could step in any time, and make Gallagher's life a little tough, if not miserable. Watson was a political cop like Deputy Chief Barnes. They had one other thing in common; they both were extremely jealous of Gallagher.

Every cop in Philadelphia worth his salt liked and respected Gallagher, if not personally, then by reputation. Gallagher was a legend, and all the political cops hated him for it, even the ones that outranked him.

They hated him because he was probably the best cop in The Department; and he wouldn't pal up to them, or kiss their asses. If Gallagher wanted to play their game, he could be an Inspector, and then a Chief in no time, test or no test. But Gallagher stayed the course. He had his twenty years in; and that meant anytime he wanted, he could retire on fifty percent salary for the rest of his life. And the political assholes that knew about his personal life really hated him.

Gallagher had no mortgage. His father had left him two houses. Gallagher lived in the one in Roxborough, and rented out the other in Tamaqua, Pennsylvania. It was on a lake in a closed community. He let a realtor handle the details, and when he wanted it for a couple of weeks, he just let the realtor know. From the car dealership he had also inherited, he took three new vehicles, and sold off the dealership. When his father died, this had all been a huge surprise, because he thought his mother would inherit everything. But she just took a lot of cash, and moved to a retirement community in New Jersey. She told Gallagher that that was what she wanted, and his father had worked the will to her wishes. His mother was still relatively young, and she had friends in the community she moved to. Gallagher saw her often, and everything was copasetic there.

In short, Gallagher had none of the problems and headaches that most cops did. Even the good guys envied him this. Thousands of Philly cops faced a tough day in the City of Brotherly Love; and then went home to unrelenting bills, nagging wives or husbands, and screaming or sulking kids. They managed; barely, but they managed. But it did mean there was an awful lot of firepower in the hands of some pretty stressed out cops. But Gallagher wasn't one of them. Still, the first phone call would be tough.

He dialed the office of Inspector Earl Watson. He got his secretary.

"This is Lieutenant Gallagher for Inspector Watson, please."

"He's not in, may I take a message, please?" the secretary replied.

"Please just tell him I called," Matt said.

"Very well Lieutenant," said the secretary, and Matt hung up.

Matt felt better about the next call now. If Watson had been in, Matt would have told him he needed help. Watson eventually would help as he saw fit, because it was official business. But first he would tell all of his fellow assholes that the great Gallagher had called for help. He couldn't handle one investigation. Professionally, it would hinder the investigation; and Matt could do without that. He quickly dialed Chief Inspector Maxwell Loudin, Chief of Detectives for The Philadelphia Police Department.

"Chief Inspector Loudin's office," came over the phone.

"Hi, Miriam, it's Matt Gallagher. Is he in?"

"He just walked in. Hold on, Matt." A short pause and then Loudin came on the line.

"Lieutenant ABLS," Loudin boomed over the line. "How's my favorite celibate Policeman?"

Any tension that Gallagher may have felt instantly melted away.

"I need help, Chief."

"You need to get laid, my boy. But that's beside the point. Whaddya need?"

"I need a floater for a partner. You know what's goin' down, right?"

"Yeah, and it sounds like a wild one. Deputy Chief Barnes is heading your way. He's gonna do a press conference on the front steps of the station house. Fair warning."

"Actually," Matt replied, "I'll be glad to let him do the media thing with this. I like watching guys like that shoot themselves in the foot."

"Easy, Matt. This line is unsecure, and besides, he outranks both of us. Respect!"

"Yessir," Matt replied. "He's already torn a new one off one of my guys."

"Let me guess. Gonzales."

Matt had to laugh. "Is it just me, or does the whole Department know my squad inside out?"

"No, it's not just you," Loudin replied. "You're the best cop in the city. You've got the best detective squad I've ever seen. You've got a Limey, a Vietnamese, a mother of three, and two Italian subordinates who rape you with their eyes every time you walk by. Just to mention a few."

Gallagher was openly laughing now, and didn't care who heard it.

Loudin waited for Matt to settle down and said, "What happened when you tried to get in touch with Watson?"

"He wasn't in. I left a message. I know I should wait but this isn't personal. It's professional. Yes, he's my superior; but he'll saddle me with a real dickhead. I need a Sergeant; I need a partner and I need it right away."

"Alright, Matt," Loudin said. "I'll talk to him. He's gonna be pissed you called me, but you're covered. There's just one thing."

"Yessir?"

"You absolutely have to catch this asshole. There's a definite consensus on that. Three black kids maimed for life? Shit, the Very Reverends, the Very Concerned, and the Very Everybody Else are all gonna be up in arms about this."

"Right. Just so you know for reference purposes, these kids were the Booze Bandits; and they were stalked and set up."

"I'll be goddamned!" Loudin replied. "Catch him, Lieutenant. I'll be in touch."

"Yessir. Thank you, sir."

CHAPTER SIX

Smythe and Gonzales had headed up 9th Street in their Crown Vic. Before leaving the station house, Gonzales had called the SEPTA Police Department Headquarters, and found out that the officer on duty around the transfer point on the evening of May nineteenth was named Mike Givens. And he would be on duty again, this night on the four-to-midnight shift. The duty officer offered to call Givens and have him call the Three-Four; but Pablo declined the offer. They would personally talk to Givens in the late afternoon or early evening.

Detective Winston Smythe was silent in the passenger seat. He rarely initiated a conversation; but he was a keen listener, an astute people watcher, and had a never-ending thirst for knowledge of his adopted country in general, and Philadelphia in particular.

Philadelphia absolutely fascinated Smythe. It was a city that had everything you could want in a metropolis. Of course, Philadelphia came with a lot of baggage he could do without.

Gunfire resonated throughout some of the worst neighborhoods every night. A murder a day was the norm, along with uncountable muggings, burglaries, and theft. Rape was a constant danger to those women who had to commute alone late at night in bad neighborhoods. And bad neighborhoods, Smythe had come to learn, ran the racial and ethnic gauntlet—from black neighborhoods and projects in North and West Philly, to Puerto Rican communities in Kensington. Chinatown, near the Reading Market, was no bargain for a stranger caught in the wrong place at the wrong time. And there were white neighborhoods in Kensington, Port Richmond, and Bridesburg that could be just as dangerous to white outsiders, let alone someone of color.

The drug problem in Philadelphia was as bad as in any other large United States city; and crack cocaine had absolutely devastated some neighborhoods.

In a city of one-and-a-half million people, it was estimated that there were around one hundred thousand uninsured motorists, and who knew how many driving without a license or any papers at all. It was a nightmare for law-abiding citizens who, as a consequence, paid some of the highest auto insurance premiums in the country.

Air pollution in the city wasn't as bad as it was in Liverpool, England, where Smythe was born. But sometimes, with the traffic and the various industries still thriving in the city, the air could get pretty bad, pretty quick.

And the traffic! Smythe could recite the commuting nightmare (as could most Philadelphians who drove) as well as any television or radio traffic chopper reporter. Morning rush hour: 95 South backed up from Girard to Bridge Street or as far north as Cottman Avenue, all lanes; the Schuylkill Expressway East backed up from 30th Street to Belmont Avenue, and sometimes as far as Conshohocken; West River Drive and Kelly Drive backed up to Falls Bridge, and on and on. Evening rush hour: reverse all of the above. Smythe could well understand why Gallagher used The System, as his Yank colleagues called it.

But the bad things couldn't drive Smythe away because there were so many good, and more than a few great things, about the City of Brotherly Love.

Philadelphia, first and foremost, was where it had all started, of course. The Declaration of Independence—written and signed here. The Constitution—drafted and re-drafted here until Jefferson and the lads were confident in getting enough votes for ratification. First Capital of the United States. *First Capital of the United States to be captured by an enemy,* Smythe chuckled to himself. Washington, DC came later in both instances.

This was a modern city, a bustling seaport. It was also a hard-drinking, hard-core sports town. The first part was fine by Smythe. He loved to bend his elbow, and could hang with the best of them. He refused, however, to drink some of the watered down piss the colonials dared called beer. He had happened upon Yuengling Lager by chance one evening, and always made a point to have at least a case in his fridge. He also sampled, in his wanderings, some of the new micro brews cropping up around town. This tabled neatly with his people watching, a never ending sport with him. Smythe was no snob, but he was continuously amused in his traveling in and around the city.

The sports were something else entirely. The Flyers, the Phillies, the Eagles (the Iggles, as they were more commonly called) and the 76ers all had enormous and enthusiastic fan bases. The Phillies were the talk of the town this summer with a win/loss record of 27-11 at this time, which was definitely not the norm. The fans were holding back a touch, because they didn't want heartbreak this early in the season; but there was a definite buzz in the air. Smythe could hear baseball talk anywhere and everywhere he went in the city.

Smythe still followed the Liverpool Reds and the Everton Blues, two local soccer teams of his birthplace. Hated rivals Manchester and United still stirred his fire a bit when they had matches with his Liverpool teams; but acclimation by osmosis had turned his sports interest to the Philly pro teams, especially the Phillies. He just loved this Lenny Dykstra chap, "The Dude." Dykstra was the Phillies center fielder. Smythe had been to several games this year and had tried different seats at each game.

On April 22nd, he had been sitting in the 700 level of Veterans Stadium, in left-center field. From his vantage point, he could easily see the huge puddles of tobacco juice Dykstra created by continuously spitting on the field. Late in the game, the San Diego Padre in center field was playing deep because Pete Incaviglia was at the plate, and Incaviglia was always a threat to "go yard," as they say. "Inky" had got under a fastball, and popped it up to shallow center field. The San Diego center fielder had come charging in and dove for the ball, making a spectacular sliding catch; of course, he was sliding right through Dykstra's massive puddles of tobacco spit. The player got hurriedly to his feet. It was the third out; and he just stood there, dumbfounded. He was saturated with Dykstra's goo. He was taken out of the game; and his Padre teammates later said he was still throwing up in the clubhouse long after the game was over.

Smythe was very happy with his adopted town, but as with all transplanted native sons, he missed his home city. Comparisons between the cities were unavoidable and inevitable.

Philadelphia's City Hall was an enormous structure with four huge clocks high above the streets.

The Royal Liverpool Building had a tower clock that was the biggest in Great Britain, beating old Ben by two feet, six inches.

The Liverpool Cathedral was the largest Anglican Church in Britain.

There were several hundred places of worship in the Philadelphia area, some of them quite spectacular buildings of stone.

Liverpool was chartered by King John in 1207 A.D., and started off as a fishing town; but gradually evolved into a world-class trading center.

In 1700, Philadelphia was a town of 4400 people, occupying 2 square miles of land very close to the Delaware River. On February 2nd, 1854, the General Assembly passed the Act of Consolidation, expanding the city to 129 square miles, its present size.

But for modern wide-world impact, there was one thing Philadelphia couldn't compare to, couldn't match. Of course, no other city in the world could either.

The Beatles started in Liverpool, and started playing in an underground café called "The Cavern," in 1960. They played there in the early Sixties over three hundred times, until they were "discovered" by Brian Epstein, in November of 1961. And the rest, as they say, is history.

Gonzales was turning left on Samson Street, and Smythe noticed the massive lunch time throngs already starting to flood the downtown sidewalks. As they drove across Broad Street Pablo said, "I'm gonna make a Ralph on Sixteenth, and we'll park up near City Hall. How's that?"

"Righto, Matey," Winston replied, greatly exaggerating his English accent.

Pablo laughed. He was fascinated by Smythe's accent, and loved it when Winston went overboard with it. Pablo broke his balls occasionally about being a Limey; but Smythe didn't mind. Gonzales was a good partner, if a little hot tempered. Smythe suspected that even Pablo knew his temper and his mouth would get him in deep shit one day, especially with higher-ups like Butthole Barnes only too happy to accommodate him.

Smythe knew that political wonks like Deputy Chief Barnes liked to break a career now and then, thinking it made them look good to their superiors. But Barnes and his ilk weren't totally stupid. They just waited until someone like Detective Gonzales, otherwise an excellent cop, stuck his foot in his mouth. Then they just handed him the salt and pepper to complete the meal.

The two cops parked in an official space at City Hall, threw their "Get Out of Jail Free Card" on the dashboard, and set off for the Subway entrance. They descended down into the underground that spread out in all directions under City Hall. Both men instinctively looked at all the food kiosks and little cafes that were immediately in view. All were packed with the usual lunchtime crowds.

"What say we case the joint, and eat when we're done?" Pablo asked.

"Fine by me," answered Winston without a trace of accent. Pablo looked at Smythe and laughed. "Always fuckin' wit me, aincha, Limey? C'mon, let's go."

* * *

Matt Gallagher was at his desk writing an attack plan for the investigation into the booby-trap incidents. He knew that eventually someone in the squad room or elsewhere would come up with a catchy nickname for this case; but until then he would call it what it was, an unsolved whodunit.

Captain Parmalee had come back in around 12:30 P.M., and told Matt that Parmalee and Barnes would handle the press conference for 2:00 P.M.

"You don't have to be there, Matt."

"Thanks, Cap. In that case, I'll stay right here. Since you'll be out front, I'll call my boys, and tell them to stay away for awhile."

"That's fine. Afterwards though, there's gonna be an official meet. Me, you, Watson, Loudin, Barnes, and your new partner."

"And who would that be?" Matt asked.

"I don't know, Matt." Parmalee replied. "I believe Loudin's still working on that; and Watson's raising a stink because he didn't hear from you first.

"I called him. He wasn't in."

"I know," Parmalee said. "Don't worry about it. He would've tried to saddle you with a loser, one of his. Me and Loudin got your back on this all the way, Matt." Parmalee lowered his voice. "The Commissioner took me aside after the meeting at Headquarters, and said he's behind you too. Are you going to the Vet tonight?" The "Vet" was Veterans Memorial Stadium, the Phillies home field in South Philadelphia.

"Yes," Matt said. "I figured I'd take my new partner down."

"Good. The Commish said to mosey over to his box for a chat."

"O.K., I'll do that."

"Good. See you after the press conference."

"Yessir."

Gallagher picked up his squawker, and flipped to the squad frequency.

"Pablo, Winston. Gallagher here."

"Go, boss."

"Stay away 'til around three o'clock. Then you can come in and start the official paperwork on this case. Check with Operations about the parents or guardians of those kids at Sinai."

"10-4."

"Vargas, Trung. Gallagher here."

"Talk to me, boss."

"When you're done down there, go to the Red Eagle bar, 6th and Tasker. See what you can dig up."

"O.K., Jefe. Jeet?"

"No, Joo?"

"Not yet. O.K., we'll head to Pat's on our way back for some cheesesteaks. Want one, boss?"

"You bet," Matt replied.

"With or without?" Vargas asked.

"Dumb question."

"O.K., Boss. Later."

* * *

Julio and Nguyen left Juvenile Court in a hurry. They had finally managed to get a junior DA to take Gerald Hanson off their hands. This was after much discussion (loud at times) as to why the little Bandit hadn't been read his rights. Every time somebody in Juvenile asked this, Sergeant Vargas handed over one of Lieutenant Gallagher's cards.

Gerald was really starting to enjoy himself. He listened to everything, and missed nothing, a quality which had made him so valuable as the Booze Bandit's point man in the first place. He realized he was going to get away scot-free. He would only have to face his grandparents, who were raising him. He could deal with that.

Before Vargas and Trung actually stepped out of the building, one of the junior DA's said, "I will call Gallagher's boss. This is inexcusable. These little bastards mugged and robbed their way across Center City for months, you catch one, and before he confesses you don't Miranda his ass? And we ask why, and you hand me one of Saint Matthew's cards? That's bullshit!"

"That's why we gave you the card, ma'am. Take it up with Lieutenant Gallagher."

As they made their way to the Red Eagle Bar, Trung broke a long silence. "I got questions, Sarge," he said.

"And you know, in this squad, you can always ask them," Vargas replied.

"Right. O.K. How many of those people will actually call the Captain or the Loo about the kid getting off?"

"Oh, for certain, one of the junior District Attorneys down there will call. The Booze Bandits coulda been a career maker for one of 'em.

But their bosses will realize that, with three of those kids maimed for life, it would look real bad goin' for a fifteen year old. Everybody, cop and citizen, will realize that we gotta find the bomber. Every black organization in the city is gonna be watchin' this case like a hawk; and if The Department doesn't make every effort to find this lunatic, heads will roll. If this was an election year, they probably would've turned the whole case over to the Feds, and said, 'thank you very much'."

"O.K.," Trung said. "Question number two; what was that Saint Matthew crack all about?"

Julio sighed. Sometimes the political infighting and back-stabbing in The Department and the City amazed even a grizzled old veteran like him.

"Pure jealousy," he said. "Pure green, pure evil, jealousy. Matthew Gallagher is the best cop in The Department. He's a really decent human being. He's a war hero. A medal of honor winner. And he's a widower. And there are people who can't stand him because of all that."

"So, those cards you gave out; is Matt daring those people to call?"

"No, and once and for all, you younger guys are gonna see what he's really all about. He had me give those cards out so people would call, and he really would tell them that the decision to let that kid talk without Miranda was his and his alone; and none of us will suffer for it. I mean, you guys knew he was a great boss; but during this case you're really gonna see it. And with Matt leading us, if we can't find this asshole, nobody can. Next question."

"Where do you think he'll strike next?"

"I don't know and neither does Matt—yet. But it shows you're sharp. You knew he would do it again. Even the higher-ups, assholes and otherwise, know that if this guy's a serial, we won't get 'im until the third or fourth incident." Vargas sighed again. "But I'll tell you what. Dollars will get you doughnuts that Matt will have us staked out in the right areas for the second or third bomb. It doesn't mean we'll catch him; but we'll be close."

If Trung had any more questions, he kept them for later. He was smarter than any of them, Julio knew; but he lacked what almost every Philadelphia cop had by nature—street smarts. It was why he would be encouraged to go for higher rank in administration or operations. Good people were needed in those areas too, if for nothing else than to keep some of the shit off of the regular cop's heads.

They reached the bar at 6th and Tasker and parked in front. The door was open. It wasn't really hot in Philly yet. That would come later. They walked in, and took seats near the door.

"What'll it be, Officers?" asked the bartender, a middle-aged black man, with huge arms and a large beer belly. He could smell a cop a mile away.

"Two mugs of Shlitz," Vargas said.

Trung pulled his chair out a little further from the bar. He would watch the door and the other patrons while Julio questioned the bartender. It wasn't really dangerous to be in any Philadelphia bar during the day; the real mayhem didn't usually start until around 10:00 or 11:00 P.M. But cops were always looking; and Trung and Vargas were cops, as the bartender had noticed.

"I'm Vargas, he's Trung," Julio said, he and Nguyen flashing gold while the bartender slapped their beers on the bar. Trung put a five on the bar.

"They call me 'Whitey', replied the bartender. "And the first one's always on me."

"O.K.," Julio said. "You know my first question's gotta be ..."

Whitey laughed. "Yeah, yeah. Look." He lifted his pullover up to his collarbone. A streak of pure white hair ran down the center of his chest and disappeared into his pants.

"It's been like that since I been fifteen years old." He pulled his shirt down. "Whaddya's need?"

Vargas slugged down half the mug. It was frosty cold and delicious. "You own the place?"

"That's a fact."

"I'm looking for the night man for last night."

"That would be Mugs. He's over in the corner eatin' lunch. He's a pretty decent citizen, chief."

"He ain't in no beef with us. We're looking for a patron been drinkin' here for two or three weeks after work."

"Help yourself." Whitey moved to the other end of the bar. Julio got up and moved towards the back corner, where a young black man was chowing down. As he passed Whitey, he raised his eyebrows. Whitey was very sharp.

"We call him Mugs because every night from four to nine he draws mugs at a pace you wouldn't believe. Nobody ever has to wait for a beer. He's gotta be the fastest draw in town."

Julio laughed and moved on to the corner booth. "I'm Detective Sergeant Vargas," he said, once more flashing the badge. "I have a couple of questions to ask you. Mind if I sit down?"

Mugs pointed a large half-eaten rib at the empty side of the booth. "Long's you don't mind I keep eatin'."

"No problem. White guy, tan sports coat, jeans, new kicks. He had a tan Jeff, wore glasses, and had a beard and a mustache."

"With that description, sounds like you got 'im already. Yeah, he's been in here last couple, three weeks."

"Could you tell me his routine? What he drank? Anything he said or did that stuck out?"

"He stuck out just bein' here. I mean, he didn't bother nobody, and durin' the rush I didn't pay 'im no mind, 'cept to mug 'im. Oh yeah. That's one thing. He drank Yuengling Lager. I don't draw a lotta that, but it's good brew. I drink it myself."

"He ever meet anybody, start conversations with others at the bar?"

" He wouldn't a got much response if he did. Boss says serve anybody—white, black, or purple—long's their money's green. Most nights he was the only honk … I mean, the only white guy in here. But we got a good crew comes here. Nobody bothered him."

"He sit in the same seat pretty much?"

"Yeah. Right under the TV. Usually left around ten, ten-thirty. Good tipper."

Mugs finally finished his ribs, and started cleaning himself up. Julio could dig it. There was only one way to eat ribs. Damn the mess, and full speed ahead. Clean everything up later. He stood up and dropped a card on the table.

"You think of anything, gimme a call. Thanks, and sorry for interrupting your lunch."

"No problem. You mightta noticed I never stopped eatin'."

Vargas laughed. A true chow hound was a man after his own heart. He walked over and put his mug on the bar.

"'Nother, guys?" asked Whitey.

"No thanks, compadre. Hasta luega."

Trung and Vargas walked out onto Tasker.

"Yeah. Later, Paco," muttered Whitey. Somethin' was comin' down. But he ran a straight joint. No dope, no pimpin', no hookin'. He had his poker video games, but those assholes in South Philly made him take them in. They made him money; but they made him nervous. Oh well, another day of Brotherly Love.

"Ready for Pat's?" Trung asked.

"You betcha, hombre. Greasy, saucy, and cheesy. I can feel my arteries hardening already." Vargas jumped in the passenger seat. "Let's ride, Clyde. I'll fill you in on the way. But there ain't much. I know this is a stretch, but our 'honky' has to be wearing a disguise."

"Of course he's wearing a disguise, my boneheaded Sergeant. Geez, you're sharp."

Vargas laughed as Trung headed deeper into South Philly for the best cheese- steaks in the world.

* * *

Deputy Chief William "Butthole" Barnes fidgeted with his uniform; but of course it was immaculate already. He was on the top level of the outside stairs of The 3/4 District building. Captain Parmalee stood behind and to the left of Barnes. Inspector Earl Watson, the supervisor of South Division Detectives, as well as Central and West Divisions, stood behind and to the right of Barnes. Chief Inspector Max Loudin stood behind them all, his perpetual bemused look spread across his face. He wore this expression 99 percent of the time, which was very significant, because occasionally the expression changed. Anybody and everybody who knew this man, and were still in his vicinity when the changeover to the 1 percent was completed, deserved anything that happened to them.

Captain Parmalee had a strong premonition that today he was going to see "One Percent Max." He also foresaw that the cause for the changeover was at the podium preparing for the press conference. Parmalee didn't know how much Barnes had leaked to the press and various civic groups already; but it didn't matter. No one in their right mind would sit on this. There were two reasons: this was one of those "We need the public's help cases," and because hiding something like this would only explode in their faces later. Except for specific details about the booby-traps, the public would know all about it by the evening rush hour. Parmalee looked at his watch; 1:59 P.M. *Showtime*, he thought.

Barnes looked out at the assembled media people. "Ladies and gentleman," he began, "can I have your attention please? I'm going to read a statement, and then I'll take questions. Last night, the nineteenth, around 22:30 hours"—Parmalee, Loudin, and even Watson rolled their eyes at Barnes' use of military time—"four teenagers came upon a briefcase and a wallet."(They weren't officially the "Booze Bandits" yet; not until, or if, one of the older three boys was Mirandized and charged).

"The boys separated, with one taking the wallet, and two taking the briefcase. The fourth boy took neither, which was very fortunate for him, as you'll see."

Barnes paused for a breath and a stealthy look at the cameras, to see if they were trained on him. They were.

"The two boys with the briefcase took it to the playground you see across the way behind you, the Wharton playground. Apparently both youngsters were leaning over to look into it when they opened it. When they did open it, two CS canisters exploded in their faces. These two young men are in very serious, but stable condition, at Mount Sinai Hospital. Both have permanently lost their eyesight. They also have very serious burns on their upper chests, necks, and faces. These two young men are Jamal Woodson, sixteen, of four-eighteen Fitzwater Street, and Reshawn Deeds, also sixteen, of five-eleven Montreal Street.

"The teenager with the wallet, Michael Jefferson, seventeen, of eight-nineteen Woodstock Street, is at Saint Agnes Hospital. The wallet exploded in his hands, apparently when he opened it up in a shed behind his house. He lost two fingers from his left hand, and parts of three fingers from his right. He lost the use of his right eye. As you might imagine, we have yet to thoroughly question the three youths in the hospital. The unharmed youth, one Gerald Hanson, of twenty-one-oh-three Ellsworth Street, was briefly brought in for questioning, and was released from Juvenile Detention about a half-hour ago." As he looked at his watch, Barnes flashed a sinister look at Captain Parmalee. Parmalee ignored it. "I'll take questions now."

Barnes pointed to Clevus Capstone from the black weekly newspaper *POW* (*Pissed Off at Whitey*). Everyone there, Capstone included, knew it was to get brownie points from the black press. It never worked with Capstone or his editor. They were slanted and biased, and proud of it. After briefly reporting the facts, they would hammer Whitey hard and often. Never mind that not even Clevus Capstone believed that these four hapless young black men had "found" the booby-trapped items.

"Have all their kin been notified?" asked Capstone.

"I don't know about all," replied Barnes. "But their parents or guardians were notified as soon as we knew who the youths were. Otherwise, I wouldn't have just identified them."

"Will the press be allowed to see the injured teens?" Capstone followed up.

"That's up to the docs, but I doubt it. At least for awhile."

Barnes just blew that one, Parmalee thought. If the relations of these kids said no press, that was the end of it. But he would bet his last buck that these same relations would all speak to the press, especially the television folks. They'd get all gussied up for the cameras and their fifteen minutes of fame. He'd seen it time and time again; and it sickened him. That settled it. He was going to the driving range tonight and pound some golf balls.

Barnes pointed to MaryLou McBride of *The Philadelphia Inquirer*.

"Chief Barnes," she started, "are we to understand that four teenagers just happened to find a briefcase and a wallet, and both of these items were booby -trapped?"

"That's correct."

"And you're stating that for the record, Deputy Chief Barnes?" she continued.

"That's correct." Barnes pointed to Tony Brice, *The Daily News* police reporter.

"Have the three hospitalized youths been questioned?" Brice asked.

"They are too heavily sedated for questions at this time."

"Could these be the Booze Bandits?" Brice asked.

"I can't comment on that at this time." Barnes pointed to Troy Gillespie, of "Action News."

"Who's in charge of the investigation, Chief?" Gillespie asked

"That would be Lieutenant Gallagher and the Special Tasks Unit."

"Why isn't Lieutenant Gallagher here, Chief?" Gillespie persisted.

"Must be on lunch." Barnes chuckled. So did some members of the press. Parmalee glared at Barnes. Watson looked uncomfortable. The face of Chief Inspector Loudin began to change; imperceptively at first, but it was changing.

"What about my baby?" a voice called from down on the sidewalk.

The press all turned to see who had spoken. It was a black woman, hanging on the arms of the very Reverend Marvin Jefferson Quintade of the First African-American Church of Philadelphia, and Lawrence Steele, President of the Philadelphia Chapter of the NAACP.

"Who's your baby, ma'am?" asked Christina Stamp of KYW Radio.

"Her son is Jamal Woodson," replied Reverend Quintade. "And his injuries are horrendous."

Deputy Chief Barnes turned around and said, "Take over Captain Parmalee." He then left the podium and entered the station house.

"What about it, Mr. Policeman? What about her son?" asked Lawrence Steele.

"You can rest assured that we will hunt down and find this individual," replied Parmalee, stepping behind the podium. "As for the injured young men, their fate is now in God's hands, wouldn't you agree Reverend Quintade?"

The Very Reverend was very pissed off that somebody mentioned God before he did; but he wasn't very stupid. He segued smoothly into his response.

"Yes, Captain Parmalee, that's true." These two had a history. "And God is all powerful and all seeing. And he'll be watching this investigation very closely."

This was a not so veiled threat. As clownish as he sometimes appeared, looks were very deceiving. The Very Reverend Quintade could mobilize many thousands very quickly; and Parmalee and every civic leader in the city knew it. Parmalee liked to piss Quintade off, but it was a dangerous game. In a city of a half-million people of color, summer time was dangerous enough without this added aggravation.

"Well, you can help," Parmalee said. "This investigation will be handled by The Police Department in a thorough and professional manner. The public can help by calling their Neighborhood Watch Captains or their local Districts if they see anything suspicious. Don't touch suspicious objects or packages. Call us; that's our job. Now, we have work to do, so this press conference is over."

Parmalee walked down the steps to converse with Mrs. Woodson. Chief Inspector Loudin, expression still slowly changing, walked down the far side of the steps to greet someone just arriving. That someone was Detective Sergeant Yvonne Wallace, Gallagher's new partner. With red hair and green eyes, she was an absolute stunner, and she knew it. She tried to subdue it with low-accent clothing and no makeup, but it was a lost cause.

"Hello, Sergeant Wallace," greeted Loudin. "Let's go inside and get you introduced, and then we've got a meeting to attend."

"Lead the way, Chief," she replied, and many eyes followed this new arrival up the steps.

"Who the hell is that?" asked *The Inquirer's* McBride.

"That's one of Chief Inspector Loudin's floaters," Brice of *The Daily News* replied. "They get sent where the heavy action is."

The "floater" accompanied Loudin inside to the squad room; and you could have heard a pin drop. The squad all knew Gallagher was getting a partner for this case, and since she walked in with Loudin, they knew she was it.

"Good afternoon, everyone," Loudin boomed. "This is Sergeant Yvonne Wallace, Lieutenant Gallagher's partner for the duration of the booby-trap case. After a quick meeting, she'll be back out to get up to speed. Say hello to the nice detectives, Sergeant."

This got giggles from Sergeant Eileen Johnson, and an outright guffaw from Sergeant Farrel. He didn't have to look to know that Irene Costello and Imogene Patrillo were looking daggers at Gallagher's new partner.

"Hello, everyone," greeted Sergeant Wallace as she and Loudin walked up to Gallagher's desk. Matt had followed the whole scene since they had walked into the building.

Loudin made the introductions. "Lieutenant Matt Gallagher, this is Sergeant Yvonne Wallace. She's the best I could dig up on short notice."

This got a wry smile from Wallace, and a huge grin from Gallagher.

"He just has a way with words doesn't he, Sergeant?" said Gallagher, extending his hand. "I've heard of you. Word is, you're a great cop."

"Thanks, Lieutenant. I've heard the same about you, and a bit more," Yvonne replied.

"Oh, puh-leeze!" This was from Sergeant Imogene Patrillo.

"I'm going to the ladies room!" This from Detective Irene Costello.

The two females loudly made a show of gathering themselves together, and heading for the door. The door leading *out* of the building.

Sergeant Mike Shincock followed them to the door, and held it open as they left. "The bathroom's not out there girls; and you can't pee on the sidewalk. It's against City Ordinance, and it would just piss off Big Ed. He's very big on sanitation." "Big Ed" was Mayor Ed Rendell.

"Sanitize yourself, Fuzzball. You can start with a bath," came a faint, but stout reply from outside.

The detectives left in the squad room were all in various stages of subdued hysterics. This was going to be one interesting investigation.

"Did I say something wrong?" asked Sergeant Wallace.

"No, Sergeant. This is normal for this nuthouse," replied Loudin. "I try not to come here more than once or twice a year. Matthew will take you back to the conference room. I'll be with you shortly."

As Matt and Yvonne left, Loudin turned to face the squad room. He walked slowly to Detective Pasqualez's desk. They all noticed now that Loudin's bemused look was doing the glacial changeover known throughout the Detective Bureau. As he approached Pasqualez, Juan started to panic. *Oh shit! He knows!* Juan thought.

"Pull it out, Detective."

"Pull what out, sir?" replied Pasqualez, nearly swallowing his Adam's apple.

"The ABLS action calendar, dumbo. My money's as good as anybody else's, ain't it?"

"Yessir."

Still not quite believing it, Juan pulled out a large, thin cardboard sheet from under his desk blotter. The heading on the sheet said: "WHEN WILL ABLS GET LAID?"

"Whaddya got for the rest of the summer?"

"July, August, and September are wide open, Chief Inspector."

"And the price of poker just went up, Detective," Loudin replied, indicating with his head the direction Sergeant Wallace had gone.

"Yessir, it has," Juan said, finally relaxing. "It's twenty dollars a date. I only take five bets per date, and nobody can have more than three dates in any given week. It's about as fair as we could make it without inside information, if you get my drift."

"Yeah, yeah, I get your drift. Gimme July third, fourth, and fifth."

Pasqualez took the sixty bucks, made the entries on the cardboard calendar, and gave Loudin his betting slips.

"Keep up the good work, people." Loudin said as he exited the room. Everybody breathed a sign of relief.

CHAPTER SEVEN

Chief Inspector Loudin paid a very quick courtesy call on Jane Wilson, and then made his way to the conference room. He entered, closing the door behind him.

"Maxell," said Captain Parmalee. "I'd just like to start by briefing Lieutenant Gallagher and Sergeant Wallace on our meeting at the Roundhouse; and then Matthew can bring everyone up to speed."

"Fine by me, Cap. Let's roll." Both Matt and Yvonne simultaneously noticed that the changeover in Loudin's demeanor was happening. *Uh-oh*, they both thought.

"O.K.," Parmalee continued. "Matt, this is now officially Task Force Gallagher. You are to use your Special Tasks Unit exclusively to hunt the bomber. Your chain of command stays pretty much intact; myself, Inspector Watson, and Inspector Loudin. Deputy Chief Barnes is, of course, cleared for all information. All available resources of The Department are yours to use. Special units have been notified.

"If you need K-9, bomb experts, specialists from the academy, extra Uniforms, whatever; a phone call is all it should take. If anyone brushes you off, let us know; but that shouldn't happen. The Commissioner has let everybody know that the Wrath of God will descend on anyone who doesn't cooperate. I've said it before, Lieutenant Gallagher I've got your back all the way on this." Parmalee looked around the room. "Also, if you feel anyone is hindering your investigation, or standing too far in your shadow, let me know."

"What's that supposed to mean?" This from Watson.

"Funny you ask, Carl," Parmalee replied. "Deputy Chief Barnes, this goes for you too. You two are pure political animals. But you're also supposed to be Philadelphia Police Officers. I expect you to act as such, around my District and my people."

"You go too far, Captain," said Barnes. "I talk directly to the Mayor almost daily. I got pull you can only dream about."

Chief Inspector Loudin bulled his way into the conversation. "Yeah, well, pull this!" he boomed. Loudin looked at Parmalee. "Excuse me, Captain. I'd like the floor, please." It came out as a low growl.

It was frosty courtesy, because Parmalee knew Loudin was taking the floor with or without permission; by now it was clear to everybody in the room that the changeover in Chief Inspector Maxwell Loudin's demeanor was complete. Parmalee silently indicated assent with his hand. "One Percent Max" had the floor.

"To start off with, Barnes, as a professional courtesy to you, I'm letting you know that I called His Honor earlier this afternoon. We made a date to quaff a few cold ones together tonight over at The Olde Ale House on Germantown Pike. And I'm definitely gonna mention this conversation. In short, I'll match your pull. And believe me, it's checkmate, mister."

Loudin shifted very noticeably in his seat, and Gallagher, an astute reader of body language, thought actual violence might be imminent. *Oh baby!*

Loudin continued. "I've already instructed my subordinate, Inspector Watson, on his expected behavior in this investigation, and now I'm gonna instruct you."

"How dare you talk …" Barnes sputtered, but Loudin thundered, "BE SILENT!"

Sergeant Yvonne Wallace stood up and made as if to leave the room; but Loudin, without taking his eyes off Barnes, pointed emphatically to her, and then to her chair. Yvonne sat back down.

"Deputy Chief Barnes, you happen to be in the same room with the best cop in the city, and it ain't me." Loudin pointed at Gallagher. "If you fuck with this man and his troops, other than to get your 'Liaison' information, I'll publicly challenge you to a roll on the mats at the Academy. Fully supervised and fully legal; but if you don't show up, everybody will know that, too. I'll use *my* pull to have *The Daily News* headline read, 'Butthole Barnes backs out'. "

The room was unmoving, the meeting participants in frozen tableau. Barnes' face couldn't decide whether to be white with shock and anger, or red with embarrassment. Gallagher decided that it looked like a full compromise. He was a little embarrassed for Barnes.

Loudin wasn't finished. "And if that doesn't work, I'll wait until the investigation is over, resign, and beat the shit out of you." Loudin leaned back in his chair. "If you don't believe me, Barnes, try me."

Barnes was rendered physically speechless; and a remarkable transformation took place in Loudin. The intelligent, bemused look was back, along with the bright twinkle in the eyes, eyes that a moment before had looked like coal from the deepest fires of hell. Gallagher had seen it before; but it was still remarkable to behold.

Everyone started to fuss and shuffle his or her feet. Everyone but Loudin was trying to make like the incident hadn't happened.

Parmalee nodded at Gallagher. "Matt, why don't you bring everybody up to speed."

"Right," Matt said. "Well, as you all know, we caught a break, if you want to call it that."

Matt went on to describe how, with The 17th District's help, the "Booze Bandits" had been identified. He finished up by acknowledging he had intentionally not "Mirandized" Gerald Hanson, and told the group that his troops were out on the streets, where he would be as soon as the meeting was over.

"I have a question, Lieutenant," said Inspector Watson. "You've been looking for these 'Booze Bandits' for months. Now, because of your deliberate actions, it's doubtful any of them will ever be prosecuted. How do you justify this, as opposed to a successful closing of the case?"

"I'm not going to justify anything," Matt replied. "Three of these kids are totally messed up. The fourth will be back. We'll get him for something else, eventually. If I had read the little bastard his rights, he would never have said anything. Now we have a description of the bomber, albeit he was surely in disguise. But we know he tracked these kids before they started stalking him. I take full responsibility for my actions, as always."

Gallagher turned slightly in his chair, and addressed the entire group. "If nobody minds, I'd like to get moving. I can't help this investigation by staying indoors."

"Alright, Matt," Parmalee replied. "Go get 'em. Good luck. Sergeant Wallace, stick close to Lieutenant Gallagher. When his nose is close to the trail, he sometimes forgets to look over his shoulder. The bomber is unknown, and unpredictable. Watch the Lieutenant's back."

"Yessir," replied Sergeant Wallace, and she and Gallagher took their leave.

They made their way to the squad room where Matt grabbed the keys to his police Crown Vic. As they were leaving, Sergeant Farrel said, "Welcome to the Three-Four, Sarge. Watch our Lieutenant's back, please."

"Will do. It seems to be a very popular back."

That got her a smile from the rest of the squad room.

As they made their way to the lot, Matt looked over at his new partner and asked, "Jeet?"

"Yes, I had lunch earlier. Joo?"

"No, but the boys are bringing me something when they come in. I can wait."

"O.K., where we headed?"

Matt opened the passenger door for Yvonne without conscious thought. This small gesture impressed the hell out of her. Manners, too? As Matt got in and started up the car, she again asked their destination.

"I want to go over to the Jefferson place on Woodstock Street," he said. "We'll never get a search warrant for the house, but the shed is an official crime scene. I just wanna look around. Then we'll go back to the squad room. I'll brief the guys on the meeting, and introduce you. Then I wanna go to Sinai and Agnes, and see these kids. I need to make sure I have them pictured in my mind at all times." Matt was quiet for a moment as he made his way west on Wharton Street. Then he asked Sergeant Wallace about herself.

"Well, I guess it's Catholic girl makes good or goes bad, depending on your point of view," Yvonne started. "Born and raised in Robindale. Went to Our Lady of Calvary and then Ryan for Girls. Average grades, I guess."

She pushed a wisp of red hair from her eyes. *Emerald eyes,* thought Gallagher, taking a quick glance.

"I did two years at Bucks Community," she continued. "Two days after I got my Associate's Degree in Criminology, I took the police exam. I had been on the list since I was nineteen, but my parents didn't know. I passed, and was accepted into the next Academy class."

Gallagher turned left on 21st Street.

"My mom threw a fit," she went on. "But my dad backed me all the way. I thought it was gonna be just the opposite. Mom came around, though. They really were great about the whole thing, actually. I stayed with my parents until I was twenty-two. When I was assigned to The 17th District, I got an apartment in Morrell Park." Matt turned left on Dickinson. "And as we're almost there, the rest, as they say, is history, and can wait for another time."

"Right," Matt acknowledged, pulling in behind a 17th District patrol car between Woodstock and Capital Streets. "Let's see what we can see."

* * *

After Gallagher and Wallace left The 3/4, the action really picked up; and it wasn't police work. The first to stop by Detective Pasqualez's desk was none other than the prim and proper Jane Wilson, Captain Parmalee's secretary.

"Can I help you, Miss Jane?" Juan asked.

"Yes, Detective," she said. "Let's see what you have for early June."

"I don't know what you mean, ma'am," he replied.

"Can it, Fuzzball," she came back. (All narcs were "fuzzballs." They had to look unkempt and dirty for the job they did). "Get your calendar out."

Everybody was watching now. Pasqualez got out the calendar, and Jane laid twenty dollars each on June 5th and 6th. "That will give them time to become properly acquainted," Jane said, as she took her betting slips. She gently mussed Juan's already mussed hair. "Thank you so much, Detective," she said, and left the squad room.

The detectives were in collective shock. "Well I'll be dipped in sheep shit," observed Sergeant Shincock.

Loudin, Barnes, Watson, and Parmalee had just walked into the squad room, unseen by Shincock.

Jack Miles, who *had* seen them come in, egged Shincock on. "That's right, Mike. And what do we do when we smell sheep shit?" he asked, sotto voice.

Shincock took a deep breath, and all alone, he yelled, "GET DA FLOCK OUTTA HERE!"

Shincock was momentarily stunned by his solo performance. Then, realizing he had been set up, he slowly turned around to see who had entered the squad room. It was more brass than he usually saw in a month of Sundays. As a narc, he avoided them and they avoided him—unless he fucked up, like now.

"Is there a problem, Detective?" asked Parmalee, as the rest of the squad, and even Loudin, tried to keep a straight face. Inspector Watson just looked startled.

"No sir, just talking to myself," answered Shincock.

"More like shouting to yourself," said Loudin, as he made his way to the door. "Good day everyone, and keep up the good work. Relax, Sarge," he said over his shoulder to Shincock. "You were set up by a pro."

Shincock just glared at Miles. *Payback's a mother-fucker*, he mouthed silently.

After Inspector Watson followed Loudin out to the street, Captain Parmalee walked up to Pasqualez's desk. *Not another one,* thought Pasqualez.

"I know just what you're thinking, Detective. But I know everything that goes on in my District. That's how I stay a Captain. Show me the sheet."

Juan sighed, and pulled the cardboard sheet out again.

"Gimme the fourth of July, and August seventh and ninth. No reason," he added, reading the look on Juan's face. "Just a guess, like everybody else."

"Yeah," Pasqualez replied. "And ever since the centerfold walked in, the guesses are pilin' up."

Parmalee just laughed as he took the receipts and headed to his office. As word spread about Matt's new partner, he imagined Pasqualez was going to be very busy indeed. He might even have time to bust a dealer or two. *Police life in Philadelphia!* he thought. *You couldn't even write a book about it. Nobody would believe it.*

* * *

Gallagher and Wallace walked to the back of the Jefferson house. They were mildly surprised to see Detective Robinson of The 17th poking around.

"Hi, Mike. Find anything interesting?" asked Matt.

Robinson looked startled. "I just got here. Officer Whitcomb has been watching the scene," he replied, indicating the uniform.

"Hi ya, Jason," said Matt. "And this is Sergeant Wallace. Yvonne, this is Officer Whitcomb and Detective Mike Robinson."

Everyone shook hands. Whitcomb was amazed. He had never met the famous Lieutenant, and the guy knew his first name. Even in small ways, the legend kept growing.

"Officer Whitcomb, this crime scene now belongs to my task force, and we're gonna have a look-see, O.K.?" Matt asked.

"Be my guest, Lieutenant."

Mike, Matt, and Yvonne all stepped over the yellow crime scene tape, and all three men tried not to look at Sergeant Wallace as she hiked up her skirt to do so. She was peripherally aware of this, but she had long ago gotten used to it. As long as her fellow police officers didn't drool, and treated her professionally, she didn't mind. Every once in a while she had to zap a Neanderthal for going too far, and she actually enjoyed that. It kept life interesting. All three walked through the open gate into the yard.

Matt led the way to the shed just as Paul Jefferson came out of the back door of the house. The shed was small, but Matt and Yvonne went in, and Robinson stopped Jefferson at the crime tape. Jefferson said, "I wanted to get in there earlier, but I wasn't allowed."

Robinson introduced everyone, and Matt turned on the overhead light. From a pocket he pulled out a small, but powerful flashlight to highlight what he wanted to look at.

"I have to think that your grandson was using this shed to stash his loot," Matt said. "I'm sorry Mr. Jefferson; but there's no doubt your grandson has a long string of muggings behind him. It's no reflection on you. He got away with it for so long because he was intelligent, methodical, and diligent. Unfortunately for everyone involved, he was stalked by someone with the same qualities and more."

"Lordy!" said Jefferson. "Are you tellin' me these boys was da Booze Bandits?"

"That's right, sir. Now we're going to be busy for a few minutes. Officer Whitcomb, please escort Mr. Jefferson further into the yard."

Matt was standing in a corner and moving his flashlight slowly across the walls, and then the floor. He thought he saw it immediately; but as he always did, he marked the spot in his mind, and continued looking for other possibilities. It was a point he hammered home to his squad time and time again. When you find what you think you're looking for, don't stop. Mark that spot, location, or clue in your mind, and continue looking. There always is something else, and many a good cop had missed an important clue because he stopped looking past the first one.

Alright, he thought. *There are two spots*. The first one he had seen was under one of the legs of the workbench. The rear right leg of the bench didn't quite sit on the flooring like the others. The floor was two by four planking, and this particular board was cut halfway between the front and rear legs.

The second spot was on one wall where gardening tools were hung. Two of the boards making the wall had no nails.

Matt moved to this spot first. Removing the tools from the suspect area, Matt lightly touched the two boards. They didn't move so much as give a little bit. He pushed one hard in the center, and pulled it out as it sprang back into his hand. Now he pulled the other one out. The flashlight wasn't needed, but it sure did highlight the find. The light revealed, and was reflected by, a large parcel, tightly wrapped in plastic.

"Sergeant Wallace, please remove that," he said. "Mike, come in here hold up this end of the bench, please."

Robinson complied, and Matt quickly pried up one board from the floor under the rear leg.

"One more second, Mike," he said, reaching into a large depression under the floor and removing a large parcel that was also tightly wrapped in plastic. "O.K., Mike," he said, getting up. "Set 'er down. Now, let's see what we got."

Gallagher took the other bundle from Sergeant Wallace, and placed them both on the bench. He whipped out a pair of latex gloves and put them on. Wallace did the same. Mike was embarrassed that he didn't have a pair but he didn't hesitate to ask a question.

"Why the gloves now, Loo?"

"Well," Matt said, unwrapping the parcel. "If I had put them on first, I might have dropped one, or missed feeling something else. We already know who put these here. But the stuff inside the plastic is gonna have all kind of prints all over it. I don't care how sharp these kids were, there's no way the loot was wiped clean. By the time the Jefferson kid got to this point, he'd be so wound up he would just scan the loot, and put it away for leisurely perusal later."

Leisurely perusal! thought both Wallace and Robinson.

Matt had the contents of the package out on the bench on top of the plastic wrap. There was a lot of cash, and a large assortment of jewelry, including gold wristbands, gold neck chains, several Rolex watches, a few stick-pins, and other expensive trinkets. There were credit cards, but not many. Mike commented on this.

"They would move the cards quickly. There's a big market for that shit. You get the right fence involved, and you can get two, three hundred a card. The kids didn't get caught with the plastic, and that's why there's so much cash here. Even with the drunks they were hittin', there's no way they'd get this much cash. An intelligent drunk thinks he's O.K., because he just carries sixty, eighty bucks. But the idiots carry fortunes around their necks and wrists, and in their briefcases." Matt quietly counted the cash and whistled.

"How much?" asked Yvonne.

"Almost forty grand."

"Say what!" exclaimed Mike.

"Yeah, they been at it a year or more. Say two takedowns a week, and the credit cards add up. The fence for the credit cards is most definitely a 'wise guy'. As soon as they get 'em, they ring up humongous sales, and then ditch the cards. The credit card companies are gettin' better; but until they clamp down on massive splurges by any one customer, it's gonna keep happening. Even if they catch it two days after the mugging, it's too late. The wise guys are already callin' the cable companies to hook up their new eight thousand dollar, sixty-inch TV. And their wives are already wearin' new clothes and jewelry without spending a dime. O.K., Sergeant Wallace. You can do the honors on that one."

As Yvonne started unwrapping the other bundle, Matt leaned out the door of the shed. "Officer Whitcomb," he called.

"Yeah, Loo."

"Would you please go to my Crown Vic and get me a large evidence bag? They're in the flap on the driver's door."

"Right."

Matt pulled his head back in the door, looking sheepish. "I forgot it," he said.

So he is human, Robinson thought. But he was a generous man. "If that's the worst thing you do today, you still got a shot at being promoted."

Sergeant Wallace quickly gave Mike a disapproving look over her shoulder. Seeing this Matt said, "I get it all the time. If somebody didn't bust my ba … I mean, if I didn't get teased a half-dozen times a day, I'd be unfulfilled. Whaddya got there?"

"Well," said Yvonne. "I'm far from an expert; but there's lots of transferables here."

"Transferables?"

"Yeah. Paper instead of cash: payroll checks, stocks, securities. They'd need more than a regular fence for this stuff; but it's very moveable. And once it starts moving it practically disappears. It's kind of ironic; but moveable paper leaves almost no visible paper trail. You just bundle it into other large transactions, and after the first transfer, you can pretty much forget about it."

"Well," Matt said. "I'm glad you're up on that stuff because it's all pretty much Greek to me. If it's anything but cash or credit cards, I find th …"

"HOLY SHIT!" Yvonne screamed.

Matt and Mike both jumped a bit when Yvonne shouted. "What!" they both exclaimed.

"Sweet Jesus Louizes!" Yvonne turned to the men. She was visibly flushed. Her nostrils were flared, and she was practically panting. Matt and Mike were unable to stop themselves from getting slightly aroused.

"It's a Three-Pack! It's a fuckin' Three-Pack!" She looked to be having an orgasm.

"What the hell's a Three-Pack?" asked Matt, reining himself in a little bit.

"Bearer bonds!" She made a visible effort to calm herself. "Ten large a pop. And thirty of 'em makes a large pop." She leaned back against the workbench. "There's three hundred thousand dollars here."

"Get Da Flock Outta Here!" Matt yelled.

Officer Whitcomb was back from his little errand. "Everything O.K. in there?" he asked leaning in. *Do I smell sex?* he asked himself.

"We're alright, Officer," Matt replied. He turned back to Sergeant Wallace. "O.K.," he said. "I've heard of these things. No ID required to cash them, something like that?"

"That's right," she replied. "Any bank in the free world, and just about anywhere else for that matter. If you found one of these on the streets, you could walk in, slap it on the counter, and walk out with ten grand. It's the only exception to the IRS rules about reporting large cash transactions. I have a feeling this kid researched this and found this out. That's why they're still here." Yvonne wiped her brow and continued. "He hits adulthood and the heats off, and the Booze Bandits are on easy street. Unbelievable."

"O.K.," Matt said. "Let's bag it up, and get it right to Property. Me and you together. Dual receipt. No offense."

"None taken."

They finished up and left the shed. Sergeant Wallace headed for the Crown Vic with the evidence bag.

"Officer Whitcomb, escort Sergeant Wallace to my vehicle, and stay there until I get there. That's an order."

"Yessir," Whitcomb replied, stepping close to Sergeant Wallace. He took another subtle whiff. *Holy smokes*! he thought. Yvonne was still so stoked up she didn't notice, lucky for Whitcomb.

Gallagher waited until they were out of hearing range and gestured for Mike to come into the shed. "Detective Robinson, a word please."

Oh shit! thought Robinson. He knew what was coming.

Matt looked directly into Mike's eyes. "Good job all around today. You helped break the Booze Bandits. But don't ever poke around one of my crime scenes again, unless me or one of my people are there. Understood?"

"Yessir. I apologize. It won't happen again."

"Alright. You're a good cop. Don't put yourself in a hole this early in your career."

"Thanks, Loo."

"O.K. Now, I gotta head out. If I need extra people I'll give your boss a call. See ya later."

"See ya." Robinson shook his head. *Jeez!* One second he was quaking in his boots; the next he felt ten feet tall. *This Gallagher was something else.* Now he didn't know if he wanted to work for him or not. He didn't know if he would measure up. He wouldn't want to let the guy down.

Detectives Smythe and Gonzales were standing in the catacomb-like tunnel that was part of the free transfer point between the Market-Frankford EL and the Broad Street Subway. They had an hour or so until SEPTA police officer Mike Givens arrived for his shift. They had walked the entire route from each end of the huge station to the transfer point. They could see how it had gone down so easily.

Before the "victim" had made the turn up into the concrete hallway, he would have gotten off the subway car, and started walking up a sloping platform. Between the end of the station platform and the turn into the "catacomb," the Booze Bandits had taken him down. According to the report filed by SEPTA Officer Givens, a concerned citizen claimed to have seen an assault from the southbound platform.

Apparently the "victim" had then casually gotten up and headed for the Market- Frankford train. The other man yelled out to the "victim" and, getting no response, had headed back to the Market-Frankford train area himself. According to Givens' report, by the time he got up there, the "victim" had disappeared. All that the Good Samaritan had seen was a man standing on the eastbound EL platform waiting for a swiftly approaching train. And he claimed that this individual looked nothing like the muggee.

Pablo and Winston had debated back and forth for an hour about this just to check it through for flaws. The citizen had run to Officer Givens to tell what he had seen, and no one fitting this description was anywhere in the area; and certainly no one like this had passed Givens.

There was only one conclusion. The "bomber" had pulled a quick change act, probably as he walked through the platform's revolving gate to the Market EL platform. Once on the train, he could've gotten off at any one of seventeen stops, and simply disappeared.

Knowing this didn't make them feel like super-sleuths. It was the only way it could have gone down. Once they talked to Givens, they would head back to the shop and pow-wow with everybody else and compare notes.

* * *

By the time Matt and Yvonne had cleared Property and reported to Captain Parmalee, the chaos was starting to abate a bit. With the jewels, cash, and bonds, they had deposited somewhere in the neighborhood of four hundred thousand dollars in the "Cage." It was a big haul by any standard, and Parmalee was on the horn with the District Attorney of Philadelphia. He wanted this loot out of here as soon as possible. The DA promised to send some detectives assigned to his office.

"ASAP, please" said Captain Parmalee into his phone. "This place is a big enough circus right now as it is."

"O.K., Cap, O.K.," replied the DA. "I'll send an armored car with driver, guard, and two dicks. They'll be there in fifteen minutes. Think you can hunker in your bunker 'til then?"

"Alright, alright. I know I'm excited. But hell, this shit's temptin' me and I ain't even seen it. And I don't wanna see it, except on the way out of my building, thank you very much."

"Right. Later, Cap."

Christ, thought Parmalee, *maybe it was time to pull the pin and retire.* His ticker was strong; and he wanted to keep it that way. *Much more of this shit*, he thought, *and they'll be carryin' me outta here on a plank.*

There was a short rap on his door, and Jane Wilson walked in and handed him a small blue pill.

"What's this?" he asked.

"Just take it. Here." She handed him a cup of water she had just drawn from his personal buffalo.

"Is it legal?"

"It is if nobody but you and me knows about it. It's a Valium. It won't hurt you. Take it … that's a good boy."

Jane left, and Parmalee leaned back and sighed. What a day!

CHAPTER EIGHT

It was 6:00 P.M., and while the excitement of the new development had not exactly dissipated, things were winding down a bit in the squad room.

Vice and Robbery/Homicide had left for the day. Their workdays and hours were staggered according to duty requirements and their current case loads.

Sergeant Vic Taggert and Detective Pamela Smith were out on the streets. Sergeant Mike Shincock and Detective Juan Pasqualez were still at their desks. Both were catching up on enormous loads of never-ending paperwork, and would hit the streets later in the evening.

Friday was a big day for narc work. Casual users and hard-core addicts would be out looking for dope. Crack was hot, and would be for years. It was flooding the city by rail, air, and highway. Washington, DC dealers would come up on Amtrak, drop off loads to their middle men, and be headed back before 9:00 P.M. The plane riders had been arriving since Wednesday. Again, a quick drop off. These were mules, carrying large loads of pot, heroin, cocaine, and crack. The big dealers used the mules to move their loads because it was too risky for them. Once the dope was dropped off, the mules would lay low for a couple of days, and head back, usually to Florida, with or without large cash loads, depending on how the financial arrangements were made. The big boys changed this on a regular basis to keep law enforcement hopping. It was a never-ending game, and mules were lost fairly often; but they were lined up hip-deep for the job, because you could make anywhere from five to twenty grand a load. It was easy money, unless of course, you were caught. But ten or twelve trips could put you on easy street for life if you had the balls for it.

Road transport was the biggest problem for the cops: local, state, and federal. They couldn't check every car or bus coming into the city even if they could legally get away with it. Even though there were only a few major highways coming into the city because of its location on the

Delaware River to the east and the Schuylkill River to the west, a diligent map reader could find dozens of roads leading quietly into Philadelphia. And the roads, of course, were how the majority of the drugs came in.

Some of the drug couriers who were stopped, checked, and caught, were incredibly stupid. They would do eighty-five miles per hour coming in on a highway with ten pounds of marijuana in the car, and call the cops who pulled them over "racist pigs."

The successful couriers obeyed the traffic laws coming and going, and cheerfully rooted for the cops to keep chasing down their nincompoop brethren, which kept the heat where it belonged—off of them.

* * *

Task Force Gallagher (and Matt was *not* happy about the unit's name) was in the interrogation room. Matt had convened the meeting after visiting Mount Sinai and Saint Agnes Hospitals to see the kids. It was a sobering experience.

Sergeant Vargas and Detective Trung reported their findings, confirming what Matt already knew; the "Bomber" had stalked the "Bandits" by osmosis. He just bided his time. He knew he would be "hit," and this is what really worried Matt. This guy had studied the newspapers and, Matt suspected, had somehow seen police reports. Although this was a stretch, he wouldn't rule it out.

"You may be right, Jefe," said Pablo, when Matt made this point. "But there were several analysis's - is that the word? - and think pieces in the papers about the Booze Bandits. He might not have needed much more than that."

"O.K.," Matt replied. "And the word is analyses, I think."

"Thanks."

"De nada."

There were chuckles all around.

"O.K., youse guys," Matt said, pointing to Smythe and Trung.

Trung nodded to Smythe.

Winston looked at his notes. "We walked the area of the Underground where the lads took out the 'victim'. It was pretty much as the point man told us. The bomber was probably up and moving no more than thirty seconds after the takedown. The witness from across the tracks probably only saw the kids leaving and the bomber on the ground, and then making his exit." Smythe checked his notes. "By the time the witness got up to the main platform, our boy was gone, or so he thought. Nguyen?"

Trung took up the narrative. "Of course, this all comes from SEPTA Officer Mike Givens. When the witness got to the main drag, the "Bandits" and the "Bomber" were both gone. But there was a man getting on an eastbound EL. While the witness didn't get a great look at the 'victim', he was sure that the man on the El platform had no beard, no hat, and no glasses; of that the witness was certain." Trung paused, and leaned back in his chair. "Officer Givens smelled booze on the witness's breath. Once Givens started really pressing the man for details, the guy backed off. When Givens asked for ID, the guy declined, and headed back to the Broad Street Subway. Givens didn't stop him. He really had no reason to, and I'm not going to question his actions. That's about it."

Gallagher and Wallace both started to talk, and stopped.

"Go ahead," Matt said. "You're part of the crew."

"O.K.," she said. "Did Givens make a report?"

"Yes," Winston replied. "He made it part of his end of watch report. SETPA faxed us a copy." He pointed to a sheet on the table. "As you'll see, he remembered seeing some black youths; but they were just part of a small crowd moving up to and around the main part of the concourse. He paid them no mind. And when he saw no 'victim' and heard no cries for help, he figured the witness was mistaken. And he was bloody well right as it turns out."

Yvonne quickly scanned the fax. "Let's see. Average height, average build. White male, dark hair." She was reading the witness's vague description of the man on the eastbound El platform. "That narrows it down," she said sarcastically, tossing the fax back on the table.

"But," Matt interjected, "he ain't no superman. He cut it too close. If that El hadn't been coming his way, the SEPTA cop might've walked over and questioned him. Our man might have kept his cool, but the adrenalin would've been flowin' like all get out. At the very least, Givens would've gotten a good look at the guy. If the guy freaked a little bit, Givens might have asked him to wait for the next train so he could ask him a few questions. The guy was walkin' a serious edge."

The old hands sat back and waited. Yvonne stirred, but several hands went up simultaneously to head her off. The men in the room knew Gallagher's police brain was firing on all cylinders, and they knew better than to try to slow it down at this point.

A minute passed. "O.K.," Gallagher started back up. "Obviously, once he got on the EL, he was pretty much home free. At that point, Givens and the witness had finished their conversation; and the cars were already past the platform and gone. Our man became a needle in

SEPTA's haystack." Gallagher stopped again and this time he leaned forward with his elbows on the table. "Yvonne, you had something?"

"Well …" she hesitated. "It was an idea that died abornin', I guess. I am a little rusty. Putting out a description of his clothing before and after the takedown would waste a lot of time. We'll never see any of those clothes again; unless or until we catch him, and if he's stupid enough to keep them. And unless he really wants to be caught, he sure as hell won't be back in this neck of the woods anytime soon." She stopped, realizing they were all smiling at her. "Did I say something funny?' she asked, slightly irked.

Now they all laughed, and she flushed flaming red. *And that was something to see*, several of the men thought.

"No, you don't amuse us, Sergeant," Matt responded for all of them. "We're just pleased to know Max didn't let us down; not that we thought he would."

"Thanks. I think."

"Rusty or not, Sarge," Vargas said, "You're on our frequency, and it's good to know."

"Bloody right," chimed in Smythe, and they were all nodding.

"O.K.," Matt said. "I'm getting' ready to lay down the way I want us to go, and the way I think our boy is gonna go. I need to know right now about any and all personal problems, appointments, professional exams, qualifications, etcetera. Once I work out my main battle plan, I'll probably … hell I will … call for reinforcements. Anybody?"

The room was quiet while everybody thought hard and/or checked notebooks.

Trung spoke first. "I have writtens on June Fourth and orals on the Eighth. I took personal days for both. I could reschedule for September."

"Absolutely not," Matt said firmly. "You worked too hard for this. I got both days marked in bright red on my desk calendar, and you ain't missin' 'em. That's a direct order."

"Yessir," Nguyen responded. These tests coming up were for his doctorate in international relations. "My mom *would* kill me if I missed them."

"Yeah!" Matt laughed. "And then she'd come after me." Matt actually shivered. "No thank you."

Smythe spoke up. "I have annual qualifications for the Glock next month. I'll schedule that for one of my off days. I like to dabble a bit with the other ordinance anyway."

The Police Academy, where everybody qualified with their weapons (or not; some did fail), was open all year, except major holidays. Instructors and range people were always available.

"O.K., Winston, that works. I appreciate it," Matt said. "Who else?"

Vargas was next. "I got the last two weeks in July for vacation. Shore bound with the family. Margate." Vargas did not volunteer to reschedule this. He might not get it back this summer.

Gallagher started to say something, but Julio held up a hand.

"Hear me out, boss," Julio said. "I done this before. The arrangements are all set. I'll have the family down on Saturday, the seventeenth. I'll commute if need be. In fact, I want to. I get on Maria's nerves because I can't sit still anyway. And the kids are getting to the age where they don't want me around the whole time anyway. They're too busy checkin' all the hormone action on the beach. I'll be fine."

"Alright, Julio." Gallagher had to laugh. He'd known the Vargas family for years; and one summer Maria, Julio's wife, had actually called Matt during their vacation, and asked if he would give Julio a hot case to work on in Philly for a few days. So Matt brought him back to the city, and they golfed for three days.

"Anybody else?" Matt asked, looking particularly at Sergeant Wallace.

"I'm fine," Yvonne said. "I need a good whodunit, and my calendar's clear for the summer, although I hope we get this guy soon."

"Right," Matt said. "Alright, here's my initial plan of attack, with some flexibility and some room for change built in. Prepare to copy, folks."

The large legal pads were passed around, and everyone took a few sheets. It was easier to write big and sloppy, and then copy everything later into their smaller personal notebooks.

Gallagher started dictating. "Myself and Yvonne are gonna go Friday thru Wednesday, 8:00 A.M. to 6:00 P.M. We'll take Sundays off. Pablo and Winston will take Tuesday thru Saturday, 2:00 P.M. to 11:00 P.M. Sarge, you and Nguyen also take Tuesday to Saturday, 2:00 P.M. to 11:00 P.M." Matt paused to write his own notes and let everybody catch up.

Wallace couldn't believe it. He was doing this on the fly. She would have needed some prep time, at least a half-hour.

"I'm bringin' Eileen in on this." Eileen was Sergeant Eileen Johnson from Vice. "I'm gonna grab Mike Robinson from The Seventeenth and team them up." He stopped and looked up. "Any problems with that? I gotta know now."

Gallagher was in full command mode. He wasn't asking for their approval. They all knew Sergeant Johnson (except for Yvonne); but Detective Robinson was an outsider, an unknown thrown into the equation.

Smythe spoke up quickly. "I say, Leftenant. Jolly good show on his part. He knew more than us, before us, as far as the booby-traps are concerned. He may have gotten lucky; but he did well, and he seems to have his 'shit together', as you Yanks are wont to say. He should be a plus."

This was a major speech for Winston, and his colleagues took note. People-wise, his instincts were better than anyone else in the room, including Gallagher. This settled it for everybody.

* * *

Wallace sensed the mood of the others on this, and started to feel more comfortable as time went on; but she would make sure before they left this room.

"That clinches it for me," Matt said, acknowledging Winston with a nod. "They'll be goin' 10:00 A.M. to 7:00 P.M., Monday thru Friday. I'll get two Uniforms, and put 'em in plain clothes for the duration. They'll be gophers, and this will be made clear to them. And I'll only take volunteers. They'll also go 10:00 A.M. to 7:00 P.M., Monday thru Friday." Matt paused again to let everyone catch up with their notes.

"I say, Leftenant?" Smythe said.

"Gawhead," said Matt.

"It hardly seems cricket for you to take a six day shift, as opposed to our five."

"Don't worry about it. As I said, we'll take off Sundays. I'm just using these hours as a guide and a reference for my official battle plan. Number one, Yvonne and I will be splitting some of our shifts into early morning and late evenings. Number two, if I need time, I'll take it."

"You're only human Matt," said Sergeant Vargas. "Don't burn out on us."

"I won't. Emma and Eileen will be watching me like mother hens. They'll keep me rested."

There were laughs around the room because they all knew it to be true. But truth be told, they all watched Gallagher, because they all cared.

"Sergeant Wallace and I are going to start with a little research over at the Roundhouse," Matt said. The Roundhouse was Police Headquarters at 8th and Race, but everybody called it the Roundhouse, civilians included. "Pablo and Winston, dig out your walkin' shoes. Starting Sunday, I want you to sniff out the Bomber's route. Start from Tasker, where the kids started stalking him. Now, I know the trail ends under City Hall, but I want you guys to pick up the eastbound EL, and get off at every stop 'til Bridge Street." This was the end of the line for the Market-Frankford Elevated. "I want you to get a feel for each stop. Maybe even question some SEPTA people. See if you can make an educated guess about the stop where it would be easiest to get lost the quickest."

Smythe spoke up. "That's some serious gumshoe, Leftenant."

"I know," Gallagher replied. "Try it for a couple of days. And I know this is a real shot in the dark, but ask the driver of the eastbound train on duty that night if he might remember our man."

"I'll definitely be breakin' out my Chuck Taylor's," piped in Pablo.

"Good. Julio and Nguyen, I want you to canvas the neighborhoods around the Red Eagle Bar. See if anybody ever saw this guy prowlin' around. Also go to the Red Eagle again, this time at night. Ask around, you might get lucky.

"Right, Loo," Sergeant Vargas responded, while Trung nodded his acknowledgement.

Matt continued. "I'm gonna have Sergeant Johnson and Detective Robinson be our central clearinghouse. Send all your reports to her; and let her know what you're up to via squad frequency. And I'll tell her vice versa if she has some good info to pass on. Anybody can use the plainclothes cops, but clear it with Sergeant Johnson first. O.K.?"

Heads nodded around the table.

"O.K., everybody finish clearing off your desks. Everybody go home at six o'clock. Get some good rest, and eat some good chow. We're all gonna need some extra energy for this caper. Questions?"

Sergeant Gonzales lazily raised a hand. "Yeah, Jefe. Not to bust your chops or anything, but are these hours written in stone?"

"You're asking about overtime, right?" Matt replied.

"Well, yeah. I ain't gonna shut down on a lead or a good tip just 'cause it's time to punch out."

"I don't want ya to. If you're over, put in for it, and I'll approve it until the desk jockeys in finance whack my pee-pee. But if nothin's happenin', go home on schedule—everybody."

Again, heads nodded around the table. They knew Gallagher wasn't telling them not to fudge their hours. He was telling them to go home on time so they could spend time with their families or whomever. Even on a hot case like this he wasn't going to let them or their personal lives go into the tank. He was looking out for his troops, and they all loved him for that.

"Now," Gallagher said. "Here's what's on my mind. We all know that this guy's gonna do this again. For the thrill, for vengeance, for lack of anything else to do, whatever. This asshole knew what he was doin'. Aside from wearing those brand new Air Jordans, he dressed right—low key white man. And other than risking being questioned on the EL platform, everything worked for him."

Matt leaned back in his chair, flipping his pen as he spoke. He never looked at it, but he *never* dropped it. Everybody was listening intently. The best cop in Philly was thinking out loud.

"He's gonna look for patterns of crime. I say within a month, there's gonna be another incident. And unless we've got that particular area staked out, or he gets real careless, we're gonna have more stalkers as victims. That's where me and Sergeant Wallace are gonna start. We'll be lookin' at patterns, and I'm gonna get inside his head." *Not try, but going to*, Yvonne noticed.

Detective Trung lifted his hand slightly.

"Go, Nguyen," said Matt.

"One thing bothers me about this guy, Loo," Trung started.

"Just one, lad?" piped up Smythe.

Trung blushed. "You know what I mean."

"Keep going, Nguyen," Matt interjected. "Our Limey's just bustin' your balls. Oops, I mean your chops."

Sergeant Wallace blushed again, and then she smiled.

"O.K.," Trung continued. "It's not like he's Sherlock Holmes. We tried to lure the Booze Bandits out ourselves, by playing the lush after work bit. I even did it. Between the four of us, the Special Task Unit, I'll bet we had someone on the street for a total of forty-to-fifty nights. Those kids had to have seen us. But not a nibble could we get. Then, apparently this guy gets 'em hook, line, and sinker in a few weeks of trying." Vietnamese or not, Trung spoke like what he was—American born and raised.

Sergeant Vargas pursed his lips and nodded through Trung's rather long, question-like statement. He glanced at Gallagher, and Matt indicated the floor was his.

Julio looked over at Trung, and leaned forward. "It's like this, Nguyen. These young black kids from the poor neighborhoods have a talent like you're never gonna find in any other ethnic group. When they're up to shit like this, they can spot a cop a mile away, and smell 'im from two. Remember when we walked into the Red Eagle this afternoon?"

Trung nodded yes.

"Two guys walked out the backdoor before we sat down. And Whitey knew we were 'The Man' as soon as we walked in. It don't matter what we're wearin' or what we're doin', these folks know. Have you ever talked to Larry Johnson?"

"Just in passing."

"Some day next week we'll meet him for lunch. Now that I think of it, we'll ask him to meet us at the Red Eagle Monday after he goes off shift. It'll be his dinner and our lunch. It'll be an education. Nobody can chow down like him. And he's been on the streets of Philly all his life. The man's a walking encyclopedia."

* * *

As the discussion in the conference room started to wind down, two men walked into The 3/4 squad room. One wore sunglasses. He never took them off; so you couldn't see his ever-moving eyes taking in everything in sight. He was the Mayor's driver and bodyguard, an anonymous police Sergeant. The Mayor followed him in, and then the driver/bodyguard went back out to watch the car, a new loaded Crown Victoria. The Sergeant had just been just checking for trouble—yes, even in there. That was his job.

"Afternoon, everyone," greeted the Honorable Ed Rendell.

Phone calls ended, typewriters went silent, and conversation stopped.

"Is Lieutenant Gallagher here?" the Mayor asked the room in general.

"He's in the interrogation room, Mister Mayor," Sergeant Farrel replied. "I'll get him for you."

"No, no. That's all right. I'll wait. It'll give me time to speak with Detective Pasqualez. Is he here?"

Juan stiffened in his seat. *This was getting unreal,* he thought. "Here, sir," he said, standing up.

All eyes were on the Mayor as he moved to Detective Pasqualez's desk. When he got there, he turned and surveyed the room. Everyone quickly found something to do. Or appeared to, anyway.

Mayor Rendell looked down at Pasqualez. "Let's see your chart, Detective."

"Chart, sir?"

"Yeah, yeah. The chart. As in the ABLS jackpot."

"I'm sure I don't know what ..."

"Detective Pasqualez, my money's as green as everybody else's. Now get out the damn betting chart."

"Yessir." Juan pulled out the chart, and the Mayor sat down next to his desk.

"O.K.," the Mayor said. "Run it by me."

"Yessir. Sir, you can bet any day you want, but no more than three days in one week. Twenty bucks a pop."

"O.K., gimme all Labor Day weekend, Friday through Monday, and October first, second, and third. And, lemme see ... gimme October eleventh, twelfth, and thirteenth."

"Anything else, sir?"

"That's it. Two hundred, right?"

"That's right, sir. Two C-notes." Pasqualez took the money, and quickly made out the betting slips, and handed them over.

"One thing, Detective."

"Yessir?"

"If Midge finds out, we're all goin' down the tubes."

This brought out loud guffaws throughout the squad room. Rendell once caught hell from his wife when he was seen on TV throwing snowballs at Santa Claus during an Eagles game. It was a not-so-secret joke throughout the city.

Rendell pocketed the slips. "Thank you, Detective."

"My pleasure, sir."

The Mayor got up and turned. "Sergeant Godwin. How are you today?"

"Fine sir," Emma replied. "And how is Mrs. Rendell?"

Marjorie Rendell had founded, and now managed, the Avenue of the Arts Incorporated to develop South Broad Street into a world-class artistic venue. She was also a partner in the law firm of Duane, Morris, and Hecksher. A busy lady indeed, and word was she was being seriously considered for a Federal judgeship.

"Swamped with work, which actually keeps her out of trouble. She doesn't have time to find out about my shenanigans."

Everyone in the squad room laughed again. The Mayor, like all good politicians, loved an audience, private or public. One big difference here was that he was genuinely liked by the people of Philadelphia, and especially by cops and civilians in The Department.

The door to the interrogation room opened, and Matt was first out.

"Mr. Mayor, what a pleasant surprise," said Matt.

The Gallagher and Rendell families had known each other for years. Rendell and Matt were actually friends, but neither one talked publicly about that. This didn't stop the armchair warriors in the Department from being pissed off about it, though.

"Pleasure's all mine, Matthew."

"I think you've met all my detectives, sir," Matt said, indicating the squad room and the others who had followed him out of the interrogation room.

"I thought I had," Rendell replied, indicating Sergeant Wallace.

"Mayor Rendell, this is my new partner, Sergeant Yvonne Wallace. Sergeant Wallace, Mayor Rendell."

Yvonne blushed deeply, and this transformed her beauty into outright radiance. However, the Mayor looked slightly crestfallen as he shook her hand. Matt noticed this, but not Yvonne. She was instantly hooked by the Mayor's charisma, as he small talked her practically into a curtsy.

The Mayor turned back to Gallagher. "A word, Matthew," he said firmly but politely.

"Yessir. Jeet?"

"No, Joo?"

"No, but I think I have a cheesesteak around here we can split."

"Actually, Lieutenant," chimed in Sergeant Vargas, "When we heard you had a new partner comin' in, we gotcha two of 'em. Both with fried o's and sauce. They're in the fridge."

"You can have mine, Mister Mayor," Yvonne said. "I've eaten."

"Thank you, Sergeant. Matt?"

"This way, Mr. Mayor," Matt said indicating the door to the interrogation room. He started to walk toward the refrigerator to grab the sandwiches, but Emma had them out already, and handed them to Matt. She quickly walked into the interrogation room, and placed two cold birch beers and napkins on the table.

"Eat hearty, boys," Emma laughed as she closed the door behind her.

"She still mother you, Matt?" asked the Mayor.

"Yeah, all the time. But actually, I kinda like it. She's a great cop, and a really good person. She never does it to embarrass me. It's been like that since Susan died."

Gallagher's wife had been killed in January of 1992, when a drunk trucker rear-ended her on the eastbound lanes of the Schuylkill Expressway near the Gladwyne Exit. She was stopped in traffic because of an accident up ahead. The truck slammed into Susan's car, and in turn, she was smashed into the car in front of her. Her airbag deployed and her car was accordioned between the other two vehicles. With that and the initial whiplash, the doctors told police, she was surely dead before the car's gas tank erupted, engulphing the vehicle in flames. Because of the traffic mess, Belmont Hills Station 22 was called, and they barreled down the eastbound shoulder the wrong way, and got there in eight minutes. It was still too late. The vehicle burned down to the frame before they got the fire out. Everyone tried to emphasize to Gallagher that she hadn't suffered, that the double impact had killed her before the fire started.

The truck driver was tried and convicted of DWI and vehicular homicide, and was doing eight-to-fifteen at Graterford State Prison. He had expressed tearful remorse throughout the trial; but examples were starting to be made all over the United States; and the judge took the prosecutor's cue, and maxed him out.

Gallagher didn't attend the trial. In fact, he never met the trucker. He didn't want to. Susan was dead, and he didn't want to look into the eyes of her killer. It would just have magnified his grief beyond tolerance. He would never get over it; but he was coping. He had to. There was no other way.

"You holding up, O.K.?" asked Rendell as they sat down and unwrapped their steak sandwiches.

"Sure," said Matt. "I have my days, but having a squad like this helps. They're great people, the salt of the Earth."

"Good. Midge said to say 'Hi' the next time I saw you."

"Please tell her the same, sir."

"It's Ed when we're alone Matt."

"O.K., Ed."

"So, gimme the rundown," said Rendell as he took a big bite of cheesesteak. He and Matt were true Philly boys. They could enjoy a steak sandwich from Pat's, or anywhere else in the city for that matter, hot or cold. At least when it was cold, you didn't have to do the "Philly Lean" to keep the sauce and grease off your clothes. By this time the roll had absorbed all the juices.

Matt brought the Mayor up to date, including the meeting he had just had with his task force.

Rendell listened intently, never interrupting. When Matt was finished, he said, "I've already talked to the Commissioner, and I'm seeing

Max Loudin tonight. Needless to say, the heat's on. This asshole has to be caught, and we need our best people on it. You and your people are the best."

"Thank you, Ed."

"Later on, you might not thank me. Matt, we go back a long time, and I've never let our friendship interfere with your career, for good or bad."

"I know, Ed. And I've always been grateful for that."

"Right. I know. But this is gonna be tough for both of us." The Mayor paused, and took another bite of his cheese steak. After swallowing, he continued. "He's gonna do it again, right?"

"No doubt, sir. The way I see it, even if he originally intended it to be a one-time thing, he'll be flushed with the success of it. He knows that if we get him even on just the first one, he's lookin' at years of hard time. He'll just say 'fuck it', and go again." Matt paused and finished his own sandwich. "Damn, these things are good."

"Best sandwich in the world, kid."

"You bet. Anyway, I think he's got a master plan. He's gonna go again because he planned it that way. I gotta get inside his head, and figure which ongoing caper he's gonna latch onto next."

"Any ideas?"

"A few, but I'm gonna go through records at the Roundhouse tomorrow before I narrow anything down."

"Your Total Access up-to-date?" Rendell asked. As a former DA for the city, he knew what Matt needed. With a Total Access Clearance, you could go anywhere, read anything, either at Police Headquarters, or the DA's Office.

"Yessir, and so is Sergeant Wallace's. I checked."

"O.K.," the Mayor said, getting up. "I'll try to quietly keep some of the shit off your back, Matt. But I have to tell you, the black community is gonna be up in arms. It's gonna be all I can do to keep the Very Reverends and the Very Concerneds in front of the cameras from stirring up the people."

"I know, Ed. All I ask is room to do my job. He'll hit again. Three weeks, a month … I don't know. I can't catch him if I'm worried about polit … I mean other considerations."

Rendell smiled. "Politics is not a dirty word, Matthew. Now politicians …"

They both laughed and moved to leave the room. Before opening the door, the Mayor turned and winked at Matt.

"She's quite a looker, Matthew. Watch your cookies."

"Geez. Et tu, Brute?" But Gallagher was smiling broadly.

Rendell laughed. "You know, Costello and Patrillo are gonna go ape shit. I wish I could be here to see it."

"Stop, willya!" but Matt was openly laughing now as they left the room.

The Mayor took his leave.

"Take'er easy, folks. I'll stop by in Ninety-Five when I run again."

This got the Mayor another laugh as he made his way to the exit. As he passed Pasqualez's desk he murmured, sotto voice, "There's two hundred clams down the drain."

Pasqualez and others snorted laughter, and Gallagher pretended not to notice.

"O.K., everybody," Matt said loudly. "You know the drill and ya got the will. Everybody go home and play with the wife and kiddies, or the husband and kiddies, or whatever the case may be." He reached into his drawer. "Sarge, you and Julio, Jr. wanna go Sunday?"

"Sure Loo. Thanks," Vargas said, accepting the Phillies tickets.

He didn't offer payment because they had all tried numerous times to reimburse Matt, and he wouldn't hear of it. In fact, to lay down a little law, Gallagher announced one day that if they didn't stop offering money for the tickets, he would stop giving them out. The attempts at reimbursement stopped immediately. Shit, 200 level seats during a pennant race? They weren't going to mess up this gift horse.

As everyone was gearing up to leave, Matt turned to Sergeant Wallace. "Feel like seein' the Fightins tonight? The Expos are in town and Schilling's on the hill."

"Sounds good to me," Yvonne replied. "You got an itinerary or what?"

"Such a big word. Well, I always take the subway. What say we freshen up here, and walk over to the Tasker Street stop? We can eat down at the right field restaurant."

"Plus you can scope out Tasker Street, above and below."

"Right," he laughed. "Just to get a feeling."

CHAPTER NINE

While Lieutenant Gallagher and Sergeant Wallace were cementing their plans for the night, Randle Macjewski was driving east on Hunting Park Avenue after leaving his job at the Tasty Baking Company—home of Tastykakes.

Tastykakes were as much a staple of Philadelphia as beer, sports, cheesesteaks, and pretzels—soft pretzels. In fact, people have been known to live on a diet of just these "staples." And generation after generation of Philadelphia school children have gone to school with a Tastykakes in their lunch boxes. It was part of growing up.

Macjewski (pronounced Majooski) was not thinking about any of this as he drove; nor did he have any plans for this night. He was still five miles high from the mayhem he had created last night.

Once someone at work had heard the breaking news on KYW News Radio, it had rapidly spread around the plant. A Bomber? Teenagers maimed?

It wasn't that anybody was surprised about the crime. Not when some neighborhoods were serenaded to sleep at night by the sound of automatic weapons fire. Not when people—and not just females—were afraid to walk the streets at night.

It was the uniqueness of the crime. After breaking the story of the afternoon press conference at The 3/4 District, KYW, the all news radio station (at some point in their day, everybody listened to KYW), updated the incident at 4:00 P.M. Apparently, the kids maimed were the Booze Bandits, the terror of late evening Center City drunks.

Except somebody had turned the tables on them. *Damn right,* thought Macjewski, as he crossed Germantown Avenue. *And that someone was* me*!* He was scared as hell, but exhilarated at the same time. He needed to get home and relax. He needed to think; and he needed to watch the news. He needed to hear what the police were letting the public hear. Then try to read between the lines, as it were.

He knew if he was a suspect, they would've pulled his ass right out of work, right in the middle of a fresh batch of Krimpets. But they didn't. He was still just an average baker, albeit a master one, at an above average baking facility.

Thank God he didn't blush, or sweat profusely. Every conversation in the bakery during the later afternoon has been about the booby-trap incident. He could only exclaim in wonder with the rest of his co-workers.

"Who would do such a thing?"

"Why would anybody do such a thing?"

"Those poor kids!"

"Those little bastards got what they deserved!"

And the chorus had gone on and on, until he thought he would go mad. But he had dared not ask to leave early, or feign illness.

But he was almost home, he thought, as he turned right on Castor Avenue. Home to several frosty cold ones, and "Action News." *They got action all right. And the little bastards did get what they deserved*, although he hadn't joined several of his colleagues in expressing this opinion.

He took Castor down to Richmond Street, and made a right, and then turned left onto Wensley Street, and parked across the street from the S & B (Shots and Beers) Bar, which he owned, and which was attached to his house.

His house was a row home, but larger than the average Philly row home. The house faced south; and his living room entrance was one story above street level. A high, banked lawn was barricaded by a large, L-shaped wall, with little ramparts spaced a foot apart. The part of the wall facing Richmond Street gave way to the entrance of the bar, which was long and narrow.

He walked into the bar and felt the momentary rush you get from entering an air-conditioned room after being in the summer heat. Denise Reilly, his daily 4:00 P.M. to closing bartender, saw him come in, and pulled a bottle of Yuengling Lager out of a large ice bin used just for keeping bottles of beer ice-crackling cold. None of this ice was used for mixed drinks or anything else. Macjewski ran a sanitary bar.

He pulled up a bar stool, greeted Denise and Jim Richards, his daytime man and overall manager, and took a long pull of his beer. Before he finished his second gulp, Denise was grabbing another out of the ice. She brought it over and said, "Rough day, boss?"

"Hot and sticky all day at the bakery," Randy replied. Fans were in abundance and located throughout the plant, but there was no air conditioning at Tastykake, except in the offices. With all the ovens running full time, AC was a waste of money, and surprisingly, was never an issue with the workers or the union. The company paid very well, and the benefit package was excellent. There weren't many complaints from Tasty Baking Company employees.

Denise clucked in sympathy, and moved on to serve customers. She always wondered why he just didn't quit the bakery, and live off the bar. She knew it took in a lot of money, and he owned the whole property free and clear. He had taken over the mortgage payments after his mother died in 1976, of grief some said; and as of January 1984 was debt free, and the bar was never not busy.

Jim Richards came down the bar to Randy. "Evening, boss," he said.

"Hi, Jim," Randy returned. "Anything special I need to know?"

"Nope. Everything's running smooth, from the taps to the urinals."

Randy laughed. Everything his customers drank went right down the plumbing.

"Let me have it," he said, indicating the stack of bills and delivery slips next to the till.

Jim handed it over, and Randy swung around to his right to catch the news on the corner TV. There were three of them: one at each corner of the bar, and one mounted near the ceiling in back. All were large Zeniths. Randy, and many others, insisted they were the best TV's ever made, bar none. Some said the only way they would die was to shoot 'em. And that's exactly what happened one day.

A customer watching USC play Notre Dame at The Los Angeles Coliseum one year had Notre Dame and six points. With Notre Dame winning by one, USC had marched the length of the field to score a touchdown late in the game; and when USC kicked the extra point the customer fired a .38 right into the center of the TV tube. Randy had never pressed charges; and the man had gotten off with discharging a weapon in the city limits.

"Action News" at five-thirty was coming on with its famous music intro. It always grabbed your attention, which was the whole point.

The lead story, of course, was about the bombing. Lisa Thomas Laury, the early edition anchor, announced to the city that the police had designated the unit assigned to the case as "Task Force Gallagher" from The 3/4 District. Lieutenant Gallagher wasn't giving interviews; but "Action News," quoting an unnamed source high up in The Police Department, brought the city up to date.

Two of the alleged Booze Bandits were in very serious, but stable condition, and in induced comas. Jamal Woodson and Reshawn Deeds, both sixteen, were blind and horribly disfigured, according to doctors at Mount Sinai Hospital.

The apparent leader of the little gang, Michael Jefferson, was in guarded condition at Saint Agnes Hospital. He was in better shape than the other two; but that wasn't saying much. He had lost sight in one eye and fingers, and parts of fingers, on each hand. The youngest member of the gang was not injured.

The DA's Office—again, this was from an unnamed source—had recovered a substantial amount of money and valuables from the Jefferson place. And the DA was furious about the point man not being read his rights after being yanked out of school, or after being handed over to Gallagher. Heads were going to roll, etc., etc.

"We will keep you apprised with continuous updates," promised Lisa Thomas Laury. "Back after this."

"Isn't that terrible," said Denise, halfway down the bar. "Those poor kids."

"Yeah, pretty bad," replied Randy, still excited, but very cool. The beers took the edge off. Yeah, pretty bad, and that was damn good. Fuck the little bastards. He finished his beer and stood up. He handed the paperwork back to Richards, who had been standing there behind the bar, watching TV with him.

"The parents are probably basket cases," Jim said.

"Probably. It's a damn shame. Well, I'm heading up for a shower. I'll come down later and write the checks for the bills. I'll leave them in your box, Jim." Randy's out box was Jim's in box.

"O.K. boss. Take'er easy."

"Yeah. Later."

Randy walked back outside, leaving the excited buzz of conversation now being hollered back and forth by his customers. He didn't trust himself to sit through that. He walked around the wall, and climbed the steps to his front door. A shower and another beer, and then he had work to do. He was ready to start planning his next assault.

* * *

Matt and Yvonne were walking up Tasker Street after walking past the vacant lot that had been the old Moyamensing Prison, demolished in 1968. They were walking slowly, just looking, getting a "feel." They knew, of course, that they wouldn't find anything.

"I wonder how many times he walked up this street," mused Sergeant Wallace.

"I'm guessing at least four," Matt replied. "The kids would've watched him two or three times before they hit 'im, according to Gerald Hanson."

"He took a big chance that they didn't really whack 'im upside the head."

"Yeah, you're right. Plus he would've been fairly tipsy no matter how well he holds his booze. According to the bartender at The Red Eagle, he usually got there around six or so, and left a little after ten o'clock. But maybe the adrenalin took the edge off the beers."

"I agree. He must've ..." her voice trailed off as they heard someone shouting Gallagher's name.

They turned around and saw a young woman hurrying up the street after them.

"Know her?' asked Yvonne.

"No, can't say I do."

The woman caught up with them. Catching her breath, she gestured for them to wait a second.

"My name's Theresa Altez," she puffed. "I'm with SEPTA police." She flashed her badge, as she was in civvies. *Hastily thrown on civvies from the looks of it*, Yvonne thought.

"What can we do for you, Officer?" Matt asked.

"I'm off today. I been so busy I just haven't had the time to read the paper. I turned on the early news, and saw the story about the Bomber. I think I saw him."

Matt and Yvonne simultaneously whipped out their notebooks, both subconsciously noting the other's actions.

"Alright. From the top, Officer, please," said Matt.

Officer Altez said she had called Matt's District right away, and was told he was gone; and when she pressed for his whereabouts, was told he was on his way on foot to Tasker Street, and the Broad Street Subway.

"Last night about ten-thirty, I see this guy walking up Tasker, drunk as a skunk." She went on to relate how she made sure he was headed in the right direction, and described the "victim."

"That's him, alright," said Matt. "Officer, I'll call your boss in the morning, and let him know I need you to come in and make a full report for us, and compare notes with my team."

"That's fine. You already had his description?" she asked.

"Yeah, from one of the kids."

"I guess you think I should've called him a cab or something; but these foolish people do this stuff all the time. I see it on the EL, the buses, the trains ... it's unbelievable."

"Don't worry about it, Officer," Matt said. "You didn't do anything wrong. You couldn't have known. Come in and see us tomorrow. Are you on duty tomorrow?"

"Yeah, one-to-ten."

"O.K. Say around noon or so, before you go on duty. I'll clear it with your boss."

"O.K. Thanks, Lieutenant. I hope it helps."

"So do we. Enjoy your evening, Officer."

Gee, what a nice guy, thought Theresa as she turned and walked away. *Handsome, too. Wonder if he and his sexy partner are getting it on.*

"Well, now there's no question, no speculation. She just corroborated the kid's story," said Yvonne.

"Yeah," Matt replied. "It's funny. The guy passed by two cops, and didn't bat the proverbial eyelash. That really makes me nervous."

"Well, you've done enough for today, Loo. Take me out to the ball game," Yvonne said, laughing.

"Buy me some peanuts and cracker jacks," sang Matt, as they headed across Broad Street to the subway entrance. Now they were both laughing. You had to keep your sanity somehow.

* * *

Randy Macjewski walked out of his front door, down the steps, and around the wall to his bar. It was 8:00 P.M., and as always, even on a Thursday, the place was hopping. Not like Friday or Saturday night would be, but business was booming nevertheless.

He waved his hand and nodded greetings to his regulars. Moving to the far end of the bar, near the golf machine (and wasn't that a money-maker), he lifted the serving hatch and went behind the bar, closing the hatch behind him. *Always close the hatch*, he told himself, as he had told his employees. Never make it easy for somebody to get back there. Just in case though, there was a baseball bat three steps from the hatch. This was the obvious deterrent.

The secret deterrent was a sawed-off double-barreled twelve gauge halfway between the hatch and the register. It fit snugly under the rounded edge of the large industrial sink against the wall. All his regular employees knew about it except Denise and Theresa Barnes, his weekend bartender. It may have been chauvinistic on his part, but he was afraid of the women getting in trouble with would be robbers, or even the police in case of an itchy trigger finger. Besides, the panic button near the ice tub ran right to his living room, and would bring him down in seconds; and he always had a loaded M1911 Colt ready to go.

He unlocked a small cupboard, and pulled down his business checkbook. Grabbing the bills from his in tray, he pulled a Yuengling from the ice, and moved to the rear of the large open area past the bar.

He sat at a table near the pool table, and quickly paid some bills. Out of habit he subtly scanned the room, looking for trouble. But, as usual, everyone was behaving as well as could be expected, given the product he served.

He, and his bartenders, rarely flagged anyone; but many times they had taken car keys and called cabs or loved ones to get customers home safely. His father had always done this, and passed the wisdom down to his son. With liability laws as they were now, it was a good thing. He wasn't going to lose his business because a customer had a wreck. A large sign on the wall behind the bar said: "WE WILL NOT LET YOU DRIVE DRUNK. GIVE US YOUR KEYS WHEN ASKED OR WE WILL CALL THE POLICE."

When he first put the sign up, he brought his insurance agent in to see it, and got a twenty percent discount on the spot. And none of the regulars gave him a hard time about it. Most of the locals now went home from work first, and then walked to the bar to get loaded. Now the biggest problem was people leaving and falling off curbs, or pitching face first into walls or the sidewalk; but Randy could live with that.

Wrapping up his paperwork, Randy moved to the hatch, went behind the bar, and placed the checks and bills in his out tray. He then moved to the pool table, plunked down four quarters, and waited his turn. Two beers and two wins later, he said his goodnights and went back up to his house. Some people couldn't handle four or five beers without dinner; but he could, easily. He could drink half a case before he started really getting looped.

He made himself a large sandwich with a glass of milk, and headed for the basement. He walked to the corner where the main bus box was, set his milk and sandwich down, opened the fuse box door, and removed a screw-in glass fuse. Instead of a contact there was a key hole. Inserting a large key, Randy pushed hard against the paneling and turned the key. An entire section of paneling swung open on hidden, inner hinges, revealing a small, but functional rectangular workshop.

Years ago, his father had sealed off a store room in the bar by removing a door, and filling the hole up with brick and mortar. None of his regular customers or employees knew about this. The brick and mortar had long since been dry-walled and painted over, and now was indistinguishable from the rest of the bar.

Randy picked up his sandwich and milk, went in and closed and locked the door behind him. The circuit box, of course, was a fake. Everything about it was real except for the main line that came out and bored into the paneling and stopped there. It was a line to nowhere. The real fuse box was behind a refrigerator in the utility room. His friend and comrade from "Nam," Dickie Howsten, had done the real and fake wiring for him several years ago, when Randy had paneled the basement. In return, Dickie got a free pass at the bar for life, whether Randy was there or not.

When Dickie had gotten sick in '91, he had given Randy a key to his house so Randy could let himself in when Dickie was feeling too poorly to answer the door. The VA docs said they didn't know where all the cancers that were killing Dickie came from; but Randy and Dickie knew. They had walked through jungle and fields so full of Agent Orange their fatigues had become sopping wet from it.

Randy had been as exposed to it as anybody else. He was healthy now; but he didn't see himself living to a ripe old age. If some kind of cancer, or other Agent Orange related disease didn't get him, the police eventually would. He wasn't going to stop his one-man vigilante war until the cops stopped it for him.

When Dickie Howsten was on his death bed for good, Randy had asked him if he could help himself to some of Dickie's "supplies" down in the basement. Randy had been a medic in Dickie's company; but Dick Howsten was a full time 13B; a grunt—a foot-slogging, doggie infantryman. Like many of his long suffering comrades-in-arms, Dickie had shipped some interesting stuff home from Vietnam. Since mail wasn't censored, no sense to it since the press had full access to every unit in-country, parcels weren't checked either.

Dickie had shipped home M-16's, AK-47's, several Colt .45 pistols, a Thompson, a case of grenades, several pounds of C-4, and two claymore mines, plus various other little niceties of destruction. Before Dickie died, Randy had emptied his cache of arms, and hidden them in his little workshop.

The CS booby-trap had been his first little personal vengeance sortie. It was actually a working test run. Randy figured that if the CS went off prematurely, he could just drop the briefcase, and leave the area quickly. If the wallet had gone off though, he would have lost a large chunk of his ass.

His next mission was going to be a little more serious. He was going for a kill. And his research had steered him to his next target. Two weeks of observation should do it. The recon would start June 5th and continue until successful. This one would involve great personal danger; but he was prepared for that. This time, some son of a bitch was going to die.

* * *

Meanwhile at the Vet, Curt Schilling was cruising through the Expos batting order; and thanks to Pete Incaviglia's first inning grand slam, he could consistently challenge them with his heater. *Here it is, guys. It's my best. Can you hit it?*

They couldn't. Not this night, anyway. The Vet was rocking.

The fans hadn't been treated to a pennant race for ten long years, and they were really getting into it. Beer sales were off the charts, and the players were psyched. Macho Row, a row of cubicles in the clubhouse, was the talk of the town. And plenty of fair weather fans were jumping on the band wagon.

Lieutenant Gallagher and Sergeant Wallace had eaten in the right field restaurant, and were relaxing in their box seats near the Phillies dugout. The Phillie Phanatic was stomping on the top of the dugout, and the crowd was going wild.

"Amazing, ain't it?" asked Gallagher. "All your troubles seem a galaxy away when you're here."

"I'll say," replied Wallace. "I've never been this close to the field. A girl could get used to this."

Matt quickly searched her face when she said this. He thought he saw real interest there; but since he had never dated anyone but his late wife, it was hard for him to tell. She held his gaze for a moment, and then turned towards the field.

"Hey Phanatic," she yelled. "Get your fat behind outta there. I can't see."

"Now you did it," said Matt. "Here he comes."

Indeed, the mascot had leaped off the dugout, and was doing his infamous predatory walk toward their seats. When he was three feet away, he suddenly leaped on Yvonne. After smothering her in a bone-crushing hug, he pulled her up and led her playfully to the dugout roof. She tried to resist, but what with her giggling and the fans egging her on, she jumped up and joined the Phanatic on top of the dugout.

The PA system immediately let loose with a familiar rock tune, Queen's "Another One Bites The Dust," the '93 Fightins unofficial theme song.

The Phanatic led her into a chaotic, hot tango that had the whole ballpark rocking with laughter. By the end of it, she was flush with embarrassment and excitement; and as she made her way back to her seat, Matt thought he had never seen a more beautiful woman. As she sat down he handed her a cold one. She nodded her thanks and took a long, grateful gulp.

"Boy, that was fun. But I think it's time for Stinky to wash that costume. At least I hope it was the costume; otherwise that guy under there has a real problem."

Gallagher laughed, and took a pull at his own beer.

"You ever meet the Commissioner?" he asked.

"Not up close and personal, no."

"Well, now's as good a time as any."

"No, wait … you mean here … now?"

"Sure, he's right over there in the one-hundred corporate box." Gallagher pointed to a field level seat.

"Oh my God! He saw me dancing with the Phanatic."

"Him and every hormone-ravaged male in the place. C'mon. You'll like him."

They got up and walked down to the Commissioner's box. Augustus Phillips saw them coming.

"Matthew lad," he greeted loudly. "Good to see ya, boy. Does the Phanatic know you're seein' his girlfriend?"

Yvonne blushed pure crimson.

"Commissioner, I'd like you to meet my new partner, Sergeant Yvonne Wallace."

"My pleasure, Sergeant. Max Loudin speaks highly of you."

"Thank you, sir."

"C'mon in. Sit down," Phillips gestured to the empty seats near him. "Matt, you know Nat Holmes."

"Sure, we've met. Good to see ya, Nat."

"Likewise, Loo. Good evening Sergeant Wallace," Nat said, shaking hands with both of them.

"So," said Phillips. "A cold one?"

"Sure," Matt said. "If you're having one."

"I certainly am, lad." He handed a Schmidt's to each of them.

Nat Holmes was not drinking. He was on duty as long as the Commissioner was awake. He was his bodyguard, and he looked the part. He was as large as Larry Johnson, and about fifteen years younger. Matt knew he carried at least three guns and one knife, and all were well hidden. He wore very loose clothes. Once the Commissioner was in his house, a night man took over and spent the night awake and watching. It wasn't a perk. Phillips had many enemies, some still in jail, some on parole. When he took the job, Mayor Rendell had made the protection an order.

"So Matt, are these guys for real this year, or what?" Phillips said, as they all took their seats.

"They look good this year, they really do. They got lots of power from both sides of the plate, the defense is better than average, and they got a lot of live young arms. I think it's all going to come down to Mitch on the mound somewhere, the bases loaded, and the Phillies ahead by one. The guy gives me myocardial infarctions on a regular basis."

Mitch Williams was the Phillies' closer.

"Yeah, me too," the Commissioner replied, "and with my ticker, one of these nights he's gonna pitch me right into intensive care."

"Well, that's why they call him the Wild Thing."

Phillips turned to Sergeant Wallace.

"So, Sergeant. You been over to Matthew's madhouse yet, meet the folks?"

"Yessir. They mostly seem nice; but I seemed to have upset a couple of them without saying anything."

Phillips looked at Matt. "Let me guess. Costello and Patrillo?"

Matt shrugged helplessly, visibly embarrassed.

"Don't fret, Sergeant. They both got a crush on our lad here."

"Commissioner ..."

"Can it, Matthew. She needs to know." He looked at Yvonne. "They see you as competition, Sergeant."

"Competition?"

"For the heart of our blushing boyo here."

"Oh my Lord."

"Don't worry about it, Sergeant. Just watch Matthew's back, and the rest of the squad will keep those two on a short leash." Phillips turned to Gallagher. "So, Matthew. Brief me, please."

Matt brought him fully up to speed on the booby-trap case. The Commissioner did not interrupt.

"Any ideas?" he asked when Matt was finished.

'Sure," Matt said. "He's gonna case another caper, and take down more bad guys. Only question is, which one?"

"Well, he sure has a cornucopia to choose from."

"Well, yeah, but we can pretty much eliminate rapers, bank robbers, and anything else where he would physically stop a crime. He's gonna be a 'victim' again. This is what scares me. He's gonna go in serious harm's way to get his muggers. He's risking a serious shot to the noggin, or worse. And he seems alright with that."

"Right," the Commissioner replied. "Pure fearlessness, as opposed to courage. Meaning it's gotta be all about vengeance."

"That's the way I see it."

"Any thoughts, Sergeant Wallace?" asked Phillips. Nat Holmes might have been invisible for all he was paying attention. Besides, he constantly scanned the crowd.

"We gotta be where he is next time," Yvonne said, "and I don't see it happening yet—no offense, Matt."

"None taken. Please continue."

"We'll probably need to put three teams out at three different places," she said. "Then be patient. If we're not right on the next one, we do it all over again. Maybe different spots, maybe different times. I say we don't get close until the third, maybe fourth incident."

"Matt?"

"She's right, sir. There're probably a dozen ongoing serial crimes in the city right now. We're gonna need manpower, patience, and a lotta luck."

"Well the first two, ya got. The other one's outta our hands."

The crowd roared. Lenny Dykstra had just poked a base hit into right field.

"Alright, you two," the Commissioner said. "Keep us posted. I know you've heard it several times today; but you gotta catch this asshole. You have no other priorities. None. Understood?"

"Yessir," they chorused in reply.

"Good. Go enjoy the ballgame." It was a polite dismissal.

Matt turned his back to leave the box. There was a crack, and Matt's neck hairs stood up. He instinctively knew a foul ball was heading right at him. He heard several people yelling, "Heads up!"

Yvonne, who had kept her eyes on the field, reached out with both hands and started spinning as soon as she caught the ball. Matt turned, and saw her complete several revolutions. She stopped and held the ball high. The crowd went wild.

"Great hands, Sergeant Wallace," roared the Commissioner. Even Nat Homes was applauding.

Matt was laughing, perplexed. "I take you out to one ballgame ..."

She laughed and presented the ball to Matt. The crowd cheered again. Two pitches later, Darren Dalton homered to deep center, and it became pure pandemonium.

"What was the spinning all about, Yvonne?" asked Matt, as they headed back to their seats.

"I was bleeding off kinetic energy."

"Oh, spare me!"

"No, it's true. Otherwise I'd have two black and blue hands."

"What a day!" Matt said flopping into his seat.

"It sure has been interesting," replied Yvonne.

* * *

Back in Port Richmond, Randy Macjewski sat in his workshop. He had a disarmed hand grenade in front of him. The charging lever and pin were in place, but he had removed all of the explosive and the fuse.

He was placing it in a plastic mold he had made, charging handle up. He then placed the fitted mold in a briefcase. Using a thin, but heavy strip of steel, he held the handle down, and pulled the pin. Then he slowly closed the lid until it contacted the metal. Then, very carefully, he slid the steel strip out thru the opening, held the lid down, and closed both clasps. It worked. *It should,* he thought. It was about the twentieth time he had practiced it.

Starting Monday, he would use a real grenade. Before he went to work, he would drive to the bus station on Filbert Street, between 10th and 11th Streets. He would deposit the briefcase in a luggage locker; and it would be ready when he needed it.

He would scout for two weeks. He would drive his car to the Allegheny EL stop, and take the subway to Spring Garden Street, walk to Dave and Duster's on Delaware Avenue—it was now officially Christopher Columbus Boulevard, but nobody called it that—and start the mission. When he had his marks, he would start getting off at 11th Street, and walk to the bus station and retrieve his briefcase. Then he would walk to Dave and Buster's and it would really begin.

For this next mission, he chose to be bald, with a mustache and wire-framed glasses. He would wear a nice suit, subdued and slightly out of style. He had about ten suits of his own to choose from, and Dickie's wardrobe had yielded another three. Plenty enough clothes to dress different every night.

At the Red Eagle he had just registered as a white man. The clothes didn't matter.

But at Dave and Buster's, he would stick out if he wore the same clothes every night. So he would switch suits nightly, and carry a legitimate briefcase stuffed with meaningless paperwork. Until he needed the other briefcase. The lethal one.

Someone besides a mugger might get hurt in this one. He truly hoped not, but it wouldn't stop him. Only the police or death would stop him now.

CHAPTER TEN

June 1st, 1993

Lieutenant Matt Gallagher walked into his squad room at 7:45 A.M.

Detective Winston Smythe pulled out his typing slab as Matt walked by. Smythe looked at Sergeant Emma Godwin. She looked closely at Sergeant Yvonne Wallace, who was seated at her recently installed desk. Then she looked at Gallagher.

Sergeant Wallace, of course, was not let in on the ongoing wager. Emma caught Sergeant Vargas' eye and shook her head no. Vargas looked at Matt, and agreed. He gave the no-good wave off, and Smythe crossed off May 31st on the calendar. *The pot must be enormous by now,* he thought.

"Good morning, everyone," Matt called.

"Morning, Loo."

"Hey, Boss."

"Hello, Matthew."

Emma moved to Matt's desk with his cup of tea—two tea bags, a splash of half and half, and two sweet 'n lows.

"Emma, how many times ..." Matt started in.

"It does seem like forever," she laughed.

"Thank you, Sergeant. Everything smooth for you today?"

Sergeant Godwin had temporarily taken over the squad while Matt worked the booby-trap bomber case.

"Nothing I can't handle. If you want, the reports are on my desk."

'No, I know you got everything covered. My main worry is the bomber, of course. But I'm still here for advice."

"We're fine, Matthew. Larry and Ralph check in often to see how I'm doing. They don't overdo it, and I always appreciate it."

Larry Robinson and Ralph Halston were the patrol lieutenants, and they were available to Sergeant Godwin for help and advice. No order had been given for this. It just happened. The 3/4 District was the smoothest functioning District in the city. By writ or happenstance, good cops gravitated to this building. Captain Parmalee and his Lieutenants were bosses that cops loved to work for.

"O.K.," Matt said, sipping his tea. "Boy, that's good. How're Max and the kids?"

"Just fine, thank you. We went to Wildwood for the holiday. It was great."

"Good, glad to hear it." His normal meetings with Captain Parmalee, Halston, and Robinson were no longer. He briefed Parmalee about the "Booby-Trap Bomber" privately each day.

Matt quickly arranged his notes and folders, and then walked over to Robbery/Homicide. "Mornin', folks. How's tricks?"

"Funny you should ask that, Matthew," said Sergeant Imogene Patrillo. "I was wondering the same thing." She cast a none too subtle look at Sergeant Wallace, who returned the look in full.

Tensions between these two had begun to be noticeable, and Sergeant Wallace was at a loss. She had kept her relationship with Matt on a professional basis. She did not deny a personal interest; but she kept that separate. They spent a lot of time together, but so did all police partners. It came with the territory.

"Imogene," said Irene Costello, "put a lid on it."

"A lid on what?" Patrillo asked innocently.

"You go too far."

"Too far where?"

Matt, exasperated, turned and walked away; and Emma Godwin was suddenly looming over Imogene Patrillo.

"Sergeant," Emma hissed. "I'd like a word in private."

"Certainly, Sergeant Godwin."

The two female sergeants made their way to the bathroom, as everyone pretended not to notice.

Matt nodded at Sergeant Wallace, and she picked up her notes and followed him out of the squad room. Passing through the main lobby they waved at Sergeant Council, who grunted good morning in reply.

Lieutenants Halston and Robinson were leaving Captain Parmalee's office.

"Gentlemen," greeted Matt.

"Good morning, Lieutenants," said Yvonne.

"Hey, folks. Catch the Booby-Trapper yet?" asked Robinson, not in jest. It was his way of asking for an update.

"Well, we struck out on all three stakeouts last night. Again."

"Hang in there Matt," said Halston. "You'll get 'im."

"I know. I feel we will. But how many maimed citizens later is what worries me."

"He's due, ain't he?" asked Robinson.

"Yeah," Wallace replied. "I feel this week or next."

"Well, good luck."

"Thanks. Later," said Matt.

Matt and Yvonne moved to Jane Wilson's desk.

"He's on the phone. Just a moment, please," said Jane, looking at them, especially Yvonne, most intently.

The last week or so, I've been one scrutinized individual, Yvonne thought. She didn't pretend to herself that she didn't know why. She just wondered why it was so intense. *Oh well,* she thought. *I'll just have to measure up.* She had never seen such genuine care and concern by an officer's peers and subordinates, not to mention his superiors. She felt that if something happened to Matt, she had better be dead or wounded. It was a bit rankling.

The blue light on Jane's telephone lit up, and as she waved them into the Captain's office she gave them one last subtle glance. *Not yet,* she thought. Her bets were still good. Only her principles, such as they were, prevented her from egging them on.

"Good morning," Parmalee said. Parmalee indicated seats, and punched a button on his phone. "No calls please, Jane," he said into the speaker.

"Yessir," came the faint reply.

"So, talk to me," said Parmalee.

"Right," said Matt. "We drew a blank again last night."

"Same areas?"

"Yeah. Trung and Vargas in West Philly, Gonzales and Smythe in South Philly, and Yvonne and I around Temple University."

Detectives Trung and Vargas had been staking out University City for the past week. There had been a string of book bag snatchings on the grounds of the University of Pennsylvania. Apparently, several young Hispanic males had been ripping off late night students on their way back to dormitories after classes or study halls.

Gonzales and Smythe have been hanging out near 19th and Mifflin Streets. Young black males had been mugging drunks coming out of the Sit On It Bar. This used to be unimaginable in the old days. The wise guys would have taken care of it themselves. But many white Italians had left the neighborhood, and their presence was not as keenly felt as it once was.

Matt and Yvonne had holed up at the Temple University campus. White and black muggers were the problem here. It was a tough campus to police, because many students had to actually leave the campus to get to their dorms. The short walks off campus were dangerous.

"I still feel we've got about a week before he hits again," Matt summed up. "As I've said before, we probably won't get close until the third or fourth incident. Unless he makes a serious mistake, which I feel is unlikely."

"Well, it's like this," said Parmalee. "The news people may have let up a little bit, but Steele and Quintade haven't. They're both preaching serious fire and brimstone if we don't make some progress here."

Steele was the president of the Philadelphia NAACP and Quintade was the head minister of the First African-American Church of Philadelphia.

"I know, Cap, and I know ya been keeping some of the heat off us. You know I won't nail this guy until at least after the second one. The next one's gonna happen, and it's gonna happen soon."

"He's right, Captain, "Yvonne chimed in. "It sounds horrible, but we have to wait until the second one to get more clues."

"It does sound horrible; but I agree." responded Parmalee. "Actually, I see my job as preparing our official response to the hue and cry that's gonna come with it. That's O.K. Just drive on; and we'll deal with it."

"Starting tonight," Matt said, "we're gonna change tactics a little bit."

"How so?"

"Smythe is gonna start drinking in the Sit On It. Once people hear his accent, they start talking to him. He'll be looking for someone that doesn't fit, someone studiously keeping to himself. If he thinks he's got something, he'll follow the individual, and Pablo will trail them both."

"O.K., go on."

"Nguyen Trung is gonna start walking around Penn's campus. He knows the turf intimately, and he's got the look of a student anyway. He'll look for someone out of place, maybe trying too hard to fit in. Julio will have him in sight constantly."

"And you two?"

"This was my idea," said Yvonne. "I'm gonna be the bright young professor walking on and off campus late at night."

"You two are putting in some late hours," Parmalee observed.

"Well, sir," Yvonne replied. "We've been knocking off at lunch time, and coming back later. Splitting the shift."

"O.K., I guess that works. Be careful and keep me posted."

"Yessir." They rose to leave.

"One thing," Parmalee stopped them. "This is gonna sound stupid; but I gotta say it. We don't have carte blanche. If you got a suspect, fine. Take him down. But we can't pull in every one walking the streets late at night. Caution the younger officers. We don't need more civil trouble than we already have."

"O.K., Cap. Catch you later."

As if on cue, as Matt and Yvonne took their leave, Parmalee's phone lit up.

"Deputy Chief Barnes on one," Jane said.

"I'm glad I'm not taking that call," murmured Matt as they were leaving.

"Roger that," said Yvonne.

"Bye, Detectives," waved Jane.

"Later, Jane."

Randy Macjewski stood in front of the large production kettle at the Tasty Baking Company. He was overseeing the production of another large batch of Krimpets. The machines and robots did most of the work; and his job was more of a quality controller than a baker.

As he monitored batter load and oven temperature on the moving line, he considered last night's happenings.

He had spent several hours at Dave and Buster's, sitting at the street-side bar looking down on Delaware Avenue. Across the street were the dark parking lots under the elevated roadway of I-95.

At 11:00 P.M., he had tipped the bartender, and exaggeratedly weaved his way from the pier-side bar and crossed Delaware Avenue. He wandered the parking lots for twenty minutes, and then left the area by way of the Spring Garden Elevated stop. He knew they would hit him. It would probably be Friday night; but he would work the area all week just in case.

During his second week of scouting, he had finally seen it go down.

On Thursday last, he had watched several men exit the bar and cross the street. Two headed for their cars near Front Street. The third, carrying a briefcase, headed for a parking lot under I-95, right past the intersection of Spring Garden and Green Streets.

Randy's gaze wandered back to Front Street momentarily, and then he caught a quick motion out of the corner of his eye to the left. Two young white men dressed in dark clothes and dark shoes were heading in the third man's direction at a steady gait. They quickly disappeared into the parking lot under the highway. Randy got goose bumps on his skin and butterflies in his stomach. This was it. He knew it.

Sure enough, less than thirty seconds later the men emerged from the lot; this time one of them had a briefcase. They quickly made their way to the steps leading down to the small boat landings on the Delaware River. At this point they were out of his sight, but moments later a small speed boat appeared. It headed directly east, and then north when it cleared the piers.

He now had it all. These cretins stalked the parking lot for drunks, and made their getaway on the river. But how bad had they hurt the victim? He needed to wait and see that.

The victim finally reappeared from under I-95, and staggered to Delaware Avenue, whether from too much booze, a blow to the head, or both. He stumbled to a taxi, and off into the night he went.

Randy had scanned both daily newspapers the next day, but had found no report of the mugging. That didn't mean the man hadn't reported the crime; but Randy didn't believe he did. Assaults and robberies along this stretch of Delaware Avenue had been news lately, and he thought it would have made the papers if the man had gone to the police. Many people did not report such incidents, preferring to tell their boss or their spouse that they had simply lost their briefcase, wallet, or laptop, or whatever.

In any case, it was time to hunt the hunters. Randy was prepared. He knew he was probably going to take a serious blow physically; but he was wiling to risk it. Hell, yeah! For you Mom, for you Dad. These assholes are coming to the Pearly Gates for judgment. Grab a ringside seat.

* * *

In the squad room, a somewhat subdued Sergeant Patrillo avoided looking at Gallagher or Wallace as they came back to their desks. Sergeant Godwin had calmed down, but still looked a little ruffled.

Once in the bathroom with Patrillo, Emma had let it all hang out.

"This shit has got to stop," she started in on Imogene.

"What shit?"

"You know perfectly well what I'm talking about."

"Look Godwin, you may be temporarily in charge of the squad room; but you need to stay out of my personal business."

"Keep your personal business out of this squad room and I'll stay out of it."

"Fine. Chill out."

"Chill out, my black ass," Emma said. "If you don't can this raging hormone crap, me and you are gonna go."

"Yeah well, we'll see. At least I have hormones."

"What's that supposed to mean?"

"It means maybe you forget what a sex life is."

Emma struck a pose. "Honey, my man gives me all I want, and then some. You should be so lucky."

"Luck ain't gonna have anything to do with it. If I ever get the high sign from Matt, I'm going for it."

"Well, until that day comes, keep it professional in the squad room."

"Sure thing, sister."

"I ain't your sister."

"You got that right," taunted Imogene as she left the bathroom.

* * *

"How'd they do last night, Jack?" Matt called out as he sat down at his desk.

"Reds beat 'em six-to-four, Boss. Anderson blew a one-run lead in the eighth. He balked, and Dalton and Fregosi got thrown out for arguing. Schilling pitched a great game. Seven innings, three runs, and seven K's."

"Feast or famine. They pounded the Rockies Sunday."

"I know, but their thirty-four and fifteen. They might be the real deal this year."

"We can only hope," Matt said. He turned to Sergeant Wallace.

"How about we go to breakfast. There's someone I wanna meet."

"Fine by me," she replied.

"Good. Let me make a quick call." Matt dialed a number.

"It's Gallagher," he said into the phone.

"Aay, my favorite Mick flatfoot."

"I need a meet."

"O.K., the other diner at nine o'clock." The other diner was the Aramingo Diner. The wise guys all usually ate at the Melrose Diner in South Philly.

"Right. I'm bringing my new partner."

"Whoa there, Mick. We always meet alone."

"I know. But she's my partner. You never hide things from a partner."

"Alright, alright. See ya!"

Matt hung up. "One minute, and we'll be outta here." Matt made his way back to Captain Parmalee's office. Jane Wilson saw him coming and had already told the Captain on the intercom.

"Go right in, Matthew."

"Thanks, Jane."

Matt knocked once and went in, closing the door behind him.

"Whaddya got, Loo?"

"I'm gonna go see my 'guy'. I'm just givin you a heads up."

"I still get nervous about that, Matt," said Parmalee.

"Not half as nervous as he gets. I just wanna see what the 'boys' might've heard."

"O.K., that's all I need to know."

"Right. Later, Cap."

As Matt walked out, Jane looked up at him.

"She seems like a nice girl, Matthew."

"She is. And she has great hands, too."

"I beg your pardon?"

But Gallagher was already walking away, laughing. "Score one for the home team," he called over his shoulder.

Jane just shook her head and laughed.

Matt walked into the squad room, nodded to Sergeant Wallace, and grabbed the keys to the Crown Vic. "I'll be on the squad radio, Emma," he said to Sergeant Godwin. "Please tell Eileen that the Task Force will meet at 2:00 P.M."

"Will do, Matt."

"Goodbye, Matthew," cooed Sergeant Patrillo.

"Later, Boss."

"See ya, Loo."

"So," said Yvonne as they pulled out of the lot. "Clue me in."

"Guy's name is Johnny Gambella," Matt said as he headed east on Wharton. "He's an associate of Skinny Joey."

"Skinny Joey" was Joey Merlino, heir apparent to the Philadelphia mob. If he and John Stanfa could keep from killing each other.

"So, you know these guys?" asked Yvonne

"We're nodding acquaintances, you might say. I arrested Merlino for that armed robbery. You probably heard about it—Joey's robbery and the time in the slammer?"

"I knew he did time. I didn't know you were involved."

"Yeah, I was lucky and he was careless. Funny thing is, he never held it against me. When I went to arrest him, he was totally cool about it. After I booked him, he was out in fifteen minutes. The lawyers were waitin' at the lock up. We actually got back out to the parking lot at the same time. He invited me to a softball game and barbeque later that night."

"Did you go?"

"Of course not!"

"Just kidding."

"Oh. O.K. Anyway, my dad sold a couple of cars to Angelo Bruno way back when," Matt said as he turned left on Delaware Avenue. Angelo Bruno was the head of the Philadelphia Mafia before Nicky Scarfo.

"Really!"

"Yeah. He paid cash, and my dad treated him like any other customer. The Feds wanted to give him grief about it, but my dad wasn't havin' any of it. Strictly a business deal."

"Did you ever meet Bruno?" Yvonne asked.

"Sure. My dad and I played golf with him and one of his capos. They were nice guys. You had to watch 'em, though. They cheated constantly. They couldn't help it. It's in their blood."

"When was this?"

"When I was in high school. Sixty-Six, I think. Summertime."

"You're full of surprises," Yvonne said.

"I have led an interesting life," Matt laughed. "I've never been bored."

Matt veered left onto Aramingo Avenue. "We're goin to the Aramingo Diner."

"I've been there before. Great chow."

"Yeah, and a gold mine, too. I've never seen it not busy."

Matt drove deeper into Kensington and crossed Lehigh Avenue.

"So is this Gambella guy a stoolie?"

"No, no way. His capo knows we meet. He gives me information on other stuff that affects their livelihood. I just wanna see if these guys know anything. Ya never know. One thing," Matt continued. "Please be a silent partner on this. I don't wanna spook 'im."

"No problem. I'll just eat and listen."

"Good. Thanks," Matt said. He crossed over Allegheny Avenue, made a left on Westmoreland, and then a right on Memphis, and parked in the lot behind the diner.

They walked over to the diner entrance on Aramingo Avenue and went in. Gambella was in a back booth near the kitchen door. Matt smiled to himself. It was one thing cops had in common with the wise guys. Always sit in the back near a rear exit. You could keep an eye on the whole establishment, and duck out the back way if necessary. They sat down in the booth, Wallace sliding in next to Gambella.

"Hiya, Johnny," greeted Matt. "This is my partner, Sergeant Yvonne Wallace."

"Please to meetcha," replied Gambella, practically raping her with his eyes. "You're some dish."

"Thank you. Now let's get some breakfast dishes crackin'. I'm starved."

"Woman after my own beatin' heart. Anything you want doll. My treat."

"That's not an option. I pay for all my meals."

Gambella laughed. "Scruples, too. I love it."

A waitress came over.

"Ladies first," said Johnny.

"Fine," said Yvonne, looking up at the waitress. "I'll have a four egg cheese and tomato omelet, hash browns, sausage, four pancakes with syrup and sour cream. I'd like four slices of wheat toast, and coffee, please."

Both men and the waitress stared at her in awe.

"What, no waffles?" Matt asked.

"I'm watching my figure."

"You and me both, babe." said Gambella.

"One more 'babe' outta you, and you'll be eatin' breakfast through a straw."

"Feisty, too. You're a lucky man, Mickey."

"Just order willya, Johnny," Matt said, laughing.

"O.K., O.K. Two over easy, sausage, and hash browns, no toast. Coffee and O.J."

"Right," said the waitress. "You, handsome?"

Matt ordered a light omelet, hash browns, and bacon, with tea and toast.

"O.K., Mick, what's shakin'?" asked Gambella, after the waitress left.

"The kids that got blown up," Matt said.

"What about 'em?"

"Heard anything about who done it?"

"Nah, nada."

"This guy stalked these kids and set 'em up."

"Yeah, that's what the talk is," Gambella acknowledged.

"The kids were movin' cards," Matt said. "Hadda be to one of your boys."

"If it was, I couldn't tell ya that."

"I know," Matt said. "I'm not on the Booze Bandits anymore. But the DA's got it; and someone in your neighborhood is gonna be feeling some serious heat. This'll keep the DA's name in the paper for weeks."

"Yeah." Gambella looked thoughtful. "That is the name of the game, ain't it? Anyway, thanks. I'll pass that on."

Their breakfast arrived and they all dug in, both men marveling at Yvonne putting away her massive breakfast. *Hollow leg,* thought Gambella. *She could probably drink any three guys under the table, too.* This only made her more attractive in his eyes.

Matt looked up at Johnny. "This guy used old army ordinance. Two 40 mm CS grenades."

Johnny whistled. "O.K. I'll see what I can find out. But that'll be tough. I'll have to see Joey first for permission."

"Fine. Keep me posted."

"O.K."

They finished their breakfast in silence. The bill came.

"I got it," said Matt. "You tip."

"Right." Gambella laid a ten on the table. "See ya later." He headed for the exit.

"Well, that was new," said Yvonne.

"Yeah. And he wasn't alone. See that guy leavin with him? He was by the door in a booth by himself. They call him 'The Griz'. For obvious reasons."

Yvonne saw why. The man was not tall; but he was enormous, with tree trunk arms.

"Where to, now?" asked Wallace, as they got back in the Crown Victoria.

"Let's stop over at Mount Sinai, and see the kids before we head back to the shop."

"Fine by me. Damn, that was a great breakfast."

"Where the hell do you put it all?" Matt asked.

"I have an overactive metabolism. I've weighed the same since junior year in high school."

"Sure was enough for two people," Matt said as he pulled out of the parking lot.

"I been hearing that for years," said Yvonne.

Matt laughed as he drove down Westmoreland toward Richmond Street.

* * *

Nurse Florence White was again on duty at the Mount Sinai ICU Nurses Station. Matt and Yvonne showed their badges, and asked to see the kids.

"I'm sure it's O.K., but let's check with Doctor James. Here he comes now."

"I'm Doctor James. You must be Lieutenant Gallagher."

"That's right. This is my partner Sergeant Wallace," Matt said. "How'd you know me?"

"We read the papers, Lieutenant. Your pictures been in *The Daily News* and *The Inky*."

"Right. How're the kids?"

"Better than can be expected. The power of youth, I guess. Aside from their sight, they'll make full recoveries."

"Can we see them?" asked Yvonne.

"Sure. I was just down there. They have kin visiting. I've got other rounds to make." Doctor James headed down the hallway; and Matt and Yvonne went the other way, toward the kids' room. They pushed through the door, and quietly walked inside. There was a strong odor of antiseptic. There were two black women in the room. Gallagher and Wallace introduced themselves.

Amanda Woodson sat next to her son Jamal's bed. Eloise Deeds stood next to her grandson's bed. Both boys were sitting up, the beds cranked up to an upright position.

"They're not gonna answer any questions, Lieutenant," said Amanda. "The lawyers say not to say anything unless they here."

"We're not here to ask those kinds of questions, ma'am," Matt replied. "We just came to see how they're doin'."

"Yeah, right."

"Easy, Amanda," said Eloise. "They ain't the ones hurt our boys."

"How are you, Jamal?" Yvonne said to the young Woodson.

"Been better."

"How goes it, Reshawn?" asked Matt.

"I'm blind, Flatfoot."

There was an awkward silence.

"We just want you to know we're gonna catch the guy," said Matt.

"That's right," said Yvonne. "We'll get 'im."

"What about us?" asked Jamal.

"Yeah," piped in Reshawn.

"That's up to the DA," said Matt. "Unofficially, I can tell you that it's unlikely you'll be charged with anything. Personally, I think you've suffered enough."

"Got that right," the boys chorused, and the tension dissipated a little.

"How's Michael?" asked Reshawn.

"He was discharged over the weekend," said Yvonne. "He's not bad, considering."

"That honky sure fucked us up," said Jamal.

"Hush," said Amanda. "The lawyers said."

"It's alright, mama. Reverend Quintade said they ain't gonna put us in jail."

"That's right," said Matt. "They won't. But don't count on easy street either. We recovered most of the loot from the shed at Michael's house."

"Oh shit," said Reshawn.

"Anyway," said Matt. "I'm glad you're almost up and around." He handed a card to both Eloise and Amanda. "If you need anything, please call me."

"Thank you, officer," replied Amanda, who had mellowed a bit.

"Please catch this lunatic," said Eloise. "We don't need no more people hurt."

"We'll do our best," said Yvonne. "Take care," she added as they took their leave.

"That coulda gone]worse," she said to Matt as they headed for the elevator.

"Yeah, I think it's all still a bit of a shock to everyone. Me included."

"It's definitely not a pretty situation," agreed Yvonne as they stepped into the elevator.

* * *

Randy Macjewksi signed off on this second batch of Krimpets, and headed for the break room. Several co-workers were already there.

"Mornin, Randy," said Joe Tallon. "You up for that fishin' trip this weekend? Company's payin' for it."

"Nah, I got a bar to run. 'Sides, I get seasick watchin bass tournaments on television."

"Hey," said Alan Ditch to no one in particular, as he read *The Daily News*. "Paper says the DA ain't gonna prosecute the Booze Bandits."

"Well," said Joe, "They got enough problems."

"Yeah," said Randy. "The poor bastards."

CHAPTER ELEVEN

May 20th, 1993

After visiting the kids at the hospital, Gallagher and Wallace had spent the rest of the morning in the Records Room at the Roundhouse. They were looking for more patterns, serial crimes that their bomber might take an interest in. After this week, they would change their stake-out locations if nothing went down.

It was daunting, arduous work. It was a big city, and crime was rampant. Unlike what movies and TV shows would have you believe, most crimes went unsolved. There were just too many incidents, too few cops, too little resources. It was like walking in a quagmire. You might be moving, but it seemed like you weren't getting anywhere.

"I hate to do this to you," Matt said. "But I guess you knew we would have to do it eventually. We're gonna have to start looking at relatives and kin of violent crimes."

"I know," replied Yvonne. "But with one of the new computers, we might be able to set up a program to whittle it down a little bit."

"I'm a dinosaur with those things," Matt said. "I can barely turn 'em on and off."

"I'm O.K. with them; but I was thinking of maybe getting an expert to set up a search program for us. Somebody inside, or even outside The Department."

"Tell me more."

"Well, we write out a general outline of what we want, and a programmer writes up a program, and feeds it into a computer. It'll quickly eliminate victims with no kin, deceased kin, kin who've moved away, etcetera. With the green light we have on resources, we might even try to get time on a Cray. You know, the super computer."

"I thought only the military and research facilities had access to those."

"Well," Yvonne said. "That used to be true. But police forces and other law enforcement agencies get cracks at them now. I don't know what kind of waiting list we'd have to get on; but let's see what kind of pull we got. Penn's got a Cray."

"Alright. Let me see if I can run down Mary Anne Sims. She's the computer expert here at HQ. They call her 'The Wiz'. I'll be right back."

Matt walked out of Records, and headed for the main administration section of the Roundhouse. He nodded hello to several people, and made his way over to one section that was partitioned off from everything else. A bank of keyboards was lined against a wall; and a glass door guarded the entrance to the computer room. "No Admittance" the sign on the door flatly said. Even Gallagher's Total Access couldn't get him in there without an escort.

"Is Mary Anne in?" Matt asked a woman at one of the keyboards.

"In there. Wait, please. I'll buzz her." The woman keyed an intercom. "Hey Wiz, you got a visitor."

"O.K.," came the reply over the speaker. "Right out."

A few seconds later, a properly frazzled young woman came through the glass doors. A petite brunette with a Drill Sergeant's voice, Mary Anne Sims was in charge of computer operations at Police Headquarters. With an IQ in the upper stratosphere, and two doctorates from Temple University, she could have written her own ticket anywhere in the country. She chose to stay home and work with the police; to be "where the action is" as she put it. She and Gallagher were old acquaintances.

"ABLS," she boomed. "How they hangin'?" She gave Matt an affectionate bear hug. "What's the pool up to?" she asked. A keyboard operator sniggered.

"What pool?" Matt said blankly.

"Don't gimme that crap. You know what pool."

"I don't know, and I don't wanna know. They think I don't know about it, and I don't wanna spoil their fun."

"I been meanin' to come in and lay a few bucks down myself. What brings you here?"

"Where can we talk?" Matt asked.

Mary Anne led him inside the computer room. Banks of processors filled most of the room. She led him over to a small table, and they both took seats.

"I got a tough case," Matt said. "My partner had a suggestion."

Matt outlined his needs. Mary Anne listened intently, fidgeting the whole time. When Matt finished, she stared thoughtfully into space for a few seconds.

"I got a lot on my plate," she said. "This would take some doin'."

"I got the power to pull you in if I have to," Matt said. You didn't beat around the bush with Sims. She wouldn't tolerate it if you did.

The Wiz looked into Gallagher's eyes. "Let me get this straight. You'd put me on your team?"

"Yeah. Willingly on your part, I hope. If you don't want in, I won't force it. But I need help. Could you recommend someone else?" There was a twinkle in Gallagher's eye.

"Nice try, Gallagher. I'm in. I'll clear my desk and clean my Colt."

"You still packin'?"

"Never leave home without it."

"I'm not too comfortable with that, but as long as your permit's current, I can't stop you."

"Don't try. Baby comes or I don't."

"O.K., O.K.," Matt laughed, feigning exasperation. "We have our regular Tuesday meeting this afternoon. Two o'clock. C'mon in and meet the gang, and we'll get you thoroughly briefed. I'll clear it through channels."

"Fine. See ya then."

Gallagher left the room in a whirl. He hadn't counted on something like this; but he needed the research. Without a computer, he knew, it would take a dozen detectives months to even begin to winnow a list down to a manageable number. He found Yvonne still in records.

"Let's go to lunch, and then head back," he suggested.

"Sure. Where you wanna eat?"

"Let's grab some Chinese. We're close."

Chinatown, between Race and Vine and 8th and 11th Streets, was classic in its essence. Numerous dry cleaners, eateries, and lots of above street apartments and tenements were crammed into a few square blocks.

"Sounds good."

"O.K.," Matt said. "I'll clue you in on the 'Wiz'. Wanna drive?"

"I thought you'd never ask."

"Actually, if you want it, from now on you got it."

"Really?" Yvonne was surprised.

"Yeah. I hate driving in the city in the daytime."

"Cool. I love drivin' in this town. Day or night."

"I knew you were strange."

She laughed. "Thanks a lot."

They left the Roundhouse and headed the short distance to lunch.

* * *

Vargas, Trung, Smythe, and Gonzales all arrived at the station house well before 2:00 P.M. Sergeant Johnson and Detective Robinson had been there since mid-morning, as had the new plainclothes team. They were Officers Harold Michaels and Renee Withers. They were young, full of spunk, and a little awed to be in the famous Three-Four squad room. Sergeant Johnson had taken them under her wing to ease the transition, but had given them a heavy workload.

"The way we do things here," she had explained, "is work you hard . I won't chew on you for missing something; but I will come down on you for not asking questions. If you're not sure about something, ask. Period. Just don't wander too far over towards that corner of the room." She indicated the Robbery/Homicide desks. That group, as one, had smiled and waved at the new crew. "O.K., now we work," she had finished, and work them she did. She had them take all tip calls, and sift through all the new leads. The Three-Four squad never harassed new people. They worked their buns off to see what they could handle. Then, if they fit in, they might bust their chops a little, but not before.

Matt was in Parmalee's office, and Yvonne and the rest of the squad were at their desks, when a whirlwind broke upon the room. The outside door opened, and in stormed Mary Anne Sims.

"Alright, who's the head dick or dickless around here?"

"That would be me," said a startled Emma Godwin. "Can I help you, Miss?"

"I ain't no Miss. Call me 'The Wiz'. Everybody else does. And for good reason. I'm the new computer consultant to Task Force ABLS."

"Oh, I say," murmured Winston Smythe, instantly smitten. "The cheek, the bloody, wonderful cheek."

"You say somethin', Stud?" Mary Anne boomed.

Smythe stood up. "Detective Winston Smythe, at your service, m'lady." Smythe had turned on all his considerable English charm.

The chuckles and sniggers started.

"I'll determine that," said Sims. "A Limey, huh?" There was no mistaking his accent.

"Indeed, m'lady. Lost amid the colonials. Perhaps you could help me find my way."

"Not a bad line, Limey. Take a seat."

The squad was in an uproar by now. Even Sergeant Godwin was laughing.

"Matthew will be with you in a minute," she said.

"Fine," replied Sims. "Who's the bookie?"

Dead silence.

Again Emma was taken aback. "I beg your pardon?"

"Who's takin' the ABLS action?"

Yvonne looked up. ABLS action?

The laughter started again. Who was this woman?

"That would be me, Miss," said Juan Pasqualez. "Whaddya need?"

"Is there an over/under? Before/after?"

"No. Just days on the calendar. Twenty dollars a day, no more than five bets on a given day, and no more than thee days for an individual in any week."

"Show me."

Juan pulled out his cardboard betting sheet as Yvonne moved down the aisle to see this. Action on Gallagher? To get laid? It couldn't be.

"Lemme see," mused Sims, as Gallagher entered the room unseen by Juan, Mary Anne or Yvonne. Matt averted his eyes, and quietly sat at his desk.

"Gimme Friday, Saturday, and Sunday for the rest of June," said Sims.

The room was stunned. Heads quickly bent over desks, and hands reached for reports and telephones.

"That's two hundred and forty bucks, Miss," said an awed Pasqualez. As he looked up, he saw Matt at his desk. He quickly touched Sims and Wallace to let them know. Sims quieted down, and Yvonne walked quickly back to her desk, red as a beet. Mary Anne quickly counted out the cash, and Juan just as quickly gave her her receipts and put everything away.

"What's the pot up to?" whispered Sims into his ear.

Juan wrote a figure on a sticky note.

Sims whistled quietly. "Damn, I could almost retire on that."

Matt stood up, gathered his folder and said, "Meeting time, folks."

Task Force Gallagher quickly gathered in the interrogation room. Two more gun- metal gray tables had been added. Everyone took seats.

"This is Mary Anne Sims, who everyone seems to have met."

Sims had the good grace to redden slightly.

"O.K.," continued Gallagher. "I've briefed Miss Sims on the case, and what I would like her to try for us. Before we hear from her, let's go over new tactics for this week." He looked over at Smythe and Gonzales. "Youse guys first."

"Right," said Pablo. "Winston's gonna drink in the Sit On It tonight. He'll strike up conversations, and observe everybody in the bar. I'll be sittin' on Mifflin Street. If there's somebody that rings our bell,

Winston walks out behind him and stops to tie his shoe. I'll get out of the car and tail the guy. Winston will follow in the car."

"What're you gonna be drinkin', Winston?" Wallace asked. She *was* new.

"Panther piss. American beer. I can quaff that garbage all night and walk a razor's edge."

Sergeant Vargas chimed in. "We once did a breathalyzer on 'im after a night out. And I mean a night. It came up point oh five. He's not human. No offense, Limey."

"None taken, Sarge," smiled Smythe.

"Alright, Nguyen and Julio," said Matt.

"Nguyen's gonna walk the Penn campus with a book bag over his shoulder. I'll be watchin' and trailin' on foot."

"Whereabouts?"

"Right around 41st and Walnut," said Trung. "Plenty of students in that area all night. Obviously, we'll be looking for somebody lingering, somebody out of place."

"O.K.," said Matt. "No foot chases for a bag of books, though. I mean yours, Nguyen. Some punk rips off a suspect though, run 'im down."

"Right," said Vargas. "Then I'll escort our 'victim' to the recovered bag, and ask him to open it. We'll be careful."

"I know you will. But this is a new phase. We might wind up recovering property rigged to blow." Matt looked at Yvonne. "Sergeant Wallace is gonna walk around 11th and Norris Streets near Temple. I'll be close all the time." He glanced around. "Sergeant Wallace proposes we establish an outline of what we need for a computer search of possible suspects. Then Miss Sims will write us a program; and I'm gonna try to get her a time slot on the Cray-2 Super Computer at the University of Pennsylvania."

Matt sipped his tea. "Here's where I wanna go with this. All kin and relatives of violent crimes, and the victims themselves, goin' back fifteen years."

Smythe let out a long whistle. "I say, Leftenant, even in Liverpool that would be monumental, what."

"We know," said Sergeant Wallace. "But we think we can get the list whittled down. Dead, moved away, incapacitated, etcetera. We eliminate females and black males right away."

"That's right," said Matt. "Now it's time to hear from Miss Sims. Mary Anne, the floor is yours."

Sims stood up. "Everybody please call me The Wiz or Wiz. Everybody else does. With good reason, I might add."

This comment drew arched eyebrows throughout the room. She noticed.

"That's right. I got a big ego, small tits, and a big ass."

Outright guffaws now.

"And how come everything here's so clean? I never seen a squad house so clean."

"I believe in sanitation, Mary Anne," said Gallagher, laughing. "Please cut to the chase."

"O.K., *Leftenant,*" she said, glancing at Smythe, who colored deeply.

"Here's the way I wanna go. You flatfoots gimme the general parameters you need. Then I'll write up a search program. Then you get me time on that Cray-2, and I'll tie in our computer at the Roundhouse. That'll get us a list, and you can scan that, and then give me more specifics. It'll still be a big list, obviously, but that's your problem."

"Could you tell us a little about the Cray-2?" asked Sergeant Wallace.

"Sure. Seymour Cray invented most of the hardware for the Crays. The Cray-1 could do one hundred sixty million operations per second, or one hundred sixty megaflops. It had an eight megabyte main memory, and was shaped like a big 'C', for the integrated circuits to be closer together. It used Freon for cooling. The Cray-2 is ten times faster, performance-wise. It's a shared memory, multi-vector processor. It does one point nine five one gigaflops with a four gigabyte memory. It has a foreground processor, which basically does housekeeping. This lets the four background processors do the actual computational work."

"I say, Miss Sims," said Smythe. "You sure sound competent."

"That's right, Limey. And don't forget it."

This brought more laughter. Poor Winston was so obviously smitten with Mary Anne Sims, that even she noticed. This could get interesting.

"Would you be needing any assistance, Miss Wiz?" he asked. More snickers.

"What can you do, Limey?"

"I could sharpen your pencils."

The whole group broke up laughing.

"Alright, alright," Matt shouted. "Let's calm down. Before anybody goes anywhere, put ideas on paper for The Wiz. Then check in with Sergeant Johnson. By the way, I'm gonna ask Sergeant Mitelli and Captain Summers for a couple of Uniforms. Our guys are all buried in busy work. We'll use 'em for legwork. O.K., let's go to it."

As they all left the room, Sergeant Wallace sidled up to Julio Vargas. "A word, Sergeant?" she asked politely.

"Sure Yvonne. Whaddya need?"

Yvonne waited until the room cleared and then shut the door.

"What's all this ABLS action that's goin' down?"

Vargas hesitated.

"I insist," Yvonne said intently.

"Siddown," Vargas relented, and gave her the lowdown. Then he added, "Since you came on board, the bettin's gone through the roof. That's why Sergeant Patrillo's been giving you the cold shoulder."

"I can handle Patrillo. But one more question."

"Gawhead."

"Who gave Matt the nickname ABLS?"

"Well, I wasn't there, but I heard it from a Fifth District guy. Here's how it went down."

Vargas related as to how one night a couple of months after Gallagher's wife died, which happened in January of 1992, Matt had wandered into Peck Miller's Bar on Ridge Avenue in Roxborough. He played a few desultory games of darts, and then left. A cop at the bar said to a companion, "Poor guy ain't had none since he wife died."

"So he ain't been laid since, huh," said the neighborhood drunk from a few stools down. He was called "Richard," short for dickhead. He worked at the patio furniture factory on Umbria Street, and was seen almost nightly, staggering drunk around the neighborhood.

"Who asked you, asshole?" said the cop, rising from his seat to confront the drunk.

"I didn't mean nuttin'," whined "Richard."

"Let 'im be," said the other cop, restraining his buddy. "He works for Ray Rubeo down at the PVC shop. Ray gives us good deals on patio stuff."

"Yeah, well, keep a lid on it, asshole," said the first cop.

"But anyway," said Vargas. "That's it. The two cops at the bar picked up on Ain't Been Laid Since, and a legend was born. Not to mention a jackpot worth thousands."

"You guys are heartless," fumed Wallace.

"No, it's not like that. It started as a little fun, just between us. But we did accidentally create a monster. It just grew and grew. We all love Matt. I'd die for the guy. My wife and kids think he's a saint."

"Well, I won't be layin' any money down," Yvonne said.

"I hope not," replied Julio.

"What's that supposed to mean?"

"Costello and Patrillo would go ballistic. They'd figure it for an inside job, if you know what I mean."

Yvonne finally had to laugh. "I see your point. Alright, I'm cool. And remember, I'm just his partner."

"You say so," Vargas shrugged. "Ain't none of my business. All I want from you is to watch Matt's back. Please."

"That you got. No problem."

"Good. Let's get outta here."

They opened the door onto more commotion in the squad room.

Winston Smythe had taken it upon himself to get a desk out of storage for The Wiz. He struggled it into position beside his own. Then he grabbed a phone out of storage, and plugged it into a multiple jack on the floor.

"This will be your spot, Miss Wiz."

"Thank you, Detective Smythe. But, pray tell, whose desk is that next to it?"

Smythe again colored deeply. "That would be mine."

"Limey, you're about as subtle as a sledge hammer. But I like your style. Do you bathe regularly?"

"Yes, m'lady. But I can go to two a day if necessary."

There was outright hysterics at this exchange, and even Sims laughed. Sergeant Godwin was in tears, doubled over.

"Could we get some work done, please?" yelled Matt, good-naturedly. "Wiz, could you make yourself a more benign presence, please?"

"Me!?"

"Please."

"Jesus, Limey. I ain't been here an hour, and you got me in trouble already," she whined, sitting down.

"Perhaps a cup of tea, m'lady?"

"Alright. And how about a PC while you're at it. If I ain't near a processor, I get the joneses."

"Sorry, Wiz," piped up Gallagher. "We ain't budgeted for 'em yet. But it's in the works. Probably next year."

"Recognize one of these, Dearie?" asked Sergeant Johnson, placing a typewriter on her desk.

"Christ, I ain't used one of those since high school."

"Well, perhaps Detective Smythe can be of assistance," Eileen said coyly.

Smythe blushed again. He knew he was in for some serious ball-bustin'. He cared not, though. This was definitely love at first sight. And everybody else knew it, too.

After everyone had calmed down a bit, Sims leaned over to Smythe and whispered, "How much action you got down?" She nodded toward Pasqualez.

She wore no perfume, but she smelled so womanly that Winston almost fainted. This too, did not go unnoticed. The squad knew there was a new game in town.

"I've a quid or two in the kettle m'lady," said Smythe.

"You keep callin' me 'm'lady' and you'll never get in these panties. Got that?"

Smythe almost passed out again. "Yes, Miss Wiz."

"That's better," she said, winking and rubbing his head affectionately.

Winston was now in serious need of smelling salts.

Matt, like everyone else, had been watching. "Wiz, you incapacitate my only English Constable, and I'll pull your frickin' plug."

"Alright, alright." She whispered again to Smythe, "I guess we'll have to start passin' notes."

Sergeant Johnson, acutely aware of the pheromone action, waved a strong cup of tea under Smythe's nose. Eileen had spent many hours in the Computer Center at the Roundhouse.

"Careful, Winston. I know this one. She takes a keyboard to bed every night."

"Thanks a lot, Johnson," Sims said, taking her own cup of tea from Eileen.

Gallagher just shook his head, feigning annoyance. This was a good shot in the arm for the crew. Morale hadn't exactly been low, not withstanding Sergeant Patrillo; but it was always good to be loose. If you were after a bad guy, and it was clutch time, you wanted your body ready to take the enormous adrenal surge.

Task Force Gallagher started putting ideas on paper for The Wiz, and the rest of The 3/4 Squad got back to routine business. Sergeant Shincock and Detective Pasqualez went out to start setting up the drug buy for a case they were working on. The Homicide and Robbery teams were in and out all day, chasing leads, answering the phones, and doing paperwork. Sergeant Taggert and Detective Smith left for an early dinner, before they started their nightly rounds of The District's drug corners. Sergeant Godwin changed into her hooker outfit, and she and the rest of the vice squad left to begin their late afternoon and early evening cruising for Johns on their way home from work. By 10:00 P.M. they would have the "tank" downstairs filled with weeping, woebegone males.

Since Pasqualez left, and the betting shop was shut down for the day, the squad could turn away unwanted visitors, and discuss the case back and forth without worrying about uncleared ears.

"Where do you think our man's from, Jefe?" Sergeant Gonzales asked Gallagher.

"I dunno," Matt mused thoughtfully. "Could be the Northeast, Tacony, anywhere. But I'm guessing somewhere between Fishtown and Bridesburg."

"Got a hunch?" asked Detective Trung.

"Nah, more like a feel. That area's so hard core white, that I don't even go down there." Gallagher may have been half-kidding, but not by much, especially about Bridesburg. Don't get caught in a bar there after dark unless you're a resident.

"Are you leaning towards a vigilante, Leftenant?" asked Detective Smythe.

The two new plainclothes, Michaels and Withers, weren't even pretending not to listen. They were paying rapt attention. This squad's reputation was well known and well earned.

"No, not a vigilante," replied Mat. "If it had happened in Kensington or Richmond, someplace like that, maybe. But for my money, this is pure vengeance. Somebody with a personal axe to grind."

"Like somebody whose mom was mugged or somethin'?" asked Detective Robinson.

"Yeah, somethin' along those lines," said Matt. "Somebody who doesn't want to get caught; but that's secondary. His primary purpose is to hurt bad guys. And maybe even kill a few. In fact, as this thing escalates, I think it's gonna get extremely lethal."

"Yeah," said Sergeant Wallace. "That's my take on this too. If he used army CS grenades, maybe he has some kind of arsenal cached away somewhere."

Several sets of eyebrows went up in response to "cached." Yvonne didn't notice; or if she, did she ignored it.

"May I ask a question?" piped up Officer Withers.

"Always," said Matt.

"Do you think his reason for vengeance is recent, or something further back in the past?" asked Rene.

"Let's throw that one to the floor," responded Matt. "Anybody?"

"If I may, Leftenant?" said Winston.

"Take it away, Smythe."

"What's this 'Leftenant' stuff, anyway?" interjected Mary Anne Sims.

"Pipe down, Wiz," said Matt. "Gawhead, Winston."

"Well," Smythe said. "I think he's too good. What I mean is, the booby-trap incident with the young lads was well thought out. He put himself in serious physical jeopardy with the kids. And if he was caught right away, we'd of had a lynch mob at central lock-up. No, I think he's been thinking about it for years, and planning it for months. I agree with you, Matt. Not being caught is secondary with him; but he wants to be free to keep on doing this."

"How long do you think he's gonna plan the next one?" asked Sergeant Vargas.

"I think he had several planned before he did the first one," Smythe replied.

Heads snapped up at this, and Gallagher nodded approvingly.

"My thinking exactly," Matt said. "Please continue."

"I think each incident was planned contingent on how the previous one worked out. If he had almost been 'nabbed', as you Yanks are wont to say, he would have laid low for a while. I think he's comfortable with the results of the first one, and is already stalking the next bad guys."

"Wont to say?" murmured the Wiz.

"That definitely fits what Matt has in mind," said Eileen Johnson. "Success breeds success; and this guy is definitely intelligent. I smell a killing in the works next."

"Quite so," said Winston.

Matt's phone line lit up, and heads bent back to the task of outlining parameters for The Wiz's program.

Sergeant Gonzales walked over to Mary Anne's desk and dropped off his ideas.

"You kids behave now," he said sotto voice.

"Put a bloody sock in it," said Winston.

"Such language, Detective Smythe!"

"What'd he say so bad?" asked the Wiz.

"The word 'bloody' is to the Brits like the F-word is to us," said Pablo. "So he gets away with a Limey version of gutter mouth, and most people don't take offense because they don't know."

"Say it again, Limey," said Mary Anne.

"I beg your pardon?"

"Just for me."

"Oh, bloody hell," sighed Smythe.

"That's a good Limey."

The whole room laughed again. The Limey and the Wiz? Stranger things had happened in this squad room. Exhibit A was hidden in Detective Pasqaulez's desk.

Meanwhile, Matt's phone call was from Sergeant Bruno Mitelli of The 17th District.

"Thanks for calling me back, Bruno. Let me run somethin' by you."

"Gawhead."

"I could use a couple Uniforms. Our platoon Loos are already tapped out, what with vacations and what not."

"I appreciate ya askin' first," said Sergeant Mitelli. "But I know ya got the pull to just grab 'em thru channels."

"Yeah, but that's not my style," replied Gallagher.

"I know that. I'll run it by Cap'n Summers. Got anybody particular in mind?"

"How 'bout Salt n' Pepper? They got their fingers wet in this already."

'Salt n' Pepper' were officers Maureen (Little Mo) Peterson and Casey Persons. They were partners, and the nickname referred, of course, to Persons being black and Peterson being white. They were good, young, streetwise cops.

"Only two of my best, Matt," Mitelli replied.

"I know," said Matt. "But I need the best. 'Sides, the new grads will be flowin' out of the pipeline any day now. They graduate Friday, don't they?" Matt was referring to the newest class of police cadets at the Police Academy on State Road.

"Saturday. But anyway, I'll have 'em over there tomorrow morning. Eight O.K.?" "Make it ten. I'm gonna hook 'em up with Eileen Johnson."

"Plainclothes?" asked Mitelli.

"I'd rather have 'em in uniform. For what I got in mind, it'll be easier for 'em."

"O.K., Matt. Later."

"Thanks, Mike. I owe you."

Gallagher hung up, and passed the word to Sergeant Johnson.

"What's your plan for them?" she asked.

"I want 'em to work with Withers and Michaels," Matt replied. "When they go out on the street, they'll have a little visible muscle to back them up."

"Will they be working for us?" asked Harold Michaels.

"Work *with* them," said Matt. "They might put the fear of God into a reluctant tipster. Nothin' overt, but when you're talking to a citizen, infer that he or she might get a ride downtown if they aren't totally forthcoming."

"And do we? Give them a ride, I mean."

"Clear that with Sergeant Johnson on your squawker first. We don't want a valuable tip dried up because of fear. Be subtle."

"Right."

"Now," said Matt, standing up. "Who wants steaks from Pat's? It's almost dinner time, and I'm buyin'."

They were takers, one and all.

CHAPTER TWELVE

At the Tasty Baking Company on Hunting Park Avenue, Randy Macjewski, master baker, set the kettle and line for his last batch of Krimpets for the day. After checking the temperature of the huge line oven, he shucked his apron and gloves, and headed for the locker room. It was 4:45 P.M.

To say his mind had not been completely on his work was an understatement.

He was not nervous or worried. It was the continuous adrenaline rush he had been high on since he took down the Booze Bandits. After several years of thinking about it and two months planning it, the first incident had lit a fire in his belly. And that fire was growing.

He was intelligent enough to know that this was a dangerous time for him. He had never before shown distraction at work; and he knew that for his vendetta to continue to be successful, he would have to concentrate, and clamp down on his raging emotions. He didn't want to be caught, but God how he wanted to hurt the bastards. Any bastards. All bastards.

As he changed clothes before heading to the time clock, his mind drifted back to 1968, the year his father was killed.

His father had been a rabid Phillies fan, and one night in August, Stanley Macjewski and his wife Barbara were walking to their car after a game at Connie Mack Stadium, at 21st Street and Lehigh Avenue. They were walking through Reyburn Park off of Sedley Avenue, when three large black youths accosted them. All had wooden clubs in their hands.

"Give it up, Pops!" one of them said.

"Give what up?" replied Stanley stubbornly.

"Your mother-fuckin' wallet, asshole!"

"Stanley, give it to them," pleaded Barbara.

Macjewski reached into his suit jacket and handed over his wallet.

"Thanks Pops. And this is for being a smart-ass honky."

With that the youth had smashed Stanley in the head with his club. As Stanley went down, his head smashed into the concrete support of a park bench. He lay on the ground, unconscious and bleeding heavily.

Barbara started screaming for help, rapidly going into hysterics. The nearest people were some fifty yards away.

"Shut the fuck up, bitch!" another of the youths yelled. He then pushed Barbara to the ground, and grabbed her purse. Then all three boys took off like greyhounds.

Barbara scrambled to her feet, stunned. She knelt beside her husband, and fumbled in his pocket and found his handkerchief. She desperately tried to staunch the bleeding.

"Help! Help! Oh please, somebody help me!" she shouted, sobbing.

Already, people were running their way. One man ran past her pointing to a nearby pay phone. "I'll call an ambulance," he yelled.

The ambulance and police were on the scene within minutes. When the ambulance got the Macjewskis to Temple University Hospital at Broad and Ontario, emergency personnel were ready and waiting; but it was already too late.

Stanley was quickly stabilized and typed, and then wheeled into emergency surgery. Doctors quickly drilled and cut into his skull, and installed a shunt to drain the bleeding and relieve the pressure; but there wasn't much else they could do. As they probed into his brain to get at the broken blood vessels, Stanley died on the operating table from a massive brain hemorrhage due to blunt force skull trauma.

Randy had gotten emergency leave from Vietnam, and arrived just in time for the funeral. His mother, of course, was an absolute wreck. She was never the same after that; and she died in her sleep in September of 1976. The doctors said natural causes; but Randy knew better. Those three bastards killed her that night. It just took her a little longer to die.

Well now the score was four to three; and he was definitely going to run it up—pad his stats, as it were. He knew he would eventually get caught or killed; but that was fine. Mom and Pop were saving a space at the heavenly table for him. Soon, Mom and Dad. Soon.

Randy punched out and headed for the parking lot and home. He had his Mustang today, a 1990 5.0 that hugged the road tight as a teddy bear. His other car, a 1985 Olds 98, he used at night. His vendetta wheels.

When Randy finally got home in Port Richmond, he walked into the bar; and Denise quickly slid a cold Yuengling Lager into his hand.

Jim Richards moseyed over, and together they went over some paperwork, and chatted about the bar in general.

"Little slow today," Jim said.

"It happens."

"Yeah, well, it gave me a chance to catch up on the paperwork. Once you sign the checks for those bills, all of May's invoices will be finished. As usual, you're way ahead of the game."

"That's the way I like it. You folks all do a good job for me." Randy included Denise with a nod in her direction.

"Why do you still bust your balls down at Tastykake, if you don't mind me askin'? You're set with this here."

"No, I don't mind, Jim. Simple fact is, I like it. Two more years, and I get a nice pension from the Bakers Union. Then I can sit in here and bug you all day."

"You never bug me, Boss."

"Thanks. I might even sell this place in a few years. Pull up stakes. Interested?"

"I'd buy this gold mine in a heartbeat," Jim replied.

Randy laughed. "Yeah, cash flow is never a problem around here."

Denise parked another frosty Yuengling in front of Randy, and took his empty.

"How're things with you Denise?" Randy asked. "Got your final grades yet?"

"Yep. A hard earned three point eight GPA. Deans List, magna cum laude."

Randy reached in his pocket, brought out a wad, and peeled off two Ben Franklins. "Congratulations. And this is for you."

"Oh Randy, that's so nice. Thank you." She leaned across the bar and gave him a quick kiss.

"I'll bet Daddy's proud, ain't he?" Randy said.

"I'll say. The whole neighborhood knows my grades. And when he works this weekend, the whole city will know. But I love him to death."

"When do you start your Master's work?" Jim asked.

"Classes in late August. I've already started my thesis."

"Got a title yet?" Randy asked.

"Yep. The Effect of Mass Media on the Criminal Mind."

Randy jerked upright and spilt some beer.

"You all right, Boss?" Jim asked.

"Yeah. Just went down the wrong pipe. Alright, let me go upstairs and shower, and I'll come back down and settle the bills."

"O.K., see ya in a bit."

"Thanks again, Boss," Denise said to Randy's retreating back. "You're a sweetheart."

Randy waved acknowledgement as he headed out the door.

* * *

Later that night, as Randy settled in at Dave and Busters, Task Force Gallagher upped the ante on its stakeouts.

At the Sit On It Bar at 19th and Mifflin, Detective Winston Smythe, accent in tow, was doing his damnedest to charm the locals. But South Philly locals weren't easily charmed. Some had Italian or Sicilian roots that went back centuries. Charm in South Philadelphia frequently came sprinkled on the business end of a Louisville slugger.

"Yeah, so what?" said the man they called "The Griz" in response to Smythe stating that he was from Liverpool.

"Well, I don't imagine you entertaining many British subjects in here."

"We don't entertain *no* British subjects in here. And fer good reason."

"And what would that be, my good man?"

"We usually don't let 'em in," The Griz snarled. "You musta snuck in the back door."

This was certainly not going according to plan, thought Smythe. *Some of these Italian chaps are being downright unsociable. Maybe if I bought a round of...*

"Maybe if you bought a round of drinks, some of these guys would thaw out," said Ray Rubeo, clapping an arm around Smythe. "Tell you what," continued Rubeo, "I'll get a round to start things off, then it's your turn."

"That's awful decent of you, old chap. It's been frightfully hard to get conversation going around here. Even some Phillies talk doesn't seem to break the ice."

"That's because everybody here keeps makin' book on 'em to lose. And they keep winning."

"You mean to say you want them to lose?" asked Smythe incredulously.

Rubeo called for a round before turning back to Smythe. "That's right. If that's where the action's layin'."

"You colonials certainly are an odd lot."

"That may be. But here comes the great equalizer—Zambucca. Salut!"

With that, Rubeo emptied a shot glass and indicated with a nod that Smythe do the same.

"Down the hatch," Smythe said, draining his shot. He sighed contentedly, chased it with a gulp of beer, and ordered another round for the bar. "Maybe this will loosen things up," he opined.

"Don't worry about it," said Rubeo. "Ever since I moved to Roxborough, half of 'em don't talk to me either. At least until I buy a couple rounds."

Outside, a few parking spots down from the corner on 19th Street, Sergeant Gonzales tried hard to stay awake. He wondered how the other stakeouts were doing. They were probably as bored as he was.

* * *

At the student quadrangle in the heart of University City at 40th and Walnut, Detective Nguyen Trung appeared to be a student in a hurry—backpack of books slung over a shoulder, a brisk stride through the chill winter night, with quick glances at his watch. In fact, he was as bored as Sergeant Gonzales in South Philly. He knew, they all knew, success was unlikely. But until the bomber struck again, they had to try something. He actually wished someone would grab his backpack, or better yet, another student's. Then he could chase the snatcher down while Vargas stayed with the "victim." He could only hope.

* * *

Across town, in North Philadelphia, Lieutenant Matt Gallagher surreptitiously shadowed Sergeant Yvonne Wallace as she flitted on and off Temple University's sprawling campus. It was 9:30 P.M. and he was getting hungry and tired. He hadn't jogged in a while, and there had been too many cheesesteaks in the interim. And he was thoroughly pissed off at himself for wearing the wrong shoes for this. His feet were killing him. He was walking east on Berks Street, twenty yards behind Wallace, when he heard a shout up ahead. A middle-aged man was standing near a stairwell, empty-handed, looking toward a young black male running with a briefcase.

Bingo, thought Matt, breaking into a run. He quickly passed Wallace. "Detain the victim," he yelled. "I got the perp."

"Right," she shouted, breaking into a run herself. She had had the foresight to change into sneakers. She ran quickly to the victim, a balding, middle-aged professor of History named Felix Hopine.

"Are you alright, sir?" she asked, holding out her police identification.

"Yes, Officer. He didn't touch me. He just grabbed my briefcase."

"Right. Let's see if we can locate my partner, and see if he nailed the little bastard."

Gallagher had pursued the suspect further east down Berks Street. The suspect came up against a dead end at 12th Street. He had a red light at the crosswalk, and traffic was heavy. Pausing momentarily to get his bearings, the youth turned to see what was obviously a cop in civvies pursuing him. He had waited too long. The cop had his gun out, and was screeching to a halt ten feet behind him.

"Freeze, asshole! Police!"

The youth hesitated, and started leaning toward making a break for it, north on 12th Street.

Gallagher cocked his .45 Colt.

"Stay right there, man. Now slowly, and I mean slowly, set down the briefcase."

The young man complied, and then instinctively raised his hands above his head.

"Now beat it," said Matt. A small crowd had gathered to watch the excitement.

"Say what?" the stunned youth asked.

"You heard me. Beat feet. Get outta here."

The youth turned quickly and took off. As he headed up the street, he looked over his shoulder and shouted, "Dumb honky cop."

"Yeah, yeah," muttered Gallagher.

"You just let that clown go on his merry way?" a startled onlooker asked.

"That's right," said Matt. He raised his voice. "Everybody clear outta here. Police business." Matt uncocked and holstered his Colt.

"Well, I never!" exclaimed an elderly woman as she walked off.

"Sorry to hear that," Matt replied.

"I beg your pardon?"

"Just keep movin', lady. Everybody clear out."

By this time, Sergeant Wallace and the owner of the briefcase arrived.

"You got it back," said Professor Hopine, wonderingly. "Where's the kid?"

"He didn't wanna stick around," said Matt. "What's in the briefcase?"

"Papers and personal stuff. Why, Officer?"

"Are you willing to open it?"

"Certainly."

Matt and Yvonne both took a step back. "Please do so."

As the man reached for the briefcase, Matt and Yvonne both placed their hands on their weapons. The professor didn't notice, and leaned down and picked up and opened the case. The two cops drew near and saw papers, a sandwich, and a copy of Playboy.

"It's a good issue this month," said Hopine. "Last month they did a spread on lady cops." He looked leeringly at Sergeant Wallace. "You would've been a natural, Officer."

"In your dreams, Baldilocks. Take a hike."

"Well, thanks for recovering it. It has a full class of term papers in it. Students don't generally retain copies of their work, and it would have been a great inconvenience."

"Glad we could help," said Gallagher.

He and Sergeant Wallace started walking south on 12th Street.

"My feet are killing me," said Matt. "Let's grab a bite and call it a night."

"O.K.," said Yvonne. "Certain higher-ups hear you let that perp walk, you're gonna hear about it."

"The good higher-ups got my back. The rest of the desk jockeys can kiss my white Irish rectum."

"You sure are different," said Yvonne as they ducked into a small café at 12th and Montgomery.

"I don't try to be. I yam what I yam. A cop. With the wrong shoes on."

They both laughed. They ordered a couple of sandwiches, and sat at a small table. Gallagher pulled out his squad radio. "Let's see how the boys are doin'."

* * *

One of the boys, Winston Smythe, was in an unusual, but fascinating discussion with Ray Rubeo on the subject of bookmaking.

"You mean all you chaps do this for a living?"

"Not me, I own a patio furniture business. But most of us grew up doin' it. It's what we did instead of homework. Most guys around here can do arithmetic faster than a calculator."

"Hey Ray," said The Griz from the other end of the bar. "Be careful. You don't know who this guy is."

"If he's a cop, I'll eat my shorts."

"If he's a cop, you'll be eating my shorts, Dickweed."

This got a laugh from the crowd at the bar. The Griz was the only one who could talk to Rubeo like that. Rubeo had spent a good deal of his young manhood beating up wise guys all over South Philly. It had taken direct intervention from young Sal Testa, an up and coming youngster in the Philadelphia Mafia, to get Rubeo to stop beating up the mob's foot soldiers.

"So," said Smythe, "what happens when a chap can't or won't pay up on a losing bet? Where I'm from, booking's legal, and you can pursue a chap in the courts."

This got another laugh from the bar. Since Smythe had bought a couple of rounds, things had lightened up considerably.

"In the old days," Ray replied, "they'd get a visit from somebody like The Griz over there. And then they'd pay a visit to the emergency room."

"What happens these days?"

"We cut 'em off, and pass the word around town that they're deadbeats. Around these parts that's as bad as gettin' a leg broke. Eventually, they come crawlin' back for more action. If they start makin' payments on their losses, we let 'em back into the fold."

"You chaps take installments?" Smythe asked incredulously.

"Sure. Cash flow is as important here as it is anywhere else."

Smythe ordered another round of Zambucca. "You colonials certainly are an odd lot," he said, not for the first time that evening.

"I'll drink to that, Limey," agreed Rubeo. "Salut."

* * *

Nguyen Trung and Julio Vargas were calling it a night. Nothing. Not even a nibble.

"My mom's got a late dinner on. Care to come?" Nguyen inquired of his partner.

"Sounds good to me. Let me call the missus," replied Vargas. He walked over to a pay phone, and Trung sat on a bench. *No luck tonight*, he thought. *Oh well.*

* * *

Gallagher got reports from his stakeout teams, and turned back to eating his tuna sandwich.

"We gotta get that computer help," Matt said around a mouthful of tuna on rye.

"What's the scoop on that?" asked Yvonne, who was munching on an egg salad on wheat. She had already polished off a corned beef on rye.

"I ran it by Captain Parmelee this afternoon. He's gonna run it through channels. If he hits any roadblocks, I'll get Max Loudin to call Big Ed. That'll get the ball rollin'."

"You sure got friends in high places. How long have you known the Mayor?"

"We worked a case or two together when he was a junior DA back in the seventies. We been close every since. Marjorie and my wife became good friends. Marjorie delivered the eulogy at my wife's funeral."

"Is that difficult to talk about?"

"Very."

"O.K. Tell me about Vietnam."

"Whaddya wanna know?"

"Everything. I know it sounds morbid; but it fascinates me. America fought a war twelve thousand miles away, and the rest of us stayed home and protested, or went to school, but we basically went on with our lives. It was a crazy time."

"You got that right," Matt agreed.

"So tell me, if it won't hurt," she prodded.

"No, it won't hurt. I lost friends and saw some bad shit, but my head's alright. I don't have nightmares or flashbacks, or anything like that."

"Were you drafted?"

"No. I probably woulda been. But I didn't want to wind up an infantryman, sloggin' through the jungle. So one day I went down to the recruiter's office, and he suggested artillery. I still wanted to go to Vietnam, do my duty. I just wanted to increase my chances of coming back. I figured artillery guys were always behind the lines. Little did I know."

"Whaddya mean?" Yvonne asked.

"There were no lines. I trained at Fort Sill, Oklahoma as a fire direction specialist, and got to 'Nam in September of Sixty-Eight. I was assigned to a self-propelled howitzer battery. One-five-five millimeter. They were down in the Delta, southwest of Saigon at a place called Khanh Hung. It was right near one of the mouths of the Mekong River."

"How big's a one-five-five shell?"

"The caliber's a little over six inches. They weighed around ninety-six pounds a piece."

"That's a pretty heavy weight to sling around," Yvonne remarked.

"Fortunately, I didn't have to do much of that. I was in FDC—the fire direction center. We computed the data for the guns. We had our own tracked vehicle—a five-seven-seven. It's an armored personnel carrier with a higher ceiling, and mounts for generators and stuff. We ate in it, slept in it, you name it. Every week or so we had to hose it out to get the funk out. In the Delta, water was everywhere; and we hooked a pump up to a generator and let 'er rip."

"Earlier, you said there were no lines. Does that mean you were attacked?"

"Constantly. The VC tried to overrun us on a regular basis. We had an infantry company attached just to keep them off us while we fired joes."

"Joes?" she asked.

"Projoes—projectiles."

"Did you ever get hurt?" she asked.

"I was wounded two separate times. The first time I got hit in the ass. A round went through both cheeks. They guy was so close when he shot me and the round had so much velocity, it never expanded. It just punched four new holes in my butt."

"You're kidding!" she said, stifling a laugh.

"No, I'm not," Matt chuckled. "You can laugh. It is kinda funny. The gun bunnies used to call me 'asshole'. After that, they called me 'new asshole'."

"How long were you in the hospital?"

"About a week. They just cleaned it all up and stitched up the holes. I was lucky. They were very small, clean wounds. I couldn't sit at all, though. I spent my convalescence standing up at bars all over Saigon for a month."

"What about the second time?"

"That was different." Matt got a faraway look in his eyes. "The VC attacked in strength. That battle lasted two days. The guns lowered their barrels, and were firin' beehives right into the gooks."

"What's a beehive?"

"It's a flechette round. You put a high charge behind it to get it out of the tube fast, because you set the fuse for a half-second. As soon as it comes out of the barrel, the shell opens and expels thousands of steel darts. They actually used to find guys pinned to trees. It was nasty stuff."

"How'd you get hit?" Yvonne asked.

"It was a tough battle. It was the summer of Sixty-Nine, August. I had about a month to go on my tour. It was really fierce. During those two days we were in hand-to-hand combat several times. I was all over the place. Fire direction wasn't needed, because the guns were firing point-blank all the time. I would go to different spots, help plug VC breakthroughs, haul wounded, fire Fifty-Cals and M-Sixties. Whatever was needed. I was mannin' a Fifty-Cal. They were comin' at us in waves.

They were all drugged up, had to be. I hit one guy, and he went down. He got back up, and I hit him again. I could see pieces of him flying off. I finally hit him with a big burst, and he disintegrated right before my eyes. I turned to help get another belt for the Fifty, and took an AK round in the left shoulder. It came through and broke my collarbone, and left a big hole in front. That knocked me out cold. I woke up next to a pile of dead and wounded, and was medivaced as soon as the choppers could get in. It was bad. Two or three got shot down trying to get in. One full load of wounded going out got shot up, and crashed and burned. I actually saw it go down. That was pretty bad."

"Where'd you wind up?"

"They got me to a field hospital; and after some quick surgery, I was flown to Japan. I got out of the hospital in January of Seventy. I was flown to Fort Sill, and finished my hitch as an FDC instructor. I was discharged in September of Ninety-Seven."

"Never though about making it a career?" Yvonne asked.

"I thought about it. But the peace time army is all about inspections and mickey-mouse crap. I wasn't into it. I got back to Philly in the fall of Seventy, and got into the Academy in November. The rest, as they say, is history."

"Show me your scar."

"Not here. Some other time."

"It really doesn't seem to bother you, being through that," she said.

"Well, I never had nightmares. It was pretty brutal at times. But the guys I killed were trying to kill me. It was pretty cut and dry. I did my share, got home more or less in one piece, and got out. End of story."

"And a wild story it was."

"Yeah, it was." Matt finished his sandwich. "Let's get outta here. I wanna go home and soak my feet."

"No System for you tonight. After we get back, I'm driving you home."

"I'll take that offer. But I can take the Crown Vic home anytime. Just ride me home from here. It's quicker."

"Alright. Let's go."

As she started up the car, she asked, "What's the best way?"

"From here, just head up Broad and take a left on Lehigh Avenue. Lehigh dead ends into Ridge. It's a pretty straight shot from there."

So they headed north on Broad in comfortable silence, neither saying anything until they were climbing The Ridge into Roxborough.

"Stay on Ridge down past Walnut Lane. When we pass the library on the right, we'll take a right on Gates. I live in the middle of the block."

They finally pulled up in front of Matt's place, a large two story house, with a huge lawn and large enclosed front porch.

"Wanna come in for a quick brew?" Matt asked.

"Sure," she said. "I could use it."

They parked and walked up the long steps to the porch. Matt collected his mail and unlocked the massive front door.

"Jeez, it's huge," she said, referring to the door.

"I know. It's steel reinforced. All the doors are. The storm shutters are cast iron, and damn near impregnable. My dad had everything done that way."

"I know The 5th District. Lowest crime rate in the city. What gives?"

"He just wanted to be secure. Everybody knew he owned a car dealership; and he wanted protection. Ya never know."

They walked through the foyer into a huge living room. There was a massive couch fronting a huge entertainment center with a large screen Zenith TV and a stereo system with Bose 901 Series IV speakers. Yvonne whistled appreciatively.

"Very nice," she said.

"Thank you. I have Heinies and Yuengling Lager."

"A lager, please."

"O.K., make yourself comfortable. I'll be right back."

She sat on a lounger and kicked back. She heard Matt in the kitchen, and he came back shortly with two frosty bottles. He handed her one.

"Wow, are these cold or what?"

"Yeah," he said. "I have a small fridge for just beer. I keep it at thirty-four degrees. I like my brew cold." Matt put an Allman Brothers tape on, and then sat down on the couch. He loosened his tie, and took a long pull at his beer.

"So this was your old man's place, huh?" she said.

"Yeah. He left it to my Mom, and she gave it to me. I was lucky. I never made a mortgage payment in my life."

"That is lucky. My rent's a real drain on my paycheck."

"You said it's in Morrel Park?"

"Yeah, right off Academy on Canterbury road. They call them townhouses, which is just a way of charging high rent. But it's nice. Two floors and a quiet neighborhood.

"Yeah, I know the area. Clean."

"That it is."

There was a short silence.

"Matt, I heard why they call you ABLS."

"Oh?"

"I won't insult your intelligence. You gotta know about the pool."

Matt took a sip of beer. "Yeah, hard not to. I don't pay it no mind. If it keeps morale up, I'm all for it."

"But it's such a bizarre thing to bet on."

"I've heard of worse. Some Districts have Heimer pools."

"Heimer pools?"

"Yeah. In Eighteen-Twenty-Eight, Steve Heimer was the first Philadelphia Police Officer to be killed in the line of duty."

"That's nuts."

"Yeah. They size each other up, and bet whose gonna be the next Heimer."

"Oh, brother."

"Want another beer?"

"No. I'm gonna go." She stood up.

Matt rose to his feet. "Head back to Green Lane, and go towards the river. You'll hook right up with 76."

"I know. I been down this way before."

"Take the Vic home. Your car's alright down at the shop."

"O.K." She moved close to Matt, and he caught a strong scent of lovely woman.

"Is there no one in your life, Matt?"

"I've never dated anyone but my wife."

"I heard how she died. That was horrible."

"Yeah, it was pretty rough. It still is."

She moved quickly into his arms and kissed him briefly.

"It doesn't have to be," she said huskily.

"I'm just not ready," he said softly. He disengaged from the embrace and walked

her to the door.

"Thanks for the ride," he said smiling.

"Anytime. Thanks for the beer."

"Ditto. Drive safe and I'll see you in the morning."

"O.K." She kissed him again, quickly, on the lips. "You're a sweet man."

"And you're an incredibly beautiful woman. You'll make some guy very happy."

"But not you."

"Not me. Not now. Goodnight, Yvonne."

"Goodnight, Matthew." She sighed as she left Lieutenant ABLS standing in his doorway.

Matt closed the door, and turned around and leaned against it.

"Holy shit!" he exclaimed as Duane Allman belted out "Statesboro Blues."

CHAPTER THIRTEEN

June 4th, 1993

Matt Gallagher was deep in thought. He was in a comfortable seat on the R6 train from Norristown that ran through Northwest Philadelphia. He had gotten on at the Manayunk Station where the Route 35 bus had dropped him off. He varied his ways to and from work not from any heightened sense of security, but strictly for the variety so he wouldn't get too bored. He always bought a no-limit monthly SEPTA rail pass that allowed him access to any bus, train, or subway in The System. Looking out the train window at backed up traffic on the Schuylkill Expressway, Matt laughed to himself. *You can't beat The System!* he thought.

Two more nights of stakeouts by the three teams of Task Force Gallagher had yielded more negative results. He was going to go to three different crime areas starting tonight. He would assign Vargas and Trung to the area near Penn's Landing on the Delaware River. His research had shown some late night muggings and robberies around there that seemed to have a common thread. Again, it seemed that recently some businessmen and women had been mugged after leaving bars in the area between 10:00 P.M. and midnight. He would have Vargas and Trung just scout the area this first weekend. If nothing happened, he would then have one of them do a little bar hopping with the other partner waiting in a car, and ready for any trouble.

He was going to have Smythe and Gonzales patrol the area north of 34th and Market Streets. In recent months, some youths posing as students had been robbing and mugging real students and professors out late on Drexel University's sprawling campus. Again, they would just observe first. Next weekend, one of them would pose as a professor out late on campus.

Himself and Sergeant Wallace were going a little out of jurisdiction. Northwest of the city, Villanova University had been having some problems recently. On their campus, it seemed that people with the new laptop computers were being singled out for snatch and run thefts. He had had Captain Parmalee call the Radnor Chief of Police, and the head of security at Villanova, to ask permission for them be in the area. It had taken some persuading, but both individuals had finally relented to having two armed Philadelphia police officers roving their territories. They had insisted on being in on any arrests; and Parmalee had readily assented. If they scored here, neither Parmalee nor Gallagher cared what jurisdiction wound up with the bomber. Once he was behind bars, any bars, they could sort everything else out later though channels.

Gallagher stirred in his seat as the light-rail train pulled into Market East Station. Matt stood up, nodded to the conductor, and moved to the exit steps. The train slowed to a halt, and Matt stepped down and headed toward the Broad Street Subway, making his way through the vast subterranean network under the city.

It really was amazing, he thought. Though not as large as the underground areas of New York or even Atlanta, it was quite extensive. Many people worked and shopped underground in Philadelphia.

Matt made his way past shops, kiosks, and cafes, passing under JFK Plaza, and headed for the turnstile of the City Hall stop of the Broad Street Subway. As he ran his card through the turnstile slot, a southbound train was just pulling in. *No seats on this baby,* he noticed. Not this time of morning. He squeezed his way on a car, and held onto an overhead bar for the short trip.

He knew the bomber was getting ready to hit again. He also knew he didn't have a prayer of guessing where. He could only try different areas and wait. Yesterday he had gotten a call from the FBI's Philadelphia field office. Special Agent-In-Charge Gary Souderton had wanted to know how the investigation was going.

"Since it was old army ordinance, we could officially take the case off your hands," Gary said. "But I got enough on my plate, Matt; and my higher-ups aren't gonna press it."

"Thanks, Gary. We got carte-blanche on any resources I might need throughout The Department," Matt said.

"Fine. If you need us, you know where to find us."

"Right, Thanks. Goodbye."

Matt knew that some higher-up desk jockeys would love to pass the case on to the Feds, just to be able to say that he couldn't handle it. But unless they yanked the case out of his hands, that wasn't going to happen. He was going to keep this one right down to the wire. He was going to get this guy. Of that he had no doubt.

Matt got off at the Ellsworth-Federal stop, and climbed up the steps to the street. He walked east on Federal Street, and then south on 11th Street, eventually arriving at the station house on Wharton Street.

It was 7:50 A.M. when he walked in the door to a chorus of greetings. Emma Godwin met him at his desk with a cup of tea.

"Emma, thank you. You won't ever stop, will you?"

"Not unless one of us transfers outta here, Matthew. And that won't happen at least 'til I pass the Lieutenant's exam."

"When you takin' it? Decide yet?"

"September twenty-fifth. I figure by then I'll be ready."

"You're ready now," Matt said. "But I know, I know; you wanna max it."

"That's right, buddy. And I will."

"I'm sure of it. We'll have a big party when you do. That's an order."

Emma laughed. "That's one order I'll gladly follow." She walked back to her desk.

Yvonne Wallace came out of the bathroom and sat at her desk, next to Matt's.

"Hi," she said.

"Good morning. What's new?"

"We got a call from The Wiz. She's got a program set up. Wants to see us over at the Roundhouse."

"Fine. Let me finish my tea, we'll go see Cap, and off we'll go."

"O.K. by me."

Matt gulped his tea down, not unnoticed by Sergeant Godwin.

"That perfect cup of tea was meant to be savored, not chugged like a beer," she yelled.

"Sorry Emma. Gotta go." Matt grabbed the case file, nodded at Yvonne, and they headed for Captain Parmalee's office.

They got the usual grunted greeting from Sergeant Council as they passed through his lobby. As they approached Jane Wilson's desk, they encountered Lieutenants Halston and Johnson coming out of Parmalee's office.

"How they hangin', guys?" Matt asked.

"High," said Ralph Halston.

"Low," said Larry Johnson.

Everyone laughed, including Jane Wilson.

"How goes the Lunatic Bomber case?" asked Ralph.

"Slow," Matt replied. "I'm changin' stakeouts tonight. We'll see what shakes out."

"He's about due, ain't he?" asked Larry.

"Yeah," said Yvonne. "Any time now. I get goose bumps just thinking about it."

"How're our new plainclothes couple working out?" asked Halston.

"Fine. Eileen Johnson piled the grunt work on 'em, and she says she ain't heard a complaint out of 'em," Matt replied.

"Yeah. They're good kids," Larry said. The blue light on Jane's phone lit up.

"He's ready for you, Matthew," she said.

"Right. Later, guys."

"See ya, Matt."

"Good luck, Matt."

Yvonne and Matt went into Captain Parmalee's office after Matt gave a polite rap on the door.

"Good morning Lieutenant, Sergeant," Parmalee greeted, indicating chairs with a wave of his hand. "Whaddya got?"

"I'm changin' stakeouts tonight," Matt started. "I'm sending Vargas and Trung to Penn's Landing. Smythe and Gonzales are gonna be up around Drexel University. Yvonne and I will be headin' to Villanova; and by the way, thanks for clearing that for us."

"That's what I'm here for Matt. Chief Ribaldi in Radnor and I go way back. He beats my brains out on the golf course on a regular basis, so I whined a bit, and told him he owed me one. Jack Gallanty at the Villanova security office was no problem. He's pissed about the snatch and runs they been havin'."

"Yeah. It's a long shot. They're all long shots. But I gotta strong hunch on this one. Our boy might want to spread the action out a little bit to keep us off his trail."

"Good," Parmalee said. "Anybody been bothering you lately?"

"No," Matt replied. "And I find that a little strange. Disconcertingly so. It's like the calm before the storm."

"Yeah," Yvonne said. "Knowing Chief Barnes and the Very Reverends and the Very Concerneds, I thought we'd be inundated with garbage by now."

"Disconcertingly! Inundated! You gotta stop using these big words," Parmalee said.

They all laughed, relaxed.

"The way I see it," Parmalee said "is they're gonna wait until the next incident, and then we'll hear from them big time."

"Yeah," Matt nodded thoughtfully. "Then it'll be like day one all over again."

"Jeez, I can't wait," said Yvonne.

"Don't worry about it," said Parmalee. "I got your back, same as before. If Barnes decides on another personal visit, just keep Pablo from steppin' on his stringer. Barnes would love that."

"I'll ride herd on 'im," Matt laughed. "But he just can't help himself. He hates Barnes with a passion."

"He's got lotsa company. But most of us bite our tongues, remembering how powerful Barnes is, pain in the ass that he is. All right. Anything else?"

"The Wiz called," Yvonne said. "She's ready to hook into the Cray."

"Oh, good. We got lucky there. There's a Doctor Ken Lavitz in the Computer Department at Penn. Apparently, he's big on law and order. And to top it off he has fond memories of our own Detective Trung."

"And Nguyen thought he had no influence," Matt said.

"Our boy's too modest," Parmalee replied. "Apparently he's famous on campus for graduating in four years with a BA and a Masters. He's got his doctorate exams coming up, doesn't he?"

"He's taking the written today. He has orals on the eighteenth. He offered to postpone the exams, but no way."

"I know," Parmalee said. "Besides the fact that he deserves it, his mom would tear us all a new one if he missed them."

"Got that right," Matt visibly shuddered. He liked Mrs. Trung, but she protected her boy ferociously. Matt had seen her on the warpath once, and it wasn't pretty. No thanks.

"O.K.," Parmalee said. He handed Matt a sticky note. "Here's Lavitz's phone number. He's waiting to hear from you. Keep me posted."

"Right, Cap," Yvonne and Matt chorused. They stood up and took their leave.

"And how are you too getting along?" Jane asked innocently, as they passed her desk.

Matt noticed Yvonne turn flaming red. It made her look incredibly beautiful.

"Fabulously, Miss Wilson. How nice of you to ask," Matt replied, looking hard at Jane.

It was Jane's turn to blush. "Have a nice day," she said quickly, turning back to her work.

"You too," Matt replied, laughing as he walked away.

* * *

As Matt and Yvonne re-entered the squad room, Matt noticed that Irene Costello and Imogene Patrillo had their heads together in deep conversation. They broke it up when they noticed Matt had come back in.

"How goes it, Matthew?" cooed Imogene.

"Hi, Boss," said Irene.

"I'm fine, ladies. How are you?"

"Oh, couldn't be better."

"Me, too," chimed in Irene.

"We've missed you around here, Lieutenant," said Imogene.

"Well, you know I've been busy," Matt said, as he moseyed over to the Robbery/Homicide corner. Yvonne had gone on to her desk, but was watching closely. "And you know we've been staggering our hours, what with the stakeouts and all."

"Yes, we've noticed," purred Patrillo. "We've been wondering what you've been up to. And with whom," she added slyly.

Yvonne sighed, and buried her nose in some paperwork. Sergeant Emma Godwin was now monitoring the conversation.

"Just me and Sergeant Wallace," Matt said.

"Is she any good?" asked Imogene. "At police work, I mean?"

"That's it!" snapped Sergeant Godwin. "I've had it with you two!"

"I'll handle this, Emma," Matt said, and his bright blue eyes went hard and cold.

"Know this, Sergeant Patrillo and Detective Costello," Matt stated in a cold, steady tone. "Sergeant Wallace is a fine detective; and she's been a great partner during this investigation. I don't wanna hear any more sly, under the table innuendo and insinuation about me or her. Got that?"

"Yes, Lieutenant," said Costello, dropping her eyes.

"I didn't hear a response, Sergeant," snapped Matt again.

"I hear and obey," said a slightly intimidated Patrillo. "No offense meant."

"My Irish rectum!" Matt rejoined

The squad room was in a slight state of shock, Emma Godwin included. Gallagher had never before publicly chewed someone out. He rarely even did it private.

Matt turned around, and raised his voice. "Everybody hear this. Everybody seems to be slightly carried away with this ABLS bullshit. Chill out or I'll confiscate the kitty and donate it to the Police Athletic League."

Matt paused, and took in all the dropped jaws. He knew he had to release the tension he had just built up.

"It's been starting to smell too much like sheep shit in here. And what do we do when we smell sheep shit?"

"WE GET DA FLOCK OUTTA HERE," everyone shouted, including Sergeant Wallace. The tension dissipated somewhat, and Matt turned to Sergeant Wallace.

"Ready, Sergeant?" he asked.

Yvonne grabbed the Crown Vic keys off the hook behind her desk.

"Ready, Lieutenant," she replied.

"And your whereabouts?" asked Sergeant Godwin. "For Sergeant Johnson's information."

Matt's eyes twinkled, and he smiled broadly. He hooked his arm through Sergeant Wallace's, and started dance stepping to the door.

"We're off to see the Wizard, the wonderful Wizard of Oz," he sang, and it brought down the house as he left the building.

* * *

Randle Macjewski finished his monitoring of the morning's first batch of Krimpets at the Tasty Baking Company on Hunting Park Avenue. He was high on adrenaline and getting higher. *Tonight was the night,* he thought. He could feel it as surely as a Krimpet had butterscotch icing. The grenade was set in its nice little plastic mold; and the briefcase was safely stashed at the bus station at 11th and Filbert Streets. He would go home, check the bar, and dress for the kill, with mustache and slightly balding black wig. He would drive the Olds to the Allegheny El stop, don the disguise, and take the El to 11th Street. He would walk to the bus station, claim the briefcase, and head east to Delaware Avenue and Dave and Buster's. After the incident that he knew would happen, he would strip off wig and mustache, and walk, he hoped, to the Spring Garden El stop, and head home.

Yeah, Mom and Dad. Tonight's the night I send two of the bastards straight to hell!

Matt and Yvonne arrived at the Roundhouse around 9:30 A.M., and made their way to the computer area. Matt knocked on the glass door, and Mary Anne Sims, 'The Wiz', opened the door and let them in.

"Good morning, Officers," she said jovially. "How they hangin'?"

"Mine are fine," Matt laughed.

The Wiz arched an eyebrow at Yvonne.

"Mine are still fairly upright, thank you," Yvonne said.

All three laughed at this.

"Show us what ya got," said Matt.

"Right," said Mary Anne. "Over here."

They followed her to a desk stacked with printouts. The Wiz picked up one huge pile and said, "This is it."

"It's friggin' huge," said Yvonne.

"Yeah, it took some doin'. The worst part was typing it up into the computer. These other two piles are extra copies, and I saved it on three floppies. Here's one for you and this one's for the Cray. The other I'll lock in the safe here."

"Outstanding," said Matt.

"We got Cray time?" asked Mary Anne.

"Let's find out right now," Matt said. "Where's a phone?"

"Over by the door," Mary Anne indicated a small desk. "Help yourself."

"You know Ken Lavitz at Penn?" Matt asked.

"Oh, sure. I've attended some of his lectures over there. He's some smart cookie."

"Good. He's our contact. Let's see what we can get."

Matt dialed the number. A secretary answered.

"Dr. Lavitz, please. This is Lieutenant Matt Gallagher, Philadelphia Police."

"One moment," the secretary replied. "He's been expecting your call, Lieutenant."

"Thank you."

"Dr. Lavitz here, Lieutenant. How can I help you?"

"My Captain informs me, Doctor, that you're aware of our agenda, and our needing time on the Cray."

"That's correct," Lavitz replied. "Are you ready?"

"Doctor Sims seems to think so."

"Mary Anne Sims? The Wiz?"

"Yeah," Matt laughed. "That's her."

"Wonderful. She's a bona fide expert at programming and just about everything else involving computers. May I speak to her, please?"

"Certainly." Matt handed over the phone. "He wants to talk to you."

"Hi, Doc," Mary Anne said into the phone. "How they hangin'?"

"Brash and impertinent, as ever," Lavitz replied. "And I love it. It's always a breath of fresh air."

"Thanks, Doc. I try to stay loose."

"Got a boyfriend yet?"

"Actually, I might at that. A Limey. He works with Matt." Mary Anne winked at Gallagher. "We're goin' out for a few beers tonight. We'll see who can bend a bigger elbow."

Lavitz laughed. "Good for you. You ready for the Cray?"

"Got the old floppy right here as we speak."

"Great. How about, say, 10:45 A.M. I'll meet you at the computer room security desk. Bring the Lieutenant."

"He and his partner wouldn't miss it. See ya then." Mary Anne hung up and relayed the information.

"Good," said Matt. "And what was that about my good English constable?"

"We got a date tonight, ABLS." She reached up and tweaked Gallagher's cheek. "You oughtta try it sometime."

Both Gallagher and Wallace blushed at this, and The Wiz laughed. She again arched an eyebrow. "You two?" she asked slyly.

"Don't you start," Matt said sharply. But he couldn't keep a straight face. "I've already had enough of that this morning."

"Aw, I was just bustin' on ya. You're still my favorite flatfoot. And besides, you two look great together."

"Oh, brother," Yvonne blushed again.

"O.K.," Matt said. "Let's go. You wanna ride with us?"

"In a real cop car? You bet. And in the back. I want people to think you're takin' me in."

Matt and Yvonne both laughed, and they gathered up their stuff and headed for the door.

* * *

Doctor Ken Lavitz was a tall, lean man who was all smiles as he greeted them at the security desk guarding The University of Pennsylvania Computer Center. It was in a large building at 37th and Walnut Streets that housed several university departments. The Computer Center occupied the third and fourth floors of the building.

Introductions were made all around, and The Wiz got right down to cases. She was visibly excited.

"Is Big Boy ready for us?' she asked Lavitz, referring to the Cray-2 Super Computer.

"Yes. I hope you're ready for it," he replied, indicating the floppy disk in her hand.

"I'm ready. Lead the way."

The security guard gave them all badges that gave them access to the facility, as long as they stayed escorted by Dr. Lavitz. The guard pushed a button, and the door buzzed and clicked open. Lavitz let them inside.

"Your input station is right down this hallway. Last door on the left."

They entered a small windowless room with a half-dozen workstations, five of which were occupied. Lavtiz waved Mary Anne to the empty chair. She quickly picked up a phone attached to a modem, and dialed up the code to connect her to the Roundhouse computer. Gallagher and Wallace were silent, slightly intimidated by the cathedral-like atmosphere.

"The Cray can handle all these inputs at once?" whispered Yvonne to Lavitz.

Lavitz whispered back, mindful of the people at the other work stations.

"These and six dozen other sections scattered throughout the facility."

"How long will it take?" Matt asked as The Wiz inserted and loaded her disk. She was now "talking" to the Cray-2.

"Five, four, three, two ..." before Lavitz hit one, a printer in a corner, one of six, started chattering. "Thar she blows."

Gallagher and Wallace looked at each other, unabashedly awestruck. Mary Anne removed her disk, hit a few keys, and stood up.

"The printing will take ten times longer than the processing did. I used the rest of the space on this disk to record the results, also."

"Unbelievable," said Matt.

"Ditto," said Yvonne.

"We are proud of Big Boy," said Lavitz. "He is so talented. By the way, how is Nguyen Trung doing? Does he take well to police work?"

They were all still talking in low tones.

"He's taking his written exams today for his doctorate, as a matter of fact," Matt informed him. "And he's a fine Police Officer. He'll go far if he wants to."

"I'm glad to hear that. Please tell him good luck for me."

"I'll do that," Matt said. "And thank you for the Cray time."

"No problem. There'll be a small charge that we'll bill The Department."

"O.K. You ready Wiz?"

"Almost," Mary Anne said. "Two more pages."

Soon they said their goodbyes, and made their way back to the security desk. As they were handing in their visitors' badges, The Wiz took Doctor Lavitz aside.

"We'll probably need another shot or two at Big Boy, once the detectives winnow the list down a bit."

"No problem," said Lavitz. "You're on the list now. Just give us a call."

"Thanks again, Doctor Lavitz," said Yvonne.

"Right. Stop back and see us."

"Cool," said Mary Anne, as they left the building. "Now when I ride in the back, you really will be takin' me downtown."

"You're so weird," Gallagher said.

"I know. Ain't it great?"

On the ride back, Gallagher perused the list. Sixteen-hundred and forty-three names and addresses. Last known addresses, anyway.

"Well, don't keep us in suspense," said Yvonne as she drove east on Chestnut Street. "How many names?"

"Sixteen hundred and change," Matt said. "Enough to keep us busy forever." Matt sighed. "We'll need copies of this," he said, looking back at The Wiz. "Twelve paper, and you can keep one floppy and make me one."

"Right. Drop me at the Roundhouse, and I'll come by this afternoon. Say around two o'clock."

"What a coincidence," Matt said. "Right when Winston Smythe comes on duty."

"Don't knock it till you try it, ABLS. Maybe next time I'm on Big Boy, I can have him print out a list of eligible ladies. Just give me your personal parameters."

"No thanks," laughed Matt. "I'll know when I'm ready, and the right one comes along." He cast a sidelong glance at Sergeant Wallace, who studiously watched the road as yet another blush climbed her neck.

The Wiz smiled with twinkling eyes, but said nothing. *I hope and pray for you, Lieutenant ABLS,* she thought. *Give the guy a break, Lord. Please. Just one lousy break.*

After dropping off The Wiz at the Roundhouse, Matt asked Yvonne to drive them to the Jefferson house on Woodstock Street.

"Let's go see how Michael's doin'. A little courtesy call."

"Fine by me." Yvonne continued down 8th Street, drove past Market Street, and made a right on Lombard. She crossed over Broad Street and made a left on 19th, a right on Dickinson, and parked on the corner of Woodstock.

"I wonder if he started going back to school yet," Yvonne said, as they got out of the Crown Victoria.

"We'll soon find out," Matt said, and they climbed the steps and rang the doorbell at number 1519.

Monica Jefferson, Michael's mother, answered the door. Yvonne and Matt automatically flashed the gold.

"Good morning. I'm Lieutenant Matt Gallagher and this is Sergeant Yvonne Wallace. Are you Mrs. Jefferson?"

"I am," Monica said. "What do you want? Reverend Quintade and Mr. Steele said we're not to talk to the police without a lawyer present."

Quintade and Steele were the head of the First African American Church of Philadelphia and the president of the Philadelphia chapter of the NAACP, respectively.

"It's not like that, ma'am. We just came to see how Michael is doing."

Paul Jefferson, Michael's grandfather, came to the door.

"It's all right, Monica. They's good people. C'mon in, folks."

He opened the screen door, and Matt and Yvonne stepped into a tidy, well-kept living room. Michael Jefferson was sitting on the couch reading a school textbook.

"Hello, Michael," Matt said. "I'm Lieutenant Gallagher. This is Sergeant Wallace."

"Yeah, so I heard."

"Mind your manners, boy," Paul Jefferson snapped. "This be a social call."

"That's right," said Yvonne. "How are you feeling?"

"Been better," Michael replied. He had a black patch over his right eye; and his hands were lightly wrapped in gauze and tape.

Monica moved to the couch and sat next to her son. "Easy, son," she said. "Talk only if you want to."

"Can I get you Officers some coffee?" Paul asked.

"No thanks," Matt said. "We won't be staying long." He turned to Michael. "Have you been back to school yet, Michael?"

"Next week. I gotta lotta catchin' up to do."

"I'm sure you can handle it," said Yvonne. "You're a very intelligent young man."

"Not that intelligent," Michael said, holding up his bandaged hands. "That honky set us up good. When you gonna catch him?"

"We're working hard, night and day," Matt said. "We'll get 'im. But he's real smart. Sick, but smart."

"What can you tell us?" asked Paul, taking a seat on a recliner.

"Not much. The CS gas used on Jamal Woodson and Reshawn Deeds was old army ordinance, as was the C-4 used in the wallet. Lots of guys mailed that kinda stuff home from 'Nam. It's almost impossible to trace. And the bomber surely wore a disguise, as I'm sure you've already guessed."

"What's gonna happen to all the stuff from the shed?" asked Michael.

"That's up to the District Attorney and the Lost and Stolen Property Office," Yvonne said. "Hopefully, most of it will find its way back to the rightful owners."

"I'dda been set for life," said Michael, a little peevishly.

"You're lucky you got your life, boy," said Paul Jefferson. "Be grateful."

"Well, we'll be going," Matt said. "I'm glad to see you're up and around, Michael. Good day, Paul. Goodbye, Mrs. Jefferson."

Matt and Yvonne took their leave.

"He can't be hurtin' too bad if he's wondering about the loot," Yvonne observed, as they walked to the car.

"Yeah. And you know, if it wasn't for our lunatic, he would've been set. All of them would have."

"That's life," said Yvonne, as she strapped in and started the car.

"Yeah," Matt laughed. "That's life in the City of Brotherly Love."

* * *

Randy Macjewski sat in the break room at The Tasty Baking Company, idly reading *The Philadelphia Inquirer*. But his mind was on tonight. The Big Night. He knew he would probably wind up with a knock on the head or worse; but if everything went according to plan, he would send two bastards to meet their maker. And then he knew things would heat up. He would bring a field-stripped M-16A1 to work on Monday, and stash it in his locker. And he always had his M1911 Colt on him, or in the car.

He was determined not to go to jail. He would not let them take him alive. If he was wounded and incapacitated, he would turn his gun on himself. And if his Maker had an open mind, he would join Mom and Dad in paradise.

CHAPTER FOURTEEN

Back at The 3/4 District squad room, Matt broke the hard news to Eileen Johnson.

"Say what!"

"That's right, Eileen. Sixteen hundred plus. All white. All male. And all needing to be ran down. That's why I brought in the extra troops." Gallagher was referring to officers Michaels and Withers, newly minted plainclothes cops from his own District, and Officers Peterson and Persons, 'Salt 'n Pepper', respectively, from The 17th District, on loan for the duration. "They can start running them down," Matt continued. "Keep them in the same neighborhoods as you cull the list. That way, they'll always be close for mutual back-up."

The four "extra troops" were paying rapt attention to this conversation. They were about to get their first real marching orders as members of Task Force Gallagher.

"Copies of this on the way?" inquired Sergeant Johnson.

"Affirmative," Matt replied.

"O.K., you four," Eileen said, turning to her troops. "Break the list into neighborhoods: Bridesburg, Tacony, the Far Northeast, etcetera. That'll take you a while. Then we'll be sending you out for some casual conversations." She turned to Matt. "Anything you wanna add?"

"Yes," said Matt. "Keep it light and low key. Find out in a casual way how they're feeling, whether they still harbor deep resentments about the crimes. I know you're not detectives, but do your best. Take lotsa notes, and mark any that you think need follow up. That'll be our job, to look harder. Have the Uniforms visible near you. Anyone that still doesn't want to cooperate, tell 'em fine—they'll be gettin' a visit from other detectives real soon. I know it sounds insensitive, but sensitive took a vacation when the bomber hit."

"O.K.," said Eileen. "Go to it."

The four took the list and went to huddle at their desks. Matt looked at Eileen. "Anything new on the tip sheet?" he asked.

"Not really. A lot of junk from the lunatic fringe. Nothing that needs your attention, in my judgment."

"Right. Keep me posted."

"Will do."

Matt walked back to his desk. Sergeant Wallace had walked down the aisle to help sort the list. Matt's outside phone line lit up.

"Gallagher here."

"Johnny G. here, Flatfoot. How's my favorite Mick cop?"

The caller was Johnny "Give it Up" Gambella, an associate in the Philadelphia mob. He was called "Give it Up," because when he went to collect for his book operations, the first words out of his mouth were, "Give it up." They were not social calls.

"Can't complain," said Matt. "Ya got somethin' for me?"

"Ya know about Joey and Nicky, right?"

"Yeah, who doesn't?"

Nicky Scarfo, the current head of the Philadelphia mob, had tried to set up a hit on Joey Merlino, the up and coming youngster, who Scarfo thought was up and coming just a wee bit too fast. In the ongoing comedy/drama that was the Philadelphia Mafia, Scarfo ordered his son to make dinner plans with Merlino at Sparks Steak House. There he would have his goons make a hit. The hit was canceled, believe it or not, when Scarfo's son couldn't get reservations at the restaurant.

"Well," Johnny G said, "Joey's more than a little pissed. We did some leg work. And he authorized me to tell ya this. In the summer of Eighty-Five, Scarfo bought an AK-47 from a guy in Kinsessing. Guy was a 'Nam vet. Had an arsenal. He didn't sell stuff as a rule, but Nicky twisted his arm."

"I don't suppose you got an address?" Matt said.

"I told ya Joey was pissed. It's Forty-Nine-Oh-One Woodland Street. Guy's name is Dickie Howsten."

"I owe ya, Johnny. Pat's Steaks on me one day."

"Big friggin' deal. Don't forget this. We won't."

"Right. Thanks, Johnny. I mean it."

"Yeah, yeah. Joey says 'Hi.'"

"Return the courtesy for me."

"Aayite. Later."

Matt hung up the phone and waved to get Yvonne's attention. She walked to his desk.

"We got somethin'. Maybe nothin'. But we might as well check it out. I'll tell you in the car."

Yvonne grabbed the Crown Vic keys, and they made their way to the door.

"Goodbye, Matthew," cooed Imogene Patrillo. "Later, Sergeant Wallace," she added, in a voice hard as nails.

Yvonne flashed daggers right back at her, but with an ice cold smile. "Goodbye, Detective."

As they were walking down the steps toward the District parking lot, Matt said, "You probably should just ignore her. I don't need any gunplay in the squad room."

Yvonne laughed. "I try not to let her get under my skin; but it's a female thing. Costello and Patrillo think we're an item."

"We're not."

"I know we're not. And that bugs me."

"That they think we're an item or that we're not?"

"Both. I like you Matthew. A lot."

"After this investigation is over. No promises, but we'll do the dinner and movie thing if you're still interested."

"I will be," Yvonne said, starting the car.

"Ya never know," Matt said, "some Prince Charming might come along and sweep you off your feet.

"Nobody like you, mister. O.K., where to?"

"South Philly. Kinsessing. Forty-Nine-Oh-One Woodland. Know it?"

"Yes, I do."

"You do know your turf, Sergeant."

"I know lotsa things, Lieutenant," she laughed, and pulled out of the lot.

Wallace took Wharton Street east to 6th Street and made a right. At Morris Street she made a left, and then turned right for the ramp for southbound I-95.

"Gonna go around the city?" Matt asked.

"Yeah. It's longer, distance wise. But much quicker. I'll take 76 west to the 34th Street exit. A left on Grays Ferry Avenue, and that dead ends right into Woodland Avenue. That'll get us pretty close."

"I'm impressed."

"I know Philly. While I was at the Academy, I bought an ADC Philadelphia Street map and read it like a book. They're great. I have one in my car. I keep forgetting to bring it to the shop."

"No problem," Matt said, and reached in a large pocket attached to the back of his seat. He pulled out a half-dozen ADC map books. "I got

Philly, Bucks County, Delaware County, Montgomery County, Chester County—and just in case—Camden County." Camden County was across the Delaware River in New Jersey. The six counties together made up most of The Greater Philadelphia area, also know as The Delaware Valley.

"I shoulda known," Yvonne said. "But how come you don't like to drive around here?"

"Just too many headaches and too much traffic. I like to think hard when I'm on a case; and I think better with my hands off the wheel."

"Makes sense." She nodded. "Alright, who's at Forty-Nine-Oh-One Woodland?"

"His name's Dickie Howsten. Once sold an AK to Nicky Scarfo. Johnny G said he had an arsenal. He's a Vietnam vet, according to the wise guys. Anyway, we can talk to him. See what we can scare up. Maybe he knows other guys who sent some of that shit home."

"You ever?" asked Yvonne, as she headed west on the Schuylkill Expressway.

"Never was even tempted. All the stuff we had was for one thing. Killing and maiming. I wanted to leave all that behind me when I left 'Nam."

"But you knew guys that did," she prodded.

"Yeah," Matt replied. "But I looked the other way. I had enough of the enemy trying to kill me, without having to worry about my own guys."

"This is a real long shot, you know."

"I know, I know. But if he won't open up to us, I'll threaten him with a same day search warrant. We'll plant ourselves on his porch until somebody runs over and gets one for us. We got pull, remember? One phone call and I'll bet we got one on his steps an hour later."

"That'll be interesting."

"Won't it, though."

Yvonne got off the highway at Exit 42, and made a left on Grays Ferry Avenue. She crossed the river, made a left, and parked at 49th and Woodland. They found the corner house immediately, mounted the steps and rang the bell. An elderly white man answered the door.

"Yes?"

Yvonne and Matt flashed the gold. "I'm Lieutenant Matt Gallagher and this is Sergeant Wallace. We'd like to speak to Dickie Howsten, please."

"Never heard of him, Officers. I've lived here since the summer of Ninety-One. Maybe he was a previous tenant."

"And your name sir, please," Yvonne said.

"Gainer, Rob Gainer. Retired from the Navy Yard."

"You rent, then?" asked Matt.

"Yeah. Rent's reasonable and there's no maintenance hassles. Landlord takes care of everything."

"And his name is?" asked Yvonne.

"John Williams. Lives right across the street at Forty-Nine Hundred. As a matter of fact, there he is now."

Across the street, a large black man of indeterminate age was getting out of a Jeep Wagoneer. The back was loaded with home construction material.

"Thank you, Mr. Gainer. If your landlord permits, would you mind if we had a look inside?"

"Not at all. I'll be here."

Gallagher and Wallace walked back down the steps and across the street. They again flashed the gold and introduced themselves.

"I'm John Williams. What can I do for you, Officers?"

"We're looking for a Dickie Howsten. Was he once a tenant of yours at Forty-Nine-Oh-One?"

"Was, is a pretty good description. He died a couple years back. Agent Orange complications. Guy had about six different cancers. Any one coulda killed 'im."

"Did he leave a lot behind in the house when he died?" asked Matt.

"Just the furniture," Williams replied. "He had no close relatives; and he told me to sell it or keep it. It was good stuff. Bedroom, living room, dinette set. I kept it, and gave him his last three months rent-free. It was a shame. He was a pretty good dude. Never a problem. His rent was direct deposited right into my checking account."

"We're investigating a crime where some old military ordinance was used," said Yvonne. "Maybe some stuff that was shipped home from Vietnam. You know if he had anything like that?"

"Not that I ever found," said Williams. "But I know what you're talking about. I did two tours in the early Sixties. Lotsa guys shipped sh … uh, stuff home. Every time we uncovered a VC weapons cache, half the stuff would be missin' by the time it got back to battalion."

"Where'd you serve?" This from Matt.

"I did one tour based out of Vinh Long in the Delta. Second time I went right back to the Delta outta Vinh Loi. Huge VC hotbeds, both areas."

"Really," said Matt. "I did an artillery tour out of Khanh Hung."

"Yeah? Then you know. There was never a quiet time around them parts."

"Got that right. I never had a full nights sleep 'til I got back to the world."

"Me neither," said Williams. "And then I'd walk around the house all night when I got back. Drove the missus crazy."

"Listen, Mr. Williams ..."

"Call me John."

"O.K., John. I know this is an unusual request; but could we take a look inside the house? Just to see what we can see."

"I suppose it's alright, LT, long's Rob don't mind. He's my best tenant."

"Got many?" Yvonne asked.

"I own six houses on this street. When I retired in Seventy-Five, property values were down like you wouldn't believe. I got all six for a hundred-twenty grand and change. Spent five years fixin' 'em up. Now it's all gravy."

"Mr. Gainer said we could look if you O.K'.d it," said Matt. "Of course, we'd like you to come with us."

"Wouldn't let you do it without me," Williams said. "No offense."

"None taken," said Matt and Yvonne together.

John laughed. "O.K., let's go."

They walked across the street and back up the steps. Rob Gainer was waiting on the porch, smoking a cigarette.

"Rob, these folks gonna take a quick look-see of the house," John said. "Hope you don't mind."

"Not at all. I'll be in soon's I finish this smoke."

Williams held the door, and Matt and Yvonne stepped inside, John following.

"Told ya he was O.K.," said John. "He never smokes in the house."

"You can tell," Yvonne said. "There's not that overpowering tobacco smell."

"Yeah. It's a nasty habit. I quit off and on myself. I go without one for days. Then I pop a brew, and the next thing in my mouth's a smoke."

The living room was large, with paneled walls, and full wall-to-wall carpeting. Two huge, comfortable looking sofas each took up a wall, boxing a large recliner.

"Actually," said Matt. "I'd just like a quick look in the basement."

"Alright. This way."

John led them through the kitchen, opened a door, and reached up and flicked on a light. He walked down the brightly lit stairway, and waited for Gallagher and Wallace to catch up. The basement was large, clean, and basically empty, except for a washer and dryer in a corner on either end of a utility sink. A quick look showed nothing that interested Gallagher.

"He get many visitors?" asked Yvonne.

"Not too many," replied John. "Least that I know of. I don't pry with any of my tenants. I vet 'em pretty good beforehand. After that, as long as the rent's paid on time, I pretty much leave 'em alone. I check each house every three months or so, just for maintenance purposes. I never have any trouble."

"Do you have any idea who helped him arrange his affairs?" Matt asked. "I mean, towards the end."

"The VA took care of the funeral and all that. There was one guy who showed up a lot at the end. Andy or Randy, something like that. They served together in 'Nam. Guy lived across town in Kensington, or one of those neighborhoods. I respected their privacy. Last thirty days or so, Dickie was on his deathbed. Between the two of 'em and the VA, everything was taken care of."

"Alright Mister ... John, we'll be going," Matt said. He handed John his card. "You ever think of anything unusual you think might help, give us a call. Somebody will always answer that number."

"O.K. But I doubt I can help. You're doing that booby-trap case, aintcha?"

"Good guess," said Yvonne.

"I read the papers. How're them kids?" asked John.

"Pretty well banged up," said Matt. "This guy knew his business. These weren't firecrackers."

"Catch that asshole, Officers. Those kids were wrong, dead wrong. But nobody deserves that."

"We agree," said Matt.

"He'll do it again," said Williams.

"You're very perceptive," observed Yvonne.

"He's got a taste for it now," said John. "I knew guys like that in 'Nam. We killed, we all did; but I hated it. Some guys couldn't get enough of it. They couldn't wait to mow somebody down."

"We'll get 'im," said Matt, as they started back up the basement steps. "It's just gonna take some time."

They heard Rob Gainer come back in the house as they moved through the kitchen.

"Find anything, Officers?" he asked, as they came into the living room.

"No," said Yvonne, "But if you do, give us a call."

Matt handed him a card. "We'll see ourselves out," said Matt. "Thank you for your cooperation."

* * *

As they headed back to the car, Matt said, "I wish he knew more about Dickie's friend. It's a long shot, but ya never know."

"Where to now?" asked Yvonne.

"Back to the shop, I guess. With a detour to Pat's. I could go for a sloppy one, with a cold birch beer."

"Sounds good to me."

"I knew it would, you chow hound."

Yvonne laughed as she headed them back to Interstate 76.

* * *

Lunchtime at Tasty Baking Company, and Randy Macjewski was so high on adrenaline he could taste it. He actually felt a metallic taste in his mouth. Anyway, he told himself it was adrenaline. Not the coppery taste of fear. No! No fear, Mom and Dad. Two bastards for you tonight.

Randy forced himself to eat the large salad he had packed for himself. He had no appetite; but he knew he had to maintain outward appearances. Everybody got three Tastykakes a day on the honor system, and Randy had eaten a Chocolate Junior. No Krimpets. Never again a Krimpet. He forced the Junior down, and was startled to find Joe Tallon had been talking to him.

"I'm sorry," stammered Randy. "What'd you say?"

"I said we got a golf outing coming up on July second. It's at Cobb's Creek this year. You playin'?"

"Probably," Randy said.

"Probably!" exclaimed Alan Ditch. "You were low gross last year. Shot what, seventy-five?"

"Seventy-four." Randy was smiling now. It was a good memory. It was a tough sport to be average at, let alone good. And a seventy-four was damn good. He had three-putted a couple of times, or he would have broken par.

"Us three on a team again," said Joe. "And we got a ringer. The new driver I been talkin' to is a scratch player. Between you and him, we'll take top team."

"Sounds good to me," said Randy. "Sign me up, and give me a reminder about two weeks ahead of time, and we'll go hit some balls."

"Good," said Alan. "You can show me that Tic-Toc shit again. You know, for chippin'."

"I'll show you right now," said Randy. He was relaxed now, the adrenaline rush just a mild burn. He stood up and backed away from the lunch table. Randy bent over an imaginary ball. "Take a pitchin' wedge. Lock you arms together around the club, and grip hard. Imagine your arms and the club are one piece—a pendulum, like on an old grandfather clock. Now watch."

Randy locked his arms around the imaginary club.

"Bring the club back. That's Tic. Swing the pendulum through the ball. That's Toc. Bring the club back to center. That's Stop."

Randy demonstrated again.

"Tic, Toc, Stop. And never look at the hole until you come back to stop. Practice that enough, and soon you'll be able to judge your arm strength for speed and distance."

"That's with a wedge, right?" Alan asked.

"That's right. From thirty feet in, just a wedge. Believe me, it works."

"You'll show us again at the driving range?" asked Joe.

"Sure thing. Just tell me when."

Alan stepped to a wall calendar. "How about next Friday, the eighteenth? After work, we'll haul ass to Cobbs Creek and hit some balls. Maybe play nine."

"Sounds good," said Randy. He looked at his watch. "Well, time to start another batch of Krimpets." Randy exited the lunch room, and smiled inwardly. A little thing like some golf talk had settled him right down. He hoped he was around long enough to play.

Mary Anne Sims, "The Wiz," rolled into the Three-Four right at 2:00 P.M. She walked right to her desk, and set down floppy disks and a dozen sets of printed copy.

"Hi, stud Limey," she said, ruffling Winston Smythe's reddish-brown hair.

"Hello m … hello, Miss Wiz."

"Stud Limey?" exclaimed several of the detectives together. Winston blushed deeply.

"A little presumptuous on my part, maybe," said The Wiz. "But not for long."

Everyone laughed, and Smythe went pure crimson. Gallagher was laughing along with everyone else.

"Can't you ever walk in here without causing a commotion?" he asked.

"Ain't my style, Flatfoot."

"That's Lieutenant Flatfoot to you. Whaddya got for me?"

"Twelve floppy copies, and twelve printouts. One for every member of Task Force ABLS."

"That's Task Force Gallagher," shot Sergeant Emma Godwin from across the room.

Mary Anne turned toward the voice. "Whatever. Holy shit, Emma! You look like a hooker on North Broad." Godwin was in a red, low-cut mini-skirt that looked like it had been painted on.

This brought another laugh from around the room.

"That's the idea, Dearie. I got vice detail tonight."

"Christ, if I went that way, I might hit on ya myself."

"Twenty bucks for a quickie, fifty for a room, buck-fifty all night. Cash up front."

"Alright," said Matt, laughing. "Break it up. Officer Withers, would you please distribute the material."

"Sure, Loo," Rene said, and got up and started passing out disks and paper.

"After everybody gets their copies, let's go in the interrogation room and have a little meeting," Matt said.

Everybody started shuffling into the room, which became quite crowded now that Task Force Gallagher had expanded to twelve people. Matt waited until everyone found seats.

"O.K. Officers Michaels, Withers, Persons, and Peterson, you have your marching orders as far as the list is concerned." Matt briefly looked at his notes. "Tonight we change stakeouts. Sergeant Vargas and Detective Trung, you'll be prowling the Penn's Landing area. We know people have been getting hit coming out of nightclubs. Just observe tonight. Next weekend, one of you can do a little bar hopping."

"Right, Loo," acknowledged Nguyen. Julio nodded his agreement.

"Sergeant Gonzales and Detective Smythe will be patrolling the north side of Market Street, up near thirty-fourth around Drexel's campus. Students and professors have been getting hit by snatch and run bandits."

"Be careful, Limey," said The Wiz.

"*We* will," said Pablo.

"Sergeant Wallace and I are going to Villanova, to see what we can see." Matt looked around the room. "They've been havin' snatch and run problems, too. Any questions?"

"I say, Leftenant," opined Smythe. "That's somewhat out of our jurisdiction, what?"

"I love it when he talks Limey," whispered Mary Anne, sotto voice.

"It is," replied Matt. "It's just a hunch, and a long shot at that. If I was him, I'd try something different to keep us off his trail."

Officer Persons raised a hand.

"Gawhead, Casey."

"Gimme some parameters, Loo. When I question these people, besides my own instincts, what trips the red flag?"

"O.K., good," Matt said. "Number one, someone won't talk to you, they get an immediate follow up from a detective team. Number two, if the printout says Vietnam vet. Other than that, attitude and demeanor. I'd like to tell you that those who cooperate can be eliminated as suspects. But our boy is smart. I'm wiling to bet he'll be a cooperative, concerned citizen. Some people that don't cooperate might just hold a grudge against the police. Maybe we never caught the perp who did their mom or pop, or whoever."

Matt paused for breath and took a sip of tea.

"For you officers on the list assignment, I won't lie to you. This is gonna be some real grunt work. But we need it done. O.K., that's it." As everyone left the room, Gallagher sat down at a table to make a few additions to his notes.

When Matt re-entered the squad room, The Wiz again had the place in an uproar. She had placed some more bets on the ABLS action, and had been accused of having inside information. She pleaded innocent.

"The only Studly I study is my Limey," she roared in defense.

Matt thought to himself, not for the first time, that Winston might have bit off more than he could chew. But he was a big boy. And as long as it didn't affect his police work, Matt had no problem with it. But he was watching the situation closely.

"Wiz, go to the blackboard and write out one hundred times, 'I will not mess up Lieutenant Gallagher's only English constable'. "

"Aw, Flatfoot," she pouted. "We're cool. I won't jump his bones unless we're at least three blocks away."

The squad room broke up in hysterics. Officers Persons and Peterson, on their way out the door, were practically doubled over in laughter.

"Wiz," Matt said, feigning exasperation, "I'm going to put your desk in the interrogation room if you don't cut it out."

"Alright, alright. I gotta go anyway. I do have other duties." Mary Anne quickly wrote a number on a piece of paper. "Call me when you're ready tonight, Studly." She pecked him quickly on the cheek. "And do be careful out there."

Matt moved to Eileen Johnson's desk. "Sergeant Wallace and I are gonna take off. We'll be on campus at Villanova around eight o'clock. Hold down the fort."

"O.K., Boss. Take 'er easy."

As Matt and Yvonne passed Sergeant Patrillo's desk on the way out, she said, "Have a nice nap, folks."

Yvonne stiffened to reply; but Matt just gently guided her to the door.

"Forget it," he said. "She's incorrigible."

"That's right," Patrillo muttered. "And don't you forget it." For this she received a none too gentle kick under the table from Detective Costello.

* * *

At 4:45 P.M. Randy Macjewski left the Krimpet production line, changed at his locker, punched out and left. He was calm and felt relaxed.

Of course, he did not realize that he was slowly descending into madness.

CHAPTER FIFTEEN

Randy Macjewski walked into his bar, the S & B, at 8:00 P.M. He put some completed paperwork in his out box, and grabbed a cold Yuengling Lager from the iced beer bin.

"How's it goin', Boss?" asked Mike Reilly, the Friday night bartender.

"Good, Mike. You?"

"Couldn't be better. Did I tell ya? Denise made the Dean's list. Magna Cum Laude. A three-point-eight grade point average." Reilly was beaming like a searchlight.

"Yeah, she told me Tuesday night."

"Hi, Boss," greeted Theresa Barnes. Theresa was his weekend daytime bartender.

"Hi, Theresa," said Randy. 'Bout time for you to knock off, ain't it?"

"Soon's I do the till, I'm outta here. Got to pick up the boys at Mama's house."

"How're Lionel and Richard?" Randy asked. "How they doin' in school?"

"Straight A's and no trouble, so far. I can only hope and pray it keeps up."

"It will. You're a good mother, and it shows. They're nice young kids."

Randy had met the boys on several occasions, and one time had brought them new school backpacks. Theresa worked nights, Sunday through Thursday, as a coin and token counter and collector for SEPTA, and worked Friday, Saturday, and Sunday at the bar. The boys' father had been killed during a drug buy gone bad several years ago. Randy paid her and all his bartenders well; and they all made good tips. Barnes was making it; but the struggle of being a single parent wore on her, and it sometimes showed.

"Gawhead and do the till," Randy said. "I'll help Mike for awhile."

"Thanks, Boss. Then I gotta pick up pizza on the way home. Can't have it delivered no more. Neighborhood punks keep rippin' off the delivery guys."

This got Randy's attention, though he affected nonchalance as he served customers at one end of the bar.

"Really. How longs this been goin' on?" he asked.

"Couple months, off and on. Some places still try to deliver; but they gotta send two guys for protection, and some just quit tryin'. All in that little section behind F and Allegheny where I live. Around Lippincott and Clementine are the worst."

"What about the cops?" Randy asked.

"They can't be bothered," Theresa replied. "There's so much other bad stuff goin' down in West Kensington, they don't even patrol back there. They say they're too busy."

"That's a shame," Randy said.

"Anyway," Theresa sighed, closing the cash register, "I'm outta here. Goodnight. See you tomorrow."

"O.K.," Randy replied. "Drive safe. Say hello to the kids for me."

"Will do."

Randy helped Mike with the crowd until 9:00 P.M. "You got it now, Mike?" he asked.

"No sweat, Boss," Mike replied.

Randy nodded. He knew Mike could handle twice this crowd. "Alright, I'm outta here."

"G'night, Boss. Have a good one."

"You too." Randy left the bar; and as soon as he started climbing the steps to his front door, the adrenaline started to kick in. He was becoming addicted to the high.

He took a quick shower, and changed into a black suit with a navy blue shirt. He folded a tie into his shirt pocket. The semi-bald black wig and black mustache went into a suit pocket. He tucked his Colt M1911 automatic into the small of his back, and headed out. He drove the Olds 98 to the Allegheny El stop. Before getting out of the car he quickly donned mustache and wig.

* * *

Detectives Trung and Vargas were sitting in their car at Front and Church Streets, facing the Delaware River. Like any stakeout it was total boredom, and it took discipline and lots of coffee to stay alert.

"Whaddya say we take a stroll, Sarge?" asked Nguyen. "Shake out the limbs a little."

"Sounds good," said Julio. "Let's go."

They locked the Crown Vic and joined the people walking up and down Delaware Avenue and dipping in and out of the bars and clubs. They saw a couple of beat cops from The 26th District, and identified themselves.

"How's the action?" asked Vargas.

"Quiet so far," answered Mike Bellows, a large, beefy ten-year veteran. "Shit don't start goin' down for a while yet. Everybody's still gettin' a snootful."

"Yeah," said his partner. "There's still a little 'Brotherly Love' left in town. Give it till about eleven or so. Then the fun starts."

"Listen," said Vargas. "You guys wanna get a coffee, we'll walk the beat for a while. We gotta be here anyways."

"Thanks, Sarge," said Mike. "We'll do that." As the two beat cops were walking to a corner deli, Mike's partner, John Ruscomb said, "You don't hear that happenin' too often. Not even from our own dicks."

"Yeah, you can tell they're Gallagher's guys. He gives a shit, and passes that attitude down to his troops."

Ten minutes later, Randy Macjewski and his grenade booby-trapped briefcase passed behind Vargas and Trung, and headed up the steps to Dave and Buster's.

* * *

Lieutenant Gallagher and Sergeant Wallace had arrived at Villanova's campus around 8:00 P.M. They checked in with Jack Gallanty, head of campus security, and then Matt had made a courtesy phone call to The Radnor Police Department to let them know they were in town.

"No problem, Loo," the dispatcher said. "Chief Ribaldi said you would be prowlin' around. I'll let our patrols know."

"Thanks."

For the next hour or so, Matt and Yvonne had wandered the campus to get the lay of the land. It was quiet, what with most students having gone home for the summer. But like any other college, there were summer classes, and some students and teachers were out and about. The Route 100 bus had two stops on campus, and Lancaster Avenue, which was State Route 30, ran right through the college. The Blue Route, Interstate 476, was minutes away. Plenty of getaway routes for any snatch and runners.

"Inner city kids do the same thing at the King of Prussia Mall,"

Matt said. "They run into a store, grab a bunch of goods, and hop in a getaway car and head right back to town. The car's stolen of course. They speed back into town, abandon the car, and an hour after they make the hit, them and the merchandise are history."

"Some of 'em been caught lately," observed Yvonne.

"Yeah. The real dumb ones. They jump on the Schuylkill Expressway at rush hour and get stuck in traffic. Nowhere to run then."

"Jeet?"

"No, Joo?"

"No, let's duck in this little sandwich shop and grab a bite."

"Good by me."

* * *

Winston Smythe and Pablo Gonzales were sitting in their Crown Vic at 34th and Cherry Streets, next to a Drexel fraternity house. Loud, thumping music echoed from the house and resonated up and down the street.

"They're all in there gettin' soused, and probably not a one of 'em's twenty-one," remarked Pablo.

"Well lad, at least they're off the streets."

"Yeah, that's somethin'," Pablo sighed. "I'm bored as shit. Turn on the Phillies game."

"Oh, good show. They're in town?"

"Yeah, they got the Rockies tonight. Mulholland's on the hill. They're seven-and a-half up on the Expos."

"Do you think they'll make your playoffs?" Winston inquired.

"Yeah, I do," Pablo replied. "Their pitchin's holdin' up, and Macho Row has been awesome."

Winston tuned in the game, and they sat back and relaxed. Harry Kalas informed them that the Phils were up one to zip.

"What time ya meetin' the Wiz tonight?" Pablo asked.

"Well, I figure we can leave post around ten-thirty, what. I'll meet her in front of Dave and Buster's around eleven or so."

"Yeah, we can leave a little early unless somethin' goes down."

"I hope not, not tonight."

"You're really hooked, aintcha?" Pablo asked.

"Hook, line, and sinker, as you Yanks are wont to say. She definitely tickles my fancy."

"Is that what they call it in England?" Pablo laughed.

"Oh, bugger off!"

* * *

Officers Bellows and Ruscomb had resumed their beat; and Vargas and Trung has moseyed along with them. They walked on the edge of the street, Delaware Avenue being a wide thoroughfare.

"Sounds like your bomber's a real looney tunes," commented Mike Bellows.

"Yeah, but crazy like a fox," replied Julio. "He don't wanna get caught; but primarily he wants to hurt bad guys. He knows if he keeps doin' it, he'll get hurt or we'll nab him."

"No offense, Sarge," said John Ruscomb, "but stakin' out certain areas is really a long shot."

"We know that," interjected Nguyen. "But until he hits again and we get a better handle on him, it's all we can do."

"When's he due again, ya think?" asked Bellows.

"Right around now," said Julio. "If he's serious, he just laid low to see how we reacted. We think he has a long-term plan, dependent on how each incident goes."

"Jeez," said Ruscomb. "I don't envy youse guys. We got our hands full just makin' sure the drunks don't get killed in traffic."

"We'll see ya later," said Bellows. "We gotta cruise further up the avenue."

"Alright. We'll be around. Holler if you need help."

"Will do."

Vargas and Trung started retracing their steps south as the two beat cops headed further north.

"It's gonna be tonight," said Julio. "I can feel it. I don't know where; but it's tonight."

"Wouldn't it be wild if it happened down here," commented Nguyen.

"Yeah, it'd be wild alright."

* * *

Randy Macjewski, in disguise at Dave and Buster's, nursed a Yuengling Lager at a front table near a window facing out on Delaware Avenue. In fact it was the very table from where he had observed the mugging on May 28th, a Thursday.

He had seen the beat cops, and what were obviously two plain-clothes cops walking with them. He watched them split up and go in opposite directions. He hoped they didn't scare off his "muggers." But it was a big street; and they didn't appear to be paying attention to the parking lots under I-95. The timing was something he had no control over. If he saw two white males in dark clothing loitering on the street, he would just have to be sure the cops were out of sight when he made his move. The adrenaline was almost making him sick; but he remained outwardly calm. He was ready. He just needed to wait.

* * *

Smythe and Gonzales were headed east on Market Street, having called it a night. It was 10:45 P.M. They had patrolled the entire Drexel campus several times, and hadn't seen so much as a jaywalker. Gonzales was in a foul mood, and not because of the limp stakeout.

"Mulholland strikes out fourteen. And then the Rockies win in the ninth. Damn, I wish we had The Big Cat on our team." "The Big Cat" was Andres Gallarraga, who had driven in the winning run with a RBI double.

"Oh, well," said Smythe. "We'll get them tomorrow."

"Yeah, I guess. You want me to drop you at Dave and Buster's, or are you going home first?" Smythe lived in a huge loft apartment at the corner of Willow Street and Delaware Avenue.

"If you don't mind, home first. I need to brush my teeth and throw on a fresh shirt and tie." On duty or off, Smythe wouldn't be caught dead without a tie.

"O.K. I'll drop you off, and go sign us out."

Gonzales turned left on 16th Street, and headed north to Spring Garden and made a right. He took that all the way to Delaware Avenue and made another right, and dropped Smythe off two blocks down.

"Good luck, Limey," he laughed as he drove off.

Smythe hurried up the steps to his loft. Letting himself in, he quickly shed coat, gun belt, and tie. He was fastidiously neat; but this time he left his clothes on his huge couch. He quickly brushed his teeth, and shed shirt and t-shirt. A quick spray of deodorant, and then he donned fresh shirts. He grabbed a blue paisley tie and knotted it in place.

Gun belt and suit coat back on, he was headed back to the street less than five minutes after he arrived. He walked south on Delaware Avenue, checking his watch. It was 11:00 P.M. He would just manage to be fashionably late.

* * *

As Gonzales continued south on Delaware Avenue, he spotted a couple of beat cops, and then further on he saw Detectives Vargas and Trung. He pulled abreast of them. "Hi, guys," he said out the window. "Any action tonight?"

"Nah. Nada," replied Sergeant Vargas. "How 'bout youse guys?"

"Bore city. Listened to the Phils. Mulholland strikes out fourteen and Big Cat wins it for the Rockies in the ninth."

"Yeah, well. We're gonna hang for a while yet. Get a handle on what it's like down here once the Friday night fights start. Where's lover boy?"

Pablo laughed. "I just dropped him off at his place. He's meetin' The Wiz down here in a couple of minutes. I'd like to be a fly on the wall for that date."

"It is an interesting match up," said Nguyen. "I doubt they'll bore each other."

"Hey Nguyen," said Pablo. "How'd the exam go today?"

"Well, I think. Thank you for asking."

"Good for you. Well, I'm gonna go park the pig and sign out. See you guys."

"Adios, muchacho," replied Vargas.

* * *

Winston Smythe arrived in front of Dave and Buster's at 11:08 P.M. He spotted Mary Anne Sims at once.

The Wiz was never late for anything. She was lounging at the base of the large building on the old pier that housed the humongous club. As she spotted him, she walked up, grabbed his lapels, and planted a quick, sensual kiss firmly on his lips.

"I'm the female and I'm on time. I'm pissed you're late. But I'm glad to see you, Limey."

"So I gather m … my impetuous friend. Shall we retire upstairs for a libation?"

"Now you're talkin', Stud. I'm toisty."

"I'm parched, myself," said Winston, lightly taking her arm and guiding her to the door. He got a faint whiff of bath water; but mostly he detected the lovely aroma of healthy young woman. He was intoxicated before a drop of alcohol touched his throat.

They climbed the long stairs to the bar level, and stopped at the stand-up tables at the large front windows overlooking Delaware Avenue. They took no notice of the balding, well-dressed businessman staring intently at the street. There were several bars scattered throughout the establishment; and the place was packed. The noise level was high; but they could talk without shouting.

"What would you like, m'lady?" Winston asked.

"Order for me. And what did I tell you about that m'lady stuff?"

Winston leaned over and quickly kissed her shapely little ear.

"You may have to get used to it."

"Alright, alright," she giggled. "Get some brewskis, will ya?"

"Righto." He turned, and politely muscled his way to the closest bar. "Two Yuengling Lagers, lad," he said when he got the bartender's attention.

The kid was quick, as all bartenders at Dave and Buster's were. It was non-stop action all night, especially on weekends. As the barman handed Smythe the beers, Winston handed him a twenty.

"Keep the change lad. And throw about six more of these on ice, please."

"You got it. And thanks."

Winston made his way back to The Wiz.

"Let's stand at one of these window tables," suggested Mary Anne.

"Fine. We can people watch while we chat."

They made their way to one of the long tables by the window. One of the occupants of the table they chose was Randy Macjewski. He did not acknowledge their presence, but continued to stare out down the street. There were several Yuengling Lager empties in front of him.

"Mind if we join you?" asked Winston.

The man looked over and absently shook his head negative.

"Good choice, that," Winston said, indicating the empty bottles.

The man silently raised his bottle in a toast, and continued looking out the window.

"Hey, remember me?" said the Wiz.

"I don't think I'll ever forget you, come what may."

She snuggled up to him. "Tell me everything," she said.

"Everything?"

"Everything. Like, what the hell ya doin' in my city in the first place."

"Alright. I grew up in Liverpool in the Sixties and Seventies and I wanted to …"

"Tell me about Liverpool," she interrupted.

"Very well. It was chartered by King John in twelve-oh-seven AD. It began as a fishing town; but over the years it developed into a world-class trading center." He hesitated. "This must sound incredibly dry."

"Dry?"

"Boring."

"No, no," she said. "I'm fascinated. Go on, Stud."

Stud, he thought giddily. "There are many interesting things about the city. We have Her Majesty's Customs and Excise Museum, the Merseyside Wartime Museum. The Tate Gallery has the largest collection of contemporary art outside London. More?"

"More."

"The clock in the Royal Liverpool Building is the largest in Great Britain."

"Bigger than Big Ben?"

"By two feet six inches. The Liverpool Cathedral is the largest Anglican Church in the Empire."

She raised her eyebrow. "The Empire?"

"Old cultural habit. We're just a small island nation now. But at one time, we controlled one-quarter of the Earth's surface, and one-sixth of the planet's population."

"Wow!"

"Yes. But when we fell, we fell hard. There's still many a people that would like to see the stiff British upper lip mounted on their mantelpiece."

"Why's that?"

"We were a brutal conqueror," Winston said. "No mercy on our subjects. We preached freedom, and subjugated large populations. Funny, though. Most of our former subject nations retain a large amount of our laws and customs. At least the ones in The Commonwealth."

"I'm still waiting," said Mary Anne.

"Waiting?"

"When the hell ya gonna tell me about the Beatles?"

"Ah, The Fab Four. I was getting to that. We're very proud of the lads."

"Ever meet 'em?"

"Not hardly." Smythe took a large swallow of brew. "They broke up when I was five years old. But my parents met them."

"Really?" Mary Anne was gaga-eyed.

"Yes. They used to perform at a place called 'The Cavern'. It was a no-liquor underground cafe. This was also when Peter Best was their drummer. He quit or was fired in early nineteen-sixty, depending on who's telling the story. One of the monumental bad luck cases of all time."

"And your mom and dad met them?"

"Sure. Before Brian Epstein discovered them, and they became famous. They used to mingle with the crowds before and after sets at The Cavern."

"That must have been something," she said, taking a swallow of beer.

"It was at that. I have pictures of my parents posing with them."

"Get outta town!"

"I surely do."

"Well, that settles the 'your place or mine' question."

"I beg your pardon?" Smythe sputtered.

"We're goin' to your place later. Now be a good Limey, and get some more brewskis."

"Yes, m'lady."

Mary Anne Sims laughed as he moved away towards the bar. She didn't notice Randy Macjewski suddenly stiffen.

There they are, he thought. Two white males in dark clothes had appeared from the direction of the boat landing. They were loitering on the street, smoking.

Randy quickly gathered up his briefcase, and moved to the stairs. He hurried down to the exit, and then stopped and gathered himself. He couldn't stop the adrenaline surge; but he did mentally prepare himself. He opened the door and staggered toward the street, going right past the two hoods. Randy made a show of drunkenly looking both ways before crossing the street. He stifled the almost irresistible urge to look behind him to see if they followed.

Not yet they didn't. But they were watching like hawks. They had their victim. As Randy reached the other side of the street, they started slowly across. When Randy entered the lot under the highway, they quickened their pace.

Randy staggered around the darkened lot, pretending to look for his car. He heard footsteps come very close, and hunched his shoulders. The blackjack glanced off his head, and struck his right shoulder. The blow was stunning, and brought him to his knees. He briefly blacked out; and when his head cleared somewhat, the briefcase was gone; and the muggers were headed back across Delaware Avenue.

Randy quickly collected himself. He tore off the mustache and wig. He put them in his suit coat pocket, and took off the coat and placed it over his arm. The gun went into the other suit pocket. He staggered slightly, for real this time, and started toward the Spring Garden El stop, stripping off his tie as he went. The tie went into his pants pocket. *To hell they go*, he thought, as he hurried away.

* * *

Winston Smythe had returned to the table by the window in time to see two men cross Delaware Avenue and hurry toward the boat landing, one of them carrying a briefcase. He instinctively looked for the man at the table that he had talked to earlier. He was gone. *It couldn't be!* he thought.

"Come quickly!" he said to Mary Anne.

"What?"

He grabbed her arm.

"Quickly! Oh, blimey! I don't believe this!"

As they hustled to the stairs he had his squad radio out.

"Three-Four, zero-one-eight to Central. Emergency."

"This is Central. Stand by Three-Four, zero-one-eight. Break. Central to all units. Clear the channels. Break. Go, Three-Four, zero-one-eight."

"Zero-one-eight. I'm in pursuit of two suspects. White males, dark clothes, heading toward Penn's Landing boat stairs. Need assistance."

Winston and Mary Anne hit the street in time to see the two men hurrying down the stairs to the small boat landing.

"Stop! Police!" Winston shouted. He ran toward the landing, shouting over his shoulder to The Wiz, "Wait here!"

* * *

Sergeant Vargas and Detective Trung heard the commotion on their radio, and also heard the shouting in the distance.

"Central. This is Three-Four, zero-zero -three. I'm right there, will assist."

"Roger, zero-zero-three. All other units in vicinity of Penn's Landing, assist detectives."

Several units were responding, but Julio and Nguyen were on the scene in seconds, seeing Winston running for the landing steps. They converged at the top of the steps, guns out.

"Whaddya got, Smythe?" Vargas asked breathlessly.

"Oh Christ!" Winston rasped. A small boat had started with a roar, and was speeding east towards the center of the river. It quickly veered north and was out of sight.

"I think they mugged our man. No! I'm bloody well sure it was him! I'll explain it later. We must stop that boat."

Vargas again yanked out his radio.

"Central. Three-Four, zero-zero-three. We need Marine One to pursue suspects heading north on the Delaware River. Small boat, at high speed with no lights."

"Roger, zero-zero-three. Break. Marine One, you copy?"

"Central. Marine One. Roger. We've been monitoring. We're down by the USS Olympia. We're gearing up. Be advised we can pursue; but with that kind of head start we may miss them."

"Roger, Marine One. Break. You copy zero-zero-three?"

"Roger, Central. I'm taking command of this situation."

"Roger, zero-zero-three. Break. All units responding Penn's Landing. Report to Sergeant from Three-Four, commander on scene."

Officers Mike Bellows and John Ruscomb, the beat cops from The 26th District, arrived on the scene slightly out of breath. Mary Anne Sims was right behind them.

"Whaddya got, Sarge?" asked Bellows.

"Stand by," replied Vargas. "O.K., Winston. Quickly."

"A man at the club. At our table. He did nothing but watch the street. I saw these men rushing across the street from the parking lot area with a briefcase; and when I looked, the man at our table was gone. It was him. I know it. My height, my build. Slightly balding, dark hair and a mustache. Black suit. He must still be in the area somewhere."

"Right," said Sergeant Vargas. "Take Trung and these two Officers, and check the lot across the street. I'll head toward the El stop." Vargas waved a follow me to two other patrol officers that had just arrived on the scene. He pointed to their patrol car. "Let's go. To the Spring Garden El stop." They piled in the car and squealed away.

Smythe, Trung, Bellows, and Ruscomb ran across Delaware Avenue. Mary Anne followed.

"You can't come with us," Winston hollered.

"I'm not lettin' you outta my sight, Limey."

Winston didn't argue, and they all together arrived under the highway. The Uniforms and Smythe drew their weapons. Sims did not.

"Spread out," Winston said. "Check anything and everybody." He stopped The Wiz with a no-nonsense gesture. "You're with me."

By now, Delaware Avenue was in chaos. Cops and cop cars were everywhere. Sergeant Vargas, in the back seat of the patrol car that was speeding away, realized his mistake. As commander, he had left the scene. But pursuit of the bomber took precedence.

"Central. Three-Four, zero-zero-three."

"Go, zero-zero-three."

"I have temporarily left scene. Am in pursuit of suspect in Booby-Trap Bomber case. Assign new scene commander."

"Roger, zero-zero-three. Break. All units vicinity Penn's Landing. Senior officer on scene to take charge. Three-Four Sergeant has left scene."

* * *

Lieutenant Matt Gallagher and Sergeant Wallace had been listening intently to the organized chaos on the radio. As soon as Vargas had mentioned his pursuit of the booby-trap suspect, they had wordlessly run across campus to their Crown Vic. Lights flashing and siren blaring, their unmarked car was now speeding east on US Route 30, which was Lancaster Avenue.

"We'll never get there in time," gritted Yvonne, as she veered in and around traffic. She hadn't done this in a while.

"I don't care! I want there, and I want there now! Punch it!"

Yvonne did a high-speed, tire squealing turn south onto City Avenue. Almost three miles later she hit the ramp for eastbound I-76 doing 80 mph. It was a long gradual access ramp, and she accelerated. She hit the Schuylkill Expressway at 95 mph and kept it there. Traffic was light, and they barreled along. The Ford Crown Victoria was responding beautifully.

* * *

Sergeant Vargas and the two patrol officers charged up the steps to the Spring Garden El stop. A northbound train was receding in the distance.

"Damn!" said Vargas. His squad radio warbled, indicating someone from The 3/4 District wanted to speak to him. He switched frequencies.

"Vargas. Go."

"Gallagher. Talk to me."

"I'm at the Spring Garden EL stop. Platform's clear. A train just left northbound. We're not even sure our man came this way. He might've had a car in the area."

"O.K.," Gallagher said. "Switch back and give Central suspect description. We're eastbound on the Schuylkill coming up on the Vine Street Expressway. We're shit hot. I'll be at Penn's Landing shortly."

"O.K., Boss." Vargas switched frequencies and gave Central Dispatch Smythe's description of the suspect.

Gallagher switched frequencies and waited for Vargas to finish.

"Central. Three-Four, zero-zero-two."

"Go, zero-zero-two."

"Please contact SEPTA Police. There's a northbound El train that just left the Spring Garden stop. Please advise suspect description and request assistance."

"Roger, zero-zero-two."

"You know," Yvonne said, "even if he's on that train, he's shed his disguise."

"I know. But we gotta try."

Yvonne hit I-95 South from the Vine Street Expressway, and quickly slowed for the Columbus Avenue exit. Seconds later they were at Penn's Landing. Gallagher and Wallace quickly exited the car, and made their way to the group of officers near the boat landing.

"I'm Lieutenant Gallagher of the Three-Four."

"I know you, Loo. I'm Sergeant Covington of The 26th. You want in charge?"

"No, I'll be all over the area. Anything from Marine One?"

"Not that we've heard."

Gallagher pulled out his squad radio.

"Central. Three-Four, zero-zero-two."

"Go, zero-zero-two."

"Patch me to Marine One, please."

"Stand by. O.K., go."

"Marine One, this is Lieutenant Matt Gallagher of the Three-Four. Be advised, suspects may have a bomb aboard."

"Marine One, Loo. That's just great. They turned their lights on a couple of seconds ago. They just turned up Rancocas Creek and … Holy Shit! They just blew the fuck up."

"Say again, Marine One!"

"There was a bright flash and a loud bang. Stand by. We'll be on the scene in fifteen seconds."

Gallagher stomped his foot in disgust. All the officers were watching him.

"Damn! Damn! I guessed right! And we still fuckin' missed him!"

"Not your fault, Matt," said Yvonne. "You did your best."

"But it wasn't good enough! Damn!"

"Central. Marine One."

"Go, Marine One."

"We're on the scene of the explosion. Debris everywhere. Two bodies in the water. Or what's left of them. Blood and flesh everywhere. Declaring this a crime scene."

"Roger, Marine One. Assistance is on the way. New Jersey State Police, Burlington County Police, and Delanco Township Police have all been notified."

"Roger, Central. We are standing by."

* * *

Randy Macjewski saw two SETPA Police Officers get on the train at the York-Dauphin El stop. As they made their way from car to car, Randy remained outwardly calm as he gazed out the window. The officers entered his car, glanced briefly at him, and continued on.

Randy needed a beer. But he could wait. Eventually the train arrived at the Allegheny stop. Randy made his way down the steps. Seeing no one around, he dug into the suit coat pocket and pulled out the mustache and wig, and dumped them in a garbage can. He got into his Olds 98 and drove home.

CHAPTER SIXTEEN

Lieutenant Matt Gallagher walked up the steps of the Broad Street Subway stop at Federal Street at 7:40 A.M., crossed Broad and headed east on Federal. When he turned right on 11th, he could see and hear the commotion in front of the station house a block away. *Big surprise,* he thought. Well, he was prepared for it; but he didn't have to like it. It was part of the job.

As he approached, he saw cameras and reporters surrounding who else—Deputy Chief Barnes. *He is in his glory,* Matt thought. As much as Matt shied away from the limelight, Barnes bathed in it. It was Matt's case, but the media would mainly quote Barnes. This was fine with Matt. As Matt started up the steps to the entrance, he was first spotted by Tony Brice of *The Daily News,* who hustled over to him.

"Lieutenant Gallagher, can you confirm that last night's explosion on the Delaware River was related to the Booby-Trap Bomber case?"

"I can't confirm anything until all the test results are in."

"Deputy Chief Barnes says the two bombing incidents are definitely related."

"I never contradict my superiors," Matt said.

Other media people joined in.

"Lieutenant Gallagher, Christina Stamp for KYW News Radio. Were detectives or other police officers in pursuit of the two men who were killed in last night's boat explosion?"

"That's affirmative."

"Why were they being pursued?"

"They were suspects in a mugging," Matt responded.

"Lieutenant, Troy Gillespie—*Action News.* If they were suspects in a mugging, and they were killed in an explosion, doesn't it follow that they were the victims of the Booby-Trap Bomber?"

"That's pure speculation, Mister Gillespie."

"But pretty good speculation, wouldn't you say?"

Matt smiled without his eyes. "Be sure to tell your viewers that your report is pretty good speculation. O.K., Troy?"

Matt hurried up the steps, ignoring Barnes and the continuing shouted questions of the news people. He entered the squad room to a small chorus of morning greetings. Acknowledging everyone with a wave and a nod, Matt moved to the coffee table and made himself a cup of tea. The squad room was relatively empty, as it was a Saturday. He had told his crew last night to keep to their regular schedules. They had all volunteered to come in early; but Matt had said no. They had all put in a long night last night; and he had told them to get their rest. He had even told Sergeant Wallace to stay out until noon. As Matt was steeping his tea, Chief Barnes came up behind him.

"Your Captain is in today. And I'm sure he wants to see you," he said to Matt's back.

Matt slowly turned around. "I'm on my way there right now. Care to join me?"

"I don't need your permission. Where the hell's the rest of your crew?"

"Keeping to the schedule their boss - that's me - gave them."

"That schedule can be changed."

Matt looked Barnes square in the eye. "If I'm relieved of duty, it sure can."

"Don't get smart with me, Lieutenant. You're on thin ice as it is."

Matt gestured to the hallway door. "The Captain, I'm sure, is waiting."

Barnes muttered under his breath and led the way.

Captain Parmalee was indeed waiting, but not in a snit, as Barnes would have liked to believe. He was simply waiting to hear from Gallagher in person, after having read the overnight reports. Jane Wilson never worked weekends, so Matt knocked sharply on the Captain's door, and he and Barnes went in.

"Good morning, Chief Barnes," said Parmalee, indicating chairs. "Good morning, Matt. Chief Barnes and I have read the overnights. Now tell us what went down."

As dispassionately as he could, considering the circumstances, Matt started relating the events of the night before. He briefly summarized what happened before he arrived at Penn's Landing.

"Dammit! I guessed right and he still beat me. One of my guys and The Wiz even got a good look at him. They'll be sitting down with a Department sketch artist later today."

"They should be doing that right now," grumbled Barnes.

"Well, Chief," responded Matt. "Contrary to popular belief, it's better to wait awhile, and let someone sleep on it. The first thing they'll think about when they wake up is what happened the night before. It was a traumatic event. Detective Smythe was beside himself that he was getting a beer when our man left the club. He knows if he'd been standing at the window three minutes earlier, he would have put two and two together immediately. But it's not his fault. He was off duty anyway."

"When's he due in, Matt?" asked Captain Parmalee.

"Two o'clock, but knowing him, he'll be in sooner. I'll call in a sketch artist as soon as I'm outta here."

"O.K., continue with your report."

"Well, as soon as I got a negative report from the SEPTA Police, I knew we'd lost him. Then I went into after-action mode."

Matt related the gumshoe details of the several hours following the explosion. They had interviewed the bartenders, who hadn't served the bomber, and the waitress, who had. She had described a balding man of medium height and build with mustache, who drank Yuengling Lager. Except for the hair, she could have been describing Smythe.

They had tracked down the SEPTA train operator who had pulled out of Spring Garden Station right before Sergeant Vargas arrived. "Hell," he had said. "All I do is make sure they're all off and all on before I give 'er the juice again. If memory serves, there were about five, maybe ten people that got on at that stop. Nobody stood out to me; but again, all I watch for is people gettin' on and off. That's my job."

Gallagher had also interviewed the SEPTA police officers who had gotten on the train at the York-Dauphin stop. They had seen no one resembling the description of the suspect, or any unusually stressed out individuals.

"Besides," said one. "We're not detectives. We're not about to roust a whole train full of fare-paying customers. Not unless one of our supervisors is on the scene, and directs us to do so."

Matt and his detectives had also scouted out the parking lot across from Dave and Buster's where the "mugging" had taken place; but it had yielded no clues. They couldn't even be sure of the exact spot where the incident had gone down.

Before wrapping everything up, Marine One had given Task Force ABLS a ride to the scene of the explosion. It had happened right at the mouth of the Rancocas Creek off Hawk Island in Delanco, New Jersey. New Jersey State Police divers and marine operators had secured the crime scene, as it was their turf. But there were to be no bureaucratic turf battles here. As soon as their work was done and the reports finished, higher-ups had decided that copies of everything would be turned over to Task Force Gallagher. Keep your lunatic bomber on the other side of the river, thank you very much.

Marine One had gotten as close as it could without interfering with the police work going on. The two mangled bodies had been laid out on the deck of a police boat, and the Burlington County Coroner had, of course, pronounced them very dead at the scene. There would be a final autopsy; but each man had suffered many massive wounds, almost any of which would have been fatal. Chunks of their torsos and internal organs were missing. The coroner, a veteran combat medic, guessed grenade, due to the multiple, slicing penetration wounds.

The muggers' boat hadn't sunk, incredibly enough. A grenade explodes up and out, and as it killed the muggers it simultaneously blew them out of the boat, which had veered suddenly left and grounded itself on Hawk Island. Forensics would check it extensively of course; and these reports would also wind up on Matt's desk.

Gallagher and his crew had finally called it a night around 3:30 A.M. Matt had gotten about two hours sleep.

"What now, Matt?" asked Parmalee.

"We go real hard on the victims list, and continue with stakeouts. I'll use my best hunch on serial crime areas; but I think our big break will come from the list or from someone who knows our guy, and sees him acting funny. This guy's mean, intelligent, and cool. He's gonna be real tough to nail; and he'll not go down quietly."

Deputy Chief Barnes had remained uncharacteristically subdued throughout Matt's description of last night's events. Now he stirred. "Tell me Lieutenant, how many more incidents do you think it will take before you catch this guy?"

Gallagher hesitated.

"It's a legitimate question, Matt," said Captain Parmalee.

"We'll probably be chasin' 'im all summer," admitted Matt.

"Well," Barnes said. "We can't throw an unlimited number of resources at this. It's a big city and there's a lotta shit goin' down. You'll just have to do the best you can."

Matt was startled to silence. Parmalee was also shocked. Barnes siding with his fellow officers, admitting crime case reality? Did the man suddenly get police religion?

"I'm gonna get this bastard, Chief," Matt gritted. "If those two clowns had opened that briefcase on Delaware Avenue instead of on the boat, we would have had serious, multiple civilian casualties. A grenade, yet. No, we'll get him. We just need time."

"You'll probably get just as much as the citizens of this town allow, Lieutenant. And we'll all just have to wait to see how much that is." Barnes rose to leave. "Deal with the press, gentlemen. The people do have a right to know."

"We'll do that, Chief," answered Parmalee.

"I'll handle it," said Matt. "Let me make a few phone calls, and then I'll go outside and meet with them. I'll read a statement and take questions."

"O.K.," said Barnes. "I'll let the press know you'll be out in a few minutes. I'll be in touch."

After Barnes left and shut the door, there was a long silence. Finally Parmalee spoke.

"This won't be too bad, Matthew—and I'll tell you why. The Reverend Jefferson and Lawrence Steele won't be up in arms about two white guys from Jersey getting waxed. They'll milk it a little for the publicity; but there won't be any crying mamas in front of the cameras for these two. Nobody deserves to die like that, but good riddance. For all they knew they were taking down an innocent citizen for his briefcase. Now it's two less Jersey rats coming across the river to bother us."

"I know, Cap. I know. But I want this guy before he hurts innocent people."

"You'll get him, Matthew. Now go do what you gotta do. Show me the statement you're gonna give to the press. Not for my approval. Just so's I know what info you give 'em."

"O.K., Cap. I'll be back in a few."

Matt made his way back to his desk. He called a Department sketch artist, and asked him to stop by around 1:00 P.M. He then called The Wiz at home and got no answer. He started to call Smythe, but let it ride. *If those two have really found each other, let them have some peace,* he thought. He wrote out a statement, made and delivered a copy to Captain Parmalee, and went outside to meet the press, as it were.

"Ladies and gentlemen, I'd like to read a statement, and then I'll take some questions.

"At approximately 11:35 P.M. last night, two men from New Jersey apparently mugged a citizen, identity unknown, in a parking lot under I-95, across from Dave and Buster's on Delaware Avenue. The two men then made their way to the small boat landing off the avenue, and headed north on the Delaware River. Just before or just after they entered Rancocas Creek, there was an explosion on board the boat. Apparently the briefcase they stole from the victim was rigged to explode upon opening. Both men were killed instantly. The mugging victim was not found. Absent any evidence to the contrary, we are going on the assumption that this was the work of the Booby-Trap Bomber. We still don't have any real leads on who this man is. His description is: white male, age thirty-five to forty-five, medium build, medium height, last seen wearing a black suit. He has black hair and mustache, and is slightly balding. We are asking the public's help. If you have seen or see this man, contact any police officer or official, and the information will be relayed to my task force. You can also call the Philadelphia Police Tip Line at one-eight hundred, nine-one-one, TIPS. Thank you. I'll take questions now."

He knew them all; but they stuck to the formalities.

"Lieutenant, MaryLou McBride of *The Inquirer*. What type of explosive was in the briefcase?"

"We're gonna hold that tight to the vest for now. That way, when we get tips, we can separate the wheat from the chaff. It'll save us from running down a lot of false leads."

"Lieutenant, Clevus Capstone, *POW Weekly*. How many more innocent people are gonna be killed or maimed by this white lunatic before you catch him?"

"I won't comment on the 'innocent people' portion of your question. As for the rest of it, we hope to catch him before he hurts anybody else."

McBride again. "Lieutenant, do you believe the bomber was in disguise?"

"We have to assume that," Matt replied. "But the description stands. Someone had to have seen this man before he arrived at the Penn's Landing area."

"Lieutenant, Troy Gillespie, *Action News*. Where were you last night when the mugging took place?"

"Myself and Sergeant Yvonne Wallace were on a stakeout at a location I won't tell you. We don't want to let the bomber know our whereabouts at any one time. After hearing the initial reports on my radio, I arrived at the Penn's Landing area at approximately 11:55 P.M.

"A follow-up, please. Did you have officers staked out in the area where the mugging took place?"

Gallagher hesitated. *Oh well, it doesn't make any difference now.* "That's affirmative." This created a stir, as he knew it would. He inwardly cringed at what he knew was coming next.

"Lieutenant, Christina Stamp, KYW News Radio. Are you saying you actually guessed right? You had this area staked out? And you still missed your man?"

"Yes. That's what I'm saying."

The reporters all hustled away to their vehicles. Gallagher could see the headlines now—TASK FORCE BLOWS STAKE-OUT—LOSES IN BOTTOM OF NINTH. He slowly made his way back into the building.

* * *

Winston Smythe awoke slowly but alertly, acutely aware of the bundle of delicious young woman in his arms. Mary Anne Sims was buried against his chest, sleeping deeply. He didn't move. He didn't want to disturb her.

They had finally arrived back at his loft apartment at around 4:00 A.M. Saturday morning. Without a word they had undressed each other in the living room, and after some passionate kissing and touching he had carried her into the bedroom, where they made love for hours. They had finally fallen asleep around 7:00 A.M. He sighed contentedly. It was, without a doubt, the best sex he had ever had. She had been delightfully uninhibited, and had seemed to enjoy it as much as he. A man could ask for no more from a lover.

She stirred in his arms.

"Hi, Stud Limey," she murmured.

"Good morning m'lady," he said, kissing her sweet smelling hair.

"You really are a stud, you know."

"Thank you. And you were pretty spectacular yourself."

"Really?"

"The best I've ever had."

She was fully awake now. "Let's qualify that. Or quantify that. Or whatever. How many have you had?"

"I will not answer that question."

"C'mon," she persisted playfully, grabbing him down low. "How many?"

"Thousands. Wilt Chamberlain type numbers."

"Liar!" She squeezed gently.

"You asked."

"What's for breakfast?" She was stroking him gently to life.

"Whatever you like." He groaned with delight. "The larder is fully stocked; and I'm an excellent cook, if I do say so myself."

"Sounds great. But first things first," she said, rising above him.

A few minutes later, they settled down in the bed. Finally she said, "O.K. Show me your culinary artistry. I'm starved."

"Right. Up you go." He literally picked her up and placed her in a standing position beside the bed, and got up and threw on a robe. "If you care to shower, I'll have breakfast ready in twenty minutes. It'll be large and greasy."

"Good by me. I'm to the showers."

He quickly padded into his large kitchen. He pulled out two humongous double-burner skillets and threw them on the stove. Into each he placed a stick of butter, and turned on the flames. As the butter was melting, he reached into the refrigerator again, and pulled out a dozen eggs, a bowl of boiled potatoes that he always had ready, and a large package of fresh-made sausage. He quickly sliced up the potatoes, and got them and the sausage going in the same skillet. He chopped an onion and a red pepper, and mixed these and the eggs in a large bowl. When the potatoes and sausage were halfway done, he poured the egg mixture into the second skillet, and let it basically cook itself, occasionally mixing it up. While he was doing all this, he managed to set the table, make a pot of Earl Gray tea, and toast eight slices of whole wheat bread.

Mary Anne came to the table wearing nothing but one of his dress shirts.

Wow! Winston thought. *Do women know how incredibly sexy they look wearing nothing but a man's button down shirt? Of course they do,* he answered himself. *That's why they do it.*

"Please be seated. There's orange juice and tea. Chow will be served shortly."

Mary Anne buttered the toast, and marveled at the size of the breakfast cooking on the stove. "My God, are we expecting Task Force Gallagher?"

"Just our little portion of it," he laughed.

Wearing large asbestos mittens, he lifted the skillets one by one off the stove, and placed them on two huge ceramic pads on the butcher block island next to the kitchen table. He reached for her plate, and filled it heaping with succulent, greasy food.

"I can feel my arteries hardening already; but give it here," she said. "That's my kind of breakfast."

"Somehow, I knew that without asking," he said, grinning. "I hope you enjoy it."

"Trust me!"

Winston fixed a plate for himself, sat down, and they ate in companionable silence. They each had seconds, and finally they both sat back, contented.

"So where do we go from here?" she asked him quietly.

"I've been thinking about that: and I'm going to leave it entirely up to you. I know I want you. I want you badly. You'll have my number; and you can call me and let me know if you want it to continue. That way, I'll know you want me too."

"I can handle that. I have a lot of think about. I haven't been in a relationship in a long time. I may need some space."

"Take all you want. You can always reach me, and professionally, we'll be seeing a lot of one another anyway."

"Alright, that'll work." She paused briefly. "The other part of last night was so unreal. I can still hardly believe it happened the way it did."

"I know," he said. "If I had made that second trip to the bar earlier, I would have seen our man go out into the street and be followed by our dearly departed muggers."

"Don't let it eat you up. You people are gonna catch this guy. I know it."

"Yes, we will eventually. He'll screw up, or someone will notice something suspicious. We'll get him." He took a sip of tea. "Let me call the shop and see what time the Leftenant has the sketch artist coming in."

"I'll clean up," Mary Anne offered.

"Thank you. I'll help you in a minute." Winston moved to the phone in the living room and called The 3/4 District, and Matt gave him the information. He thanked him and hung up.

"1:00 P.M.," he called into the kitchen. "Let me use the bathroom, and I'll come in and help with the dishes."

"I got it. Take a shower. Relax. We've got plenty of time."

* * *

Randy Macjewski had woken at 8:00 A.M. and immediately turned on KYW News Radio. The story was there. Two men killed in a boat explosion on the Delaware River. Quoting unidentified police sources, the report linked the explosion to the Booby-Trap Bomber, who had apparently let himself be mugged.

Success, he inwardly exhilarated. *Two bastards to hell, Mom and Dad. And more to follow.* But he would lay low until late August. The dog days of summer. There would be no anonymous calls or letters to the press, or any of that wacky bullshit. Let the police worry about what his plans were. He knew when and where he would strike next.

Villanova University. There had been snatch and runs there that had been making news lately. He would scout it in early August. Then he would make some more news himself.

He quickly showered and dressed. Saturday was his favorite day at the bar. He drank, he bartended, he did paperwork, he played pool and video games with customers. And he was sure there would be many discussions about the latest booby-trap caper. *This will be a good Saturday*, he thought, as he headed downstairs to the bar.

* * *

Gallagher sat at his desk, going over the crime victims' kin list. The bomber was on this list. He could feet it. But it would take weeks to winnow it down. There had to be something here that would raise his hackles. *Well,* he thought. *I have all morning.* He just had to plug away. His outside line rang.

"Lieutenant Gallagher."

"Lieutenant, this is Elizabeth Mackley, TIPS operator. I have a call I think you should take. We've been alerted about your Booby-Trap Bomber case."

"O.K., Miss Mackley. Put it through. And thank you."

"You're welcome. Go ahead, caller."

"Hello?"

"Yes, this is Lieutenant Gallagher of the Three-Four District. How can I help you?"

"Good morning, Lieutenant. My name is Doug Arnett, with All Service Security. We provide security for the bus station at Eleventh and Filbert Streets."

"O.K., gawhead."

"Last night, just before 10:00 P.M., I saw a man at the bus station that matched a description I just heard on 'Ten-Sixty'."

"Ten Sixty" was the common name for KYW News Radio, at 1060 on the AM dial, the best-known station in town. Almost everyone listened to it at some time during the day.

"O.K.," Matt said. "As objectively as you can, give me your description of the man."

"Well," Arnett said. "He was five-nine or ten. He was about one-eighty or one-ninety. He was slightly bald, with a dark mustache. He was wearing a black suit."

"What brought him to your attention?" Matt asked.

"It was what he did. Actually, it was what he didn't do. He didn't get on or off a bus."

"Are you sure about that?"

"Almost one-hundred percent. Hardly anything exciting ever happens down there, so you become a real people watcher by default. I happened to be looking at the Reading Terminal side of the station, and saw him come in. He went directly to a storage locker and retrieved a briefcase, and left by the 10th Street exit."

Matt's pulse quickened. This had to be their man. He silently pleaded to the police gods for an affirmative answer to his next question.

"Do you think he's on tape?"

"I'm sure of it."

"We need that tape," Matt almost shouted into the phone.

"It's yours," Arnett said. "I called down to the station before I called the TIPS line. I told them to seal last night's tape and hold it pending further investigation."

"That's great," Matt said. "I'll have it picked up. I'd also like you to come down to my squad room. I have a police sketch artist coming in at one o'clock."

"No problem. I'll drive down there right after lunch."

"Better yet. We'll pick you up. Gimme your address, please."

"I live in Germantown. Four-thirteen Walnut Lane."

Matt jotted down the address.

"I'm gonna have a Sergeant Yvonne Wallace pick you up at twelve-thirty, O.K.?"

"Fine. I'll be waiting."

Matt hung up, and quickly dialed Central Dispatch.

"Central Dispatch, Elaine speaking."

"Good morning. This is Lieutenant Matt Gallagher at the Three-Four. Would you please connect me to the security office of the bus station at 11th and Filbert."

"Stand by." There was a brief pause.

"Bus station security. Bob Wyatt speaking."

"This is Lieutenant Matt Gallagher, Philadelphia Police Department. I wanna send somebody to pick up last night's security tape that you're holding."

"It's all set, Lieutenant. The paper work's ready. We just need a police signature."

"Sergeant Yvonne Wallace will be picking it up somewhere around 1:00 P.M."

"That's fine. It'll be here."

"Great," Matt said. "Have you looked at the tape?"

"Yes," Wyatt replied. "Doug Arnett called in here about the tape and said he was going to call you. We looked at it right after he hung up."

"O.K.," Matt replied. "Please block access to the locker on the tape. We'll have someone dust it."

"Can do, Lieutenant," Wyatt replied.

"Thank you."

"Glad to help."

Matt hung up, briefly looked at his rolodex, and dialed Yvonne's number.

"Hello?"

"Good morning. It's Matt. Sleep well?"

"Not bad," Yvonne said. "Considering it was all of four hours."

"Yeah, it was a rough night all around. Listen, I got a mission for ya on your way in." Matt quickly gave Yvonne the details and the address for Doug Arnett.

"Looks like we caught a break," she said.

"Maybe. It's our guy. I know it. Where he came from is still the problem."

"Right. O.K., I'll see you in a bit. My squad radio is on as of now."

"Good. Later."

Matt looked over to the Robbery/Homicide area. Detective Chuck Ladders was typing a report. "Excuse me, Chuck," he said loudly.

Ladders looked up. "Yeah, Loo."

Gallagher quickly briefed Ladders. "How 'bout grabbin' a Uniform and goin' over and dust that locker. I know there'll be prints or smudges all over it, but ya never know."

"O.K., Boss."

Matt sat back and collected himself. Shortly the squad room would be a very busy place. He went back to studying the victims' kin list. The answer was there. He could feel it.

* * *

"Eight ball. Side pocket. One bank of the cue ball."

Randy carefully lined up the shot. Using a gentle side spin, he tapped the cue ball toward the far bank. It hit solidly, and came back down the table and nudged the eight ball into the side pocket.

"Game, set, and match," sighed Nick Cardle, Randy's opponent. "Jeez. You lost yet today?"

"No," Randy replied. "And I'm retirin' undefeated. I'm done." Randy unscrewed his stick, put it in the case, and placed it behind the bar where it always stayed. He moved to the small cooking area, and quickly made two fried bologna and cheese sandwiches on Kaiser Rolls. He grabbed a Yuengling Lager out of the iced beer bin, and sat on a bar stool to eat. The TV at his end of the bar was tuned to CNN.

"In Philadelphia," the anchor began, "the case of the Booby-Trap Bomber took a new twist last night in a bizarre incident on the Delaware River. Lesley Stone, in Philadelphia, has more."

Stone stood at Penn's Landing, silhouetted against the background of Camden, New Jersey. "Last night on the Delaware River," Stone began, "there was an explosion on a small boat just at the mouth of Rancocas Creek in Burlington County, New Jersey."

Stone, quoting unnamed police sources, related last night's incident and the police description of the bomber. Randy watched intently.

"Police have confirmed that they believe this was the work of the Booby-Trap Bomber. Apparently the victims had just mugged someone under I-95 on the Philadelphia side of the river. The mugging 'victim' has not been found. We'll have more as the story develops. In Philadelphia, for CNN, this is Lesley Stone."

"Shit," said Nick Cardle, who had walked up to stand behind Randy and watch the report. "Between the Bomber and the Phillies, we'll be national news all summer."

"Yeah," Randy replied. "It's gonna be one strange season."

CHAPTER SEVENTEEN

Gallagher sat back and sighed. The list was giving him a headache. But his police brain was firing on all cylinders, and something tickled the back of his mind. It was one of those unexplained hunches he sometimes got.

What had John Williams, Howsten's former landlord, said? Before Howsten died, he had had a steady visitor. An Andy or a Randy, or some name like that. From Kensington or Richmond, or one of those neighborhoods on the east side of town.

He bent back to the list, and started scanning for Andys or Randys. He found Andys and Randys alright. Five in Richmond, four in Kensington, two in Fishtown, and three in Bridesburg. They would start on this mini-list after the sketch artist was through, and they had all watched the videotape from the bus station.

He would give Fishtown to Smythe and Gonzales, Kensington to Vargas and Trung, he and Wallace would take Richmond, and whatever team was done first would take Bridesburg. It was dreary gumshoe work; but it had to be done. Besides, he always followed his hunches. They didn't always pan out, but more often than not, something would come out of it. Howsten selling the AK-47 to Scarfo was at least a lead to go on. If they could find his bedside friend, maybe he could shed some light on the subject. If he also turned out to be on the list, that would be an added bonus they could look into. Matt leaned back and stretched.

"How'd they do last night, Jack?" he asked Detective Miles.

"Oh, man!" Jack said. "Mulholland pitched the game of his life, Boss. Gives up seven hits, no walks, strikes out fourteen, and loses in the ninth. Big Cat hit an RBI double for the winning run. Final was two-to-one, Rockies."

"Musta been tough to watch."

"It was. Over forty thousand there and nobody left 'til the last out. By the way, Jack junior says thank you every much for the tickets. Me too. Those seats are awesome."

"You're welcome," Matt said, smiling. "My dad had 'em for years, and passed 'em down to me. He started with season tickets at old Connie Mack Stadium."

"That's goin' back some," Jack replied. "I don't even remember Connie Mack. I was only three or four years old when they tore it down."

"It was a nice old ballpark. Grass field, old fashion scoreboard. After the games, they would open a gate in right field, and people could leave the park that way. You got to walk in the outfield. I even ran the bases once before they chased me off."

"You don't see that nowadays," said Jack.

"Yeah," Matt laughed. "You can't get near the field, and if you do go on it, you get arrested. Who's pitchin' tonight?"

"Tommy Greene. He's seven and oh. Leads the majors in ERA."

"I'm goin' down for that," Matt said.

"Should be a good one. Not to pry, but no stakeouts tonight?"

"Nah, it's too soon. I'll wait a week to ten days or so. We can help our team with the victims' list. I'm sure he's on it."

"Got one of those feelings?" Jack asked.

"Just a hunch. But a strong one."

"Good luck, Boss."

"Thanks."

* * *

Winston Smythe and Mary Anne Sims came in the squad room at ten to one, followed shortly thereafter by the sketch artist, Rachel Conly.

Matt walked up to her and offered his hand. "I'm Lieutenant Matt Gallagher. This is Detective Winston Smythe and our computer consultant, Mary Anne Sims. Why don't you all use the interrogation room and see what you come up with?"

"Right, Leftenant," replied Smythe. "Come, ladies. Duty calls."

Matt did not fail to notice how Winston put a light, guiding hand on The Wiz's back. Mary Anne saw Matt watching, and blushed furiously.

"Can it, gutter brain!" she said.

Matt feigned shocked astonishment. "I didn't say nuttin."

"Keep it that way."

Winston, blushing now himself, led the way into the interrogation room. As he turned to close the door, Matt winked at him, causing him to turn even redder.

Matt smiled. *Good for them,* he thought.

A Uniform, vaguely familiar to Matt, walked into the squad room from the hallway.

"Can I help you, Officer?" Matt asked.

"Hi. I'm Al Talerico, outta The Fifth District."

"We ever work together?"

"I been at The Fifth for years. I was there when you passed through a few years back."

Matt had made Sergeant during his brief stay at The 5th, and had quickly been transferred to The 3/4, and had been here ever since.

"How can we help you, Al?" Matt asked.

"Well, I … that is," Officer Talerico was stammering and blushing to beat the band.

This was a switch, Matt thought. *Everybody but me doin' all the blushin'.* He pointed to Juan Pasqualez's desk. "I think you want that man there."

At the start of the conversation, Pasqualez had quickly buried his nose in paperwork. *Oh well,* he thought. If there had been any doubts about Matt's knowledge of the kitty and who ran it, they were now erased.

Talerico and Pasqualez huddled quickly, and money and receipts changed hands while Matt pretended not to notice. After Talerico had quickly left by the squad room door, Matt walked up to Juan's desk. He sat down on a side chair.

"What's the pot up to?" Matt asked.

Pasqualez had the good grace to blush, and the good sense not to ask 'what pot?'

"Over seventeen large."

"Jesus! You gotta be shittin' me!"

"Nope. Some lucky person is gonna be payin' off a mortgage soon … that is, I mean … oh well, what the hell. When you gonna get laid, Boss? I get nervous sittin' on all this money."

Matt laughed. "You'll be the third or fourth one to know." He got up and walked back to his desk just as Sergeant Yvonne Wallace and Doug Arnett walked in the door. Yvonne introduced the two men and handed Matt a videotape in a case.

"Thanks for coming down, Mr. Arnett," Matt said.

"Call me Doug please."

"Fine, Doug. Two of our people are with the sketch artist right now. I'd like you to give it a try when they're done. This way, we'll have triple corroboration. Help yourself to a cup of coffee, and have a seat, please."

"O.K."

"We'll look at the tape after Winston and The Wiz are finished with the sketch artist," Matt said to Yvonne. "Everybody else should be in by then."

"What's the new game plan?" Yvonne asked.

"We'll have a meeting around two-fifteen, and I'll go over it then."

Half an hour later, the door to the interrogation room opened and the small group came out.

"Let's see what ya got," Matt said, as Conly handed him the final sketch.

It was basically what he expected. It showed a middle age white male with dark, balding hair, and a dark mustache. "O.K.," Matt said to Conly. 'Let's get this man's version." He indicated Arnett. "Then we'll get the final draft printed and sent out. Your office will do that, right?"

"Right," said Conly. "We'll put a case number on it, and it'll go out to all The Districts with your phone number on it."

"O.K. Mr. Arnett ... Doug, would you sit at the empty desk over there and work with Miss Conly, please?"

"O.K., Lieutenant."

"Now," Matt said to the others. "Let's go in the interrogation room and watch this tape."

Matt, Yvonne, Winston and The Wiz filed inside the room and closed the door. Matt inserted the tape in the VCR, turned everything on, and waited for the first pictures to appear. After several minutes of watching people come and go, a man was seen coming in off a street entrance.

"That's him!" Smythe and Sims shouted together.

"Sounds like you're sure," commented Yvonne.

"It's him," repeated Smythe, as the bomber walked across the bus station. It was a wide view, and they watched him retrieve a briefcase from a storage locker, and leave through the 10th Street exit. Matt rewound the tape; and they all watched it again. It was grainy and in black-and-white; but there seemed to be no doubt, at least according to Smythe and Sims.

"That's the guy we saw," The Wiz said. "No doubt about it."

"O.K.," Matt said. "We'll get this to the lab and see if they can blow it up for us. We'll send out the sketch and a still picture from the video."

"Leftenant, he's using The System," Smythe said. "We know that. I'll bet he got off a westbound El at 11th Street."

"We'll definitely have pictures up there, and all over the rest of The System. Somebody else had to have seen him."

There was a knock at the door, and Sergeants Vargas and Gonzales and Detective Trung all walked in.

"Well, the gangs all here," Matt said. "Take a look at this, guys." He rewound and played the tape again.

"So that's out boy," remarked Julio.

"Picture ain't so great," commented Pablo.

"But it's him," said Winston. "We're sure of it."

"O.K.," Matt said. "We're all here. Let's have a sit-down."

They all took chairs around the gunmetal gray tables.

Matt briefly explained about the Andy's and Randy's on the list. "Pablo, you and Smythe take Fishtown; there's two names there. Julio, you and Nguyen take the four in Kensington. Yvonne and I will take Richmond. Whoever finishes first can start with Bridesburg."

"No stakeouts?" asked Julio.

"Not for ten days or so. I think we have a consensus on the fact that he's on a schedule. He won't be ready again for a couple of weeks." Matt looked around the room. "O.K., let's look at the tape again, and then I'll make a couple of copies of the sketch, and we can head on out."

They all watched the tape again, and then filed out of the room. Matt made copies of the sketch, and then compared them to the picture Doug Arnett and Rachel Conly were just finishing up. They were virtually identical.

"Yvonne, would you take Doug's statement, please?" Matt asked. "The rest of you can head out. Call on the radio if needed, and stay in touch."

Matt walked to Captain Parmalee's office, and quickly brought him up to speed. Parmalee came to the interrogation room and watched the tape.

"That's a break there, Matthew. A small one, but a break."

"Right. I'm gonna have the lab blow up the best still frame from the video."

"Why not have the sketch artist take it with her?" the Captain suggested. "That's the kind of stuff her office does. Save time."

They walked back into the squad room and Matt explained what they need to Conly.

"I'll have it done today," Rachel said.

"Please don't lose it," Matt said, as he quickly filled out the chain of custody paperwork.

"I am a cop, Lieutenant," said Rachel, as she signed the hand receipt.

"No offense meant," said Matt, somewhat abashed.

"None taken. I'll have the blowups to you later today. Those and the sketch flyers will start going out this afternoon, with copies to SEPTA and all other local police agencies."

"Thank you, Officer Conly."

"You're welcome." Conly started to make her way out, but stopped first at Pasqualez's desk, fiddling with her purse. Parmalee shook his head and laughed quietly, taking his leave.

Sergeant Gonzales waited next to the Crown Vic, while Smythe kissed his new found love good-bye. She had driven Winston and herself down to the station in her new Chevy Caprice. She got in it now and drove away.

Winston got in the unmarked car, and Pablo handed him the paper with the two names and addresses on it.

"You navigate," Pablo said.

"Righto."

"That's it? Righto?"

"Was there something else, Mate?"

"Something else, my ass! How'd it go last night?"

"Well," Winston began. "We actually saw the bastard, and he …"

"I know about that," Pablo interrupted impatiently. "But first things first, *Mate*. How'd the date go?"

Winston sighed, but happily. "Oh, very well. We had breakfast at my place, if you must know."

"I must, I must."

"That's all you'll get from me, Lad."

"Are you gonna see her again?"

"Hope to."

"Well, congratulations. It couldn't happen to a nicer guy. I mean that."

"Thank you, Pablo."

"You're welcome. NOW, tell me about the bomber."

"Fine. Head north on Delaware Avenue and I'll tell you all about it."

Pablo headed toward Fishtown as Winston gave him the lowdown on the previous nights festivities and fireworks.

"Dollars'll get you doughnuts he was on that northbound El," Pablo said.

"I agree," Winston replied. "Abeit without the disguise, of course."

"Right. But we know he's smart. He don't dump the disguise 'til he's clear. Too bad we couldn't have really searched that train. Frisked everybody on it."

"Citizens wouldn't stand for it, lad. Civil liberties and all that, you know."

"Yeah, yeah. Gimme the first address."

"Four-thirteen Livingston Street, off Columbia Avenue. Name's Andrew McNeese."

And Smythe and Gonzales marched on.

* * *

Sergeant Vargas and Detective Trung were traveling north on Aramingo Avenue.

"Twenty-one-ten Clearfield Street," said Nguyen, in response to a query from Julio. "A Randle Godder."

"O.K. I'll cut up Allegheny, cross over on Frankford Avenue, and come back down. Clearfield's one-way."

"You must have a map in your head," commented Nguyen.

"I been drivin' these streets as a cop for twenty-three years, kid. I do have a map in my head."

"So what's your take on last night?"

"I think Winston got laid."

Nguyen snorted laughter. "I mean the Bomber, my lame-brained Sergeant."

"Oh, that," Julio chuckled. "Well, we did everything right except catch the guy. I'll bet we even saw the guy and didn't know it."

"You think?"

"We definitely walked the same turf. Time frame's about right. I don't think our boy sat in that club all night drinkin' beer this time. Not with a hot pineapple in a briefcase." Julio turned left on Allegheny. He continued his thought. "Too much chance of mishap. CS is one thing. A grenade'll mess up your whole day."

"Powerful, huh?"

"You bet. One time in 'Nam, the guy in the hole next to me pulled the pin and threw one in a night fight. He shoulda waited a second or two after he pulled the pin. It hit a VC square on, about ten feet away. VC picks up the grenade and throws it right back in the guy's hole. A lucky throw. Next morning, after the battle, I look in the guy's hole. He was in pieces."

"Good Lord!"

Julio turned left on Frankford Avenue and then took the third left down. "Here we go. You do the talkin'. Consider it part of your trainin'."

"O.K."

Vargas parked the car, and they approached the house, which was on the south side of Clearfield, several addresses down from Amber Street. Nguyen knocked on the screen door. The main door was open; and they saw a woman get up from an armchair in the living room.

"Can I help you?" she asked.

They flashed badges. "I'm Detective Trung and this is Sergeant Vargas, Philadelphia Police. We'd like to speak to a Mister Randle Godder."

"I'm Amelia Godder, his wife. Is something wrong?"

"No ma'am. We're conducting an investigation and we need to ask him some questions."

"Who is it, Amelia?" a voice called from further back in the house. It was a typical row house for this part of the city. Narrow, but very deep.

"Police officers, dear." She turned back to the door. "Please come in."

"Thank you ma'am," Julio and Nguyen said in unison, stepping into the house.

Randle Godder came into the living room. He was six foot-three, and skinny as a rail. Both detectives groaned inwardly. This man did not come close to fitting the Bomber's description.

"Can I help you, Officers?" Godder said.

"You are Randle Godder?" asked Trung.

"That's me. Is there a problem?"

"No sir. Not now. We're working a case, and it has to do with people related to crime victims. We do have a suspect's description, and you don't come close to matching it. We won't take any more of your time."

"One question, please," said Vargas. "Were you related to Agnes Godder?"

Godder's face fell; and he quickly sat down on a couch. His wife moved to his side and took his hand.

"Officer," she said. "Agnes was raped and killed six years ago. It was a very difficult time; and we're still not over it. Is this really necessary?"

"No ma'am," said Trung quickly. "As I said, not now. We're very sorry to have bothered you. We'll be going."

Vargas and Trung quickly made their way out and headed for the car. Once inside, they sat silently for a moment.

Vargas sighed. "Shit. Gimme the next address."

"This is not a pleasant experience."

"You can say that again, my Vietnamese friend."

* * *

Gallagher and Wallace had interviewed two men who did not match the Bomber's description, and now were driving north on Richmond Street.

"What's the address again?" Matt asked Yvonne.

"Twenty-seven-thirty-one Wensley. Should be right past Westmoreland Street."

Matt was driving for a change. He turned right on Wensley and parked the Crown Vic. They found the address on the northwest corner. A bar, the S & B, was attached to the side of the house. They walked up the steps and rang the bell. No answer. Matt knocked hard.

"Looks like nobody's home," said Yvonne.

"Let's check the bar. Maybe somebody knows the guy."

They walked down to the sidewalk and entered the bar. A young black woman was bartending.

"What'll it be, folks?" she asked.

"Two Yuengling Lager drafts, if you got it," said Matt.

"We got it." Theresa Barnes quickly pulled two beers, and turned back to Yvonne and Matt. And two police badges were being held up.

"I'm Lieutenant Gallagher and this is Sergeant Wallace. Would you happen to know the person who lives upstairs, a Randy Macjewski?"

"I sure do," Theresa said.

"That would be me, Officers," said Randy, sidling up to the bar. "Can I help you?"

Matt's antenna quivered. Right height, right build. *Right height. Right build. Slowly. Go slowly.*

"We'd like to ask you a few questions," said Yvonne.

"Sure thing," Randy said. "Although I should warn you, I've had more than a few today. Saturday's my drinkin' day."

"No problem," said Matt. "We'll join you. Let's grab a table."

"O.K."

The group walked to the back and grabbed an empty spot near the pool table. They all sat down.

"So," said Randy. "What can I do for you?" *It's a good thing,* Randy reminded himself, *that I don't blush or sweat. This is not a coincidence.*

"This is gonna get a little personal," Yvonne began. "But we're conducting an investigation, and we have to ask."

"Ask away," said Randy, outwardly calm.

"Your father was killed by muggers in July of Nineteen Sixty-Eight, correct?"

Randy looked down for a second, and then visibly collected himself. He took a swallow of beer.

"Yeah, that's right. They never caught the guys. Are you re-opening the case?"

"It was never closed," Matt said. "That case was worked out of The Twenty-Third District, I would think."

"Well, now that I remember, that's right. After about six months the calls to my mother stopped, and the papers moved on to other news. I pestered the cops for about two years; and they always said the same thing. 'The investigation was continuing'."

"Must've been rough," Yvonne said.

They all took another gulp of beer.

"It was. It killed my mother. Literally. She died in Nineteen Seventy-Six. 'Of natural causes', they said. But those muggers killed her the day they killed my father."

"You sound bitter." Matt immediately regretted saying it.

"Bitter!" exclaimed Randy incredulously. "You gotta be kidding me! I've never not been bitter about it."

"O.K." Matt held up his hands in a conciliatory gesture. "That was a stupid thing to say."

"I'll buy that, Lieutenant," replied Randy. "What the hell's all this about anyway?"

Yvonne looked at Matt, who nodded. It was time.

"We're investigating the case of the Booby-Trap Bomber," said Yvonne. "You've heard of it?"

"Who hasn't," said Randy. "I've been in here all day; and it's been on all the news reports. I even saw your press conference, Lieutenant."

"Alright then," Matt started in. "Let's get to it. We think the guy is related to a past crime victim; and we think he's on a vengeance kick. That's the angle we're taking. And that's why we're here."

Several patrons were openly listening to the conversation now. The bar had gotten quiet. Mike Reilly, the weekend night bartender who had stayed over to drink some beers with Randy, drifted over.

"Everything O.K., Boss?" he asked Randy.

"Boss?" echoed Matt and Yvonne.

"Yeah, I own the place." Randy looked at Mike. "Everything's fine, Mike."

"Right, Boss." Reilly walked off.

"O.K.," Randy said. "Again, what's this got to do with me?"

Yvonne picked it up. "We're talking to lots of people who have close relatives who were crime victims. You just happen to be one of them."

"Yeah, well, it was twenty-five years ago. I'll never forget it; but the details are blurry. One minute I'm patching up grunts in Vietnam, and the next minute I'm at my father's funeral."

"You were in 'Nam?" Matt asked.

"Yeah. January Sixty-Eight to January Sixty-Nine. I was a medic. I got compassionate leave when my father was killed."

Matt jumped. It was time again. "Did you know Dickie Howsten?"

"How the hell did you know that?" asked Randy, genuinely surprised.

"We're asking the questions," Matt said. "So you knew him?"

"Yeah, we met in 'Nam. He died two years ago. Had all kinds of cancer. Agent Orange was what did it."

"You sound sure," Yvonne said.

Randy motioned to the bar. "Theresa, grab three of these off the ice, please." He turned back to Gallagher and Wallace. "Yeah, I'm sure. We used to get soaking wet with the shit. I'm clean myself; but I get lab work done once a year. I'm sure it's just a matter of time."

Matt kept at it. "Did Howsten have weapons in the house? Weapons he shipped home from 'Nam?"

"Not to my knowledge."

"We know you were a regular visitor at his bedside during his last few months. You never saw any 'mementos' from the battlefield?"

"If he had anything like that, I never saw it. Shit, he didn't even keep his medals, just like that guy Kerry. He threw them away."

The fresh beers arrived. Matt pulled out a ten. Randy waved it away but Matt tucked it into Theresa's apron.

"We always pay our way," Matt said. "Keep the change, Miss," he added.

"Thank you, sir," said Theresa, moving away. She never turned down a tip.

"Wait a minute," Randy said. "You said you knew I spent a lot of time with Dickie in the end. I did. He was my friend. But how did you know that? That was two years ago."

"Like I said," Matt repeated. "We'll ask the questions. You ever meet Nicky Scarfo, by the way?"

Randy snorted beer. "Nicky Scarfo! You gotta be kiddin'. He sure don't hang around this end of town. Besides, I'm a Pollock for Christ's sake."

They all laughed at this.

"Look, Officers. I don't know what you're looking for; but I ain't got it. I'm pretty toasted; and some of my customers are gettin' nervous. Is there any way I can really help you?"

Matt took a long swallow of beer, and abruptly stood up.

"We're done here, Mr. Macjewski. Here's my card. If you ever wanna talk to us, about Dickie Howsten say, give us a call."

"Don't keep the lines open, Lieutenant. Like you said, we're done here." Randy also rose from his chair and gave Gallagher a long, hard, unwavering look. Then he turned away and slapped four quarters on the pool table.

* * *

Yvonne got behind the wheel. She waited until they were southbound on Richmond Street.

"Whaddya think?" she asked.

"He lied towards the end. When I asked about weapons at Howsten's house, he said 'not to my knowledge'. He said it too quickly, too succinctly. Nobody answers a question like that if they're telling the truth. A normal response would've been, 'I never saw any', or 'how the hell would I know, I didn't poke around his closets'."

"You don't think he's our guy, do you?"

"I don't know. But we can't watch everybody, so I'm gonna watch him. We know Howsten sold an AK to Scarfo. On his deathbed he don't tell his bosom buddy that? Bullshit! Macjewski at least knows about that. And remember. Johnny G said Howsten had an arsenal. Where's the rest of it? I'll bet Macjewski knows somethin' about that, too. I'm gonna put some more of Halston's and Robinson's people in plainclothes, and watch him for awhile. We'll see what happens. Let's get to the shop. I can't talk to any more civilians anyway. Not with all this beer on my breath."

They drove back to The 3/4.

CHAPTER EIGHTEEN

When Gallagher and Wallace got back to the shop, Matt called Lieutenants Halston and Robinson at home, and got permission, a courtesy really, to use four more uniformed officers for his tail on Macjewski. He would put them in plainclothes. Robinson gave him Officers Eugene Naples and Sheila Marrows. Halston gave him Officers Maccahriah Stone and Joseph Caldwell. Matt then called over to The 17th District, and got Sergeant Bruno Mitelli on the horn.

"How many this time, Matthew?" asked Mitelli, getting right to the point.

"Bruno, I gotta put a tail on a guy. Call it a hunch or whatever. But we both know it eats up manpower. I hate to ask; but it's a lead I really need to follow up." Matt then explained to Mitelli about Randy Macjewski and his ties to Dickie Howsten, who had sold a weapon to Nicky Scarfo.

"Why not get a search warrant on Macjewski?" asked Mitelli, trying to postpone the inevitable.

"I don't have any kind of probable cause. That's why I want the tail. Then if he sneezes in the wrong direction, I can write it up and submit for a warrant."

"Alright, Matt, we're a little slow over here. How about I give ya Canatta and his partner Ruth Netters. They're both good dicks, and Alphonse was in on the first break ya got."

"O.K.," Matt said. "But then I'll still need two more."

"Alright," said Mittelli. "Lemme check the duty rosters and run everything by Captain Summers. I'll get back to ya later this afternoon. When do you need 'em?"

"I wanna start the tail Monday morning at 6:00 A.M. I figure with eight people, they can go twelve hour shifts, with four on/three off, three on/four off. That way they won't get too burned out. I'd like to have them all here tomorrow at noon for a meet so I can set everything up."

"O.K., Matthew. I'll get back to you."

"Thanks, Bruno." Matt hung up the phone.

A few minutes later a courier arrived with a package from the Delanco Township Police of New Jersey. Sergeant Wallace signed for the package and brought it to Matt's desk. Matt unsealed the package and for the next half-hour they buried their noses in the reports.

Explosive, definitely a hand grenade. The deceased died of massive trauma to their torsos. The handle of the briefcase had been found, but no visible prints were found on it, or the other small pieces of the briefcase that had been recovered.

"Same as last time," Matt said. "No prints other than the victims'."

"He's gotta be using gloves," commented Yvonne.

"Yeah, but in summer heat they'd be a dead giveaway. If he's using 'em, they must be flesh colored and skin-tight. Wait a sec." Gallagher flicked his squad radio to the Three-Four frequency.

"Gallagher to Smythe."

"Smythe here, Leftenant."

"Winston, as we all know, our man's gotta be wearing some type of gloves. Did you see any on him?"

"No, Matt. Not the obvious type anyway."

"O.K. Thanks." Matt turned to Yvonne. "He probably wears latex gloves when he sets the bomb, and then puts on another pair with his disguise. You can get that kinda stuff at any theatrical makeup store, the kind that would look natural."

"Yeah," said Yvonne. "Anything on the make and model of the briefcase?"

"Says here the make was Samsung, business model eleven-ten. According to this, they were manufactured by the hundreds of thousands. Dollars will get you doughnuts he got it second hand, like at a yard sale. No receipt, no record of the buy."

"Well," said Yvonne. "Somebody saw this guy before the hit, when he was on his way to Dave and Buster's. The flyers will help a little bit."

"Yeah, we'll see. Meantime he sets up another bombing. What's next? A claymore?"

* * *

Little did Matt know, a claymore was exactly what was next. Randy Macjewski sat at his bar and pondered the events of the last two days. *They weren't on to him,* he thought. If he were a suspect, they would've hauled him in for questioning. No, he was willing to bet they just got lucky on the Dickie Howsten lead. Then his name must have popped up on some list of past crime victims.

But still, they came to talk to him; and that meant something. He would stick to his game plan; but he would be extra alert. He wondered if they would follow him. That would take a lot of manpower, he knew. Well, let them. For six or seven weeks he would lay low. Then, in late August, he would rig a laptop computer briefcase with a claymore. He had two, compliments of Dickie Howsten. Soon, there would be one left.

* * *

Task Force Gallagher finished all their interviews, and were all back in the squad room by 6:00 P.M. Sergeant Mitelli had called Matt back earlier in the afternoon, and had given him Officers Nellie White and Joseph Rittles for his tail team. Matt called all eight officers for the tail detail, and told them to report to him at noon the following day. Gallagher informed the rest of the crew about his and Yvonne's interview with Randle Macjewski, and his plans for the tail.

"I say, Leftenant," Smythe piped up. "What say I pop over for a brew, and get a look at the bloke."

"Not now, Winston. He'll smell trouble if he's our man. I want him to feel like he's still safe. Then maybe he'll make a mistake with our tail on him, and we can take it from there. Alright, folks," Matt finished up. "I'm outta here. I'm goin' down to the Vet tonight. I want everybody to read the report from the New Jersey folks. Anybody need me, squawk on squad."

Matt turned to Yvonne. "Wanna go tonight?"

"No, I can't make it. I've got dinner with my parents tonight; and I'd never hear the end of it if I didn't make it."

"O.K. Take the Vic home, and I'll see you Monday."

'That's alright. I've got my wheels. They've been sitting in the parking lot all week. They probably miss me."

"Suit yourself," Matt laughed. "Good night, everybody."

Gallagher walked out of the squad room, and headed for the Broad Street Subway stop at Tasker Street. He'd be way early; but it had been awhile since he caught batting practice and warmups. If the Commissioner was at the game, he would touch base with him and bring him up to date.

* * *

Randy Macjewski, by now plenty inebriated, left his bar and went upstairs and crashed on his couch. He would fall asleep watching the Fightin' Phils on TV. He had no way of knowing that his nemesis would be at the game.

* * *

Gallagher was in his seat at the Vet by 6:35 P.M. Batting practice was just finishing up; and players from both teams were stretching and warming up all over the field.

Matt sipped a cup of Schlitz and pondered the case, especially the events of the past two days. He doubted he had gotten so lucky that Randy Macjewski was the bomber; but it was the first real connection in the case, and pursuing it also gave him the sense he was doing something progressive.

Matt looked down at the Commissioner's box from his two hundred level seat. Sure enough, Augustus Phillips, the Philadelphia Police Commissioner and his bodyguard, Nat Holmes, were just settling into their seats. Matt finished his beer and headed down.

"Matthew, lad," boomed the commissioner. "How's my favorite Lieutenant?"

"If the Lieutenants Association heard you say that, they'd tear up my membership card."

"Fuck 'em if they can't take a joke. Siddown, son."

"Thank you, sir." Matt relaxed in the comfortable seat.

"Brewski?" asked Phillips.

"Sure, Boss," Matt replied, taking the proffered ice cold Schlitz. "Thanks."

"How ya' doin', Loo?" asked Nat Homes.

"Fine Nat. You never sleep, do you?"

"It just seems that way, Loo. But the duty's great; and I couldn't ask for a better boss."

"Why thank you, Nathan," said the Commissioner. "You got an eval coming up or something?"

"No, sir," Nat said, as he and Matt both laughed. "Just callin' 'em like I see 'em."

"That's a good lad," said Phillips, joining in the laughter. "So Lieutenant," he said, turning to Matt. "Last night must've been rough. I've read the reports; but tell me all about it anyway."

Matt recounted the past evening's happenings, and also threw in the information about the bus station video and the report from the Delanco Township Police, and the tail he was putting on Macjewski. He then sighed and took a long pull of beer.

"And sigh you might," commented Phillips. "You guessed right on the stakeouts; and the bastard still beat you." The Commissioner pulled no punches with anybody, favorite or not.

"Yeah," said Matt. "That rankles real deep."

"That tail's gonna eat up a lot of manpower, Matthew."

"Yessir, I know. If you think I'm chasing shadows, I'll pull it."

"Lieutenant, I've never second-guessed you before, and I'm not gonna start now. It's a lead you gotta do something with. I was just talkin' like the old desk jockey I've become."

A surge of cheering and laughter from the crowd drew their attention to the field. The Phillie Phanatic, the best mascot in any sport, was making his first appearance of the night.

"By the way," said Phillips. "Has Chief Barnes been giving you any trouble?"

"Funny you should ask," replied Matt. "At first he hovered around, and I thought it was gonna be a real problem. But the last time I saw 'im, he had mellowed out a bit. Even Captain Parmalee was surprised."

"Humph," grunted the Commissioner. "Mellow is a word I never would have thought to hear about that dude. He'll make some political capital outta this caper, one way or another. Anyway, if he becomes too much of a pain in the ass, call me. That's an order."

"Yessir."

"'Nother beer?"

"No thank you. I have to pee as it is. Please excuse me, and enjoy the game."

"Night, Matt."

"Later, Loo," chimed in Holmes.

Matt made his way up to the concourse, and joined a line for the bathroom. Even though no one had come right out and said it, he knew this case could break his career. He could deal with leaving the force; but he wanted it to be on his terms.

Matt went back to his seat to watch the game. And it was a gem. Tommy Greene gave up two runs and struck out eight. He was now eight and oh, the best start for a Phillies pitcher in years. Pete Incaviglia went three for four, Dave Hollins hit his ninth homer, and the Phillies beat the Rockies six-to-two.

Matt took the subway back to the Three-Four, and took his official Crown Vic home to Roxborough. He was coming back in tomorrow, a Sunday, and traffic would be light.

* * *

June 6th, 1993

At noon the next day Gallagher had his tail detail in the interrogation room for a briefing. He passed out info sheets on Macjewski.

"Most of you know me. For those who don't, I'm Lieutenant Matt Gallagher. I need a twenty-four hour tail on an individual. He's a possible suspect in the Bobby-Trap Bomber case. I say possible, because it is a slim lead I'm going on." Matt then brought all the newcomers up to speed on the case. Then he handed out the schedule he had made up earlier that morning. He also handed out the work schedule for Task Force Gallagher's original people.

"As you can see I've set it up for four on/three off, three on/four off. I've put the more experienced people on the night shift because that's when things have been happening. This is a covert tail. If he makes you, fine. But don't make it easy for him. What I'm looking for is probable cause for a search warrant. If he does something criminal, take him down. If you see him disguised, take him down. Otherwise, just tail him. The Bomber will be due around the July Fourth holiday weekend. If Macjewski's our man, we might catch 'im in the act. The tail is your number one priority. But for those of you new to this type of duty, be advised; if you see a crime in progress along the way, you must act. The tail can always be picked back up. Any questions?"

"Yeah, Loo," said Nellie White from The 17th District. "Could you please clarify the last part about a crime in progress?"

"Sure," said Matt. "Say you're tailin' the suspect down Hunting Park Avenue. You're stopped at a light. You see a mugging go down. Forget the tail, and go after the perp. If you can't reacquire the tail, go to his neighborhood or his place of work, which by the way is Tastykake on Hunting Park Avenue. Wait on him and start over."

"Thanks, Loo."

"Anybody else? No? O.K." Matt continued. "I want everybody to have their car radios on Central Dispatch, and your squawkers on Three-Four frequency. Even off duty I'll have my squawker on the Three-Four. I'll have it in bed with me."

That brought some laughter.

"I'm serious. I'm an old Army RTO. If you call me when I'm asleep, I'll hear it. Otherwise, I'll sleep right thru the chatter. I'm call sign zero-zero-two. Your collective call sign is Tail Detail. Or just call me by name. I will answer. Anything else?"

When no one responded, Matt finished up. "I strongly suggest you night shift folks stay up thru tonight, and get to sleep around 7:00 A.M. or so. That's the quickest way to acclimate yourself. That's it."

As they were filing out of the interrogation room, Matt touched Detective Canatta lightly on the shoulder.

"Alphonse? A word, please."

"Yeah, Loo. What's up?"

"I just wanted to thank you for the job you did on Gerald Hanson. That was huge."

"No sweat, Loo. Glad I could help."

"O.K. Be careful out there."

"Always."

* * *

Matt cleared his desk and headed for the Broad Street Subway. The Fightins had an afternoon game. Schilling had the pill on the hill. He was seven and one, and the Phils were thirty-seven and sixteen with a comfortable lead over the Cardinals. The town was definitely buzzing about the team. It was making for an exciting summer.

* * *

At 2:15 P.M., game time, Deputy Chief William "Butthole" Barnes popped a Schmidt's, and settled in to watch the Phillies on TV. He was mulling over his recent change in strategy regarding the Booby-Trap Bomber Case.

Inspector Loudin's thunderous warning about interference was seventy percent of the reason for the change. The rest of it was strategy. He would lull Task Force Gallagher to sleep with his non-presence. His stoolie at The 3/4, Detective Sergeant Mike Shincock of Narcotics, kept him fairly well briefed. Shincock was retired-on-active-duty, just waiting to put in his papers. Shincock had informed Barnes about the pending tail on Randy Macjewski. Barnes would monitor the Three-Four on his squawker. The first time he heard anything concrete, he would swoop in, arrest Macjewski and get a search warrant for his house. He would beat Saint Matthew Gallagher. Oh yes. He would beat him, and beat him badly.

* * *

Mary Anne Sims lay contentedly in Winston Smythe's arms. Earlier, Smythe had made them one of his artery-hardening English breakfasts. Winston was lightly snoring.

She had always played the loud, profane career woman. That drove a lot of potential suitors away, which was what she intended. She was so much into her work as the top computer geek for The Philadelphia Police Department, that she had no chance for romance. Or so she thought. *And then along came Limey,* she laughed to herself. The only explanation she could get out of him was that it was love at first sight.

She wasn't ready to use the "L" word yet on her part; but, like the old commercial said, it sure was a real hankerin'. She wondered what Task Force Gallagher and the other cops were saying. She didn't particularly care, but she was curious. She giggled to herself as she drifted off to sleep. *The Limey and The Wiz. Whooda thunk?*

* * *

June 10th,1993

Detectives Ruth Netters and Alphonse Canatta sat in their unmarked Crown Victoria, halfway down the 3300 block of Richmond Street. Macjewski's house, on the northeast corner of Wensley Street, was clearly visible, as was the bar. Earlier in the week, Officers Eugene Naples and Sheila Marrows had ascertained that there were two ways from the house to the bar; out the front, walking down the steps, around the wall and into the bar; or exiting the house from the basement in back, and walking around the opposite side to the bar entrance.

It had been an uneventful week so far for the stakeout teams. The mortal enemy of surveillance teams everywhere, boredom, had settled in early in the stakeout. Lots of coffee was not an option, as it would mean lots of latrine calls.

Canatta sighed, long and loud. Netters just chuckled.

"That sigh is worth more than a thousand words," said Ruth. "I'm as bored as you are."

"Yeah. So far this guy's clean as a whistle. Doesn't even jaywalk."

Ruth laughed again. "So what's your take on all this anyway? Not just the stakeout, but the whole case."

"I don't know, really. Ya gotta figure the Bomber, whoever he is, is whacked out. He knows he'll be caught, sooner or later. And these aren't firecrackers he's playing with. Maybe he'll do us all a favor and blow himself up."

"Well," said Ruth, "the general thinking is, he's gonna keep doin' it. Or at least, like you said, 'til he gets caught or hurt."

"I remember a class at the Academy. Some psychiatrist came in to talk about serial criminals."

"We had it too," said Ruth.

"Right. Anyways, he said something to the effect that, the more their insanity progressed, the harder they are to catch. Up to a point, anyway. Eventually the real looney tunes start leaving love notes at the crime scene or they start writing letters to the editors. But some don't wanna be caught. They either stop, or go underground for a time to get the heat off."

"Where you headin' with this?"

"The Bomber isn't leavin' any messages at the scene or writing to the papers. No strange phone calls, no nothin'. I don't think he wants to get caught; but I think he doesn't care if he does. He's careful and smart; and I think the only way we're gonna catch him is luck, or a tip from a citizen. Anyways, that's my opinion."

"One I happen to agree with," said Ruth. "Mind if I turn on the Fightins?"

"Gawhead. Who they playin'?"

"The Mets. Tommy Green's on the hill with the pill."

"He's undefeated, ain't he?"

"Yeah. Leads the majors in ERA, too."

"You sound like a serious fan," Canatta said. "How come I never noticed before?"

"Number one, we were always working cases, doin' paperwork or somethin' to that effect. Two, you put a wall up between us. You might not know you're doin' it, but it's there."

"No," Al responded. "I know I'm doin' it. Especially around beautiful women. And you don't have to be Sigmund Frickin' Freud to figure out why." Canatta was referring, of course, to the vicious acne that covered the top one-third of his body.

"You think I'm beautiful?"

"Gorgeous."

Ruth blushed and smiled at her partner. "Please continue."

They were both peripherally aware of the background noise from the Phillies game on the radio. Greene was getting pounded; and Fregosi was on his way to the mound. Goodnight, Tommy.

"I'm not looking for pity," Al said. "But my adolescence was brutal. I had two dates in my life before I joined The Department. Naturally, I got an inferiority complex. And I don't imagine that people talk about old Pus Face. I know they do."

"The Vitamin A regimen and those wipes I gave you seem to be working."

"Actually, they are. But even so, my dermatologist warned me. After the acne's gone, I'll have craters to rival the moon. It ain't easy knowin' you're ugly and it can't be fixed."

"Give it time, Al," said Ruth. "And I don't think you're ugly."

"Well," he said. "You been straight with me so far, so I'll take that little compliment and run with it."

They both laughed.

"So you really are a big sports fan?" asked Al.

"Sure. I grew up that way. My brother and father were fanatics. I mean everything. The Flyers, Sixers, the Iggles, the Fightins. And they all golfed. Even my Mom golfed. So I had a club in one hand and a bat in the other almost before I could walk."

"You golf?"

"Yeah, you?"

"Yep. I'm not very good. Average, I guess."

"How about we go tomorrow? We got a couple days off."

"O.K.," Al said. "But let's make it right after work. I wanna keep my circadian on the same sheet of music, even when we're off."

She gave him a playful look. "Say what?"

"We're working nights. So even when we're off, I'll still sleep in the daytime.

"Oh. Ya coulda said so without the big words."

They both laughed again.

"Are you any good?" Al asked.

"I break ninety on a regular basis."

"Well, we won't be makin' any wagers on this little match. I struggle to break a hundred."

"No competition," said Ruth. "We just go for fun. Try to beat the course and not each other."

"Sounds good … oop, there he is. Comin' outta the bar."

"Yep, and right up the stairs and into the house. We'd better move in closer, in case he decides to go on a little trip."

"Right."

Canatta started the Crown Vic, and they moved almost to the corner. Their report from Task Force Gallagher had the info on Macjewksi's cars. He drove a '98 black Mustang and a 1985 blue Olds '98. Al pulled up so they could see both automobiles, and parked.

Al sighed again. It was gonna be a long night; but at least he had good company. He hoped she thought so, too.

June 18th,1993

Philadelphia Police Detective Nguyen Trung of The 3/4 District and member of Task Force Gallagher, leaned back in his chair and relaxed. He faced a slightly raised dais. At a long table on the dais sat the three professors from The University of Pennsylvania who were hearing Trung's oral exam for his PhD in International Relations. Trung had passed his written exam on June 4th with flying colors. In fact, he had maxed it.

Nguyen had just finished an hour long dissertation on the military role of the United Nations in the world today. It was a masterpiece. Nguyen knew it, and the professors knew it. But they weren't finished just yet.

The three grillers briefly conferred among themselves. They were Professors Nathaniel Boxcott, Cassandra Hawkins, and Stanton Bearclaw. They were the Department Chairpersons, respectively, of History, International Affairs, and Political Science.

Professor Hawkins took a sip of water from her glass and then looked at Nguyen. "Mister Trung," she said. "You pointedly left out the current situation in Somalia. Why?"

Trung put his own water glass down on the small table at which he sat. He took a deep breath and gathered his thoughts.

"I did leave that out purposely, ma'am. The fluidity of the situation is extremely dynamic. And, as we all know, very explosive. There is no government whatsoever; and the country as a whole is arguably the most lawless place on the planet today. UN peacekeepers are routinely attacked and killed, as are aid workers. The situation will, in my opinion, take years to play out."

There was a pause. Professor Boxcott stirred. "How do you see the role of the United States in the present situation?"

"Sir, I would hesitate to speculate on that at the present time."

"Humor us," said Professor Bearclaw. He was the highest ranking Native American ever at Penn, and was widely respected throughout the University. Rumor had it that the presidency of the University was his for the taking when the incumbent stepped down.

"Yessir," replied Trung. He took another deep breath. "The U.S. presence is large and growing. As is usually the case, the U.S. has massed massive firepower to back troops in the area. At the airport in Mogadishu where the U.S. forces are camped, the Army troops are backed by a sizable helicopter assault force. There is a Marine Amphibious Assault Ship off shore. This is basically a mini-aircraft carrier, with all that implies. Also, the Persian Gulf is about a thousand miles away, as the crow flies. There are two carrier groups there that could provide more assistance as needed."

"So, you are up on the situation," commented Professor Hawkins.

"Yes ma'am. But there is a problem inherent in the whole force makeup."

"And that is?"

"There's nothing to attack. There are no armed forces in Somalia. It's total anarchy. Eight year olds carry assault rifles. Fifteen and sixteen year olds man fifty-caliber machine guns on pickup trucks. These are called "Technicals." I read where one UN observer commented that there are more RPG's—rocket propelled grenades—and launchers in Somalia than in any other country on Earth. While it is surely an exaggeration, it underscores the point. Who do you go after? There are scores of opposing factions and warlords. So if the UN and the U.S. forces want to stop the chaos and the killing, they'll have to go after the warlords. And each of the warlords has hundreds, if not thousands of loyal followers, many of them women and children, and all of them concentrated in small population centers and refugee camps."

"Your point, please" said Professor Hawkins, not unkindly.

"If the United States goes after individual warlords, they'll do so with a large, heavily armed force in convoys. And if they get in trouble, the air power available to them would have to wipe out large numbers of innocent civilians to help them. And I don't see that happening. The U.S. is not going to kill massive numbers of women and children with air strikes. Same with artillery. It's not going to happen. At some point, I see a battalion size force of U.S. soldiers being trapped in the middle of a large number of people; and I believe they'll take very heavy casualties before they can be extracted."

After a bit, Professor Bearclaw cleared his throat. He looked uncomfortable. They all did.

"You've done your homework, Mister Trung. I have a nephew in the Army Rangers; and he's over there. I happen to agree with your analysis of the situation. Let's hope it doesn't come to pass in quite that way."

"Well," said Professor Boxcott, who was the senior faculty member of the three. "I think we are done here. However, I have a personal question to ask, Mr. Trung. And of course, you are under no obligation to answer."

"Please," said Nguyen.

"Briefly tell me how your police career is going. And if you do indeed plan to make it a career."

"Well," said Nguyen. "It certainly is an ongoing learning experience."

Everyone laughed lightly at this.

"I work for the best cop in the city—Lieutenant Matthew Gallagher. I am a member of Task Force Gallagher, which you might know is investigating the Booby-Trap Bomber case. I learn new things every day. As for a career, I am definitely leaning that way. It has been intimated to me that I have a very promising career path ahead of me, despite my ethnic background."

"Has that been a problem?" asked Professor Bearclaw.

"Not with the group I work with. But I've been told—unofficially of course—that there will be some very hard walls to knock down. I will deal with that as it comes."

"Thank you, Detective Trung," said Professor Boxcott. "You will, of course, be hearing from us."

"Thank you sirs, ma'am." Nguyen drained his water glass and took his leave. He exited the building on Locust Street, and headed east to 40th Street. He then turned north, and headed for the subway entrance at 40th and Market. He whistled as he walked. He had done well and he knew it. Mother and Father would be pleased.

CHAPTER NINETEEN

July 1st, 1993

Task Force Gallagher was assembled in the interrogation room of the Thee-Four District. It was 2:30 P.M. All members were present, except Officers Nellie White and Joshua Rittles. They had daytime tail on Randy Macjewski this day. The room was definitely crowded. A half-dozen people were standing along the walls.

"I'd like to thank the people who came in on their off-day," Matt Gallagher began. "But I believe it's just about time for our lunatic to strike again. That is, if he sticks to what I believe is his schedule. I'm trying to get into this head; and I believe he'll feel this is the perfect time to strike. Half the city will be away somewhere for the 4th of July holiday. A lotta cops will be on vacation or off for the long weekend."

Matt paused and consulted his notes.

"The tail detail, of course, will stay as is. I've settled on three new stakeout areas. My stakeout teams will work through the holiday weekend. This will mean overtime. You don't have to put in for it. I've cleared it with the Captain. It's already been approved."

Matt paused again.

"I know that for Detectives Smythe, Gonzales, Vargas, and Trung, this will be a little rough; but it can't be helped. This should be his time; and I need you out there. The stakeout areas will be these: Sergeant Vargas and Detective Trung will be assigned to the Grant Avenue train station in the Northeast. There's been a series of late night muggings there recently. Sergeant Gonzales and Detective Smythe will be at the long-term parking lot at Philadelphia International Airport. In the last two months or so, despite internal security, late night travelers have been getting mugged there. Sergeant Wallace and I will be at the Franklin Mills Mall, also in the Northeast. Shoppers have been getting hit at night in those huge parking lots."

Matt stopped once again to look at his notes.

"I've written up a little synopsis on the three scenarios for the stake-out teams. I'd like everybody set up around sunset. When not doing that, we'll continue to work on the victims list. It's a drag, I know; but we have to keep plugging away. Any questions?"

Detective Alphonse Canatta, a tail team member on loan from The 17th District, raised his hand.

"Gawhead, Al."

"Yeah, Loo. I was wonderin'. Has anybody been inside Tastykake, where Macjewski works?"

"Good question, Al," Matt replied, as several heads nodded in agreement.

"I gave that some thought, earlier, "Matt continued. "I decided against it, because no matter how discreet we would be, I'm sure Macjewski would get wind of it; and again, I don't want to spook him. Once he's there for the day, we know where he is. Even if he sneaks out, he'd have to get to his wheels. Unless he's got another car stashed around there somewhere. And I kinda doubt that."

"O.K., Loo."

"Anybody else?" Matt pointed to a raised hand. "Gawhead, Ruth," he said to Detective Netters.

"Anything ever come of the print dusting at the bus station locker?"

"No," Matt replied. "Nothing from our lab or even from the FBI lab in D.C. I must've forgotten to mention that." he said, embarrassed.

There were good-natured smiles around the room. Everybody made mistakes. Even Gallagher The Great.

"Anything else," Matt asked.

There were no takers.

"O.K., that's it. As per usual, keep Sergeant Johnson and Detective Robinson informed and up to date. Thank you."

As everyone started filing out of the interrogation room, Matt tapped Detective Trung lightly on the shoulders."

"Nguyen. A word, please."

Trung waited till everyone left, and closed the door.

"What's up, Lieutenant?"

"Nguyen, I'm sorry; but I've been really busy. But I didn't forget. How'd the oral exams go?"

Trung hadn't let anyone know because, like Gallagher, he nev his own horn. Unless someone asked. Then he was all musi

"I did really well, Loo. I haven't heard the results won't be any surprises."

"Good," said Matt. "But do me a favor. When you find out, let me know."

"Will do, Boss."

"Thanks. See ya later."

Matt walked out to this desk. Yvonne Wallace, at her desk next to Matt's, was scrutinizing their portion of the crime victims list.

"Where do you wanna start on this today?" she asked.

"We'll pick that up tomorrow morning," Matt said. "Let's take our midday break and get some rest before tonight." Since Matt and Yvonne started early in the day, they had been taking afternoons off when they were on stakeout duty.

"Alright," Yvonne said.

"I'll take the Vic home, and pick you up tonight at your place in Morrell Park around seven-forty-five."

"O.K. See you then." Yvonne grabbed her things and headed out. Matt straightened up his desk, and then grabbed the keys to his Crown Victoria. He stopped at Sergeant Eileen Johnson's desk and told her he'd be home and then on his stakeout later that night.

"Be careful," she said.

As he was leaving he called out, "How'd they do last night, Jack?"

Detective Jack Miles, like just about everyone there, was a Phillies fan and kept up on the results for Matt. "They got waxed boss, nine-to-three. The Cards were all over Tommy Greene. St. Louis scored five in the bottom of the fifth."

"Who did the damage?"

"Mark Whiten had a homer and four reebees," replied Miles.

"Greene got roughed up, huh?"

"Yeah. He only lasted five innings. Still, he's nine and two. And the Fightins are still on top by six and a half games."

"All right. Later, everybody." Matt left to a chorus of good byes.

* * *

Clevus Capstone—reporter, bigot, muckraker, entrepreneur—sat at his desk putting the finishing touches on next week's edition of Pissed Off at Whitey, or *POW* as it was more commonly known, a black run, and mostly black read, newspaper. The lead article was a particularly vitriolic diatribe against The Philadelphia Police Department in general, and Task Force Gallagher in particular. There had apparently been no real progress in the Booby-Trap Bomber investigation, even after the second incident down at Penn's Landing.

Truth be told—and he made no secret of this—he was happy that the white fucking lunatic had taken out two honkeys this time. But he was a realist. He knew that if they didn't catch this guy, he would eventually hurt more black people, even if they were thugs.

Which led to another thing. Lawrence Steele, the president of the Philadelphia Chapter of the NAACP, and Reverend Marvin Jefferson Quintade, the head of the First African American Church of Philadelphia, had been strangely silent lately.

When the bomber had blown up those young black kids, allegedly members of the Booze Bandits Gang, Steele and Quintade had been in the forefront of black outrage, parading before the news cameras. But when the white assholes from New Jersey had been blown up (hallelujah and amen, brother), they had been quiet.

Clevus saw it as an opportunity to rage against the machine some more. But not those Uncle Tommys. Hypocritical, self-righteous motherfuckers! Well, he let them have it in his article, too. He had enough hate to spread around. And in the end, that was the only game in town. Hate sold these newspapers.

* * *

Tony Brice, police beat reporter for *The Daily News*, was bored. He wanted some information on the Booby-Trap Bomber case; but there was none forthcoming. Calls to Task Force Gallagher had elicited little more response than "the investigation is continuing."

Well, he had had enough of that shit. He opened a lower drawer in his desk and pulled out a locked metal box. He pulled out his key chain and unlocked it. Inside was his secret stash of file cards for his special sources, named and unnamed. He found the card for Deputy Chief Williams Barnes and dialed the number.

* * *

The special outside line on Chief Barnes phone lit up.

"Chief Barnes."

"Tony Brice, Chief."

"Ah, *The DN's* finest. What can I do for you, Brice?"

"Well, Chief," Brice began. "Things are a little too quiet on the Western Front. What's shakin' on the Booby-Trap case?"

"Not enough, if you ask me," Barnes replied. "But that may change soon."

"Gallagher got a new lead?"

"Maybe. Maybe not. I may become a little more involved within a week or so. How'd you like to be in on it?"

"Really?" Brice's antenna quivered. Barnes involved in an ongoing investigation?

"Really. When I get ready to make my move, I'll call you. Until then we're off the record. Right?"

"Sounds good to me, Chief. I'll be waiting." Brice hung up. *Well,* he thought. *This could get interesting.*

* * *

Barnes replaced his phone and leaned back in his chair. The vague outlines of the plan that had been floating around in his head had started taking a more solid shape in the past few days. He had made what was for him a pretty courageous decision. He was going after Gallagher's suspect, Loudin or no Loudin. He outranked Chief Inspector Loudin, Gallagher's patron saint. And Loudin wouldn't really dare come after him physically. At least, he hoped not.

* * *

MaryLou McBride, police beat reporter for *The Philadelphia Inquirer,* got up from her desk and walked to the city editor's glass-enclosed office. Gary McLeod was in and on the phone. She knocked, and he waved her in. She moved to a chair and sat and waited.

Presently, McLeod hung up. "What's up, McBride?"

"Well, I'm hitting a wall on the Booby-Trap Bomber. The cops have clammed up. The only word out of Task Force Gallagher is 'the investigation is continuing'. Even my confidential sources are mum. Nobody wants to do an end around on Gallagher."

"Can't say as I blame 'em," said McLeod. "He's probably the most popular cop in the city."

"Ain't no probably about it."

"You got somethin' in mind?"

"Yeah, a think piece follow-up on the original stories. A real deep piece for an early Sunday edition. There's usually lots of filler needed for those."

"There is," McLeod replied. "What's your intention?"

"To get a reaction from Task Force Gallagher. Or someone higher-up."

"I'm almost afraid to ask; but how are you going to go about it?"

"By expanding on the obvious," she replied. "Why no apparent progress? And I have a rather sticky angle I'd like to try."

"Uh oh." Gary's stomach rumbled.

"You remember the second incident?" she asked.

"Sure. Down at Penn's Landing."

"Well, after the first incident, Lawrence Steele and Reverend Quintade were right there, a huffin' and a puffin'. Much righteous outrage and indignation."

"Yeah, so?"

"Well," McBride said, "after Penn's Landing, nothing. Not a peep."

"Oh, shit. I know where you're goin' with this."

"Wait," she said. "Hear me out. I'll be real gentle. Real thorough, but real gentle. And maybe by pryin' a reaction out of our concerned African American community, I can indirectly get a reaction out of Task Force Gallagher."

"Very risky business. I'd have to send your piece upstairs for approval."

"I know. That's why I'm givin' you a heads up."

"O.K., McBride. Can't hurt. Can't hurt me that is, because I'll definitely be passin' the buck on this. Racial divides in this goofy city are the only issues that scare me. I'll stick my own neck out for anything but that shit."

"Mind if I ask why?"

McLeod leaned forward in his chair. "Because it's the only issue you can never be right about as a newspaperman. Only wrong. Forever wrong."

"Interesting philosophy."

"Philosophy hell, McBride. It's a hard learned fact. When somethin' goes down, and we report it, either the whites or the blacks want your scalp. And the Puerto Ricans stand on the sidelines cheerin' on all the mayhem."

"Such cynicism."

"Oh spare me, McBride. Go write your piece."

"I'll have it on your desk next Wednesday."

"You'd better, if you want it in the following Sunday. Tuesday would be better. Now get outta here."

MaryLou McBride, young instigative reporter, left the office laughing.

* * *

Detective Ruth Netters, of The 17th District, and on loan to The 3/4, settled herself slightly lower in the driver's seat of her unmarked Crown Victoria. It was eight-thirty in the evening—another hot, sticky night in The City of Philadelphia. This time of year, this city could be as hot and miserable as any other big city you care to name.

She had asked for and received permission to dress for the weather.

She was in shorts and crew shirt. Light socks and comfortable running shoes completed the outfit. They were parked in the 3300 block of Richmond Street, in the Richmond section of the city. The row homes on the west side of the street had blocked the sun for some time now, providing some relief from the heat and humidity.

Her partner, Detective Alphonse Canatta, sighed disgustedly and shook his head. They were listening to Phillies game and the Cardinals were pounding the Fightins. Manager Jim Fregosi had just pulled his staff ace, Curt Schilling, from the game. The Phillies announcer, Harry Kalas, gave the line on Schilling. Two and two/thirds, eleven hits, eleven runs, seven earned, one base on balls and zero strikeouts.

"Jeez," said Al. "That ain't like Shill. He got frickin' pounded."

"Yeah," responded Ruth. "They're six and a half up on the Cards; but if they start slumpin' now, St. Louis is definitely capable of passin' 'em."

"I agree. The Phils seem to be in a little bit of a funk right now. It's a good thing they started the season hot."

"Maybe too hot," said Ruth.

Like any true Phillies fan, Ruth had taken the team's hot start with a healthy does of salt. It had been ten years since the last pennant. In the 1983 World Series, the Orioles had cleaned their clock, four games to one. And almost thirty years ago, before either Detective had been born, occurred the famous traumatic collapse of the '64 Phils.

The Phillies had been six and half games ahead of the pack with twelve games to go. They promptly went two and ten, and lost the pennant to the Cardinals by one game. This event was indelibly and forever stamped on the collective psyche of the city. The '64 team was never forgiven, and it was twelve long years before the Phils were again in contention.

Canatta turned off the game, and reached in the back of the car and pulled *The Daily News* over the seat.

"You eyes on for a while so's I can look at *The DN*?" he asked Ruth.

"Yeah, gawhead."

After twenty minutes or so, Ruth stirred in her seat and glanced at Al. "Anything interesting?"

"There's all kindsa goofy shit happenin'."

"For instance?"

"The TV networks have agreed to provide violence advisories in TV show descriptions."

Ruth laughed. "Yeah, right. That'll stop a lotta viewers from watchin' the blood and gore."

Al laughed too. "Here's another good one. The International Monetary Fund has agreed to Boris Yeltzin's request for a four-and-a-half billion dollar loan. They can kiss that money goodbye."

"Yeah," Ruth laughed. "They should save themselves some paperwork and write that loan off before the check clears."

"The Shuttle was supposed to land today," said Al, continuing to peruse the paper. "They been up two extra days so far."

"Really? I wonder how much extra food they take up."

"I dunno. Probably more than enough. This one's the Endeavor. Its next mission is gonna be in the fall. They're gonna try and fix the telescope."

"The Hubble? What a billion dollar boondoggle that turned out to be. Does it say how they're gonna do it?"

"Says here they know what they have to do. They're gonna replace a bunch of modules, and add somethin' to it to refocus the main mirror. The big problem, it says here, is that they don't know if the astronauts can pull it off. It says it's gonna be the toughest mission ever attempted. They're gonna need like a half a dozen separate space walks."

"Lotsa luck. What else?" Ruth asked, continuing to look out the windshield at the corner of Wensley and Richmond.

"Spanky McFarland died."

"Who's he?"

"You know. Those old Spanky and Our Gang shorts. They played 'em on TV when I was growin' up."

"Oh yeah, I remember now. I wasn't a big fan of that stuff."

Al lowered the paper and looked askance at his partner. "Next thing, you'll tell me you're not a Three Stooges fan."

"Not even a little bit," she said.

"Typical female."

"Oh, spare me! It's such stupid shit."

"It's supposed to be stupid. Once you accept that, it's a laugh a minute."

"Right. And now I guess I'm supposed to ask you who's better, Curly or Shemp."

"So you've had this conversation before?" he asked.

"Only with every guy I've ever met."

Al laughed. "I could watch 'em for days."

"Typical male. What else?"

"On a more serious note—action in Somalia's really heatin' up."

"What's it say?"

"Big chopper attack on a militia group. Some ground combat between our guys and the locals. Lotsa sniper action by the bad guys."

"I can't even begin to understand what we're doin' over there," Ruth said.

"Can't say as I do either. It's a real mess," Al replied. "Here. You can read for a while. I'll watch."

"Thanks."

And so passed another long night on the most boring detail a police officer could draw.

* * *

Randy Macjewski lay on his couch, watching the Fightin Phils. He was very relaxed. The Phils losing didn't bother him, although he was a fan.

His plan didn't call for another attack until late August. He would scout Villanova University earlier in the month, and keep watching the news and reading the papers. The snatch and runs had been happening around the two stops on campus of the Route-100 High Speed Rail. *Just a short recon,* he thought. He knew what he was going to do. He just needed to get the lay of the land.

Tomorrow was the annual golf outing for Tastykake employees. He was looking forward to it. He was way better than average; and he had been practicing. Once with the members of his foursome a couple weeks back after work. He had also gone out several times by himself—at Cobbs Creek, and at Juniata Park, which was closer to home. He was ready.

It was odd, though. At Cobbs Creek and Juniata—at both places he had felt his hackles rise. Was someone watching him? He had carefully scanned the parking lots of both courses. He didn't see anything out of the ordinary. He hoped he wasn't being paranoid; but he couldn't discount the possibility that he was being tailed. He had been careful, but you never know.

He dozed off to the sounds of the shellacking the Cards were putting on the Fightins.

* * *

July 8th, 1993

At 2:30 P.M. Task Force Gallagher was gathered in the interrogation room at The 3/4 District.

"Good afternoon, everybody. Everyone's here except Officers Naples and Marrows, who have daytime tail today." Matt paused and looked around the room. Some heads were down.

"I believe I know how some of you feel. Poundin' the pavement to whittle down the kin list. Sittin' in cars—hot cars—on tail detail. It's incredibly boring. And it also provides a textbook example of the horrible contradictory nature of most police work. We want action. And unfortunately, action in our line of work usually means some of our citizens are bein' abused by the bad guys."

Matt took a sip of tea.

"In our case specifically, it would mean some serious violence has occurred. Well, our man hasn't hit on schedule. At least not in our jurisdiction or anywhere close by. Maybe the heat's gettin' to 'im; but I doubt it. He's gonna strike again. Believe it. So the tail continues and the list work goes on."

Ruth Netters raised a hand. "Not to step on your toes Loo. But is everybody aware of Macjewski's change of habit?"

"Don't worry about my toes, Detective Netters. And good point. I was comin' to it. But since you mentioned it, please brief everyone."

"O.K.," said Ruth. "Last couple a three nights, Macjewski has been goin' to the Polish American Club." Ruth looked at her notebook. "It's at Twenty-Seven Fourteen East Allegheny. He's been takin' the Olds he and parks in the back off Salmon Street."

"How long's he been stayin'?" This from Officer Maccahriah Stone of the tail detail.

"Actually," said Al Canatta, "he's been stayin' pretty late—past midnight."

"Does he look lit when he comes out?" asked Joe Caldwell, Stone's partner.

"Nah, not really," said Ruth. "We did suggest havin' a unit pull him over for a suspected DUI, but the Loo put the kibosh on that."

"Indeed I did," said Gallagher. "Again, I don't wanna spook 'im. Nobody's seen 'im fallin' down drunk, so we leave 'im be. Again, that's my decision."

"What in bloody hell does he do in there all night?" asked Winston Smythe.

"I love it when he talks Limey," said Mary Anne Sims, sotto voice.

That got many good-natured chuckles around the room. That The Wiz and the Limey were an item was on all the grapevines. And everybody was happy for them.

"Well," said Sergeant Eileen Johnson, "we sent in Little Mo to take a look. Enlighten us, Officer Peterson."

Maureen Peterson was the white half of the partners called "Salt-n Pepper." Big, bad and black Casey Persons was her partner.

"I went over there the other night in civvies," Peterson started. "I told them I was thinkin' of joinin', and they gave me a visitor's badge and I took a look around.

"It's got three bars and two real big rooms: one upstairs, and one downstairs. The first bar's in a small room near the front. The second bar's in the huge room downstairs. The third bar's in the room upstairs. Plus there are other, smaller rooms for pool and card playin'. I saw a lotta that the night I was there. There was a pretty good crowd; and this was on a Tuesday. One of the bartenders told me that was normal; and he said weekends are absolutely packed. Plus they have wedding receptions, banquets, stuff like that. The kitchen's industrial, and it's huge. I guess that's it."

"You didn't mention Macjewski, didya?" asked Officer Harold Michaels.

"I ain't stupid, Michaels." Peterson glared at Michaels.

The question had also drawn a dangerous look from her partner, Casey Persons; and the room tensed. Little Mo was a very competent police officer; but Persons was protective of her. *Very protective.*

That would be a good one, thought Detective Mike Robinson. Persons was a well known badass; and Michaels was young, lean and hard. In a showdown, Robinson's money was on Persons.

"O.K.! Calm down. Everybody!" Matt wasn't having any of this in his squad room. "Anybody else got anything?"

Nobody replied.

"O.K., let's get at it."

"How'd they do last night, Jack?" Matt hollered over to Detective Miles as he emerged from the interrogation room.

"I know they won seven-to-six. But I haven't seen a paper yet, so I don't know any stats. I think they're still five and a half up on St. Louis."

"You're slipping, Detective." This from Juan Pasqualez of Narcotics.

"Can it, Fuzzball. *I* been out workin'. Not like some Narcs I could mention."

"I been doin' paperwork," countered Pasqualez.

"Yeah. And I know what kinda paperwork," replied Miles, giving a sly look at the bottom of Pasqualez' desk.

During all the nonsense, Matt had said his goodbyes. He and Yvonne had a stakeout tonight, so they were taking their long afternoon break.

Outside, Matt said to Yvonne, "I'll drive up to Franklin Mills and meet you in front of Somnia Furniture around eight."

"O.K., see ya."

CHAPTER TWENTY

Randy Macjewski set the speed and temperature on the large oven for his last batch of Krimpets. He double checked his work, and then headed for the locker room. He shed his apron, work shirt and pants and opened his locker.

As Randy dressed into his street clothes, he got a nice little adrenaline rush as he thought about the package at the back of the locker. The M-16A1 was broken down into two pieces—the upper receiver group and the lower receiver group. The bolt carrier group was locked into the upper receiver.

It would take him about seven seconds to reassemble the rifle, and load and lock a twenty-round magazine. He briefly imagined doing so at the Central Lock-Up of the Roundhouse. Then a quick two seconds on the trigger and twenty rounds would decimate the bastards. Black, white, Chinese—he didn't care. All scumbags needed to die. The adrenalin was really surging now, and he didn't hear Joe Tallon and Andy Ditch come into the locker room.

"Well, if it ain't Jack Fuckin' Nicklaus," said Alan, slapping Randy on the back.

Randy whirled around with his hands in the "port arms" position. *I need another magazine*, he thought. *Before they get me.* Then, just as suddenly, he snapped out of it. The weapon, of course, was still in the locker.

"You alright, chief?" asked Joe. "It ain't like you to be jumpy."

"Yeah. Sorry. I was just daydreamin' about the tournament. What a coincidence. We did pretty good, didn't we?"

"Pretty good?" exclaimed Alan. "We won goin' away. You and Jack Donnits tied for low net. Pair of seventy-ones." Jack Donnits was the new delivery driver that Joe had locked up for their team before anybody else could get to him.

"You guys played pretty good, too," said Randy, smiling. "You seem to have gotten the Tic-Toc chipping down O.K."

"You got that right," said Joe. "Man, if you can chip good, it sure makes the game more fun."

"Exactly. It can really suck if you're close to the green in two or three shots, and wind up with an eight." Randy slammed his locker closed and spun the dial to lock it. "Well, I gotta go. Youse guys take it easy."

"See ya tomorrow."

"Later."

Randy left the building and made his way to the parking lot. *Christ,* he thought. *I really spaced out in there. I've never done that before.*

Of course, when one was going insane, one was always the last to know.

* * *

In *The Daily News* building on north Broad Street, Tony Brice answered his phone.

"Brice."

"Deputy Chief Barnes. You got any plans for the next few nights?"

"Nothin' I can't cancel."

"Good," said Barnes. "You know the Richmond playground at Richmond and Allegheny?"

"I'll find it."

"O.K."

. It's right across the street from a WAWA. Meet me there at six o'clock. And bring your camera."

"Righto. Bye."

* * *

Barnes smiled to himself as he hung up the phone. Sergeant Mike Shincock had given Barnes all the latest poop on the Booby-Tray Bomber case, including a description of Randy Macjewski. Five-eight or nine, one-eighty. Red hair. Stocky individual.

Barnes had used his new computer to tie in with the main frame downstairs. Macjewski's parents had been mugged near old Connie Mack Stadium in 1968. His father had died of injuries inflicted by the muggers, who were never caught.

Barnes had then called The 23rd District and had the cold case file pulled and copies sent to his office. He had also told the helpful detective to keep his mouth shut or he'd be walkin' a beat in Timbuc-fuckin'-tu.

When Barnes received the file, he had closed his office door and turned on his answering machine.

* * *

Randy Macjewski had been in Vietnam when his father was killed. He had been granted immediate emergency leave, and had arrived home just before the funeral. Two weeks later, he had shipped back over to 'Nam. A footnote grabbed Barnes' attention. Macjewski had refused a compassionate reassignment or discharge. *To go back to that shithole?* Barnes thought.

The file named the detectives assigned to the case. Sergeant Nicky Deemer and Detective Frank Kearsay. Barnes had punched the names into his computer. Deemer had retired in '88, and ran a bed and breakfast with his wife June in Cape May, New Jersey. Frank Kearsay was now forty-eight years old, and was Captain ofThe 5th District in Roxborough/ Manayunk. Now the light went on. He had met Kearsay at a police function years ago. Kearsay, a black officer, had started moving up the ladder at precisely the right time and place. Affirmative action quotas had assured him a good career as long as he didn't screw up. And apparently he hadn't. Barnes called Central Dispatch and had them ring Captain Kearsay's phone directly. Kearsay had answered on the first ring.

"Captain Kearsay."

"Good afternoon, Captain Kearsay. This is Deputy Chief William Barnes."

Kearsay felt his stomach tighten. A call from this guy was generally not good news.

"Good afternoon, Chief Barnes. What can I do for you?"

"I need a few minutes of your time, Captain."

"Gawhead. My desk is clear for the moment."

"Good," said Barnes. "This goes back a ways. You and your old partner, Nicky Deemer, worked a mugging in July of 1968. It was in Reyburn Park, near old Connie Mack at Twenty-First and Lehigh. One of the victims died during surgery at Temple University Hospital."

"Jeez, Chief. You must have the file right in front of you. That's exactly the way I remember it goin' down."

"I do have the file, Captain. For security reasons, I can't tell you why I have it. But I have a few questions."

"Shoot, Chief."

"The son, Randy Macjewski, went back to Vietnam after the funeral. Remember?"

"Yeah, I do. I don't remember the individual so much; but I remember how sad it was that he chose to go back to that place. He was eligible for compassionate reassignment."

"Did you ever find out why he wanted to go back?"

"No. I don't remember ever askin' 'im about it."

"O.K.," Barnes said. "When he came back from 'Nam, did he keep in touch with you about the case?"

"Yeah. Ya know, it's really comin' back to me now. After he got out of the service around the spring of Sixty-Nine, he kept after us for almost two years. But ya know? We never came close to catching those bastards. There were three of 'em, and we never got a lead. Three large black youths." Kearsay sighed. "Never a lead."

"How bitter was the son Randy?"

"Very. He used to come down to The District every few days, and after awhile he got real nasty. We tolerated it at first, because of the circumstances. But later on we had to lay down a little law. Even after he stopped comin' down, he called us almost every week for close to two years."

"Did he ever threaten to take matters into his own hands?" asked Barnes.

"All the time. And we kept tellin' him if he did, we would haul his ass in like any other criminal. That usually set him off pretty good. But nothin' ever came of it. You said you have the file. Is it still open?"

"Yeah, it is," Barnes replied. "Well, you've been a big help."

"I don't see how."

"Well, you have." Barnes paused. "Listen, you should be coming up for some kind of promotion soon. I'll put in a good word."

"Thanks, Chief. But in two more years I'll have thirty in, and I'll be more than happy to retire on three-quarter Captain's pay."

"O.K. Please keep this conversation under your hat. You ever need anything, gimme a call."

"Sure thing, Chief. Have a good day."

* * *

After that call, Barnes had thought long and hard. *Could a man let something fester for twenty-five long years, and then go on a vengeance kick.* He decided it was possible and took the next step. It was dangerous; but hell, he *did* have his thirty years in. He decided it was a big enough cushion.

* * *

Randy arrived home around 5:30 P.M. and walked into his bar. Denise Reilly slapped an icy cold Yuengling Lager on the bar before Randy had even sat down.

"Thanks, hon. I really can use it." Randy drained half the bottle in three gulps and gave a low, satisfying burp.

"Hi, Boss," said Jim Richards, his manager.

"Hey, Jim. Any bad news."

"Nope. Just the usual paperwork. The taps are runnin' and the urinals are flowin'."

Randy laughed. They made a running joke of it, but Randy and all his employees made sure the tap lines were always running smooth. And the bathrooms were always clean, and the plumbing always flowed free and clear. He finished his beer, and Denise gave him a fresh one.

"Ya know," she said, turning around and looking at them in the huge mirror behind the bar. "Youse guys look more alike every day. Especially when Randy lets his hair grow out a little bit."

Jim and Randy looked at each other in the mirror. She was right, and she wasn't the only one who had commented on it. Both were five-nine and stocky, with short red hair. Jim's hair was longer, but not by much.

"O.K.," Randy said. "Gimme the bills and the checkbook." Randy took the offered material and his beer and headed for a back table. *Might as well do it now*, he thought. A couple of beers and a sandwich, and then to bed. He was tired.

* * *

Tony Brice turned left onto Richmond Street from Allegheny Avenue, and almost at once spotted the big, black unmarked Ford Crown Victoria in a tiny dirt parking lot on his right. He turned in and pulled up next to Barnes. It was just a few minutes to six. He grabbed his camera case and his tape recorder, and got out and locked the car.

Barnes flipped the passenger door lock, and Brice got in the Crown Vic. Barnes spotted the recorder. "You can't tape me."

"I won't," replied Brice. "It's for me. I always dictate my story, and then write it up later back at the shop."

"Oh, O.K. then. Why dontcha rig up your camera, and I'll brief you as you're doin' that?"

"Fine." Brice opened the case. It was a Canon AE-One with all the trimmings. As Brice worked he said, "Talk to me."

"O.K.," Barnes started. "Here we go. Task Force Gallagher is tailing a suspect in the Booby-Trap Bomber case."

Brice gave a long whistle.

"That's right. Now, his name is Randy Macjewski. Age forty-three. Five-eight or nine, one-eighty. Stocky, short red hair. His parents were mugged near Connie Mack Stadium after a Phillies game in 1968."

Barnes paused. Brice had finished setting up the camera.

"You wanna write some of this down or record it in your own voice, gawhead."

"That's alright. When I'm focused, and believe me I'm focused, I have an almost photographic memory."

"Alright," Barnes continued. "His father was severely injured and died in surgery that night. Randy was in Vietnam at the time." Barnes gave Brice the whole story and then leaned back. "I'm monitoring Task Force Gallagher; and I'm just waiting for the right moment. I'm gonna arrest Macjewski."

Holy shit! thought Brice. *A Deputy Chief disrupting an ongoing case? It was unheard of. If Barnes was wrong, he was through.* You didn't have to be a police beat reporter to know that.

Barnes, reading his thoughts, said, "I know it's risky; but I'm makin' my play. Macjewski's the bomber. I'm sure of it."

"Ya got a warrant?" Brice asked, immediately regretting it.

"I don't need a fuckin' warrant. I'm a Deputy Fuckin' Chief. Once he's in the slammer, I got a judge who'll give me an immediate search and seizure warrant. Then I'll raid his house and bar. If we got the goods on 'im, the DA's got a case. If I'm wrong, we let 'im go."

"You say so, Chief. While you monitor the radio, I'm gonna step outside and record all this."

"Fine."

Brice got out of the car, turned on the tape recorder, and repeated verbatim everything Barnes had just told him, adding nothing. He would add his own take on the story later, as he played back the recording. When he was finished, he got back in the car.

* * *

Randy was behind the bar making himself a sandwich, when he happened to look at the clock on the wall. It was 6:35 P.M.

"Oh, shit!" Randy exclaimed, slamming a knife down on the counter.

Jim Richards, standing a few feet away, looked up.

"What's wrong, Boss?" he asked.

"I'm supposed to take the Mustang down to Bob's garage. I completely forgot."

"What's wrong with it?"

"Nothing, really. He's gonna tune it up and change the oil and shit. Tomorrow. But I wanted to get it on his lot tonight before he closes."

"What time's he close?"

"Seven."

"You got time," Jim said.

"Yeah, but I been drinkin'. Listen, Jim, could you run it down for me. Bob'll ride you back after he locks up. It's up near Frankford and Allegheny."

"I know where it's at. Gimme the keys."

Randy handed them over. "I'll call 'im and tell 'im you're on your way."

"Right." Jim left; Randy made the phone call, and went back to making his sandwich.

* * *

Officer Eugene Naples sat up and looked hard through the windshield of the Crown Vic. He was tail detail today on Macjewski.

Sheila Marrows, his partner, noticed him tense up. "Whaddya got?" she asked.

"Lookitt that guy unlockin' Randy's Mustang. It sure ain't Randy. It's that Richards guy." They had been tailing Macjewski long enough to tell the difference.

Marrows grabbed her squawker.

"Three-Four, zero-zero-two, this is Tail Detail."

Gallagher, at home, responded instantly. "Gawhead, Tail Detail."

"Loo, we got a guy gettin' into Randy's Mustang. Not our guy. We need instructions."

"Where's he headin?"

"He's headin' south on Richmond."

"Don't bother with it. Sit tight where you're at. If we have to, we can ask him later where he went."

"Ten-four."

* * *

Brice and Barnes had been talking when Task Force Gallagher started squawking. And a half-block away was a SEPTA mini-terminal. Barnes' squawker caught some interference from SEPTA's radios.

Barnes thought he heard "Randy's Mustang. 'Got' our guy. We need instructions."

Barnes and Brice listened to the rest of the transmissions.

Barnes' face lit up in ecstatic disbelief. Super cop Matt Gallagher had just told his tail detail to let the suspect go on his merry way, unhindered. And the suspect was heading right at him. Oh, joy of joys!

"Here we go," said Barnes. "Macjewski's in a black Mustang Five Point Oh, 1990."

Barnes pulled out of the dirt parking lot, and faced the car toward Richmond Street. Sure enough, thirty seconds later, the Mustang passed by and made a right onto Allegheny Avenue. Barnes slapped a red bubble light on top of the Crown Vic and turned on his siren. Startled civilians either sped out of his way or pulled over as Barnes screeched left onto Richmond Street. Seconds later, the Crown Vic also turned right onto Allegheny, and the chase was on. And a short chase it was.

This is more than a little surreal, thought Brice. Barnes was chasing Macjewski; but he knew Barnes was really chasing Gallagher. He didn't understand it; but he put it out of his head. He had to pay attention. They were now right behind the Mustang.

Jim Richards wasn't sure who the cops behind him were chasing; but he dutifully pulled as far right as possible. Parked cars prevented him from getting all the way to the curb. To his surprise, the cops stopped right behind him.

Barnes fairly leaped out of the Crown Vic and drew his Glock. Brice got out on his side, and went around the back of the vehicle to the driver's side. This gave him a better angle for pictures.

Barnes, in full uniform and aware of Brice in his peripheral vision snapping photos, struck a heroic pose, slightly behind and to the left of the Mustang's driver side.

"Put your hands on the steering wheel!" Barnes shouted.

"What the hell is this?" Jim Richards asked in a high squeaky voice. He was scared to death. A cop slapping leather on him? Holy shit!

"I said put your hands on the goddamned steering wheel!" Barnes shouted again.

Richards quickly complied. Brice was snapping as fast as the camera's motor drive allowed. This being the tail end of rush hour, a sizeable crowd had quickly gathered.

"Now," said Barnes. "I'm gonna open your door. When I do, you step out with your hands on your head."

Jim Richards was sweating bullets. Barnes quickly reached over and opened the door.

"O.K., do it. Hands on your head and get out. Slowly."

Richards complied, visibly shaking.

"O.K.," Barnes said. "Move to the rear of the vehicle. Place your hands on the trunk and spread your legs. Wide."

Richards did as he was told. Barnes had his cuffs out and, reaching up, quickly locked up the left wrist and holding the gun in his left hand, wrenched Richards' left arm behind him. Reaching around with his right hand, he yanked Richards right arm behind him and finished cuffing him. Barnes could hear the camera's motor going almost non-stop behind him.

Richards was desperate. He wanted to scream out "what the hell is this"; but his throat had locked up and he couldn't utter a sound.

Barnes then frisked Richards. Philadelphia Police Department policy was, 'cuff first, frisk second. All he found was a wallet, a comb, and a pen. He placed these items in his right shirt pocket and holstered his gun. He turned the suspect around, and marched him to the back door of the Crown Vic. He quickly placed Richards in the back seat and closed the door.

Brice was changing film in his camera. Barnes waited until the fresh roll was in, and then reached in the front of the car and grabbed his mike.

"Central Dispatch. Admin, zero-one-seven."

"Admin, zero-one-seven, go."

"Zero-one-seven. I need a patrol unit at the twenty-six hundred block of Allegheny, near Thompson Street. I also need a police tow truck dispatched to this location."

"Roger, zero-one-seven."

Barnes hung the mike on the side of the door and turned to Brice.

"You get enough pictures?"

"Oh yeah. Beaucoup."

"Good. As soon as the patrol unit gets here to secure the Mustang, we'll head to the Roundhouse. You can watch me book 'im."

"Sounds good to me," said Brice. "He sure don't look like a lunatic."

"It's always the quiet ones. Here's my backup."

A patrol car had come eastbound on Allegheny and, lights flashing, had made a u-turn and pulled up behind the Crown Vic. Two young officers got out and approached Barnes.

"Whaddya need, Chief?" asked one.

"I want you guys to secure that Mustang 'til the tow truck gets here. Tell the tow guy to bring it to the back of the Roundhouse, and put it in one of the temporary impound spaces. And escort him there. Once you see him finish the job, come into the booking area and let me know it's done."

"Yessir," the two cops chorused.

"O.K., Brice. Let's go."

Brice jumped in the passenger seat, and Barnes got in, turned around in the seat, identified himself, and read the suspect his rights. He then removed the bubble light, made his own u-turn, and then turned south on Richmond Street. He would pick up Delaware Avenue south, eventually go west on Race Street, and run right into 8th.

Jim Richards still couldn't speak. He couldn't believe this was happening. He had never been in a cop car in his life, let along done something to be arrested for.

By the time Barnes was on Race and coming up on 8th Street, Richards had worked up enough saliva to speak. "What the hell is all this about?"

"As if you didn't know, Macjewski," Barnes replied.

"Macjewski?"

"Don't start, scumbag. I know who you are."

"So do I. My name's Jim Richards."

Hello! thought Brice. *Did Barnes have the wrong guy?*

A flicker of doubt flew through Barnes' mind. *Nah, it couldn't be.* "Just be quiet, Macjewski. We'll be at the lock-up in one minute."

Jim Richards settled back in the seat, mind racing. *He thinks I'm Randy. He thought he was arresting Randy.* Jim had heard about Randy's interview with a Lieutenant Gallagher. Something about relatives of crime victims. Something relating to the Booby-Trap Bomber incidents. *Oh my God! They thought Randy was the Bomber!! And they think I'm Randy! Holy fuckin' shit!*

Barnes pulled into the back of the Roundhouse and parked next to the door to the lock-up. He got out and helped Richards out of the car. Brice got out and followed them inside.

The booking Sergeant was mildly surprised. Deputy Chief Barnes making an arrest?

"Sergeant Gerard, I want you to book this individual as a suspect in the Booby-Trap Bomber case."

"O.K., Chief." Gerard buzzed his door lock, and Barnes walked Richards into the booking room. Gerard looked at Brice. "You can't come in here, sir."

"He's with me," said Barnes.

"O.K., Chief." He indicated a chair next to his desk and told Richards, "Sit in that chair."

"You guys are making a big mistake," said Richards, sitting down.

"They all say that, Bub," replied Sergeant Gerard, sitting down at his desk and rolling an arrest report into his typewriter.

Here we go, thought Brice.

"These are his personal effects," said Barnes, placing the items on the Sergeant's desk.

"Right, Chief." He turned to Richards, hands poised over the keys. "Name?"

"Jim Richards."

"Oh, bullshit!" said Barnes. "His name is Randy Macjewski."

Gerard picked up Richards' wallet, opened it up, and the first thing he saw was Richards' driver's license. "That's not what this says, Chief."

Barnes grabbed the wallet, and Richards spoke up again.

"I'm Jim Richards. Randy Macjewski is my boss. He owns the S & B Bar in Port Richmond. If you dial four-two-six, three-eight-six-one, chances are he'll answer the phone. He's covering for me while I was taking his car to a repair shop." Jim Richards had totally recovered now and was absolutely seething.

Barnes had turned white, Brice noted. What a story this was gonna be. Anyway you shaded it, Barnes had fucked up. Big time.

Sergeant Gerard picked up the phone and dialed the number.

"S & B Bar."

"Yes, may I speak to Randy Macjewski, please?"

"Speaking."

"Yes sir, we have a mix up concerning your car. My name is Sergeant Gerard of The Philadelphia Police Department. Will you be at this number for a while?"

"Yes," Randy replied. "What the hell's wrong with my car?"

"Sir, I'm gonna call you right back about that. Please stay by the phone." Gerard hung up, sat back, and looked at Barnes with a carefully neutral expression on his face.

"I just talked to Randy Macjewski, Chief. Whaddya wanna do now?"

Barnes was speechless. He looked at the Sergeant, and then at Richards, who stood up.

"You can remove these cuffs anytime now," he said angrily.

Just then the two patrol officers came in. "The Mustang's in the lot, Chief Barnes," one of them said. "Here's the keys."

Barnes, still white as a ghost, moved stiffly behind Richards and unlocked the handcuffs. "This man is free to go," he said.

Richards was livid. "That's it. No apology? Nothing?"

Barnes didn't reply. *Smart move,* thought Sergeant Gerard. *Don't say nothin'.*

He took the keys from the officer through the portal under the glass. He gave these, the wallet, and the other items to Richards. "You're free to go, sir."

Richards moved to the door. Gerard buzzed him out. As he opened the outer door, he looked over his shoulder. "You'll be hearing from my lawyer, Barnes." Then he left.

Brice stirred. "Would you buzz me out too, Sergeant. I'm done here."

"Who the hell are you, anyway?" asked Gerard as he pressed the button.

"Tony Brice. *Daily News.*"

Holy shit! thought Gerard. *Not only had Barnes stepped on his stinger; but he had done it in the company of a reporter. The doo-doo was sure gonna hit the fan.* He looked at Barnes, who now was turning from white to red. Barnes left through the Sergeant's internal office door. *Oh baby!* thought Gerard. He picked up the phone and again dialed the number for the S & B Bar.

* * *

Brice had quickly recovered his camera case and tape recorder from Barnes' Crown Vic. He then caught up with Richards, who was getting into the Mustang.

"Mind riding me back to Richmond?" he asked.

"Kiss my ass, Officer!"

"I'm not a cop, I'm a reporter." He extended a hand. "Tony Brice. *Daily News.*"

Jim hesitated. Then a slow smile came to his face, and he shook hands with Brice. "No shit," he said.

* * *

Randy slowly hung up the phone. This Sergeant Gerard had said there had been a mix up concerning his car and Jim Richards. What the fuck's going on? He went back to helping Denise with customers. *Jim should be back soon,* he thought. Then he'd find out what the story was.

* * *

Richards dropped Brice off at his car, and headed back to the bar. Brice had got some background information from Richards on the ride back. He had told him that he was coming to the bar to talk to Randy. Well, that was up to Randy, he had told Brice. He parked the Mustang and walked into the bar. Randy saw him and came over.

"What the hell happened?"

Richards scrutinized the man he thought he knew. "Let's talk outside, Boss."

Randy followed Jim out of the bar. They both leaned on the retaining wall, and Jim gave Randy the whole story.

"They think you're the Booby-Trap Bomber, Boss."

"Yeah, right. And you're Mother Theresa."

Just then, a Chrysler LeBaron convertible turned onto Wensley Street and parked.

Jim indicated the car. "This is the reporter, Boss."

Brice fairly hopped out of the car and hustled across the street. "Mister Macjewski, I'm Tony Brice of *The Daily News*. I wonder if I can have a few minutes of your time?"

"Mister Brice, I don't think that's a good idea. Mister Richards here is considering legal action against the city; and I don't wanna compound the situation."

Brice persisted. "Deputy Chief Barnes thought he was arresting you. He considers you a suspect in the Booby-Trap Bomber case. Care to comment?"

"No, I don't." He turned to go into the bar. "I've got work to do."

"Your name will be in the paper."

"Whatever." Randy went inside.

Brice started to follow him in, but thought better of it. "That's it then. Later, Richards. Thanks for the ride."

"No problem."

Brice got into his car, and headed back to the shop. Unless one of the other cops leaked the story to someone, he had a hell of an exclusive. Barnes had screwed up royally. When the story broke in the morning edition of *The Daily News*, Macjewski would know he had been the subject of twenty-four hour surveillance. Gallagher would not be too happy about that. Among others.

He whistled happily as he made his way back to work.

CHAPTER TWENTY-ONE

July 14th, 1993

"O.K., let's get settled folks," said Lieutenant Matt Gallagher. "We've got a lot to cover."

Task Force Gallagher was assembled in the interrogation room at The Three-Four District. It was 2:30 P.M.

"You may be wondering why Officers White and Rittles are here this afternoon," Matt began. "And wonder you might. As of today, per orders from higher-up, the tail on Randy Macjewski is terminated." This caused quite a stir. Many people started talking at once. Matt patiently waited, letting them get it out of their system. "Now," Matt said. "Let me give you the real skinny on what's been goin' down and put all the rumors to rest."

The room grew silent.

"First. Yes, it's true. Deputy Chief William Barnes has been suspended, pending an investigation into his actions last Thursday evening."

The room erupted in cheers. Matt also let this outburst run its course.

"Personal feelings aside," Matt said, "there's no doubt this puts a crimp in the investigation. Is Macjewski still a suspect? Absolutely! And so are several hundred people on the list of relatives of crime victims, some of the ones we've gotten to, and all of ones we haven't gotten to. Matt paused to look at this notes. Detective Alphonse Canatta raised a hand.

"Gawhead, Al."

"What's the status of The Seventeenth District people?"

"Believe it or not, that was next on my agenda," Matt replied. "Officers White and Rittles, and Detectives Netters and Canatta are officially released from Task Force Gallagher as of now. Sergeant Mitelli is expecting you over at your shop." Matt paused and looked around the room. "I believe I speak for all of us when I say thank you, you've been a big help. As we all know, Detective Canatta gave us our first break in the case. Again, thank you and be safe, folks."

There were handshakes and goodbyes all around as The 17th District people took their leave. It took more than a few minutes; and Matt certainly wasn't going to rush it. When the door finally shut on the exiting officers, Matt cleared his throat and started again.

"O.K. I'm going to go over the events of last week in detail so we're all on the same sheet of music. I'm sure all of you have read, or at least heard about, Toni Brice's story in last Friday's *Daily News*. Unfortunately for Chief Barnes, it was not a second hand account of what went down. Chief Barnes did in fact invite Brice along for the ride. What his motives were is speculation on my part. And I'll leave it at that."

There were several outright guffaws at this; and Matt smiled too. They all knew Barnes had set out: number one, to embarrass Gallagher, and two, to bring glory on himself. And it had all exploded in his face. He was gone; and they all knew it. He would either resign voluntarily or be forced out. Good riddance.

Matt continued, and related all the accompanying hubbub and chaos that had resulted from Barnes actions.

* * *

Brice and *The Daily News* broke the story in the morning edition on Friday, July 9th. Neither Sergeant Gerard at Central Lock-Up nor the two officers who had assisted Barnes had spoken to the press or leaked the story anywhere else. Gerard wanted to retire in peace, thank you; and the two young officers were not about to fuck with a Deputy Chief. And Barnes himself had not said anything. He just waited for the story to break. He didn't even attempt to call Brice off the story. It certainly would have been an exercise in futility.

Barnes had received the summons from Commissioner Phillips at 9:00 A.M. on Friday. And it was not a request.

As he was riding the elevator to the top floor of Police Headquarters, Barnes tried to swallow huge lumps in his throat. He would immediately offer to resign. He would take his thirty years, and retire on three-quarters Deputy Chief's pay. It was a huge chunk of change, and he and his wife would have full medical and dental for life. *It could be worse,* he thought. *Much worse.*

Little did he know.

He got off the elevator, headed left, and after a short walk he presented himself to Corretta Shiponski, the Commissioner's secretary.

"Good morning, Mrs. Shipnoski."

"Good morning, Chief Barnes. Please go right in. They're expecting you."

"Thank you," said Barnes. They? Oh, shit! Barnes moved to the Commissioner's open door and knocked twice.

"Come in," boomed Commissioner Augustus Phillips.

Barnes, for all his faults, was a high-ranking officer; and he certainly knew procedure for this situation. He marched to within three feet of the Commissioner's desk, came to attention, and saluted smartly.

"Deputy Chief Barnes reporting as directed, sir."

"At ease, Chief Barnes," said the Commissioner. "Chief Barnes," he continued, pointing to the two individuals seated on a leather couch, "this is Ronald Shapiro, from the DA's Office. The man on the left, as I'm sure you know, is Inspector Donald Platt, from the Fraternal Order of Police."

Nobody stood up or offered to shake hands.

The Commissioner indicated a high-back leather chair cater-corner to the couch. "Please sit down, Chief." Phillips' face was unreadable. Barnes sat.

"Deputy Chief Barnes," Phillips started. "This is not an official hearing. That will come later. But this *is* for the record. Do you wish legal representation at this time?"

Barnes was a prick; but he wasn't stupid. He had no intention of antagonizing anyone at this point. "No sir," he answered.

"Very well." The Commissioner settled back in his chair and relaxed a little. His face was still blank. He hadn't risen to this high office without a poker face.

Phillips continued. "I read the article in *The DN* on the way in this morning, Chief. To say I am concerned is an understatement. I have been in contact with Sergeant Fred Gerard; and he confirms the part of the story that he was involved with. You did, in fact, start arrest proceedings last night on a mister Jim Richards, correct?"

"Yessir."

"Excuse me, Commissioner Phillips," said Inspector Platt.

"Go ahead, Inspector."

"Chief Barnes, I would strongly advise you not to answer any questions at this time. And I would also strongly suggest you retain legal counsel before you say anything further."

Barnes looked at Commissioner Phillips. "Sir, am I up on charges?"

"Not yet."

"Then sir, I would like to offer my resignation at this time."

"That's not an option for you right now," replied the Commissioner.

Barnes turned to Platt. "Inspector, I respect your position and appreciate your help. But at this point, I'd like to continue."

"O.K." Platt shrugged his shoulders. "I certainly can't stop you."

The Commissioner stirred. "Chief Barnes, the investigation you involved yourself in comes under the purview of Task Force Gallagher. You were certainly aware of this. Aside from blatant interference in something beyond the scope of your normal duties, you may have brought a civil suit against The Department. Am I clear so far?"

"Yessir." Barnes was sweating.

"Very well. As of this moment, you are suspended from all duties. Also as of this moment, I am referring the matter to the District Attorney's Office to see if criminal charges are warranted." Phillips paused, and looked at Assistant DA Shapiro. "Mr. Shapiro, the paperwork is being taken care of as we speak. I would like you to have that paperwork before you leave the building, sir."

"I won't leave without it, Commissioner."

"Thank you." Phillips turned back to Barnes. Barnes knew what was coming.

"Deputy Chief Barnes. Please place your badge and your gun on my desk."

Barnes stood up; and his humiliation was there for all to see. He removed his Glock, dropped the magazine into his left hand, and pointing the weapon to the floor, he pulled the slide back to insure the chamber was clear. It was. He stepped up to Phillip's desk and placed the gun and magazine on it. He removed his badge and did the same.

"Deputy Chief Barnes, Mr. Shapiro and Sergeant Wilsky, who is waiting outside, will accompany you to your office. You may remove personal items. You will not touch your phone or your computer. Understood?"

"Yessir."

"Very well. Please give me the keys to your office and your Crown Vic."

Barnes pulled out his keys, removed several, and placed them on the desk.

"Are there duplicates?" asked Phillips.

"Yessir. I keep a spare set at home."

"Very well." Phillips pressed a button on his speakerphone. "Mrs. Shipnoski, please send in Sergeant Wilsky."

Seconds later there was a sharp rap on the door, and an enormous man in a well-tailored suit stepped into the office.

"Yes, sir?" he said.

Commissioner Phillips stood up. "Sergeant, you and Mr. Shapiro will escort the Chief to his office. He is to remove personal items only. Then, Sergeant, you are to drive Chief Barnes home in this Crown Vic." Phillips held up three keys and Wilsky stepped forward and took them. "Once there, Sergeant, Chief Barnes will hand you a duplicate set of those keys. Understood?"

"Yessir." Wilsky was all business. A block of granite would have shown more emotion.

Commissioner Phillips looked at Barnes. "Deputy Chief Barnes, you are dismissed."

Barnes stepped back and started to bring his right hand up in a salute.

The Commissioner's deep bass voice boomed out again. "Do not salute me, Deputy Chief Barnes. You are suspended. You are not privileged to either render or receive a hand salute."

Barnes' humiliation was now complete. He turned and left the office, accompanied by Shapiro and Wilsky.

"Inspector Platt," said Phillips. "A word, please."

"Yes, sir?"

"For the record, are you satisfied with the way these proceedings went?"

"Yes, Commissioner. Professional from beginning to end."

"Good. Please shut the door."

Platt did so, a quizzical look on his face.

"Off the record, Ron?" Phillips asked.

"Sure, Commissioner. Gawhead."

"I don't want his pension. Nobody who puts in thirty years deserves that, unless they're crooked. For all his faults—and they are legion—Barnes is not crooked."

"I agree with that, sir."

"Good." Phillips sat down. "Having said that, I want you to know that I'm going to put the fear of God into him, and through him, all the other assholes of his ilk. Gallagher's the best cop in town, and having a political animal like Barnes screwing up his investigation is simply intolerable."

"Gotta say I agree with that, too," said Platt.

"O.K." said Phillips. "The DA's Office will take their cue from me on this. If we split hairs, we could probably find something to prosecute him for; but I ain't goin' there. With me so far?"

"Yessir."

"Good. We'll stay inside The Department. I'm gonna bust 'im down to Captain. Then I'll take his 'voluntary' resignation. You guys wanna fight it, fine. We'll fight. But I wanna send a crystal clear message to all the political animals on the force. This is the perfect opportunity. And I'm gonna take it."

Phillips stood up. "O.K., that's all I got."

"Thank you, Commissioner." Platt stood up and let himself out, leaving the door open.

Phillips punched the intercom button on his phone.

"Mrs. Shiponski, please get me Chief Inspector Ellison of Internal Affairs."

"Yes, Commissioner. Standby, please." Several seconds later, a line lit up on his phone. "Line two, sir," said Mrs. Shiponski.

Phillips punched the button and picked up his handset. "Robert, Commissioner Phillips here. Read *The DN* this morning?"

"Yessir," replied Ellison. "Me and everybody else on the force."

"Good. Here's how I want this to go down."

* * *

Gallagher looked around the room. "I don't know the final consequences of Barnes' actions as far as he is concerned. And frankly, I don't care. But, of course, there is more."

The past week had seen a lot of activity concerning the investigation in general, and Randy Macjewski in particular.

On Thursday evening, July 8th, Randy had called his lawyer, James McDonnell. McDonnell had come straight away. He, Randy, and Jim Richards had gone up into Randy's house. Randy had started first. He told of the day Lieutenant Gallagher and the Sergeant, whose name he couldn't remember, had come into the bar to question him. Then Jim had told of the events earlier this evening. McDonnell heard them both out.

When Jim finished, McDonnell handed him a card. "This is the card of a colleague. If you wish to pursue legal action, he can help you. Please call him."

"O.K."

"Now if you don't mind, I'd like to speak to Randy alone."

Jim left, and Randy grabbed a beer from the refrigerator. "You want a beer?" he shouted from the kitchen.

"Sure," James yelled back.

Randy came back into the living room, handed James his beer, and settled in his lounger. McDonnell was on the couch.

"I just don't believe this shit," Randy said. "Poor Jim."

"He'll be fine. It's you I'm worried about."

"Why?"

"What the hell do you mean why?" McDonnell shouted. "You're a suspect in the Booby-Trap Bomber case!"

Randy took a swallow of beer. "Look, they said they were looking at people who were relatives of crime victims. In this city? There's gotta be thousands of people who fit the bill. Christ, tens of thousands even."

"Alright," McDonnell said. "Calm down. As crazy as it's gonna sound, I am morally and ethically bound to ask you the question."

"What question?"

McDonnell turned to face Randy squarely. "Are you the Booby-Trap Bomber?"

Randy stared right back. "Hell no!"

"I hadda ask. Let me hear what you wanna do. And then I'll tell you what I think we should do."

Randy pulled at his beer. "I want 'em to leave me alone. The way I see it, they have no reason to bother me. The thing with my parents happened twenty-five years ago, for Christ's sake."

"Alright. I'll go see 'em—the cops, I mean. But it'll have to be next week."

"What!"

"Hear me out, Randy. You know that guy Brice is gonna put you in the papers. I wanna see how that plays out. Then Monday I'll go to the DA's Office. I'll tell 'em to have the cops back off or I'll got to court to have them cease and desist. I can have that done by Wednesday, if the cops won't back off."

"Alright," Randy sighed. "So people are gonna see this in the papers. Half the city'll laugh. And the other half'll think I'm fuckin' nuts."

"We can't stop Brice," McDonnell said. "He came by his info legitimately. But I'll take care of the cops. If they have no evidence against you, they'll hafta stop. Or tail thousands of people."

Randy snorted beer.

"I wanted you to laugh. See. It'll be all right. Think of it this way. You'll probably have to hire some more bartenders."

"How's that?" Randy asked.

James laughed. "Are you kidding? People will be flocking to your bar. You'll be a celebrity overnight."

Randy looked startled. "I hadn't thought of that. Sweet Mary Mother of Jesus!"

* * *

Gallagher stopped talking, and took a long sip of tea.

"Well, it's official. I met with Macjewski's lawyer and Dale Botham from the DA's Office on Tuesday. I stalled 'em a little, to give us a little extra time on the tail, hoping something would go down. No dice. I saw the DA and the lawyer McDonnell again this morning. I had nothin' to show 'em. It was either leave Macjewski alone or go after everybody left on that frickin' list. So that's where we stand. We gotta leave Macjewski alone. If we do anything to bother him, we get slapped with a harassment suit. And after what Barnes did to that Richards guy, the politicos don't want anymore shit to hit the fan."

Many sighs and much head shaking accompanied the end of Matt's narrative.

"I say, Leftenant?"

"Gawhead, Winston."

"How many names are left on the list?"

"Almost six hundred."

Everyone groaned.

"I know," said Matt. "But that's where we go from here. We'll also continue the current stakeouts as they are. That's all folks."

Julio Vargas hung back as everyone filed out of the room. He then closed the door.

Matt arched his eyebrows. "What's up, compadre?"

"Boss, Barnes was an asshole. But he's got lotsa friends. And some of those friends are gonna look for a way to take you down."

"Yeah, I know. But I got my twenty years in. After this case is done I may pull the pin anyway."

"If you go, I go."

"I appreciate your loyalty, Julio. But let's put that on the back burner for now."

"O.K," Julio said, and both men left the room. As Matt sat down at his desk, his inside line lit up as the phone rang.

"Gallagher."

"Matthew, it's Jane Wilson. The Captain would like to see you."

"O.K. Thank you." Matt hung up, and looked over at Sergeant Wallace.

"Yvonne, why don't you head on home. I'll see you at Franklin Mills tonight. Same time, same station."

"Alright," she said. "Later."

Matt made his way to Parmalee's office. Jane nodded at him and said, "Go right in, Matthew."

"Matthew me boy," said Parmalee. "You've had a rough week. Whaddya say we shake out some of your cobwebs?"

"Whaddya got in mind, Cap?"

"I'm gonna take my perimeter walk in a few minutes. Why don't you come along?"

Parmalee periodically walked through his District to meet the people and chat with his troops. He called it "walking the perimeter."

"Sounds good," Matt replied. "I'll go clear my desk, and you can pick me up on the way out."

* * *

Charlie Therber was restless. He was sitting in the lone chair in his room in the flophouse at the northwest corner of Broad and Wharton. He was tired of running, tired of hiding, tired of life. He was no good and he knew it. Rotten to the core.

Therber was from California. He was wanted there for armed robbery; and he had barely gotten away. He had been up the river twice already for violent crimes. California's three strikes law meant that, if they caught him now, he would get life without parole.

Charlie was thirty-six. And he had decided he was not going back to jail. No way was he going to spend forty or fifty years behind bars. And then die there. No way. He was going out his way. And *his* way was in a blaze of violent glory. And today was the day.

He grabbed his gun, a Charter Arms .357 Target Bulldog. It held five rounds. He checked the cylinder. Fully loaded. He stood and tucked the gun into the front of his pants. He then put two full speed loaders in his left front jeans pocket. He pulled his t-shirt over the weapon. Ready! Or almost ready. He grabbed a half-full bottle of Jack Daniels off a small night table, and took a long pull. O.K. *Now* he was ready.

He went down to the sidewalk, and headed south on Broad Street. He felt oddly at peace now. The booze helped, of course. But it was more than that. He knew he would soon be dead. And he now welcomed death. He strode with purpose, looking for a cop. Any cop would do. He would take one out, and then go down with gun blazing at any other cops that showed up. Unknown to Charlie, there was actually a clinical name for this. It was called Suicide by Cop.

* * *

Captain Richard Parmalee and Lieutenant Matt Gallagher were strolling leisurely south on Broad Street. They were on the east side of the street. Charlie Therber was walking down the west side of the street.

Lieutenant Larry Johnson, in charge of the daytime foot patrol officers, was also on the west side of the street. He was standing against the backside of the Tasker Street entrance for the southbound Broad Street Subway. He was talking to Neil Walker, a young officer fairly new to the job. Walker's partner Chip Posner, a ten-year veteran, was fifteen feet away, talking to the owner of the corner newsstand.

Therber had his man. A big black cop, who had his back to him. The cop was leaning against the waist high back wall of the Subway entrance. He was fifty feet away.

Gallagher and Parmalee had stopped at the northeast corner of Broad and Tasker. They saw the cops on the northwest corner, and started across the street to the talk to them.

Therber was now twenty feet away from Johnson. He pulled out his Bulldog, and quickly closed the gap.

Gallagher saw Therber, and time slowed down. For Gallagher, it practically stopped.

What Matt saw was a man with a gun walking up to Larry Robinson. He was just feet away. A shouted warning would do no good.

In one fluid motion, Matt drew his .45 Colt, snapped off the safety, and thumbed the hammer back. He crouched.

Several things were happening at the same time.

Captain Parmalee saw Gallagher in his firing crouch, and followed Matt's line of sight. Holy shit! A man was about to shoot Larry Robinson. Parmalee yelled, and reached for his own gun.

Officer Chip Posner, at the newsstand, dropped his coffee, released the catch on his holster, and shouted "LOOK OUT!" as he started to draw his weapon.

Larry Robinson saw Officer Neil Walker's eyes grow wide, as Walker's right hand went to his holster. Before Robinson could react, Gallagher fired.

The round entered Charlie Therber's left cheekbone, and exited above his right ear, taking most of the right side of his head with it. The impact slammed him against a storefront. He bounced off and landed face down on the sidewalk.

Now there was pandemonium. Johnson, gun out, was down on one knee, pivoting left and right, looking for trouble.

Posner was standing over Charlie Therber, his own weapon in both hands pointed down at the now lifeless body.

Captain Parmalee was running towards Robinson.

Matt Gallagher was already there. Officer Neil Walker, wide-eyed and shaking, had his gun trained on Lieutenant Gallagher.

Parmalee came up to Walker, and gently pushed his gun arm down. "Easy, son. He's one of the good guys."

Chip Posner had nudged the Bulldog out of Therber's hand with his foot. Posner, besides Gallagher, was the only one who had seen the entire incident from start to finish.

Officer Walker, who had just heard his first up-close gunshot outside of a firing range, was now mumbling "Holy shit!" over and over.

Captain Parmalee had scanned the area, and determined there was no more danger.

"It's alright, Larry. We're clear north, south, east, and west."

Johnson stood up, took one last look around, and secured his Glock. "Holster your weapons, guys," he told Walker and Posner. "That guy ain't gonna get no deader."

Posner looked at Johnson. "I thought you were the one gonna be dead. This asshole had his gun two feet from your head. Lieutenant Gallagher saved your life."

Johnson was staring hard at Gallagher. "Yeah. I'm beginnin' to see that."

Matt said nothing. He gently eased the hammer down on his Colt, flicked the safety on, dropped the magazine, and pulled back the slide. Robinson deftly caught the ejected round. Matt handed the weapon and magazine to Captain Parmalee.

"I guess I won't be needin' this for awhile," he said.

"That's alright, Matt," Parmalee said. "It was a righteous shoot. But you're definitely on admin leave for the foreseeable future."

Parmalee squawked for a crime team to come secure the area. Walker, slightly recovered now, helped Posner start to clear people away from the scene.

Matt walked over to the newsstand, and asked the startled and shaking owner for a bottle of water. As he handed the man a dollar bill, he looked at his hand. It was steady as a rock.

CHAPTER TWENTY-TWO

August 26th, 1993

Task Force Gallagher was once again gathered in the interrogation room of the 3/4. And once again, their leader was among them.

There had been cheers and applause that morning. Rousing cheers and applause. Everyone not yet on the streets had gathered in the detective squad room. The graveyard shift people were all still there. Even some detectives and officers who were off duty had come in. And of course, all of Gallagher's squad was there. Also, and this pleased many people, there were several officers and detectives present from The 17th District.

Lieutenant Matt Gallagher, on his first day back from administrative leave, had stepped in the door at 7:55 A.M., and the place had absolutely erupted. It was jubilant pandemonium. It had brought tears to Matt's eyes. Truth be told, there were many wet cheeks that morning.

After it had all settled down to just chaos, Sergeant Emma Godwin, openly weeping, had presented Matt with a cut of hot tea—two Lipton tea bags, half-and-half, and two sweet 'n lows. Matt had playfully glowered at her.

"Sergeant Godwin, how many damn times have I told you to stop bringing me my tea?"

Emma grabbed the cup back from Matt, set it on a desk, and threw herself into his arms. "I'm so glad you're back," she sniffled into his chest.

"Easy, Sarge," Matt said, gently patting her back. "We can't have our toughest vice hooker blubberin' all over the place now, can we?"

Emma did a crying laugh as only a woman could, and disengaged herself.

Matt looked over her shoulder, and there stood Lieutenants Halston and Johnson, and a woman Matt had never seen before. An attractive, middle-age black woman.

"How they hangin', boys?" Matt yelled good-naturedly.

"High," said Ralph.

"Low," said Larry.

Everyone laughed.

"Matt," said Johnson, "this is my wife Louise, and she ..." Before he could finish, the woman stepped forward, grabbed Matt's upper arms, and kissed him firmly on the mouth. She then pulled back and looked at him with velvety, chocolate eyes.

"Lieutenant Gallagher, words could never possibly express my gratitude for saving my husband's life. I always pray for all police officers; but I will say a special prayer for you every night for the rest of my life."

"Thank you, Mrs. Johnson." Matt was red as a beet.

She placed her hands lightly on his chest. "From now on, you must call me Louise," she said.

Matt smiled warmly. "O.K. And please call me Matt."

"I'd rather say Matthew. It's such a beautiful name."

"Thank you again."

"Now," said Louise, stepping back. "I want you over the house for dinner in the near future. And I won't take no for an answer."

"Sounds good to me," Matt replied. "I never turn down a home-cooked meal."

"Good. What's your favorite meal?" She popped her massive husband in the belly with her tiny fist. "Take notes."

Johnson dutifully pulled out his notebook. There were stifled snickers throughout the room. No one there had ever seen big, bad Larry Johnson so humbly acquiescent.

"That's easy', said Matt. "Meatloaf, mashed potatoes, corn, baked beans, and stewed tomatoes."

No one noticed Sergeant Imogene Patrillo and Detective Irene Costello also writing down Matt's favorite victuals.

"O.K. Larry will let me know when's a good time for you."

"Sounds good, Louise."

* * *

Matt had eventually made his way to his desk. His in box wasn't too bad, since all his normal duties had been disbursed to the squad's Sergeants when Task Force Gallagher had been formed. And, of course, Sergeant Yvonne Wallace had kept him very current on the Booby-Trap Bomber case.

* * *

Back in the interrogation room, Matt surveyed the group. He cleared his throat and spoke. "I hope everyone's been well since I've been gone.

It's good to be back. Now, before we start the meeting, I'd like to introduce everyone to the newest PhD out of the University of Pennsylvania. Ladies and gentlemen, I give you Doctor Nguyen Trung."

Lots of cheers and whistles greeted this announcement. Trung blushed furiously, and for a Vietnamese, that was saying a lot. But Nguyen graciously accepted the handshakes and attaboys from his fellow officers. Truth be told, he was proud as hell; and these people were also his friends.

Once everyone had settled down, Gallagher started in.

"I know everyone's been working on the list. We got it down to about two hundred names left. That's outstanding work, people. Another few weeks and we'll have it done. Then we go back to the ones we've tagged for further questioning."

"Now, we'll keep the stakeouts the same as last month. You've had a few weeks off from that. I'd like to restart them tomorrow night." Matt looked around the room. "O.K. Questions, comments, gripes or bitches?"

Winston Smythe raised a hand.

"Gawhead, Winston."

"I say, Leftenant," said Smythe. "Our lunatic certainly has changed tactics on us, what?"

Matt waited. And here it came.

"I love it when he talks Limey," said Mary Anne Sims.

Everyone laughed. These two were more than just an item now. As far as everyone could tell, they were both totally head over heels in love. And they didn't care who knew it.

"Well," said Matt, "our boy's sick, dead, or layin' low. And I'm leanin' towards the layin' low. But obviously, I've been wrong about him before. And I've had a lotta time to think about it, as you all know."

Smiles around the room. Matt's administrative leave after the shooting was standard procedure. But they all knew that a police shooting never took six weeks to investigate. The desk jockeys had taken their revenge on Gallagher after Deputy Chief Barnes had been reduced to Captain, and "voluntarily" retired from the force. The political animals were legion throughout The Department, and they were powerful. But Gallagher never played their games, and pretty much ignored them, which was one of the reasons he pissed them off.

"But," Matt continued. "He's smart and cunning; and I have no doubt he's gonna strike again. Unfortunately, we only get clues after he hurts people. We just gotta keep pluggin'."

Trung raised a hand.

"Gawhead, Doc."

Nguyen blushed again, and everyone knew that, intentionally or not, Matt had just given Trung a nickname that would stick forever.

"Got any hunches about the next strike, Boss? I mean, aside from the stakeout areas."

"I think," Matt replied, "that the next one's gonna be outside the city somewhere or at least out in the far suburbs. That's what I'd do. To throw us off the scent a little bit. Anybody else?"

The Wiz shot a hand up. "May I make a suggestion?"

"Anytime."

"After you get the list winnowed down, let's get a new scenario together for Big Boy." "I would suggest," The Wiz continued, "that we ask it to look for individuals who have undergone psychiatric treatment, have been committed to institutions, have been in jail, etcetera. I'm sure youse guys can come up with better criteria than I can."

"Not to steal your thunder, Wiz," Matt responded, "but I was gonna do that. And I guess now is a good time as any to start." Matt paused, made a note, and looked around the room. "Everybody can contribute on this. Put your ideas on paper; and we'll gather everything together and consolidate it. Anybody else?"

No one stirred.

"O.K, that's it. Before your stakeouts tomorrow night let's keep workin' on the list."

Everyone filed out of the room, and Matt and Yvonne returned to their desks.

"Is your car here?" Matt asked her.

"Actually, it's in the shop. I've been usin' the Vic."

"That's fine. Gawhead and keep usin' it. I'll meet you at Somnia Furniture at eight o'clock."

"O.K.," said Yvonne. "You want a lift home?"

"No. I'm gonna stick around and clean the place up a bit. It needs it."

Yvonne knew that Matt did this on a regular basis, usually on Tuesday nights. But he'd been away for a while. Still, it was heard to believe that a Lieutenant—a twenty-year veteran, no less—actually cleaned bathrooms and such. The guy was unbelievable. And after this case was settled, she was definitely going after him. And she would pull out all the stops.

"Alright," she said. "See ya tonight."

* * *

Matt went downstairs to his locker, and changed into some old sweats. He then went back upstairs and commenced cleaning. Even the cops that had seen him do this before shook their heads in amusement. Fuckin' Gallagher!

* * *

Sergeant Pablo Gonzales and Detective Winston Smythe were headed to Southwest Philly in their official Crown Vic. They would check the names on the list from this part of town before they headed for their stakeouts at the airport the next evening.

"The Loo looked good, didn't he?" said Pablo.

"Yes, he did," replied Smythe. "Good color, slim and trim. I venture to say he worked on his golf game and his tan."

"Actually, word I got, he was at the computer room at the Roundhouse most days. He definitely took advantage of the situation. He'd golf in the morning, and work a twelve-to-eight shift over at HQ. He wanted to bring himself up to speed on computers. We'll all be getting desktop models soon, you know. Late this year or early next."

"About bloody time," Smythe rejoined. "It's been so long since I took computer courses, I had to sign up for a refresher at LaSalle University."

"LaSalle? Christ, that's way over in the Logan section of town, ain't it?"

"That's right, lad. Everything closer to home was all booked solid for the fall semester. So I took what I could get, what?"

"You gonna drive or use The System?" Pablo asked.

"Drive, definitely. It's Tuesday nights, eight-to-eleven. When classes end, I want to vacate the area as quickly as possible."

"I hear ya," said Pablo. "That area's pretty bad at night. The University's got more guards than some prisons. O.K., what's our first address?"

* * *

Sergeant Julio Vargas and Detective Nguyen Trung were northbound on I-95. They were going to get off at Cottman Avenue, and check some Northeast residents on the list.

"I'm so fuckin' proud of ya, I could spit," Julio said to Nguyen. "I'll betcha aced the friggin' tests, didn't ya."

"Yes I did, my loveable, boneheaded Sergeant. You know, I hate to say this. But it was a breeze to me."

"I know it was," said Julio. "Refresh my memory. What was your dissertation on?"

"Such a big word for you, Sergeant."

"Quit breakin' my fuckin' balls and tell me, goddammit!"

"O.K., O.K.," Trung laughed. "It was called 'The Military Role of the United Nations in the World Today'."

"Boy, that's timely. I'll bet Somalia came up a lot."

"Actually," Trung said, "I left that mess out."

"Why?"

"I'm not sure that I, or anybody else, have a handle on that situation. It's very volatile. Secretary Aspen has just ordered the deployment of a large Ranger Force, supplemented with Special Ops people from all the services. I'm sorry to say our boys might wind up taking substantial casualties."

"How ya figure?

"Well," said Nguyen, "they're gonna go after the warlords, somebody like Adid. And they'll have to go in with a large force, right in the middle of a big concentration of civilians. One of those times, they're gonna get trapped in there somewhere, and have to fight their way out. It'll be very bad."

"Jeez, I hope you're wrong."

"So do I, Julio. So do I."

* * *

August 27th, 1993

Matt Gallagher parked his 1987 Buick LeSabre in the parking lot of Somnia Furniture at the Franklin Mills Mall complex. The car was green with white leather interior. It was in mint condition. The Buick was one of the three cars Matt had kept from his fathers dealership before he sold it. Matt was, in a word, rich. But he didn't flash it; and he never talked about it.

He walked over to the sidewalk in front of the store and waited. It was a few minutes until eight, and sure enough Yvonne pulled up in the Crown Vic.

"Evening, gorgeous." Matt cursed, and looked away. "I'm sorry, Yvonne. That was inappropriate."

"Well knock me over with a feather. It only took you three months to say something like that." And then she smiled like the sun. "And I thank you for the compliment."

They were both blushing. Matt got in the car.

"Look," said Yvonne. "We can't deny the attraction. Would it be so wrong to follow up on it?" She pulled out of Somnia's lot and headed for the huge parking lots on the other side of the complex.

"I guess not," Matt replied. "But I think I've told you this; I've never dated anyone but my wife."

"Yes, you did tell me." She stopped at a stop sign, and turned and looked at Matt.

"Listen. My folks have a place in Sea Isle City." This was on the Jersey shore. "What say we go down for a day or two after Labor Day? September's the best month to go down the shore. The crowds are all gone, the weather's good, and the ocean is still warm."

"Alright. It's a date. We'll see how things go. We'll go down on a Sunday and stay for a day or two."

"Perfect," said Yvonne. She guided the Vic to a spot against a curb, rear end in. They could see a lot of acreage from here.

"You wanna listen to the Phils?" Yvonne asked.

"The Fightins are off tonight. They're headed to Cincy for a three game set."

"How they been doin'?" Yvonne, like everyone in the city, knew the Phils were almost a lock for the playoffs. She followed them; but she wasn't a fanatic about it.

"They're eighty and forty-seven, about eight games up on the Cardinals and Expos. Even if they go five hundred the rest of the way, they got a great shot. They beat the Rockies eight-to-five last night. I was down there with a neighbor. Schilling pitched fairly well, and the Phils had eleven hits. It was great. There were over forty-six thousand people there."

"It *is* getting wild," Yvonne said. "Even my mom's into it. And if you knew my mom, that would be a big surprise."

They sat together in companionable silence for a while, eyes front and heads swiveling to see all they could see.

"So," Yvonne said eventually. "Do you still feel like a dinosaur on a computer?"

Matt laughed good-naturedly. It was no secret he had spent most of his administrative leave at the Roundhouse in the computer center.

"I feel competent now, but just barely," Matt said. "The Wiz suggested I buy a McIntosh or an IBM PC. I'm gonna do it. If I wait for one to appear on my desk in the squad room, I'll be hopelessly out of practice."

"It's a good idea," she said. "And not to stick my nose into your finances, but I would get a laptop, too. You can afford it. Then you can plug in at certain places away from home. There're not many of them yet; but I see the day when they're everywhere, like in cafes and bars and hotels and places like that."

"Ya know, The Wiz said pretty much the same thing. I told her though, that I'm taking her with me when I buy."

"Good idea."

"Jeet?" asked Matt.

"No, Joo?"

"No. I should've brought something."

"Look in the back," said Yvonne.

Matt turned around in his seat, and saw a Styrofoam cooler on the floor. He grabbed it by the handle, and pulled it up and into his lap.

"You're too good," he said. "What'd ya bring?"

"Hoagies and Tastykakes. Chips and ice tea."

"Outstanding!" Matt started breaking out the chow.

* * *

Randy Macjewski sat on a bench at the Villanova Station of the SEPTA Route 100 light-rail train. It was one of two stops of the line on the Villanova campus. The other was the Stadium Station. Randy had parked his Oldsmobile '98 on Lowrys Lane, on the east side of a set of railroad tracks. The next street up was Lancaster Avenue, also called US Route 30. He was ready for a quick getaway if necessary. And he definitely hoped it was.

He had started this little mission yesterday. He would sit at one stop for a while, then get up and walk on Aldwyn Lane to the other, moving slowly. The news reports had said most of the snatch and runs had been in this area. The crooks would wait until after dark, when the train stops and the immediate area were relatively deserted.

Randy was dressed in light gray slacks, and a short sleeve dress shirt with a black tie. He had on a full blonde wig, with matching fake mustache. The flesh colored theatrical gloves completed the disguise. He carried a light-brown, laptop computer briefcase. And it was the most devastating booby-trap yet.

Inside the briefcase was a Claymore mine, a particularly vicious anti-personnel weapon. Randy had gotten two of them from the late Dickie Howsten's little collection of illegal weaponry that he had mailed home from Vietnam, a piece at a time.

The Claymore was a crescent-shaped, rectangular device, with two holes in the back for a detonator. Either hole could be used. Also redundant was the printed message under the word FRONT, on the front side of the mine. It said, "POINT THIS SIDE TOWARD ENEMY."

Inside the metal case of the mine, was a solid slab of C-4, a plastic explosive. The C-4 was embedded on the front, convex side with seven hundred streel ball bearings. It was meant for at least a squad-size element.

Randy hoped no innocents got hurt; but during his slow descent into madness, this concern had mattered less and less. Unless the device was opened with no one but the robbers around, there was bound to be "collateral damage," as the military so judiciously put it.

A train came into the station; and Randy got up and walked out with the few departing passengers. He headed south on Aldwyn Lane to Ithan Avenue, and turned left toward the Stadium stop of the Route 100 train.

* * *

Paulie Gizzuno and Richie Nittino were headed for the same location. They had been trolling this area all summer. Pickins' were slim, but that was O.K. They didn't want big crowds around when they did their thing.

Sometimes they just grabbed and ran. Other times one of the youths would pull a switchblade, and the other would demand the briefcase. Sometimes both would pull their knives. They only went for the thinner cases. These had the most potential to be one of those new laptop computers. The boys in South Philly paid top dollar for these items.

Paulie was twenty, Richie nineteen. Since boyhood both boys, like many an Italian youth in South Philadelphia, had longed to become an associate for one of the capos who ran the various factions that made up the Philadelphia branch of La Cosa Nostra.

* * *

The Philly Mob was in the midst of uncertainty, as it were. With Nicky Scarfo in prison and out of the picture, the leadership was up for grabs. Joey Merlino and John Stanfa were fighting it out; and the rest of the made membership was waiting for the best man to win. Or the luckiest.

Skinny Joey had escaped one hit attempt by Scarfo, before Scarfo had been sent to prison. The hit was canceled, believe it or not, when Scarfo's son couldn't get a dinner reservation at the Sparks Steak House, the planned hit location.

Stanfa then took his shot. On August 5th, Merlino and his friend Mike Ciancaglini were ambushed on a corner in South Philly. Joey was shot in the ass, and Ciancaglini was killed. This really heated things up. Skinny Joey had many backers, and Ciancaglini had many siblings and relatives. It was now war between the Stanfa and Merlino factions. Paulie and Richie didn't care who won. They just wanted in, and then, in a few years, a chance to make their bones.

* * *

Randy arrived at the Stadium stop, and sat down on a bench. He hadn't been there for more than a minute, when he heard what were almost two simultaneous clicks from behind him. He knew what that noise was. He owned several switchblades himself.

Two youths came around the bench. Both boys were breathing rapidly, and their faces were flushed. Randy was cool as an iceberg. *Two more, Mom and Dad. Here come two bastards for judgment at the Pearly Gates.*

Paulie said, "Give up the briefcase, man, and you won't get hurt. And do it quick." Richie looked around nervously.

"Take it," Randy said. "Just please don't hurt me." He handed the briefcase to Paulie.

"Let's go," said Richie; and the two youths took off. This was a mugging, Italian style. Never hurt the victim if he cooperates.

As soon as they left, Randy stood up and headed for his car on Lowrys Road. He saw the two robbers disappear up Barleycone Lane. He hoped to be long gone before they opened the booby-trapped briefcase. It was dark, and as he walked, he shed mustache and wig, and removed the gloves. He bent over quickly, and threw them down a sewer. Then, five minutes after the incident, Randy was eastbound in his car on Lancaster Avenue, heading home.

Richie and Paulie, young and fit, had been much quicker. Three minutes after the heist, *they* were on Lancaster Avenue, headed home. They were in a stolen car, of course.

* * *

Earlier in the evening, they had taken the Broad Street Subway north from the Oregon Station. They got off at City Hall, passed under that massive edifice, and came up into Suburban Station at 15th Street. They took an R-6 train, and got off at Ivy Ridge Station in Manayunk. There they had quickly boosted a car. It was a blue Olds Calais that had seen better days. They had driven to Villanova, and parked on a small side street that connected to Lancaster Avenue. After that, it was just a matter of time. They had been successful every trip so far. But this was the last one. They didn't want to press their luck. Besides, school was starting soon; and there would be too many people around, even at night.

* * *

Now the two mob wannabes were westbound on Lancaster Avenue. Paulie was driving, with Richie in the passenger seat, briefcase in his lap. Paulie took the on-ramp for I-476 North, also called the Blue Route. It was a long access ramp; and Paulie accelerated smoothly into the right hand lane of the highway. Traffic was light. After a moment, Paulie looked over and said, "Let's see what we got."

Richie angled the briefcase slightly towards Paulie, and opened it up. As the lid came up, the wire attached to the lid came up with it, and closed a small, battery-operated electric switch. The two young men never knew what hit them.

* * *

Lance Brickman had his eighteen-wheel rig northbound on the Blue Route, I-476. He had just passed Exit 5, and he estimated another half-hour, and he would be home in Manayunk. In a few minutes, he would be on I-76 East, and then the Belmont Exit and home.

A small car (all cars were small to truckers) pulled smoothly onto the highway about an eighth of a mile in front of him. His mind recorded this data automatically. Lance reached for the dashboard to tune to WYSP FM on the radio. He looked back up just in time to see the vehicle in front of him explode in a tremendous thunderbolt of flame. *HOLY SHIT!*

The Claymore decapitated both young men when it exploded. The force of the blast blew the roof to shreds, and the splattered pieces of both youths' heads rocketed skyward, vaporizing as they went. The car actually left the road for a microsecond; and it was enough. It veered left upon re-contact with the highway, threw up dust and gravel as it rode the left shoulder, and came right again. It started to leave the highway, but veered left once more, and this was one veer too many.

The pilot-less Oldsmobile turned sideways, and starting flipping. On one flip, the gas tank came partially loose and began leaking.

At first, Lance Brickman was transfixed by the sight of the car exploding. Then he came to his senses, and started braking and downshifting. But he had been doing seventy; and the car had immediately lost speed. He moved right when the car moved left. Then he went left when the car veered right. But the Olds had then jumped left with him. The car had started flipping and the rig was still doing 25 mph when it smashed into and ran over the car just as the gas tank blew.

The force of the explosion lifted the front of the rig three feet off the road, and threw the flywheel right into the driver's compartment. It came into the cab on an angle and slammed into Lance Brickman's torso. He was sliced and diced to pieces before he could burn to death.

CHAPTER TWENTY-THREE

September 2nd, 1993

Gallagher called the meeting to order. The folks in the 3/4 interrogation room settled down. Matt looked slowly around the room.

"Some of you might have heard about the horrific accident on the Blue Route last week. Traffic was light at the time. While no one came forward and said they saw it happen, there were plenty of witnesses afterward."

Matt paused and took a sip of tea.

"There was almost nothing left of the two individuals in the car, which was roasted to a cinder and crushed by the truck. The trucker was sliced up by his flywheel; and he too was burned to the bone. The victims have all finally been identified. The two in the car are, or were that is, Paulie Gizzuno and Richie Nitinno from the Passyunk neighborhood of South Philly. The trucker was a Lance Brickman of Manayunk.

"This morning I received two important phone calls. An investigator for the Pennsylvania State Police who handled the accident, said his team discovered odd bits from the crash site—steel ball bearings and a piece of casing, which their lab determined to be metal from a Claymore anti-personnel mine."

Whistles and jaw drops accompanied this news.

"That's right," Matt continued. "And small pieces of another material turned out to be what they are certain is parts of a briefcase. That's why he called me. It looks like our boy has struck again."

Winston Smythe raised his hand.

"Gawhead, Winston."

"I say, Leftenant. Are we sure about this?'

"That question brings me to the second phone call. It was from a very reliable source I can't identify."

Only Gallagher, Sergeant Wallace, Captain Parmalee, and Chief Inspector Loudin knew the source's identity. Matt had not told Inspector Watson, his immediate superior in South Division Detectives, for obvious reasons. The man would have gone public with it to embarrass Gallagher.

Matt continued. "My source tells me that the two youths killed in the car were responsible for a series of snatch and runs around Villanova University."

"Wow!" said Sergeant Vargas.

"Ditto that!" chimed in Sergeant Wallace.

"Why'd your source let you know this, Matt?" asked Detective Mike Robinson.

"Well," said Matt. "He hinted to me that if we ever identify the Bomber, the boys in South Philly would like first crack at him. He said, and on this he and I are in complete agreement, he said nobody deserved to die like that."

Matt let the hubbub die down. "Kind of ironic that these guys want to take the law into their own hands, much as our lunatic Bomber is doing. Needless to say, I told him that was never gonna happen. However, it raised a red flag. Certain individuals may decide to start following us to get a lead on the case. Watch out for tails. If you are positive you're being followed, arrest the individuals, and we'll charge them with hindering a police investigation. I don't care whether the charge sticks or not. Just do it."

"Now," Matt said. "Keep at it with the crime victims list. It's almost finished. The new stakeouts are as follows: Sergeant Vargas and Detective Trung will be at the Bridge Street EL terminal. There's been some late night muggings there recently."

Vargas and Trung took their notes.

"Sergeant Gonzales and Detective Smythe will be at the 69th Street terminal of the Elevated. Same thing's been happenin' down there. Myself and Sergeant Wallace will be in the parking lot at 30th Street Station. Late night problems down there recently." Matt looked around the room and saw that everyone was done taking notes. "O.K. Questions?"

"Yes, Matt," said Nguyen Trung. "About the stakeouts. Isn't it too soon for him to strike again?"

"At this point I don't know," Matt replied. "I was wrong on this one. He changed up on us. We gotta keep pluggin'. Anybody else?"

There were no more questions.

"O.K., that's it," Matt said. "Go to it."

* * *

Randy Macjewski worked his last batch of Krimpets for the day, and double-checked his line and oven settings. Satisfied, he stripped off his apron and headed for the locker room. He wanted to get home and watch the news. He had heard snatches of conversation in the break room that indicated police had determined some kind of bomb had exploded in that car on I-476. Before the truck had rolled over it. He changed clothes hurriedly, and punched out and headed for the parking lot.

* * *

Denise Reilly saw her boss, Randy Macjewski, walk in the door of the S & B Bar, and pulled a Yuengling Lager out of the ice. Randy sat at the bar and Denise slid the beer in front of him.

"Thanks, Denise." Randy drained the beer in three gulps and Denise was right there with another.

"Rough day, Boss?" she asked.

"Just hot," Randy said.

Jim Richards came over and placed the latest paperwork on the bar.

"Whenever you can get to it, Boss," he said. "As usual, you're way ahead on your bills."

"Thanks, Jim." Randy grabbed a remote from just behind the bar, and flicked the TV to channel six. The early edition of "Action News" was on. After a few minutes, the latest on the Blue Route accident came up.

Lisa Thomas Laury, the early edition anchor, relayed the latest information. There was some kind of explosive device in the car that went off first. The gas tank exploded as the car was flipping sideways, just as the truck was plowing into the wreckage. The truck's diesel tank also eventually erupted. Police said all three victims were dead before they were burned.

Randy slowly sipped at his beer. So, he had finally taken the life of an innocent person. That hurt. But he would not be deterred. Not now. He was going right back into action.

Randy took hold of the paperwork and asked Denise for the bar's checkbook. He quickly signed the invoices over Jim's signature, and made out the appropriate checks. He finished his beer. "Goodnight folks."

"See ya, Boss,"

"Later, Randy."

Randy went up and into his house, made a sandwich and grabbed a beer. He went down to the basement, opened the fuse box and unscrewed one of the glass fuses. Inserting a key into the uncovered slot, he turned it and simultaneously pushed on the wall panel. The fake panel swung open on internal hinges. Replacing the fuse, Randy closed the box. Grabbing his sandwich and brew, he entered his secret little workshop and closed the door behind him.

Randy took a bite of sandwich and a swallow of beer, and set them aside. He reached over for the pizza box—sans pizza—and placed it before him on the workbench.

The Claymore mine was already in place and glued down. Randy had used a ton of Gorilla glue to accomplish this. The front of the mine was facing up, and the detonator was already inserted into the back of the mine. Randy taped down the detonator wire and the electric switch it was attached to. The switch was powered by a watch battery. The pull wire was taped down to the inside of the box lid.

Randy pulled the lid down, and inserted the hook that dangled from the wire into a little eyelet on the switch. He then closed the lid all the way. The bomb was now armed. Randy then used some plumber's tape to secure the lid at the front corners. He would remove this tape when he went into action.

Randy finished his sandwich, and got up and opened the workshop door. He placed the plate and empty beer bottle on a little side table, and then reached inside and very carefully picked up the booby-trapped pizza box. He walked it into the basement proper and placed it gently on a coffee table. He then closed and locked the fake wall panel, and hurried up the stairs with the plate and bottle. He placed these on the kitchen table, and went back downstairs.

Randy stared for a long time at the pizza box. The next one to open the lid was a dead man. He carefully picked it up. *Actually,* he thought, *it was safe now.* The lid couldn't come up until the tape at the corners was removed. He carried it upstairs and out to his Oldsmobile. He locked it in the trunk and went back in the house.

Jim Richards was behind the bar, and happened to look out the small side window that faced out onto Wensley Street. He saw Randy lock what appeared to be a pizza box in his trunk. *Wonder that that's all about,* he thought. *Oh well, none of my business.*

* * *

8:30 P.M. that Thursday found Lieutenant Gallagher and Sergeant Wallace in the 30th Street Station parking lot in West Philadelphia. Gallagher was reading *The Daily News* while Yvonne watched the area.

"Anything interesting in there?" she asked him.

"Lots of follow up articles about the gunfight on I-76. Hard to believe those guys could be that stupid. The citizens are definitely up in arms."

* * *

On August 21st, a car carrying Joey Merlino and his pals had met up with a car carrying John Stanfa and his crew. On The Schuylkill Expressway in broad daylight, the two cars from rival factions of The Philadelphia Mob erupted in gunfire. Stanfa's son was shot in the face in what appeared to be the only casualty. Traffic had been heavy in the area of the shootout, and citizens and politicians had been enraged. Of course, in front of the TV news cameras, each politician had tried to out-enrage his or her colleagues.

"Yeah," Yvonne said. "The heat's definitely gonna be on those idiots now."

"Right. Any of those goofballs so much as jaywalks, they're goin' down. Says here that the FBI, the BATF, and the city's own task force on organized crime are all doing surveillance on these guys, and they're not even tryin' to be discreet about it."

"Brice is probably pissed off," Yvonne observed.

"Why's that?"

"All his stuff on the Bomber is now relegated to the deep inside pages of *The DN*."

"Yeah," agreed Matt. "I noticed that. But he had his time in the sun. Him and McBride at *The Inky*, and Capstone at *POW*, all had lots to say about us and the Bomber the last few weeks. I oughtta call Skinny Joey and thank him for hoggin' all the publicity lately."

"Yeah," said Yvonne. "Why don't you watch awhile and let me see the paper?"

"Here ya go."

"Thanks."

* * *

September 4th, 1993

Randy Macjewski woke up at 10:30 P.M. to the sound of his alarm. Saturday was his drinking day; and he had stayed the course. He didn't want to give anybody reason to wonder why he wasn't in the bar today. He had left the bar at 5:00 P.M., and headed upstairs for a nap. Now it was time for the mission.

He dressed in old jeans and a collared polo shirt. His Air Jordan's completed the casual ensemble. He grabbed his Colt M1911, placed it in his back waistband, and pulled the shirt over it. He headed outside, jumped in the Olds, and left the immediate neighborhood.

On Ontario Avenue he stopped the car, reached under the seat, and brought up a paper bag. He pulled out a grey wig and a pair of eyeglasses with plain glass lenses. After taking a quick look around he donned his disguise. He cheeked again, the coast was clear. He got out of the car and opened the trunk. He slowly lifted out the pizza box, and then walked to the passenger side front door. Leaning into the open window, he gently placed the box on the front seat. He then very carefully removed the tape from each front corner. Tossing the tape away, he quickly went around the front of the car, got in and drove away.

Randy made a left on Kensington Avenue, and then turned right on Clearfield Street. It had started to rain, and there were sharp cracks of thunder. He made a right on F Street, and parked at the corner of Clementine and F. He got out, checked the wad in his left pocket, and went around and retrieved the pizza bomb.

Randy started to walk slowly down Clementine Street, pausing now and then to look up as if searching for an address. It was very dark and now the rain was really coming down. Most of the streetlights in this neighborhood had been shot out long ago.

Nothing so far, he thought. Randy reached the end of the block and turned right on E Street. It was almost totally dark here. He turned down Lippincott Street, and continued his little charade.

After a few seconds, he heard soft footsteps behind him.

"Hey, man!"

Randy turned around and saw what looked like two Puerto Rican young men.

"Can I help you guys?" Randy asked.

"You sure can, Puto. That's my pizza."

"I don't think so, sir. It's for an address on this street."

One of the youths pulled out a snub-nosed revolver.

"It's my pizza, man. Give it up."

Randy handed over the box.

"And your wad, man," said the youth without the gun. "All you delivery guys got a wad."

Randy slowly reached into his pocket and produced the money, which was quickly snatched away.

"Please don't hurt me," Randy said, tamping down an urge to draw his Colt and waste these punks before they wasted him.

"Just take off," said the one with the gun. "And I mean now."

Randy walked rapidly down Lippincott to F Street, and covered the short distance to his car. Quickly looking around and seeing no one, he threw the wig and glasses down a sewer. He jumped in the car, and headed up F Street to Allegheny Avenue. He turned right and made for home.

* * *

The two pizza thieves retraced their steps, crossed E Street, ran up the stairs to a deserted, vacant house, and let themselves in. They quickly ran down to the basement and turned on two flashlights they always kept down there.

"Damn," said one. "This frickin' pizza's heavy. Must have all the toppin's. How much loot we get?"

"Almost two hundred," replied his companion. "That stupid puto. Carryin' all this money in our neighborhood."

They both laughed.

"Well," said one. "Let's eat."

The other young man raised the lid, and there was a tremendous explosion. Simultaneously, there was also a loud crack of thunder. What was left of their bodies wouldn't be found for five days.

* * *

September 9th , 1993

Matt Gallagher was on his way to convene a meeting of his Task Force, when his outside line lit up.

"Lieutenant Gallagher."

"Loo, this is Sergeant Todd May of Explosives."

"What can I do for you, Sarge?"

"I'm at thirty-nine-oh-one E Street, in West Kensington. Earlier, a couple of bodies were found in the basement here. When the dicks from The 24th District saw what they had, they called us in. These kids were killed by a Claymore mine."

"Oh my God!"

"That's right, Loo. I figured you'd wanna know about this."

"Got that right," Matt said. "What was that address again?"

"Thirty-nine-oh-one E Street. If you're comin' over, I suggest boots and gloves. It's a real mess."

"O.K. Thanks, Sarge." Matt hung up and went into the interrogation room. He got everybody's attention. He related the latest news.

"Me and Yvonne, and Trung, Vargas, Gonzales and Smythe. We're all goin' to this crime scene. Get gloves and over boots from downstairs, and we'll all meet there. Let's go."

* * *

The basement of the little house had gotten somewhat crowded.

With the floodlights, crime scene technicians, bomb squad people, and detectives from The 24th District all there, it didn't leave much room for Task Force Gallagher. But they crowded in anyway.

"I'm Jake Gaston from The 24th, Loo."

Matt extended a hand and they shook.

"What a mess," Matt said.

"Yeah," said Gaston. "There's pieces of these guys all over the basement."

"Any ID yet?" Matt asked.

"Nah. That's gonna take awhile."

A man came up to Matt. "I'm Sergeant May."

"Do you mind?" Matt asked Gaston.

"Not at all," said Jake. "I know all about your Task Force. You can have it."

"No, it's yours. I'll just need a copy of your report, and I want some info from the Sarge here."

"Gawhead."

"O.K.," Matt said to Sergeant May. "Whaddya got?"

"It was a Claymore in a pizza box. We found the bottom of the box almost intact. It was rigged to explode upon opening. They never knew what hit 'em."

"As before, please have your office forward a copy of your report to my Task Force."

"I'll handle that myself," replied May.

Matt turned to Gaston. "Have there been problems with pizza delivery guys around here lately?"

"Yeah. But with all the other action around here, it was given a low priority."

"O.K., folks," Matt said to his Three-Four people. "Take a look. And when you're done, meet me outside."

* * *

September 16th, 1993

The Thursday afternoon meeting of Task Force Gallagher broke up and Vargas, Trung, Smythe, and Gonzales left to grab some chow before heading for their stakeouts.

Matt's outside line lit up as he approached his desk. "Lieutenant Gallagher,"

he said into the phone.

"Lieutenant, my name is Jim Richards. I'm the manager of the S & B Bar over in Port Richmond."

Matt's hackles rose. That was Macjewski's bar.

"What can I do for you, Mister Richards?"

"Well, we know about that incident in West Kensington last week."

"Go on."

"Well," Richards continued, "the weekend night man called me this morning when he read the paper about it. Apparently, the cops over there finally released the details involved."

"Actually, I approved that release," Matt said. "But please continue."

"Well, the night guy, Mike Reilly, told me that several months back, he overheard a conversation here at the bar between my boss, Randy Macjewski, and Theresa Barnes, a night bartender."

"Keep going," Matt said.

"Well, Theresa told Randy that she couldn't get a pizza delivered to her house because delivery guys kept gettin' ripped off. Around F Street and those little streets like Clementine and Lippincott. And one night about two weeks ago, I saw Randy put a pizza box in the trunk of his car."

Richards paused and audibly cleared his throat.

"Well," said Richards. "I hated to make this phone call. But I know you people were following Randy and all. I thought you needed to know this."

"And you were right," Matt replied. "Do you know where Randy is now?"

"I imagine at Tastykake."

"Thank you, Mr. Richards. If he shows up at the bar before we see him, call me at this number. Someone will always answer." Matt hung up and called Sergeants Emma Godwin and Eileen Robinson and Detective Mike Robinson over to his desk.

"Eileen," Matt said to Sergeant Johnson. "I need you to stay here and man the phones,"

"O.K.," she said.

Matt quickly told them about the phone conversation.

"We're goin' to Tastykake. Emma, I want you and Mike to go to the back of the building and ask somebody where Randy's work area is. Yvonne and I will go in front and ask the same thing. Everybody put their vest on beforehand. Let's go."

They all met outside and jumped in Crown Vics. Matt let Yvonne take the wheel as usual. No sirens, Matt had told them. Just follow Yvonne.

Yvonne went down Wharton Street to Front Street, turned left and got on I-95 North near Pemberton Street. She then picked up the cross town expressway, I-676, and headed west. She got on I-76 West, and took it all the way to the Ridge Avenue exit. She headed south on Ridge, and made a left on Allegheny Avenue. Several blocks later she made a left on Hunting Park Avenue, and shortly after turned into the Tasty Baking Company parking lot. Matt and Yvonne waited for their backup. Godwin and Robinson were right on their heels.

"O.K.," Matt said. "Weapons check."

They all brought out their weapons, jacked a round into the chamber, and put the weapons on safe. Then they gently let the hammers down and re-holstered them.

"O.K.," Matt said. "You know what to do. Let's go."

Matt and Yvonne headed for the main entrance, and Emma and Mike headed for the back.

Matt and Yvonne went in, and were directed to a supervisor's office. They knocked on the door.

"Can I help you?" asked a woman behind a desk.

Matt and Yvonne flashed their gold. "Yes," Matt said. "I'd like you to show us to Randy Macjewski's work area."

"Is there a problem?"

"We just need to talk to him, ma'am."

"I could call him down here."

Yvonne placed her hands on the desk and leaned forward. "Show us the way. Now!"

* * *

Randy Macjewski was leaning on the rail that protected his work area. He happened to look down, and saw the superintendent and Lieutenant Gallagher and Sergeant Wallace come out of the office.

The jig is definitely up, he thought. Not wasting a moment, he ran down the short hallway and into the locker room. He quickly unlocked and opened his locker, and reached in the back for an item wrapped in a large towel. Ten seconds later he had the M16A1 assembled. He slapped in a twenty round magazine, and put another in his pocket. He pulled and released the charging handle and placed the selector switch on auto. He ran back to his work area and leaned over the rail.

Gallagher and Wallace had told the supervisor to hang back after she pointed out Macjewski's work area. Matt and Yvonne were both looking up, and both saw Macjewski at the same time. He had a rifle trained on them.

"Oh shit!" Matt exclaimed. He quickly pushed Yvonne toward a half-empty supply pallet. They both took several running steps and started to dive over it for cover.

Randy had the selector switch on the M16A1 on full auto. He aimed, held tight to the hand guards with his left hand, and pulled the trigger for a three round burst.

An M16A1 on full automatic pulls high and right. Randy's burst caught Matt and Yvonne mid-dive.

The first round caught Yvonne in the back of the skull just above the neck, propelling her over the pallet and several feet beyond. The second and third rounds, moving high and right, caught Matt in the left and right shoulders above the vest. One punched a fairly clean hole through the left pectoral. The other round broke his right shoulder and collarbone, and an explosion of blood, tissue, and bone burst through the right side of his chest. He was also propelled beyond the pallet.

Emma Godwin came running up, weapon drawn.

"DROP THE WEAPON!" she screamed up at Macjewski.

Randy brought the weapon around to bear on Godwin. Emma, already in a firing crouch, put three 9mm slugs in his ten ring. Macjewski was slammed against a wall, and was dead before he hit the ground.

* * *

Gallagher was vaguely aware of more shots being fired; but his immediate concern was to get to Yvonne. He tried to raise himself up by his arms. He screamed in agony and passed out.

EPILOGUE

October 10th, 1993

Lieutenant Matt Gallagher was dozing in his bed in a private room at Temple University Hospital. It had been over three weeks since the shooting.

His wounds had been severe; but the right side wound was more serious. The exit wound was so large that it couldn't be closed by stitches. Doctors had finally taken a skin graft from his thigh to his chest. It was healing, but slowly.

There was a knock on the door, and Matt came groggily awake. "Come in," he called out weakly.

In response, three men came into the room. They were Mayor Ed Rendell, Police Commissioner Augustus Phillips, and Chief Inspector Maxwell Loudin, Head of Detectives for The Philadelphia Police Department.

Matt reached for his control box, and raised his bed to a sitting position. "Good afternoon, gentleman," he said.

"Matthew," responded the Mayor.

"Matthew lad," greeted the Commissioner

"How ya feeling, Lieutenant?" asked Loudin.

"I've been better," said Matt. "I know you've all been here before; but I just vaguely remember it. They just stopped sedating me during the day. Now they just give me something at night to sleep."

"We figured that," said the Mayor. "We asked the Docs to let us know when you'd be alert. We just found out today, so we thought we'd stop by."

"I appreciate it."

All four men were silent for a moment. Matt cleared his throat and took a drink from his water glass. "I might've asked this before; but like I said, I don't remember. How was the funeral?"

"Top notch," said Phillips. "There were thousands of cops there from all over. She was sent off in style."

"That's good to hear." Matt briefly closed his eyes in grief. Oh Yvonne!

"The Docs tell us you're healin' good," said the Mayor. "They say you should be out of here in a week or two."

"How the Phils doin'?" Matt asked.

"We brought up *The DN*," Rendell replied. "They got hammered last night. Mulholland got rocked. The Braves were poundin' the ball. Lemke, McGriff, Pendleton—all of 'em. The Phils are down two to one."

The Mayor was referring, of course, to the NLCS, the Phils and the Atlanta Braves. The pennant was up for grabs.

"They play tonight?"

"Yeah," said Loudin. "Danny Jackson against John Smoltz. Smoltz is gonna be tough."

"Well, we won't stay," said Phillips. "We just wanted to check up on you."

"You're up for several commendations," said Loudin.

"That won't bring Yvonne back," said Matt.

Again, there was an awkward silence.

"I'm sorry I said that," Matt apologized.

"It was a tough loss for all of us, Matt," said the Commissioner. "Look, get well. We need you."

The men murmured their goodbyes and took their leave. Matt gave a long sigh and teared up a little. Oh Yvonne!

* * *

October 13th, 1993

Matt Gallagher had been watching the Phils pound Greg Maddux. They were up three games to two in the series. Tommy Greene had pitched well. West had pitched a perfect eighth inning. It was Wild Thing Time.

* * *

In the lobby of Temple University Hospital, Sergeant Imogene Patrillo and Detective Irene Costello were waiting for an elevator. They were here for a surprise visit. The victim was Gallagher. As soon as they had heard he was consistently coherent, they made their plans. It wouldn't have been kosher to seduce a comatose patient.

The elevator arrived, and they got in and pushed the button for the 12th floor.

"O.K.," said Irene. "You flip."

"Alright," said Imogene. "You call."

Patrillo flipped a quarter through the air, caught it, and slapped it down on the back of her left hand.

"Well. Call it."

"Heads," said Irene.

Imogene uncovered the coin so both could see. It was heads.

"Slut!" said Patrillo.

"Bitch!" said Costello.

"Two out of three?"

"No fuckin' way. I won fair and square. If he's up for it, you can have seconds."

"No thanks, slut."

The elevator stopped at the 12th floor, and they got out and approached the nurse's station. They both flashed their gold shields, and Sergeant Patrillo spoke for them.

"We're here for Lieutenant Gallagher."

"I'm sorry, Detectives," said the head nurse. "Visiting hours are over."

"There have been threats made against the Lieutenant," said Patrillo. "Until further notice, there will be one officer in his room, and one outside in the hall. Can we have a chair for that, please?"

Another nurse produced a chair, and the two detectives made for Matt's room.

* * *

Matt, with a mild buzz on from his nightly sedative, watched the Phillies closer, Mitch Williams, prepare himself. He hoped he was not wild now. The Fightins were three outs from their first pennant in ten long years.

There was a knock on the door, and Matt was surprised to see Irene Costello walk in with a beautiful smile on her face. He was even more surprised when she locked the door behind her. And he was absolutely flabbergasted when she started removing her clothes.

"Don't fight me, Matthew. I'll be gentle."

One out!

Irene, naked and radiant, moved to Gallagher's bed, unbuttoned his pajama bottoms, took hold of him, and brought him gently to life.

Two outs!

Matt was beyond astonishment.

Irene climbed on the bed and straddled him.

"Relax, Matthew. I'll do all the work." Slowly at first, then with increasing speed, she arched up and down. Matt was close. After all this time he was ready to go off like a mortar.

Two strikes! Any second now.
Strike three!
Pennant! Orgasm! Ecstasy!

* * *

November 16th, 1993

The Honorable Ed Rendell, Mayor of the City of Philadelphia, stood on the VIP tarmac of Philadelphia International Airport. It had been awhile since he had last seen his friend.

Air Force One majestically moved to its stop point, and stairs were immediately rolled to the door. Secret Service Agents were everywhere.

The President emerged, and quickly descended the stairs. There were no crowds to wave to, so he just walked up and shook hands with the Mayor.

"Big Ed. Long time no see. How they hangin'?"

"Just fine, Mr. President. The old pendulum still hangs and it still swangs. How the hell are you, sir?"

"Been better. But I'll get over it," responded the President, as they moved to the armored limousine.

They climbed in, and the motorcade, sirens blaring, took off. In the quiet of the car, Rendell turned slightly in his seat.

"Yeah. What with the Midwest flooding, the hurricanes down south, and the Somalia thing, you've had a rough couple of months."

"It hasn't been pleasant," said the President.

"Jeet?"

"What?"

"Jeet? Did you eat lunch yet?"

"Not yet," replied the President.

"How about a nice sloppy cheesesteak with fried onions?"

"Sounds good to me." The President pressed a button on the console in front of him. The glass divider slid down.

"Harry?" the President said to the Agent in the front passenger seat.

"Yes, Mr. President?"

"The Mayor's gonna give you directions. We're headin' for lunch."

"O.K., Sir," replied Harry. "Where to Mister Mayor?"

"We're goin' to South Philly for cheesesteaks."

"Pat's?"

"You know it?"

"South Philly born and raised, sir. My last name is Stonetti."

"Pat's it is," said Rendell.

Agent Stonetti got on the horn, and informed the motorcade where to go. He also used another channel to inform Philadelphia Police of their plans.

"Thanks, Harry," said the President, raising the partition. He turned back to the Mayor, who had a big smile on his face. "What's the shit-eatin' grin for?"

"This," said Rendell, pulling a fat envelope out of his inside suit pocket.

"What's that?"

Rendell opened the flap on the envelope, revealing several hundred in cash. "Lunch is on me. I'm treating the whole motorcade. Everybody."

The President laughed. "What'd you do, rob a bank?"

"No," said the Mayor. "I got a little story to tell you."

A few minutes later, the President was laughing to bust a gut.

Rendell was laughing, too. "I gave away most of it to the Fraternal Order of Police for the Widows and Orphans Fund. This is what's left."

"I wanna meet this Gallagher." The President's mood had improved considerably.

"That can definitely be arranged."

"What happened to those two female detectives?" the President asked.

The limo hit I-95 North, and picked up speed.

"Commissioner Phillips busted 'em to foot patrol for six months. He figured they had too much time on their hands."

Both men were now laughing again as they headed into The City of Brotherly Love.

Printed in the United States
128914LV00004B/1/P